A Scarlet COLLECTION of MONSTERS and MADMEN

BELLA Bloodlust

The Collection

A Debauchers Dedication

It is absolutely unmistakable to my gothic soul, as to whom this ode of eternal gratitude and this scarlet collection of monsters and madmen ultimately belongs to:

Kyle L. Burnett

Without your endless love, support and mentored guidance and wisdom along the very long, dark road into releasing my demons over the past thirteen years that it took to create this anthology of erotic horror tales; I never would've found the courage or strength needed in this lifetime to overcome so many obstacles to bring this bloody nightmare to life.

I am a better woman and writer because of your profound presence in my life, thank you for being here every step of the way. I hope that this tribute to the awakening that took place over a decade ago in the sentiment of immortality for our favorite demon and muse will be a small token that is just the beginning of all that my soul owes to you for setting this captive free.

    ***

To Aunt Mary Shelley and Uncle Lord George Byron, it was in that moment when I discovered your hidden lineage of eccentric bastards and gothic blood that flows in this writer's literary veins at the tender age of nine that I knew my life was destined to be so much more than it was at the miniscule time. Aunt Mary, thank you for being the strong female voice of your era to inspire, shock and frighten those who were too afraid to love into a profound gothic awakening that has spanned and stood the test of time.

Uncle George, I am eternally grateful for your living, breathing and rebellious libertinage that inspires me every single day to defy the societies I live within and to live each day to the fullest with endless passion and vivacious confidence. If it wasn't for your work transforming vampires into their romantic and lustful natures that have also stood the very test of time since generations past; I would not be here sharing my own debauched views about how sensual corpses can be, as the wolves howl in the pale moonlight.

From your wild parties, exiled existence from the royal family and so much more filth and depravity that embodied the very nature of your being for centuries now to notorious levels of infamy; I never would've captured that wild spirit of liberation for myself in this day and age as a modern courtesan and professional misbehavior and for that my dear uncle I am eternally proud to be your bastard niece and writer of eternal gothic perversions.

To you both I hope that this series does my ancestral heritage justice, as I do look forward to haunting minds and boudoirs for centuries to come with my very own tales of blood, lust and immortality.

Preface

In autumn of the year two thousand sixteen, I gave morbid birth to;

A Scarlet Collection of Monsters and Madmen

A book that's taken me nearly a decade to complete with the brilliant help and collaboration of real life monsters and madmen. The very same monsters and madmen who I fell head over heels in love with, and who captured me and released me long before their dark personal urges buried me in the garden to grow among the wild roses.

A midst their darkness and passion I was introduced to my own dark existence, which is an introduction that I never fathomed nor expected along the road to hell. For those who have desired to descend into the insanity and to know the deepest parts of my gothic soul, and where I hid the blood soaked corpses along the road of vice and transmutation this collection of horrorotic tales awaits your prying and most curiously debauched eyes.

Acknowledgments

To the endless monsters and madmen and some insane women that conspired and coerced this living breathing nightmare into existence with your blood, sweat and tears as well as pieces of your sacrificed soul that went into the pages of this scarlet collection of horror, I owe you my sincerest and eternal gratitude.

Frank Avitt, Cameron, Joseph, Donna Silvester and my beloved Sara Huebsch without stumbling across you a midst our star-crossed paths in this lifetime this book would not be what it has become in the most deranged fullness of its entirety.

Kyle L. Burnett without you this idea never would've transformed into the *scarlet collection of monsters and madmen* that *Darkeel* inspired from the very start and who has become my greatest obsession and darkest muse to have ever infiltrated the endless layers of my horrorotic writer filled mind.

A special thanks to Sarah Macias for sending me countless songs and albums over the years to awaken my mind plagued by writer's block at the time to finish what I originally started.

Trent Reznor without your brilliance, music archives and Nine Inch Nails this book never would've found its dark rhythmic cadence. Your work has inspired me and changed me not only as a woman and human being but as a writer. For this I am eternally grateful.

An ode to an endless variety of organic high quality strains of cannabis, without this miraculous plant, not only would I not have finished this scarlet collection due to an excruciatingly long three year imprisonment in hell suffering from a plague of writer's block, but without you I literally wouldn't be here to provide you my dear reader with this anthology without her lifesaving, cancer curing and pain soothing side effects that allowed creativity to take hold which guided me towards my escape from Hades and into the fiery rivers of literary creation itself. A true Prometheus reborn.

...And to those endless faces, souls and beating bleeding hearts with names that are too many to list, your words of encouragement in times when I felt this book wasn't worth finishing as it might never truly be read was the fuel to my fire that I absolutely needed to keep going to ensure its insanity one day arrived to you the reader in its most profound completion.

For all of you over the years that I've crossed paths with for better and for worse, you have my eternal gratitude and a taste of immortality.

You Are Mine

WRITTEN BY BELLADONNA

THEY met in the blink of an eye, "Follow me to my bedchamber". The words spilled from her mouth with the greatest of ease.

He followed her, hypnotized by her alabaster skin, sexually aroused by the glow of her flesh, he eagerly trailed behind her. Thoughts raced through her abstract mind as she showed him to the bed. He was eager; ready for the chase, hell, he longed for it.

He laid down on the silk sheets and listened to her heels against the tile floor. Illicit thoughts trailed his mind and the outcomes appeared on his face. She was dressed in a crimson silk cape, thigh highs and stilettos. She crawled on top of him to grant his every wish.

He stared deep into her eyes as she slowly unbuttoned his shirt and trousers. Her hands trembled from the tension within.

He ran his hands through her hair to calm her nerves. A smile appeared on her face as the blood rushed to her cheeks. Intoxicated by his stare for once in her life she didn't know what to do, what to expect, what to think. He ran his strong thighs up her virgin flesh and up along her body. She bit her lip and trembled. He untied the silk thread of her cape and let it fall to her shoulders.

With each touch her pulse increased. He held her face close to his lips.

He brushed the hair from her face and whispered into her ear, "You're all mine."

She moaned in vulnerability for the first time in her life she was completely at another's mercy. Her mind a clouded haze. He placed her beneath him and kissed her succulent lips, she grazed her hands on the back of his neck. She'd never been so scared in her life. Her body craved his touch, she felt like and addict desperately waiting for her drug to course through her veins.

Her body trembling he whispered once again, "You mustn't be frightened little one trust me."

As his breath escaped his lips her body released. He reached for the bindings she brought for him, never did she think that she would be the one tied up. He grabbed her wrists and tied each one at opposite ends of the canopy bed. Her arms completely immobile, he inched his way down her body and kissed her neck. He went to her ankles and she struggled with all her strength to fight him.

He laughed, "You want to fight do you?" "You'll learn to regret that."

She started to beg but it didn't help, if anything it made him work faster at his tedious task of binding her. Her face was pure fear like that of a doe caught in headlights. He trailed his hands down her right thigh and grabbed for her ankle, she tried to fight him but underestimated his strength. He grabbed her ankle with full force and tied it to the bedpost. She gasped under his touch.

He laughed and she heard the words, "By the time I am done with you there will be no fight left."

An evil smile appeared on his face that pierced her to the very depths of her soul. She fought with all her strength but the bindings were too tight. He made his way over to her free limb and grabbed her leg.

She desperately begged to be free; "Please let me go, I promise I won't make a sound."

He firmly grabbed her leg, and tied it to the bedpost. She screamed in pain and ecstasy again and he spoke:

"My sweet girl, by the time I am finished with you your screams will fill this room."

Thoughts flooded her mind of ways to escape, he smiled.

"There is no escape my love." Her eyes wide she looked in shock, he laughed and tapped his temple with his index finger:

"I can read your thoughts, your soul, there is no escape." The tears streamed down her face as he kissed them.

"Don't cry my love, it'll all be over soon." She looked at his lips and there they were two glistening fangs, her heart raced.
"I've been watching you for years, reading your thoughts, watching you sleep, waiting for the perfect moment to make you mine; forever."

Her lips quivered and his long nails brushed her neck, her entire body shook:

"Why so scared my love, you've wished for this your whole life."

"Please…" she said "Don't kill me."

A smile appeared on his face, his teeth shining in the candle light. "Be careful what you wish for, you just might get it."

He pulled her head to one side and she felt his teeth dragging down her neck, felt his tongue flick the soft flesh of her chest.

"Oh god I want it, but please let me go." He kissed her stomach and teased her clit, her body writhing as if possessed by an unnatural state of existence.

He drug his nails down her chest and the blood appeared staining her porcelain skin. She gasped at the sight of it but couldn't help but moan. He stopped at the flesh just above her pussy and bit down with such force that it took the breath from her lips. Her eyes rolled back into her skull and he slowly drank from her pure skin.

"You taste divine, I shall savor every last drop, and soon we will be one."

His face stained in her blood, her pulse weakened and her breath grew shallow. She knew the end was near and that her mortal life was in his hands. His cat like eyes glowed while he fed, she continued to moan as the tears stained her cheeks. He slid his long fingers under her hips and lifted her up. He seemed to float over her body effortlessly. He stopped feeding long enough to whisper to her in an ancient tongue.

He chanted louder and louder saying it over and over again, until it engulfed her soul. She closed her eyes and his voice pulsed throughout her body. Louder he chanted flashes of ancient cities and the origins of empires flooded her mind. She saw him in each vision unchanged and reaching his hand for her. A bright light filled the room and he plunged himself deep inside of her. She gasped and moaned from bliss that she had never felt before. She reached for his hand in her mind's eye, as she did he whispered;

"You are now mine for eternity." She smiled as she felt the bindings release her with no help from his hands whatsoever. She wrapped her arms around him and took him inside her completely. He moaned and once again his fangs appeared, he violently bit her neck and she moaned in ecstasy.

For the first time fear escaped her as death approached. Feeling her mortal life end she felt her teeth grow and her mortal soul escaping her body. They met their climax in each other's arms and he said once more:

"You…are, all mine." He brushed the hair from her face as her lips formed a smile.

The Stalker & The Psychopath

Co-written by
Cameron and Belladonna

SHE stares off into the distance watching a mysterious man standing over a corpse, before she could go unnoticed. He ignores the corpse and hungrily eyes Belladonna's delicious looking body while taking off his sunglasses. She smiles that evil grin and trails her sharp nails from her neck to her breasts. He licks his lips, and he stares into her eyes coldly as he slowly approaches, she grins and bites her lip waiting to see what's behind those shaded thoughts.

"My van is parked on the other side of the graveyard." He says as he runs his hand through her long red hair. "Will you come with me?"

Cameron asks, with no intention of hiding the carnal desire in his eyes. She walks to the van and makes sure he trails behind her stride to see the swank of her hips.

Without his knowledge she grins that evil smile knowing that he has no idea what is in store for him in that van.

The two head through the graveyard in silence. He lights a cigarette and is mesmerized by the walk of this strange and sexy girl. If only he knew the erotic thoughts that shaded her mind. *Would he be up for it? Or would he run as fast as he could from the most interesting night of his entire life?*

"Will she be loud, will she scratch? Does she bite? Will she cry? Will she scream?"

Cameron asks himself, in eager anticipation as he continues to eye her lustfully. Her tight corset dress shows off all the right curves in all the right places, she leans against his van and waits for his next move, will he be able to handle her? Or will he run in horror from the events he just partook?

He flicks away his cigarette butt; tired of the anticipation, he can't hold his urges back. He puts one hand on her waist and grabs her hair with the other. Pulling her head back slightly as he roughly kisses her neck. Belladonna smiles and trails her long pointed nails down the back off his neck, gasping with delight she urges him to bite as hard as he wants. Evil thoughts race through her mind, does he have the slightest idea of what she is? Another victim for the taking? We'll see. Or maybe she'll give him the dark gift. He has to earn it first.

He bites her and holds her firmly to his body. His breath gets shorter; he slides the door of his van open; grabs her wrist and pulls her inside where he lays her on his bloodstained mattress.

"You are so beautiful girl." He says and ponders letting her live after he is done with her. As he bites her lips, her protruding fangs pierced his. Something that he wasn't expecting. He pulled back in pain and gave a fierce look of anger. She smiled and laughed as he slapped her hard across the face. She was pleased with his anger, and fed off his energy. She reached for the collar of his shirt and pulled him down to her neck.

"Feed." She said.

Confused and in pain, his mind rushes to his blood encrusted crowbar under the mat. *No*, he thinks, *that will wait*. Holding her down by her hair he tears at her corset. In a frenzy of lust he tears the strings as his blood drips from his lips onto her breasts. She's already read his thoughts and is well aware of what he is up to after this erotic event. She smiles as she sees the desire in his soul to conquer and control another. She finds herself pleased.

Belladonna whispers with an innocent voice of sexual undertones, dripping from the words that spill from her lips, "You can put it anywhere you want." She grins with satisfaction as her canine teeth glow with his eyes.

She grins and laughs because he finally gives her what she craves. She retracts her fangs and looks him deep into his eyes with an evil smile, spreading his legs and plunging her mouth onto his already firm cock. Determined to thrust it down as far as it will go, he closes his eyes and grabs her hair for what he thinks is utter control.

"Damn girl." He gasps as his eyes roll up in ecstasy. His mind falls apart; his mind subconsciously begins to feel that his life's end is coming. After pushing her head down making her completely swallow his cock, he pulls her hair and slaps her across the face. She drives him into sheer madness; she will not fear him! He turns her on her stomach, kneels over her and raises her head with her hair.

"Fear me bitch!" He whispers almost desperately as he pulls off her wet panties.

She's pleased that he's angry and laughs at his desperate threats but is trapped by her own desires and begs for her release. She gasps at his strength and obeys his command, smiling through his actions and getting wetter from each slap. He pulls her onto her knees and presses her head against the back window. He wipes his mouth again, for the bleeding will not stop and forces his cock into her. Her gasps as her body satiates his hunger for flesh. Cameron pounds her with all his strength, sweating and moaning profusely.

She moans, screaming his name and meets his thrusts with power and speed. She digs her nails into his back, and the pain causes him to thrust harder. She laughs at his anger as her teeth appear, she bites his neck and hears him moan. She trembles in his arms and is pleased to be submissive to this powerful mortal. Cameron pounds her harder, in pain and confusion. The blood he has lost and the energies being drained by this awesome dark creature have weakened him. He screams as he cum's inside of her. His instinct would be to grab his crowbar and finish her. But today is different, and he falls to the mattress, scared and powerless to take his weapon. He realizes the danger he is but is too weak to move.

She whispers into his ear, "It will all be over soon."

She pounds him back with urgency and pleasantly takes him inside her as he moans. She looks him in the eyes as his body lies powerless on the stained mattress. She smiles her evil grin and straddles his shaking body running her nails down his chest. She looks into her glowing eyes and he breathes heavily in fear wondering what will become of him. Belladonna smiles to show her fangs and Cameron's confusion engulfs his body and mind. His body covered in sweat and smeared blood, and his mind broken, he felt absolute fear.

His pride no more, he begs her, "Please." He gasps, "Please spare me." Trailing her nails down Cameron's chest, she laughs at his request. Her fangs making him tremble and she can read the fear from his mind.

"Why should I spare you? I've followed you for years waiting for this moment. Watching your sins and tempting myself to feel your presence within me." He continues to shake, not sure what will happen to his life, will he be spared or will he be her next victim?

"Please." Visibly shaken, his strength now completely vanished, his imaginary power gone.

"Please." He stutters, "Don't hurt me. I, I, I'll do anything baby." Tears forming in his eyes, "Please don't. I beg you."

She grabs his hand and places it to her mouth. Kissing it she asks if he wants to join her on the path of immortality. The only other choice is death. She bites his wrist and drinks slowly to give him time to decide. He's still inside her but for once sex is not the first thing on his mind.

"Please, leave me alone. Please." He begs. "I want to live." As she drinks his blood, pondering his fate, he slowly and quietly reaches for the crowbar…

"Tsk, tsk silly boy, I can read your thoughts before you even possess them." She smiled deviously licking Cameron's iron elixir from her blood soaked fingertips.

She continued, "So have you decided either eternal life? To be my mortal slave? Or do you wish to atone for all of the devilishly fun things you've done in this one?" Belladonna traces a line of blood with her nails from his neck to his groin.

"Remember young one, I can't be killed." She laughs with her evil grin of satisfaction.

Desperate, he slams his crowbar into her face. Naked and almost covered in blood, he rips open the van's door. He jumps out but alas he is too weak to run. He falls in the dirt and tries to desperately crawl away.

She laughs pleasantly as the cold crowbar against her face was more pleasurable than painful. Belladonna liked Cameron's determination. She jumped out of the van and turned his naked body over and straddled his groin. She kissed the tears from his face and felt the anger from his soul.

She laughed and said, "I shall give you one chance to make up your mind. Here you should have one of these while I wait for your decision."

Belladonna places a cigarette between his full parted lips and lights it for him.

"Either way I shall get what I want, so you better make your decision soon, your pulse is weakening and you haven't much time till my hunger urges my natural instincts."

She runs her hand down his jaw and smiles, "Such a beautiful creature, a shame to see you go to waste."

"Please," He pleads. "I don't want to die. I'll do anything, don't kill me." He coughs. "I need to live."

"You have three options. One, to be my eternal companion who can fuck and kill as many people as he wants for all eternity. Two, to die a slow painless death in my arms as I drink your soul and elixir. Or three, you can be my mortal slave, keep your life, and bring me victims for the both of us until you die."

She straddles his body and whispers, "Not to worry my pet, I know you'll make the right decision." She feeds off his exposed chest and tells him to be prompt, that the pulse is slowing and she needs to feed. Her eyes glowing green he tires from loss of blood.

"I want to live!" Cameron yells in pain. "I will be your slave, just let me live!" tears run down his face.

Belladonna smiles solemnly. "Not what I wanted to hear, would rather feed off the living with you for eternity." She whispers kissing the tears from his face. Leaning down towards him, her lips upon his earlobe, "Good boy. You have pleased me like no other and for that I shall grant you the gift of mortality."

She cuts her wrist with her long nail and holds it to his lips. "Drink, the blood will make you well again. I haven't drained you completely so you shall be mortal still my dear boy."

He grabs her wrist and feeds off of it with every ounce of strength he has left. She smiles and stroked his hair, "You learned a valuable lesson, and it only cost you your mortal soul."

Cameron drinks and feels his strength return. He lets go of her arm. Naked, full of scratches, cuts and blood. Dirt sticking to his sweat drenched body, with a vampire sitting on top of him. "Thank you for sparing me." He makes another request: "Could you please hand me another cigarette?"

She smiles and grants him another, "So pleased you made the right decision, I promise your life will be better because of it." Belladonna stands above his naked body with a grin of satisfaction.

She trails the van and tosses him his clothes. "Here you're going to need these, the night has only begun and I need you clothed for the things I have planned, well most of them anyway." She laughs and waits for her blood to return his strength, little did he know that it would make him stronger and craftier to do the things he loved the most, *kill vulnerable girls.*

Cameron puts on his clothes. "What a mind fuck." He thinks to himself, eyeing his new master's ass. "What now?" He asks as he buttons his last shirt button.

She offers him her hand and helps him up. Looking at him covered in dirt is quite appealing. Belladonna grins and pulls him to his feet, her green eyes glowing fluorescently.

"I've followed you for years now, watching you take girls physically and mentally. You have a strong taste for blood and power; with me you will have plenty of victims to get your thrills."

She continued, "All that I ask is that you bring me victims and allow me to tempt your body when I please. Follow my rules and your life shall be spared." Peering deeply into his eyes she loves that he's angered by this, "Follow me, young one. You have much to learn about death."

"Follow my rules and you shall be spared, my ass." He thinks to himself, yet he knows he is in no position to argue. For the time being at his new master's mercy, perhaps the time will come when he can flip the table.

She'll slip up sometime. He thinks, perhaps in vain. Until then he shall be wise to serve her. After all, he knows that sticking together will both keep him alive and allow him to pursue his twisted passion for preying on girls. "What now?" Cameron asks.

She's pleased that he has such determination to kill and control her. The thought of him taking lives as she watches turns on the erotic charge within her body. "Come with me, I shall give you a feast of innocent girls, and the world will eat out of the palm of your hands. You shall rule this world and all the women shall be yours for the taking." They walked backed towards the mausoleum and she discusses their contract.

Nervous, and feeling awkward in the mausoleum, he stammers: "Well tell me what to do Mistress, I haven't much choice in this matter. You want me to get you a girl now or can I have a nap? When will you feed me more of your sweet blood?" His gaze dropping to her beautiful breasts, yet he quickly raises them again for fear of angering his mistress.

Pleased by his carnal desires, she smiles her evil grin as she sees where his eyes fall too. "This is my resting place. You shall sleep here tonight and I shall bring a girl to you by dawn." She pulls him towards her and whispers in his ear, "My blood is yours all you need to do is ask, I know you crave it as much as I do. Quench your hunger and your desires. I am yours till we no longer need each other anymore."

Without a moment's hesitation, he bites her hand and hungrily drinks. He drops to the floor after drinking his fill. His body filled with her essence. He licks his lips and after a long weird day he closes his eyes and loses consciousness. If only he knew that by drinking he was slowly taking his mortal life. His mortal eyes were already beginning to glow and she placed his body into her coffin. She whispered an ancient chant into his ear and he dreamt only of blood, sex and her. She smiled as she saw the thoughts that raced through his subconscious. She left to find a beautiful girl for him to please and kill.

He awakens in the cool tomb. Completely confused he looks about. "Where did that crazy bitch go? Damn I'm out of smokes." He frantically tries to think of a way to change the power situation. He is furious at his hopeless position. He paces around the inside of the mausoleum, making fists and cursing under his breath. He wants her to feel pain, he wants her to fear him, he wants her to suffer for his humiliation. *Don't worry.* He tells himself. *I'll figure something out.* Just play dumb for now. He kicks over some candles in his impotent rage.

Dawn approaches and she brings a delicious girl to her crypt. Belladonna pushes the wall open and brings her in as she looks into her eyes filled with confusion. "You said you were pure of body and wanted to change that. Go to him. He will complete your desires."

She sends a thought to his mind, *Take her. She's all yours. Untainted and naïve just the way you like them.* He wasn't sure what to do but he took her hand as she trembled. His mind instantly forgets all his hatred for his mistress as he looks at the helpless girl. He grabs her breast ad she recoils. He grabs her and presses her weak body against the altar. She yells in fear and smiles. Cameron leaning over the alter pins her arms back behind her head. He takes off his belt and drops his pants. He looks over towards his mistress, pulling down her pants before he chooses to ignore her.

She watches with satisfaction. She grins evilly as his body snatches her innocence and takes away the purity of her soul. The girl cries in fear, his mistress laughs, "Once you finish her off you shall receive your true reward." She watches and eagerly waits to watch his killer instincts kick in. He fucks her from behind. Over and over, harder and harder. He knows he will soon be finished. He takes his belt and wraps it around her neck and tightens with every thrust.

She is pleased with his actions and wonders when he will try to kill her that way. Belladonna smiles and laughs, knowing that his anger burns inside that he wants to kill his mistress. His mistress is two steps ahead of him but still yearns to give him more strength from her crimson elixir. She knows it will end in her demise but she is pleased in seeing him satisfied with the kill.

The girl goes limp. He pulls out of her and drops her to the floor. He snarl's, turns his head and stares at her in his frenzy; showing his teeth in a menacing gesture. She laughs with pleasure his anger pleasing her, "Take what you want, I shall not deny you of your twisted desires, but I must warn you, I always know what you ponder in the darkest part of your soul. You're mine. As soon as you understand that your anger will diminish."

I will never belong to that bitch. He thinks to himself. *She will beg me for mercy.* He vows, *and I won't spare her. She will pay for humiliating me so. When she least expects it.* He opens his mouth: "Yes Mistress."

"Stupid boy. I know what your thoughts shade your mind and you shall only dispose of me at my time. Thought you'd catch on." She laughs and pulls him towards her with her strength. Her teeth protrude and quickly she drains him near to death. "Maybe that will take the fight out of you. If not you shall pay with your soul. I will make you mine for eternity if you don't learn from your mistakes." She drops him to the floor and he drifts into a catatonic state. Cameron can't speak, he is so weak again. Belladonna once again places him in her coffin, "We shall sleep now. You will not be able to move until I again infuse your cells." She kisses his lips and laughs as she lies next to him and they fall asleep entombed.

Cameron awakens to a dark tomb. Unable to move, once again he is overcome with fear. *Forgive me Mistress.* He thinks.

She knows that he still has fight in him. She finally gives him all her strength. She cuts her wrist and feeds him, they are equal now. Will she live to regret this or will he use his strength to help the both of them thrive?

Cameron is terrified. He knows not his own strength, he only knows that his mistress is cruel and will not tolerate any back talk. Even back thinking from him. He falls to the floor.

"Please forgive me mistress, I will do as you say. I have learned my lesson." His eyes to the floor, he wonders if his fate is sealed by this beautiful yet terrible creature.

"We are now equals my love. We shall rule the world together. Or you can dispose of me if you wish, you are no longer my slave. I am yours to take now and only you have the power to dispose of me." She smiles and runs her fingers down his jawline, "I know you shall choose wisely. To have such strength alone is quite…lonely." She pulls him to his feet and pierces her tongue as she forces it into his mouth. He drinks once again from this immortal fountain.

Cameron draws back. *Is it true? Did this creature really give him the strength to dispose of her?* He wonders. He licks the blood from his lips. *Is this a foul trick? Will she punish him if he angers her again?* Afraid and suspiciously he eyes her, *I cannot trust her. Could she really have put herself in such a weak position?* He curiously runs his hand along her face, lips, neck, breasts, waist and ass. Probing her reaction.

She pulls him close to her. Belladonna's body reacts to his touch like a moth to a flame. She pulls him close and sighs, "Such a good one, I chose this time. I know what your thoughts have shown and yes you are my equal, I trust that you shall use it to your advantage." She offers her neck and closes her eyes to see what will become of her.

Cameron begins to softly kiss her neck. Confused as never before, yet with each kiss his fear diminishes. He holds her firmly and for a moment he ponders biting her neck and draining her blood and having his revenge. He knows now that she knows all his thoughts. He clenches her hair, pulls her head for her eyes to meet his. He needs to see her eyes emotion. *Is she afraid? Is this really no ruse?* He lick's his lips and pulls her head closer, peering into her eyes deeper than he ever has before.

She returns his stare with a sociopathic glance, no guilt, no shame, no emotion. Her eyes glow brightly green and he is fear stricken to see this so close to his face. "I am at your disposal if you wish to have your revenge. But think wisely young one. Do you want to start your journey utterly alone with nobody to help you?" These mind games sickened him, leaving him torn between revenge, and the fear of being utterly alone in a world that is strange to him.

He thinks on the matter. He hates her, yet needs her. He kisses her neck softly. He refuses to let his thoughts decide; revenge and bloodlust are far from his mind. As his gaze changes from her eyes to her lips, from her lips to her neck. He kisses her neck again, savoring the mixed emotions he feels. "Get on your knees." He demands. Searching for her reaction in her eyes.

She's pleased with his demands and grins at him with her evil and captivating glance, eyes glowing he sees his blood coursing through her veins. Heavy breathed her breasts rise and fall under her tight bodice. She slowly runs her fingers down his neck and chest looking him deep into his eyes and uttering. "As you wish." She seductively falls to her knees and looks up at her master.

His lips slowly begin to form into a smile. "Put your hands behind your back." He commands.

She smiles her evil grin and slowly puts her hands behind her back. Seductively forcing her breasts upward, she looks him in the eyes and slowly licks her lips.

"So beautiful, and dangerous." He runs his hand over her breasts, and places a finger in her mouth as he takes off his belt.

She moans and indulges in his touch. She takes his finger into her mouth completely and flicks her pointed tongue all over it. She smiles and returns his touch with her hands exploring every inch of his thighs eagerly waiting to see what will happen next.

"I said no hands." Cameron firmly states as he pulls his finger out and grabs her cheeks. His hunger for her flesh grows, he remembers the last time he enjoyed her body.

She places her hands back behind her and smiles again pleased with his anger and dominance. She laughs knowing she'll get what she wants for the both of them. Eyes glowing she's weak in his hands. She remembers the power of what is between his thighs and she yearns to please him and feel him once again.

"I'm yours for the taking, use me however you wish, I am here to please you."

Without a second of hesitation, he unzips and pulls her mouth onto his hard cock. "This pleases me girl."

She closes her eyes and indulges in the taste of his firm cock between her lips. She purrs causing him to moan in passion. She forces every inch down her throat and he's amazed that she refuses to choke. She slowly flicks her tongue all over the head and tip and feels his body tremble. She desperately wants to touch his body and feel him stripped naked and writhing beneath her.

For a moment Cameron forgets his worries of turning into a vampire. He doesn't care about the revenge; his mind completely dissolves at her sucking. She sucks harder and faster, until the pleasure of her tongue causes him to steady his balance on her shoulders. Eyes glowing so bright that the crypt is florescent green. She hears him moan, heavy breathed and screaming; she ever so slowly reaches her hands for his thighs hoping to please her master.

He pulls her to her feet by her hair. "You'll do well to do as I say woman." He says, trying to keep his breath. "Take off your clothes."

She flashes her grin, feeding off his rage and cruelty. She trails her sharp nails down her clothes and cuts the strings with the edge of her nails. She slowly seductively takes her shirt off and stands in front of him stark naked with a devilish smile and eyes glowing she strongly places her hands on her hips throwing her head back and laughing at his antics.

His thoughts wander. *Does she not know who I am? Has she forgotten my lust for revenge? Does she not sense my growing rage?* "Turn around and grab your heels." He commands.

She feels the anger growing within his soul. She slowly turns around and takes her time, she bends all the way to the ground and places her palms on the cold crypt floor. She then grabs her ankles and turns her eyes to look at him with her evil smile, "Is this what you want? To take advantage of a creature that can kill you in a one bite?"

He enjoys his view, yet Cameron's mind is tumultuous. *This girl can kill me though she says we are equal in power? I need training in the ways of a vampire, I have yet the understanding of my power to take her from her place of power.* He rubs his hand over her naked back. *Merely her lust keeps her from killing me, the time will come when I can exact my revenge; she will yet beg for mercy, but the time is not yet to come.* Remembering that the green eyed beauty before him can read his mind, he whispers "You know that by letting me live, I will kill you when the chance arises. But until then." Cameron takes his cock and plunges it inside her.

Belladonna fiercely arches her back and the echoes of her screams fill the crypt. Her fangs protrude, "Do with me as you wish. Kill me if you must, but drain me completely for if you don't I shall return and you will die a slow and torturous death!" Cameron pounds her faster as she grips the wall for support. Breath heavy and breasts bouncing, she begs for release.

He grabs her hair and thrusts harder as his own fangs protrude. "Torturous death?" He groans, "What do you know about tortuous death?" He tightens his grip on her waist. "I don't want to drain you." He pulls her head to his left roughly, exposing her neck. "I want you to FEAR me." He yells.

She fiercely screams as she reaches her climax. Thrusting his cock hard she hisses, "Give me something to fear and I might not laugh at your request." She grins and laughs loudly, the sound fills his soul the sound resonating in his head. He grows violent and more angered by her words. His yell echoes throughout the crypt as he cum's while pulling out of her. In desperation he bites her neck with his fangs and begins to greedily suck her blood.

Her breathing increases. She runs her left hand up the back of his neck and through his hair. Her other hand grips his arm, "Drink, I am eternally yours." She starts to fear that this shall be the beginning of her slow demise. Her pulse echoes in her ears. She's getting weaker by the second, trembling in his arms she moans in ecstasy.

A trail of her dark blood runs over her breast as he tastes her sweetness. He tastes his growing power and his sense of victory. No longer feeling like prey. He slows his sucking to savor this moment in his twisted mind. *You are mine.* He tells her in his mind.

She slowly feels her power fading with each drop of blood. She knows that he is now in control. She can barely stand, he holds her up with his newfound strength and begins to shake, "What are you going to do to me?" The words barely escape her lips. For the first time in her immortal life she feels fear in the darkest parts of her soul.

He drops her naked body to the floor and licks the blood off his wrist, smiling victoriously. Her energy courses through his veins and he triumphantly answers. "Whatever I want."

The glow in her eyes start to fade, she looks him deep into the eyes as her breath slows rapidly. Her teeth exposed she cannot move and knows she will not go on much longer, unless he replenishes the blood he took. She needs a victim, the evil smirk on his face pierces her soul,

"I shall die if I don't feed, please don't let me fade."

He bites his finger and lets it drip on her face, just enough to keep her from fading fast. He wants to enjoy her end. "Beg me."

Her eyes begin to fade, she looks deep into his eyes unable to move. She swallows the drop and her body craves more. The blood tears stream down her cheek, her limbs are useless. "Please, I beg of you. I need to feed. Please don't let me die." Her breath grew shallower by the second, she sends him a thought, *I will do whatever you wish of me to do for all eternity, it wasn't supposed to be this way.*

Having raped and killed many girls, yet never having experienced a moment as sweet as this, his excitement caused his cock to get hard again. He flips her onto her stomach, relishing the sight of her beautiful naked body and her helplessness.

"I am going to rape and kill you now. I will hear your begging but I will not listen." He says as he keels over her legs.

He bends over and whispers in her ear: "Laugh at me now."

Her body is excited by his hard cock, but her mind paralyzed with fear. The blood tears stream down her face as her pulse slows. Her eyes fade and her breath grows weaker. Her teeth still exposed waiting for the return of her blood.

She weakly begs for her life unable to scream, "Please, I will do whatever your body wants and whatever you need. Please don't let me lose my immortality."

The love in her voice makes him ponder, she sends him a thought. *Please, I shall never laugh again. I am weakened by fear I am eternally yours for the taking.*

He lifts her limp pelvis off the cold crypt floor and begins to fuck her. Slowly but firmly, all the while secretly weighing his choice. "I will take your body, I will take your life and your mind." He knows that he needs someone to teach him, that his revenge would have disastrous repercussions on his new life, and yet he craves retribution for the humiliation that this vampire has caused him. "I could've been your slave." He groans as he rapes her now limp body.

Her eyes close from the weight of her nearing death. She moans breathing as much as she can, her pulse pounding in her ear as she feels the power of his cock between her legs. She cannot speak. Her vocal chords cannot move to form the words. The blood tears streaming down her face, she sends him one last thought before the breath of death approaches.

I had to give you my strength, I wish to see you fulfill your darkest wishes for all eternity. Too beautiful and twisted to be my slave, I beg to be yours. Dawn soon approaches and I am almost to my demise. With her last ounce of strength she whispers, "I am yours."

"You are mine!" He says violently as he approaches climax. He pulls her head to his shoulder with her hair and thoroughly enjoys his victim's helplessness. As he cum's deep inside her body, he cannot hold back his desires and sinks his fangs into her limp neck. Hungrily sucking the last of her life from her, his arm crushingly wrapped around her.

"Goodbye. You were the best pretty victim I ever had." He drips her corpse to the floor of the mausoleum; catches his breath as he looks at her lifeless body, her sweet face covered with blood tears. He rises, dresses, and leaves her tomb. Knowing that this was an adventure he will never forget.

She feels the approach of death and hasn't the strength to fight him. Her soul escapes her lifeless body and wanders in dazed confusion. She sees her corpse and watches the one she trusted walk away with her power.

I wonder where he'll go next… Her soul disappears into nothingness.

Torture Chamber

WRITTEN BY BELLADONNA

SHE awoke in utter darkness from the loss of feeling in her arms, unable to move an inch. The pounding in her head detoured her from understanding. Weightless arms without feeling so sore, from lack of circulation; that she felt the warm tears flow down her face from the agonizing feeling of not being able to move an inch. The steel chains locked tight around her arms and secured firmly in the brick enclosed wall of this torture chamber. Cold dirt beneath her naked body, all she could manage between the pounding of her headache and her muffled tears was to figure out why she was here, before it was too late.

The wheels turning in her spinning head. She tried to remember the last place she found herself. Her head foggy in an unrecognizable haze unable to recall a clear memory of what caused her to end up here. As she tried to focus she noticed the sounds of heavy footsteps from above her head. The creaking of wood and the streaks of white light shining through a solitary crack in the ceiling, her only light source. Barely able to focus on it in the midst of darkness and haze of what she didn't realize was a drug induced state; her eyes crossing trying to make out any details of where she was. Her eyes betrayed her. Unfocused, blurring and tearing up.

She pondered intently as silently as possible trying to decipher this amnesiac state. The only image that came to mind was leaving her favorite fetish club in the middle of the night, as her heels clinked loudly down the back alley where she always parked. A special spot reserved for, Mistress Bella. She'd been in the scene for years and up unto this point mastered the ability to always be prepared for anything the world had to throw at her. From the lowliest most demented slave to the most bizarre circumstances. She always had a million different forms of foresight to prepare her for anything...except Jimi.

It vividly came back to her, she was kissing a few of her closest and most depraved friend's goodbye for the evening before taking the backdoor out to the ripperesque alley that she'd grown so accustomed too. Walking to her car as the silent breeze of three a.m. molested her soaked skin, latex always made her porcelain flesh as slick as the vinyl she wore so elegantly. Remembering relishing in the breeze she leaned her head back and felt the most intense pain slam against the left side of head. She awoke to the same darkness she fell victim to, with absolutely no idea of who was behind this or why she was brought here in the first place, all she could do now was wait.

Her limbs ached, she lost feeling in her fingers and forearms hours or days ago, whichever was accurate she couldn't be sure. Feeling the loose soil below her she heard the sounds of liquid dripping into a bucket nearby. If only she knew that each drop was a drop of her own blood, unable to feel the IV that was in her arm, milking her for every last liter of eternal elixir. Mere inches away from her were bones from past victims that didn't make it out of such hell, though she was ignorant of such things; unable to reach anything in the position she was forced into, as captive.

Her head harnessed back only allowing her to move inches away from the wall before the chain gave out and forced her to a halt. Moving her legs from underneath her pulling herself forward to see where she was, all she could feel was a wooden pillar that she was barely able to reach with the tips of her outstretched toes. She did her best to find a position to alleviate the horrifying pain shooting down her arms. Suddenly a bright light enveloped the room. She was unable to see anything, but heard Jimi's footsteps approach.

"Here, take this." The voice told her firmly.

"What is it?" Mistress Bella asked immediately.

"That is of no concern. However if you wish for that splitting headache to go away I suggest you take this."

Mistress Bella was hesitant yet unable to deny this man both from fear and blinding pain. She opened her mouth and felt a small bitter pill on her tongue, and then she felt the tip of a glass held to her lips as she slowly sipped the water, as much as she could take. So ravenously thirsty she was from the Rohypnol the water spilling down her naked breasts as she heard him sigh heavily from watching.

"I assume you enjoy it when women *spill* a little?" She asked mischievously forgetting where she was.

But before she could continue her thoughts she felt her head slammed hard against the brick wall, her mouth shoved open and his finger inserted forcing its way in probing her mouth most invasively. Gripping her hair with his hands and leaning in with the harshest most brutal tone she had ever heard from any man alive.

"Let me make one thing perfectly clear, you are no longer in charge. If you choose to defy me in any way you will reap the consequences; and rest assured these little cunts already did."

As her eyes struggled to focus Mistress Bella noticed the grouping of skulls and artistically placed bones in a pile across the opposite side of this torture chamber staring at her from a distance. Their presence tormenting her with impending doom if she crossed... a single line.

She watched as he kneeled down to the arm with the IV dripping her blood into a small glass container. She was mortified that she was unable to feel such a violation, her eyes fiercely opened her breathing increased and instantly Jimi's dark brooding gaze was upon her. His thick wolf like mane seemed to stand on end. His piercing eyes with an endless glow penetrating into her heart. She could feel him gripping her heart like a vice and letting it go with a devious smile. The sound of snapping latex gloves filled the chamber as Jimi smiled deviously into her eyes watching every moment of pain.

Her eyes rolled back and her mouth opened to reveal an emotion that was not expected, *arousal.* She moaned heaving her large pale breasts in his direction watching his mouth open and smile into the most sinisterly haunting expression. His mouth curled into a wicked grin, squeezing every last drop from the rubber tube into the glass container. He reached into his lab coat and proceeded to pull out two very large, very intimidating nipple clamps. Although altered quite sadistically with tiny needles that would leave for the most vividly beautiful blood stained breasts a sadist could ever desire.

"I may have use for you after all." He proceeded out of the chamber and once again she was left in darkness.

Her arms now a bright red and blue began throbbing. She began struggling to get out of her binds at all costs. Defying all logic or reason for safety she proceeded to shake her arms as much as possible the clanging of the chains echoed off the brick walls instantly she heard footsteps. These were not the slow calculating footsteps that she previously heard, no these were footsteps of anger; of rage that such defiance was an issue. The door slammed open and down came the swift moving legs this time with boots on, steel toed.

"Did I permit you to make noise? Do you have a death wish?" gripping her hair and forcing her to look him in the eyes, he smiled laughing as the tears welled up in hers.

"Already crying for me, what a good girl. Tears are a masochist's gift to the sadist." The warm tears streaked down her cheeks once again her lip quivering in fear and mostly pain.

She quietly spoke, "May I ask you a question?"

Most pleased with such a change of personality already the Stockholm's syndrome was working. Smiling, Jimi stated firmly and most directly while he held her chin and proceeded to place his thumb onto her lips.

"Yes you may, though you will always address me as Master. Failure to remember that and there will be severe consequences, is that understood Bella?" her eyes widened it was so difficult for a complete stranger to know her name. She despised being so vulnerable, this was the worst form of torture for her.

Whimpering from her arms, her mind racing desiring to know how he knew her by her underworld alias. But she knew if she waited any longer to beg for her arms release that her body could shut down from the abuse.

"Please Master. I beg of you, free my arms. I cannot feel them."
Master Jimi laughed, "Tell you what beautiful, not only will I free your arms but I'll also give you an opportunity for freedom."

He unlocked her arms and they fell like rocks instantly to her side. She struggled to move forward without her arms, tried to get up from her knees and started crawling towards the stairs before she suddenly fell over in a haze. Her face inches away from one of the skulls she leaned back and shook her head.

Under her breath she whispered, "You bastard, of course it wouldn't be that easy...it never is." She began to laugh somewhat hysterical at the entire situation.

"I love your determination, it's why I brought you here in the first place; along with other desires." Jimi leaned over her naked body, her limbs right next to her sides, unable to protect his approaching violations.

"Mmmm I've been waiting for you for a long time Bella and now that you're mine, I'll do whatever I desire, to fulfill my cravings completely."

Jimi leaned into her exposed neck and inhaled her sweet scent biting viciously into her neck, taking the air from her lungs in a violent gasp followed by the most satisfying moan. He pulled back and peered into her eyes with a perplexed yet excited look:

"You will be my most challenging experiment yet." Her lips so full of angst that they fell open like a swollen piece of fruit hanging from the vine aching for harvest. He leaned in closely as if he was going to satiate such a bite with a penetrating kiss. Her body betraying her she leaned in longing for the completion to such torment. Smiling wickedly, he pulled away and stood up, with a sizeable erection pressing firmly against perfectly tailored black slacks. Longingly her eyes feasted upon him as he cracked his knuckles, shook his head in a calculated movement; to center his focus once more on his tasks. His devious smile glowed while laughing to himself he immediately turned to leave the torture chamber with one last remark.

"Now don't go anywhere, I have a surprise for you."

He ran with eager anticipation to wherever it was that he was going, realizing she was left alone unchained; she stifled as best as she could to uproot her lackadaisical body. With every ounce of core strength she could muster she contracted her muscles and sat herself upright instantly falling back in a medicated daze against the brick wall,

"So fucking close I can taste it, yet so impossibly far."

Realizing the brilliance of such a sadist she leaned back and regained composure trying desperately to shake feeling into her arms; with her shoulders the only part of her extremities she could feel. Heavy footsteps from above coming from all directions, as much as she tried to focus on what he was up too; the loss of feeling was now an unbearable pain coursing hot fire through her limbs. Her obsessive mind focused more on the fact that she was unable to feel the calm replenishing feeling of a hot shower, covered in dirt and beads of sweat from this now sweltering chamber of deprivation.

The light peered in all around this hidden tomb, "It must be daylight, but what day is it I wonder."

Bella whispered to herself in her painful haze, the blood slowly made its way down her arms, the fire beginning to fade slowly in her triceps and biceps. Her forearms and fingers still ablaze.

"Come on bitch you've been through much worse than this." Shaking furiously her arms started to revive, forcing her will upon her energy she felt it course into her fingers able to feel each inch of skin more vividly than she ever had before. Her skin breathing in the air and blood like a dehydrated survivalist that just found the oasis of paradise. Not realizing the entire time that he could hear, see and practically taste her from above. If Bella only knew how well equipped not only this chamber was but this house, she would realize that escape was never going to be a reality.

Master Jimi walked downstairs with what appeared to be a laptop computer; this was one of the last things Bella expected. In the previous moments all she could think about was what her coffin was going to look like at her funeral, or the ad in the paper that said she went missing taken out by friends and family. But Master Jimi had an even more sinister idea in mind, taking this torture to an entirely different level of control.

"I see you've managed to get the feeling back in your arms. Good girl I detest having to prop up my experiments when they can so easily serve me by being self-sufficient."

Bella leaned against the wall silent as the grave, maintaining eye contact with this mysterious and enigmatic man. As completely insane as the concept felt to her on all levels, there was something about him that she was intrigued by, he was unlike anybody she had ever met before; she couldn't pinpoint it yet. He left Bella in a daze of confusion wondering what he would do to her.

"Now then let's get started." He approached her and instantly chained her to the wooden pole with no more than 4 feet of slack.

"Consider that a reward for your devotion, though only a fool would mistake this action for kindness."

Peering into her eyes with that overwhelming gaze, his smile curled into that devilish grin that she despised. Not for the fact that he relished in her suffering but that she for the first time in her life desired it. More than anything she had ever before. This mistress, this owner of flesh, madam of control; was not only enjoying every torturous moment but she wanted more.

"Now where were we? Ah yes." Master Jimi continued pulling up website screens all of which Bella was more than knowledgeable about. Networking sites where she spoke with her friends and family, her professional dominatrix site that catered to all her twisted desires; the place she created in this world to funnel every depraved individual that she longed to shape and mold into a world of beings that were worthy of this exquisite life.

"How did you...?" Bella's voice trailed off into the distance remembering what he told her about speaking without permission; her eyes instantly dropped afraid what he would now do to her, her face full of fear.

"Now we're going to make this easy aren't we Bella?" Jimi grinned mischievously.

"Yes Master." Bella instantly met his eyes and replied.

She then watched as Jimi began typing as her, using her words so perfectly as if he was actually her; convincing everybody that she was more than fine deciding to take a spontaneous and much needed vacation alone, and that she would be back when everything was sorted out that needed to be. Remarkably none of her closest friends or family even asked a single question! Bella knew that her fate was sealed. He was in complete control of her in every possible aspect of her life that she fought so hard to achieve to herself for so many years gone in a single mass email. A tear streaked down her face and she tried her best to not allow a river of angst to follow.

"You have been a much better victim than I expected, especially in your particular circumstance. Your entire life has been one of control, yet you've submitted more sufficiently than any of these whores."

Reaching his leg out in front of him and kicking one of the skulls, it fell down to the bottom of the pile to reveal a huge hole in the back of it; more than likely from a violent rage of blunt force trauma. She wondered what sort of idiotic or random unknown action would cause him to inflict such finality.

Jimi leaned in close to her ear, "Since you have learned so quickly how to behave, I have a reward for you, don't move."

Bella smirked and laughed mildly at such instruction as if she could move an inch. Jimi met and held her gaze a moment longer than she was comfortable with before standing up and disappearing upstairs once again.

Leaning back against the wall, Bella started talking to herself once more. A habit picked up in childhood due to being left alone in solitude similar to this, the only person she had to talk to was herself; a familiar yet for once unsettling circumstance.

"Bella, Bella, Bella…" Shaking her head in disappointment, "What are we going to do with you?" sighing knowing full well that the moment her friends and family accepted her fate that the final nail was in the coffin.

No matter what happened here she wasn't going to leave, and the thought of being just another skull on top of a pile of death was never an aspiration she had in life.

"I truly don't know what's worse the fact that I'm probably going to die, or the fact that all I can focus on is the fact that I probably haven't showered in days and that is the only thing I desire."

Looking into the eyes of the skull nearby her she started laughing hysterically, talking to it as if she was still alive.

"I'm sure that was the last thing you ever worried about while you were in my place."

Smiling most vividly and shaking her head at the insane world that she now lived in, she heard the footsteps of Jimi upstairs scurrying about in a frenzied excitement. His heavy boots pounding above her head matching the intensity of her heartbeat. The sweat continued to streak down her filthy flesh leaving streaks of dark brown all over her body. Curling her lip in disgust she leaned her head back and closed her eyes trying to breathe, trying to calm herself. Centering herself knowing any form of resistance was futile and chancing death.

Her mind began to trail off to forms of torture that she had implemented onto so many masochists over the years. Knowing how they relished in the pleasure of suffering for another, she had never been one of these people. She never relished in receiving pain, as her entire life up until the point where she changed her name to Bella and started this life presently, was torture. She knew she'd lost her endurance for pain, to suffer for another was now something she despised more than anything from her past abuse though for Master Jimi it was different. It didn't make sense to her at all even with the plethora of experience, and knowledge she gained by controlling and abusing others for erotic sport for the past decade. For once she was lost in another brilliant beings macrocosm, and she was the microcosm that he created.

Master Jimi tidied up his home a spacious, luxuriously comfortable home that catered to sensuality in all facets. Tapestries from countries Bella had been too over the years, antiques adorned every room each with such morbid curiosities that even the most ignorant of individuals would beg to know what story came along with each piece. The sound of his laughter echoed against the walls even though below the floorboards Bella couldn't hear a thing; nothing except his pounding footsteps.

Listening to everything she said, his cock rock hard with every gasp of pain, every sigh of discontented agony. His footsteps faintly boomed upstairs as he made his way to through his master bedroom and into the bathroom. Filling the expansive tub with hot water and adding heavily scented rose otto and tuberose to the water with a touch of lavender; for soaking and soothing her cuts, scrapes and bruises from such a violent kidnapping. With each drop that permeated the air his eyes closed. The hair stood on his neck and he smiled knowing she would make for thee most delicate sacrifice.

All the while Bella was concerned with the amount of silence that suddenly became her only focus.

"Universe please don't let me be just another set of bones on an endless pile. Somehow, someway please I beg of you. I'm not ready to leave, I have so much left to do here."

Master Jimi could here this somber confession through the secret speaker system that ran through the entire house; little did she know that every word she spoke was vividly heard with every aural detail.

"I've waited far too long for a beautiful victim that realizes the value of life."

Master Jimi smiled and continued to roll his neck and crack his knuckles as his carnal heart began to beat; faster and faster the adrenaline of the next phase in his master plan forced his arousal to an all-time high. With a wave of his highly skilled paranormal hands music began to play, the softest most romantic jazz music that any woman could ever long to hear from the depths of her unrequited soul.

Master Jimi arose and waved his other hand the entire bathroom lit up in a glow of candlelight. Staring intently at the windows all the shades drew shut; leaving the bathroom in utter darkness except for each flickering candle. Picking up a chain body harness with locks, keys and leash attachment, Master Jimi made his way downstairs to the first level on the house. Bella heard his heavy footsteps in the torture chamber and instantly her heart rate increased.

Jimi looked onto his monitor and saw her sitting there in fear once more; watching the screen tell him every medical detail about her experience was by far the most titillating. Her heart rate, beeped louder and faster with each heavy footstep, he then began to laugh as he watched her squirm with each step.

"So sensitive, this is going to be such a thrilling ride."

Master Jimi leaned in close to his monitor zooming in from cameras that were stationed all around her. Her face was so vivid, so expressive; every ounce of emotion was all consuming to his desires.

He began stomping on the ground just to see what would happen. Instantly her face contorted, she looked up and bit her lip in a worried expression hoping he wasn't angry; tears streaming down her face hoping she would not meet her fate.

"Mmmm I'm going to enjoy this more than anything I have ever enjoyed in all of my lives."

Master Jimi once again stood up rolled his neck with that intoxicating smile and cracked his knuckles picking up the steel accessories that he would need to make sure she would continue to be such a good girl.

Bella heard the booming steps come closer, with each one her heart beat faster and her breathing matched in identical cadence. Closer he came. She heard each footstep more vividly than she had ever heard any sound before. Each step, the boom, of each planting step, boomed louder and louder her heart raced with her perspiration. He could smell the fear, inhaled it. Consumed every bit of its scent as he marched with a sinister smile and his intense carnal glare that zoned in on her. Targeted her like a hungry wolf that just spotted that wild rabbit, seeing its blood pulse through its veins; coursing through one last dose of life saving adrenaline.

As soon as she saw him approach she began to tear up. She tried so hard to fight her natural instincts, so hard not to say anything but her swollen lips betrayed her;

"Please don't kill me, I'll do anything please. I don't want to die, I have so much purpose left and so many deeds that I haven't completed."

Her eyes, big and shining from tear filled glare, sparkled a bright blue green that he instantly got lost in. As he took a long deep calming breath, restraining the initial desire to backhand her so hard that she would black out for disobeying. His neck instantly snapped back and he rolled his piercing eyes down to hers;

"For once in my entire life I am going to ignore the fact that you just blatantly disobeyed me."

Anger surged through his entire being as Bella calmed for just a moment.

"Perhaps another time." Before she even realized what was happening, he backhanded her with such ferocity that she was out cold. The blood dripping from her now cracked and swollen lips, he bent down and grabbed her by the back of the head and forced a kiss onto them. Taking in the sweetest, most pure blood he had ever tasted,

"How bizarre you think such a sadistic woman would be filled with dark secrets in her, this doesn't make any sense."

Perplexed he laid her head back on the cool soft earth bed beneath her; she looked just like a corpse; with her porcelain skin and her delicate features, yet still warm and fresh. Suddenly Bella gasped as Master Jimi's voice came through between the ringing in her ears.

"Wake up, and do as you're told. I have a surprise for you, one that I know you'll enjoy."

Wafting the smelling salts under her nose she gasped and tried to focus on him, though for a moment her vision was hazy. She instantly grabbed her jaw, the pounding was severe. She looked him in the eyes not sure what to do, or think for that matter.

"Did I not tell you that if you spoke without permission that you would reap the consequences?" Master Jimi inquired.

"Yes Master." Bella replied humbly.

"Now be a good girl and take this for the pain, and let me help you stand up. There is no need for this place any longer, unless you choose to continue to misbehave then you will not only find yourself back here; but also like them."

Bella looked at the pile of bones reminiscent of the catacombs of Paris, her gaze returned to meet his. "Yes Master."

Pulling her legs towards her body she did her best to stand up, her legs and arms were of no use to her as they trembled and shook unable to support her body at all. Leaning for the wooden post and gripping to pull herself up, Master Jimi stood behind her and helped support her allowing her to lean against him and the pole to get her legs back. Bella's head gently pressed against the pillar, her hands grasping the pillar on each side waiting his further instructions.

"That's a good girl, now let's turn you around."

Grasping her right arm he pulled her around to allow her back to lean against the wooden pillar as she struggled to maintain composure and her ability to stay standing. She felt the cold steel chain wrap around her waist like a belt, he cinched it close to her body and slid a lock onto the chain. She heard the harsh click of control, her juices began to flow and she faintly moaned. He could smell her arousal instantly. His nostrils flared and his eyes dilated in a frenzied possession.

Gripping her by the hair and forcing her head back, he spoke: "Such a paradox."

Smiling wickedly he bit down violently onto her chest. Yelping from the unexpected force her legs trembled and her swollen, aching pussy dripped with such ferocity from the blood that shot down to her clit from every extremity.

As Bella opened her eyes in horror she thought, *how can I be so aroused at a time like this??* She looked down realizing these awful clamps were still attached to her painfully sore hard pink nipples.

"Such a distracting experiment." Jimi shook himself out of his intoxicated haze and grabbed another chain, this one was meant for her wrists.

"Now lean back, don't worry I won't let you fall. Put your wrists out in front of you and hold them together for Master." Bella instantly obeyed, "Good girl."

Master Jimi smiled so pleased that this sacrifice was finally cooperating. Oh how he despised having to hurt them, having to break them down into submission; when they could make it so much easier on themselves but most importantly, him.

Wrapping the chains around her wrists in the rhythm of a figure eight, he then placed a lock into the center of the chains and her wrists were bound to each other. She bit her lip, why was this causing her such erotic energy?

Master Jimi then proceeded to lock her wrists to her chain waisted belt and attached a steel collar around her neck, so cold against her flesh that it instantly dropped her temperature and her skin began to ripple all over from the frigid metal. Master Jimi then proceeded to reach for her waist, as he reached for the slack that hung from her naked body she thought to herself, *what torture so close yet so far....* Biting her lip fiercely Jimi laughed tapping into her mind ever since he brought her here, he possessed this connection. If only she knew that not even her mind was an escape from his clutches.

"Follow me my pretty piece of flesh."

With the final piece of chain attached to the center of the three O-ring steel contraption, she proceeded to trail slowly behind him right next to the pile of girls.

"Goodbye girls, I hope this is the last time we see each other, rest in peace."

Bella's thought trailed into the ether along with another warm tear hoping she would never see this part of his home ever again. Each booming step in front of her the light was piercing, she was unable to see. He stopped intuitively feeling her eyes scorched by the light, it had been nearly a week since she'd been down there, and on IV fluids and drip alone her weakened state left her vulnerable in nearly every organ.

"Take your time darling we have eternity."

Master Jimi's voracious grin, full of sinister thoughts and sinful intent; turned around and waited for Bella to continue walking up the stairs behind him.

Each step she took the light consumed her. It filled her body with a peace that she hadn't felt since she'd been there. There really was something so incredibly spiritual about light, the instant comfort was immediately felt. It permeated to the deepest parts of her endless soul and as her entire being radiated Jimi's eyes were in awe of her brilliance.

"What are you most beautiful creature?" peering deep into her now adjusted eyes, lost in pools of blue green.

Bella smiled unsure if she should answer or stay quiet, she smiled slightly in silence and as his hand gently grasped her chin placing his thumb on her pursed bottom lip. His smile matched her own. Dropping her eyes unsure if she had permission to look into his, he instantly replied;

"Yes you may. I prefer my prey to maintain eye contact."

Bella was trembling from nervousness, *how could he? It's impossible there's no way that he can….* "Read your thoughts?" Jimi replied with a smirk of amusement.

"Unfortunately you have nowhere to run or hide Bella. Even your mind is mine, and soon your body and soul will effortlessly follow."

"Now where were we? Ah yes…. Follow me."

Jimi proceeded to stomp. With every step up, each creaky step Bella followed close behind wanting so badly to appease him. Unable to describe this overwhelming feeling of service oriented submission to want to please him so completely even in these circumstances. Instead of analyzing relentlessly as to why or where this desire originated from. She for once in her life succumbed to it utterly. She couldn't see the smile on his face as he led her upstairs. He could feel her desire to be here, everything he wanted in a concubine. Yet no other understood it, not only without instruction but instantaneously with the relinquishment of her will.

She was in awe when they made it to the first level of his beautiful home. Her mind was going in a million different directions,

Wow, I can't believe he actually owns…. Bella thought.

"Please continue in words. I do so love to hear what specifically people love about my collection. As most have no desire to ask any questions from previous circumstances."

Bella's face full of awe, "I'm overwhelmed by your collection Sir. Truly I'm not sure where to start first, my eyes fall upon a tapestry that I recognize from a visit to France I took years ago. It was in the local museum in Nice if I remember correctly."

"You have a wonderful memory." Master Jimi replied. "It was very difficult to convince them to allow me to purchase it, but when I desire something I refuse to take no for an answer."

Jimi looked directly at Bella and she dropped her eyes trying hard not to let him see her blush. Lifting her chin and forcing her to look into his eyes;

"You will never hide your emotions from me, is that understood?"

Bella so vulnerably timid, barely able to muster the words; "Yes Master."

He leaned in and for the first time she felt his soft, passionate, penetrating kiss. He pressed his lips against her third eye and she breathed him in. The energy he encompassed was pure nirvana. This was profoundly perplexing to her, she smiled and laughed unknowingly from such a complete feeling that resonated from his kiss.

"As much as I would love to show you each and every piece of my collection, we have eternity for that and your surprise is still waiting."

Master Jimi proceeded to walk her up the stairs to the second level of the house and through the hallway that lead to His master bedroom, a luxurious red bed with gold trimming. *Decadent* was the closest word she could form in her mind.

"Thank you Bella, I'm very pleased you like it." Bella smiled forgetting that her mind was his.

"Yes Master very much so. You have a beautiful home filled with items that I have seen all over the world on my travels; but never imagined anybody else would love them as much as I do."

Master Jimi smiled and proceeded to continue walking her into his master bath. Instantly she was overwhelmed by the candles and the perfect combination of perfumed oils. The bath steaming hot, and a shower in the distance with the doors shut. Steam searing inside for her to wash off all the filth of being locked away in his torture chamber for the last week. She was unable to contain herself screaming and smiling;

"Thank You! Thank You! Thank You!"

Jimi laughed most amused by her gratitude, still half delusional from starvation and all she was focused on was a shower.

"Oh God! I have never been so happy in my entire life!" Bella was thrilled and Master Jimi even more amused by every word that spilled from her lips. His smile filling his sensual face, he proceeded in his instructions;

"Now my beautiful Bella, I'm going to unlock your chains, and remove your collar for your bath. I'm sure I don't need to tell you what happens to girls who misbehave."

Master Jimi's tone became serious and Bella instantly replied with a smile on her face "You have nothing to worry about Master, I'm here now."

His face full of calculated cruelty softened into a smile. "Good girl, I'd hoped we'd gotten over those previously, ugly decisions of yours." Bella's face fell to shame;

"Yes Master, my sincerest apologies for my initial disobedience. It won't happen, ever again."

Master Jimi looked at her face and eyes that fell to the floor, awaiting his response, "Look at me." Instantly Bella complied too his wishes, "I am very, very pleased to hear that."

Master Jimi began unlocking her wrists from her waist, then he took the set of keys he carried on his thick leather belt. That belt that she wanted so badly on her ass, to feel him release that fiery rage into her silky white flesh; the thought was tormenting. Unlocking the lock between her wrists and unraveling the chain that left such a beautiful imprint on her then. She'd never felt like such property before. Her pussy was beyond torturing her, pounding from the inside out, shooting an inferno of lust inside her body penetrating her being completely she was starving for him, as much as he was starving for her.

He reached down to the link of chain that dangled mere inches in front of her perfectly shaved mound. A place that typically had the most softest ginger curls a man could ever feel, though there would be an eternity to know such things about her, she was after all completely his now. His strong hands gripping the chains and pulling her towards him. She gasped biting her lip trying hard not to moan; not to show him just yet how desperately she longed for him. She desired his strength, his power, and his control. His left hand calculated which key was the correct one and placed it instantly into the keyhole, unlocking her with one fluid moment.

The chain fell heavily from her hips sliding down the back of her ass to fall to the floor in a heavy clanking pile. The most beautiful belt of marked flesh aroused Jimi to the point of a hissing serpent, ready to ravage his forbidden fruit.

"Now turn around for your owner and show me that pretty neck of yours."

Bella slowly turned around still maintaining what little balance she had feeling his hands search through her long crimson locks pulling them to one side tenderly as she felt his hands grip the steel collar to unlock it; setting it nearby on a crimson pillow of red velvet on the marble countertop nearby.

Master Jimi's arms wrapped securely around her waist, "You have been such a good concubine, would you like to shower?" moaning and leaning her head back against his strong supportive shoulder, "More than anything at this moment Master."

Bella smiled so content knowing she'd soon be washed clean again, the dirt, stench and fear of being locked up for over a week was stained on her body in a mess of sweat and earth.

"Master, may I ask a question?" Bella looked back into his predatory stare.

"Yes my pet?" Bella softly asked, "I'm unsure of my ability to stand Master. How would you like me to shower?"

Master Jimi's contented smile once again turned into that predatory grin that curled his lips, and made his cock rock hard.

"I would be more than pleased to help you my beautiful Bella."

He opened the shower door to a wall of steam that encompassed them both; he helped her into the shower placing her next to the wall where the bar was.

"Hold onto this my precious Bella, I'll be with you in a moment." Bella leaned against the shower wall feeling the water washing over her breasts moaning without conscious awareness. The steam felt transcendental, her body was sore; watching the dirt drop off of her body leaving behind streaks of white underneath. She could hear him removing his clothes, she could see his blurred silhouette.

First the long heavy dark lab coat full of tormenting devices, that she didn't even know existed. She heard the heavy clang of his thick leather belt fall to the ground and her moans grew louder, and so did his eager cock. His thick trousers fell to the floor and he unlaced and stepped out of his doc marten boots, watching every moment was sheer torture. She wanted to see him so badly, wanted to feel him take her completely and knew that it would still not happen, not yet; perhaps not ever.

The shower door opened to reveal his predatory stare sizing her up like wounded prey on the Serengeti. The cruelest most evil smile that shot an inferno of lust down to her trembling thighs, Bella's mouth dropped open as she took in every site of his beautiful naked body. His tall lean torso, his powerful legs. Shoulders so wide that he was able to be a human door for the shower he had just opened. It was shoulders like these that made Bella weak, even when she was Mistress Bella. A slave with wide shoulders always made her ripe peach drip just a bit more tormentingly.

His perfect cock, the delicious girth and length to satiate her tight wanting pussy, with that perfect curve that she knew if he took her with it... Would grind so wickedly against her g-spot that she would leave the most explosive puddle all over him and his glorious member in the possession of lust.

"Turn around, Now!" Master Jimi ordered her. Bella instantaneously turned around and positioned herself spread eagle, pressing her face against the cool tile while the steam enveloped them both. Her hands above her head on either side of her body, gripping the tile as if she were going to tear it loose, legs spread wide so that he could see her desperately writhing for sex. Her ass forced out by desire leaving her exposed like a common whore.

"Such a fucking whore you are for me Bella, most girls need to be taken, broken in, raped against their very will; to surrender to a demon like me, not only do you give yourself to me, so completely; but effortlessly, like you were made for me, my will, and most of all my cock."

Jimi was now squatting in the shower looking up at Bella and her glorious ass, smiling like the devil himself. Bella moaning desperately like a cat in heat.

"I have never before been affected this way Master. I cannot begin to describe what you do to me, and I no longer care to understand. I long to serve you, to please you, to be satiated by you, I know now that you are the only man that will ever be able to do this. So many years I've searched for a real man; a sadist so brilliant that even I, Mistress Bella could succumb to his will without resistance; a victim of pure foolishness."

Amidst this entire confession Bella was forced to think between Jimi probing her wet pussy, violating her tight ass with his calculating fingers, all the while moaning in agony.

"Oh God Master....Jimi....I need you inside me!"

Bella not realizing she spoke out of line heard a sinister laugh before he forced her hard against the wall, filling her pussy with fingers so deeply she felt completely violated by his presence inside her.

The most ecstatic moan escaped her lips, "Oh God Jimi Yes! Uh.....Uh......Yes! Mmmmm I need you Master, make me your whore!" bringing her to the point of release, he violently stopped.

Her orgasm faded instantly into torture once more and her face pressed so hard against the tile wall that she now carried the imprint on her face. Breathing heavily unable to speak her body trembling in torment, pounding blood into her swollen pussy, it hurt intensely and still she wanted more.

"Such a fucking cumslut, Master is going to enjoy this even more than I initially thought."

Master Jimi whispered into her ear and kissed her gently on her cheek, Bella returned his kiss with a moan and expression of blissful gratitude.

"Now then let me help rinse my beautiful concubine off. This is only the first phase of many to visit for what I have in store for you tonight my perfect whore."

Grabbing the detachable showerhead and rinsing Bella off from head to toe, slowly deliberately focusing on every inch of flesh with dirt. Master Jimi watching her hair drip drops of brown washing her shoulders, back, all while pressing his hard cock the entire time into the back of her ass, reaching around and washing her large soft full breasts. Each pink nipple hard as a rock with every small touch he inflicted. Reaching down around her full hips he found that perfect spot that he would make his.

Pressing his talented fingers that skillfully played her like Beethoven, He continued pressing and searching, teasing and tormenting; every nerve to align into the perfect melody, each moan, each vulgar desire she begged for played out like the most beautiful song.

"If you decide to cum without asking permission, you will be punished, understood?"

Bella looked back horrified knowing that her own game was being used against her and she was not only falling victim but desperately so. Struggling to maintain composure Bella moaned her answer to him, "Uhh....Yes Master!" gasping from such torment.

"Master I am so close!" biting her lip firmly and shuddering harder than he had ever felt a woman shudder from his touch. He cruelly pulled his fingers out and left her shaking.

"Now that you are finally back to that exquisite pallor, it's time to follow me."

Bella turned around feeling almost human again, watching him exit the shower. His strong shoulders, back and legs so tormenting, a feast for the eyes. She was lost in the image of his ass, wanting so badly to sink her teeth into it; wondering if that would best convey what an animal he had turned her into.

Master Jimi took Bella's hand and gently guided her to the bath he had previously prepared for her, still hot from the boiling water it was now the perfect temperature to calm her mind, body and soul completely. She would need to be in a calm state for what his debauched soul had in store for her. Walking into the bath Jimi sat along the backside and spread His legs, not only was this absolutely cruel to her ripe pink lady apple, but even more hell for a woman with an insatiable oral fixation.

"Now my pretty piece of flesh, I want you to sit down here and let all your worries fade away." His smile warmed along with his eyes,

"Come to me my beautiful Bella Luna I've waited far too long for you."

She walked up the two stairs accompanied by his outreached hand helping to stabilize each step, each step felt like a dissent from reality and further into his entire world. She reached the water and felt it rise to the middle of her legs, she felt lost, completely lost; unable to return to any aspect of her former self.

"Now rest your back against the tub here I desire to look down into those beautiful eyes of yours my pet."

Bella using his thighs to help herself into the tub leaning back and looking upwards into his eyes feeling; his contentment. This was the last emotion she expected from a man that kidnapped her, restrained her in a torture chamber; with a pile of former failures... drugged, beaten, naked and starved for over a week.

He began to pour perfumed water all over her hair, she sighed peacefully lying back against his crotch and stomach feeling his hard cock pressed firmly against the back of her skull. Such a fucking sadist was Jimi.

"Now Bella I want you to wash yourself for me, though I desire to have you facing me instead before you begin."

He looked into her eyes and instantly she responded coyly, "Yes Master, whatever you desire I am here to serve."

Bella leaned forward and repositioned herself thighs open lying back on the porcelain that matched her gorgeous flesh, making her red locks and green and blue glowing eyes stand out even more prominently than they already did.

"I find it interesting that you paint your nails like the color of a whore." Master Jimi smirked and spoke as Bella proceeded to wash her long crimson locks.

Bella smiled most amused, "Master I have always found that I have a lot of things in common with women of that classification, even though I myself am not one by traditional standards."

Bella tried to maintain her gentleness as best as she could, she awaited his response though dreading his reaction.

"I think we've already gone far beyond traditional standards, and you may previously not have been a whore. But like it or not, you are my whore now." Master Jimi relished every word of this sentence as he stared her down.

"Master please forgive me if I misspoke, as you are the only one I have ever been a whore for."
Biting her lip most revealing she began to lather her breasts and arms, her stomach, scrubbing every inch of skin that soaked up this godly feeling.

"If you misspoke?" Jimi's eyebrow arched most deviously. Bella's face turned every shade of red as her eyes dropped afraid of the consequences.

"Master I apologize for such insolence; I will try harder to please you." Bella's eyes so fearful of disappointing her new owner, her King, her God.

"You make it so easy, such a timid little girl inside, still shaking wondering if Daddy is going to bend you over his knee and inflict what is deserved but has been long since overdue."

Master Jimi's smile of pure sadistic delight beamed, glowed as beautifully as every candle in the room that flickered off the walls, mirrors and marble.

"Master I look forward to your every correction, to be molded, shaped and custom designed for you. For every conceivable desire that your dark soul thirsts for, hungers for, like no other; I want to be her."

Bella lifting her legs to the sky and washing them from hip to toe, twisting to her side, her ass cheeks pressed together. He relished, taking in every moment of her bath, watching her work her hands between her large round firm sensuous cheeks, cleaning so in depth, making sure every inch, every crevice was washed perfectly for him.

Lying back and soaping her wet aching pussy was by far the most difficult task at hand, so sensitive it was, pure hell tending to every inch inside and out. Unable to cum, so weak she was from lack of nourishment that she leaned her head back. Master Jimi picked her up instantly on her weakened state:

"Don't worry my precious Bella; I'll take good care of you. I always take care of what's mine."

Jimi reached towards the wall and pulled a needle out with a vile of green liquid, Bella was more than alarmed as it looked identical to anti-freeze;

"Oh God this is it, I knew this was too good to be true."

Bella bit her lip in horror as the needle went in feeling the liquid enter her body all she could do was hope and wait.

"Your fear surpasses your logic my dear concubine, do you think I would waste the time taking you up here if I intended on killing you? I could easily have done that two floors below, I've never been one that enjoys dragging dead bodies around."

Jimi laughed and waited for the elixir of health to kick in. Within moments Bella felt so alive, as if she had eaten the freshest foods from all corners of the world and they were instantly revitalizing her body with incredible speed.

"Wow Master I feel incredible! I....I....have never felt this much pure untainted energy before."

Jimi smiled most pleased that her earlier sacrifice of blood was well worth the effort.

"Bella my darling this is your blood, I simply detoxified it of all environmental particles that have been tainted inside your bloodstream due to this disgusting world we now live in. This is you if your body ran at optimal level."

Bella smiled widely, "Master is this, the reason why you brought me here? I know you earlier referred to me as your latest experiment, but the only version of that word I could imagine was something very similar to that of Hannibal Lector."

Jimi instantly laughed most amused by the comparison. "As delicious as you are my pet, I've long outgrown my days of cannibalism. I don't quite have the stomach for it anymore."

Bella replied, "I was referring more to his intelligence Sir."

"My concubine it is now time for you to rise from your bath."

Jimi stood and proceeded to help Bella stand as the water slowly drained beneath her pearlescent body. He pressed a button and a stream of water poured from the ceiling gently washing all the soap off of her body. She smelled like a dream, covered in those exotic perfumes, completely reborn. Watching her erotically enjoy each and every stream that touched her naked wanton flesh, the water stopped and she moaned in pleasure.

"Thank you so much my generous, Master. I appreciate all that you have done for me more than you know." Bella smiled most contently.

"That my perfect concubine is why you are here with me right now. You realize what glory exists inside me and you realize how fortunate you are to serve such glory."

Wrapping a long plush red towel around her and drying her off from head to toe, he reached behind her and wrapped a floor length satin robe around her bare body. There was a vanity nearby with all of her personal beauty items that she used every day before preparing for a session. Though this time she was not in charge, in control, she had absolutely no power what-so-ever and she loved it.

"There is a box in that closet for you my pet, I would like you to see you in it, and I would enjoy seeing you painted up as beautifully as you usually are at *The Scarlet Gardens*."

Bella's mind flashed back to an entire identity, which was her nightclub that she opened with her depraved family of friends years ago to create a world where she was in control. Where she could expand not only her own horizons into the dark recesses of the human soul but to drag the dark twisted roses of sadism across their exposed bodies making them bleed the prettiest drops of release upon her. A part of her soul ached to know that they would be alright without her, that they would not worry when she didn't come back now, in the near future or ever again.

"Such expressive eyes my Bella Luna, you cannot hide the fact that you are troubled. Do you forget that your thoughts are exposed to your Master whenever I please?" Bella hesitated.

"You may speak freely my pet." Master Jimi stood behind her watching her as she sat at the vanity painting her lips and face like a porcelain doll.

"It's just so hard to let go completely especially when I was unable to choose it. I realize that I built an entire world around me. A fortress that prevented it from ever happening; so I know that it would have taken this extreme of an act to help me to awaken to such blindness but I feel like I have to shut the door before I open another Master. However I do not desire for you to feel unappreciated I will forever be your tribute even though that alone cannot express my gratitude."

Jimi smiled, "That was beautiful, so honest my Bella Luna. Thank you for sharing your thoughts and feelings with me." Bella smiled, "You're welcome Master."

Her questions unanswered, she was left with a somewhat hollow feeling inside that she desired to fill with her new role in life, as his slave. It felt so natural like a puzzle piece that had been missing a hole that she never noticed but always felt deep within her. He was the key to unlocking the mysteries that she had kept from herself for far too long, never realizing after years of damage caused by a cruel past that she would ever be able to submit to the will of another human being ever again. Approaching her and kissing her gently on the third eye once more leaving her pining for him:

"I desire to see you fully prepared for your master at seven o' clock, not a moment later."

Master Jimi's predatory eyes looked into hers in the mirror while he forced her head back and bit down viciously taking the breath from her lungs once more. "Do not disappoint me."

Bella quickly turned her head to feel his lips pressed against her cheeks breathing heavily so aroused she knew how difficult it was for him to wait.

"Never again master, never again." Bella matched her breathing with his anticipation.

Master Jimi walked out of the bathroom and shut the doors behind him. Bella immediately looked up at the clock and saw that she had only an hour and a half to get ready. Instantly she opened the closet door and saw a huge red box with gold wrapping. She was in awe that he knew so much about her yet she knew so little about him but felt closer to him than anybody she ever had before.

Was she losing her mind? What was wrong with her? She shook her head and smiled for once not having a care about it, just following orders, his perfect orders.

The box was overwhelming but the custom made black latex dress that would make Marilyn Monroe faint from sex appeal left Bella in fetish heaven. Instantly her pussy dripped,

"Mmmmm Master you and I are going to get along just fine."

Smiling and laughing she adjusted the last bit of her lipstick, curled her lashes and painted her eyes into the perfect pointed cat eyes, her eyebrows screamed, *I'm ready for business.* But her eyes and lips screamed *I'm ready to please.* Sliding into the latex dress it molded itself perfectly around her hips and ass; she pulled it up over her large supple breasts that now firmly spilled forth out of this perfectly cut couture gown.

"Never ceases to amaze me."

Bella smiled as she attached the halter top dress around her neck making her breasts stand out even more dangerously than a moment before; pulling the gown down until she felt it hit the floor she then saw the seven inch black patent pumps to go with this stunning gown. Her red painted toes stepping into each heel she felt like a goddess, and couldn't wait to reveal herself to him. She walked towards the pillow and picked it up feeling as if guided there. Jimi lied in bed smiling looking through her eyes astrally. Seeing her smile in the mirror as she picked up the collar that he made just for her. He waved his hand and the doors opened, her breasts pressed together so tightly so impossibly high, her hips swishing from left to right so full, so ripe and ready to be plucked from the tree of knowledge of good and evil, his exquisite little Lilith.

"Utter perfection my beautiful concubine, I'm so pleased it fits you like a glove."

Laying back on the pillow covered bed resembling a king; master Jimi and his sizeable erection twitching, bulging full of blood, and waiting for her lips, her hips and every inch of her body. He had watched her for years now, always hidden but in plain sight. He smiled wondering if she even knew that he had been an online friend of his for years, slowly but surely pouring out every last thought innocently assuming that due to his supposed location that they would never meet.

There was always such a secure feeling in being able to tell a complete stranger all of your secrets. Bella would never guess the man dressed from head to toe in heavy latex encasement was now her owner. For years they'd spoken about everything, intimate details that she never told anybody. He was such a comfort to her in so many ways and yet she never saw his face, never knew his real name and it never seemed to matter.

He only desired to inquire, to know and understand a woman like her, and it was the only person that she'd ever came across that was so curious. Such foresight for a sadist, kindness or curiosity wasn't the reason; it was his desire all along to break the infamous Mistress Bella in as his own personal slave.

"You please your master so perfectly my exquisite Bella Luna. It would satisfy me completely if your collar was on."

Master Jimi beckoned her with his forefinger and Bella seductively walked towards him.

"As you wish…" Her voice trailing off until she leaned in close inches away from his lips "my king."

Smiling wickedly he could no longer resist her, he ravenously growled snapped the collar onto her translucent neck and locked it into place. The chain still attached to the center of the collar, the pillow dropped as master Jimi fluidly threw her to the bed forcing his lips against hers.

Unable to control himself for any longer, years had he awaited this moment. He craved it, planned every possible detail of it. Both owner and slave moaning loudly matching each other's lust with such ferocity that surely it would ignite them both in a blaze of pleasure. His lips all over her face, her neck her chest; and her large supple breasts that were now forced against his face.

As he bit violently into them with no regard for her tolerance, gasping, groaning and moaning, her pussy gushed her sweet juices all over the inside of this latex dress. She was a soaked puddle and she was still dressed! Gripping her hair tight and forcing her to look him into the eyes.

"Look at me! Do you know how long? How many centuries and

oceans of time I have searched for you?!"

Bella's eye's full of endless adoration, breathing in his eternal words, "I never knew how or if I would ever find you again."

The flashbacks from their past lives together limbs intertwined, so many lives. So many places all over the world, and still his eyes were the same. His lips, the way he kissed her. His energy that coursed through her as if it was her own.

"I have missed you so much master." Tears welled up in her eyes, Master Jimi pulled her close by her leash and collar.

"Now that I have found you, I refuse to let you go. The world and all of its women need you here, to soothe the beast within. You have and always will be the only one that has ever understood me. That took me unconditionally entirely as myself. It is the only way to prevent the body count from rising again."

Bella smiled still in awe that she had found her owner from so many previous lives, "I will never leave your side again, not even in death."

Kissing him so deeply that his soul melded with hers their heart centers alive and bursting with tantric energy; shooting down to their sex centers and forcing Jimi to rip the dress up over her luscious ass. He clawed his way up her body, screaming and moaning in pain and pleasure she took it all, everything he had to give and more. She refused to have a pain tolerance, she was lost in him completely.

His probing fingers found themselves gripping her sizeable ass and moaning from the feeling of her soft flesh,

"Fuck it's been far too long since I've felt this ass, I need it now!"

Forcing her dress up around her waist he tore her thighs open and brutally forced himself inside her, raping her tight pussy, groaning deeply from how difficult it was to tear into her. Oh how he loved that soaking wet pussy that was just for him. Moaning and gasping sharply as she felt him force his way inside her inch by inch until his hard cock stretched her to accommodate his massive blood engorged cock.

"You are mine once more Bella Luna, who owns this fucking pussy?!" gripping around her waist and finding her clit immediately;

"Who fucking owns *this spot* ?!"

Bella screamed in pleasure and pain from being stretched hard. Her ass being beaten with a wooden paddle that he impacted so sadistically hard into each cheek while pulling her head back and arching her neck making her look at the ceiling like a cat in heat.

"You do master Jimi! You own that spot! You own this pussy and you own…me…completely!" Bella moaned louder and louder.

"Oh God yes Jimi, fuck I am so close master!"

Instantly he stopped fucking her and eased his fingers off of her clit, moaning desperately wanting so badly to cum. Bella shook her ass at Jimi most mischievously.

"Moves like that will only get you harder spankings." He proceeded to grip her hair so tight, that tears streamed down her face;

"Ahhhhhhhh!"

Bella cried out as master Jimi began wailing on her ass as hard as he possibly could leaving welts, instant bruises and a trembling slave that learned it's not a good idea to tempt an already ravenous wolf.

Master Jimi out of breath; cock rock hard and wearing a smile so sinister the devil himself cowered down in submission. He leaned back and proceeded to lie down on the bed.

"You will mount your master, your king, and your God now." Smiling most pleased "And, you will not stop until I allow you too."

His tone most carnal Bella instantly spread her thighs flipping her dress around her hips so that he could take in the look and feel of her glorious ass while she rode him as he desired her too.

"Oh god master. So fucking wet; so tight for you. Mmmmm your cock fills me completely, satiating your succubus."

She took his hard dick and relished in feeling the blood coursing through it, leaning in towards him, "I want you inside me."

Master Jimi met her words with a possessing kiss flicking his tongue inside her mouth like a serpent, teasing her lips with firm bites and enveloping kisses that took her out of her body instantly. Gripping her hips he pulled her down and instantly her head fell back as she took every inch of his hard prick inside of her.

"Ooohhh God! How I've missed you!"

Gripping him close to her body his tongue licking all over the black latex as she undid the halter straps around the back of her neck. Her massive tits fell before his face and the ferocity of the lion that hunted within, went into a full blown blood frenzy. Gripping each other's hair, animalistically fucking so hard, fast and deep that death by orgasm was soon approaching, their eyes connected and he could feel her body constrict. Her moans turned to screams of pleasure, tears of bliss flowing from her face as she rode him harder and faster, deeper and deeper. He plunged his cock into her tight pussy, her juices soaking him; her muscles tightening more intensely but holding back just enough… knowing that she wanted to save it for him.

"Please master, I beg of you with every last ounce of energy I have, May I cum?!" His eyes locked onto hers, she desperately waited for his response.

"Look at me Bella don't take your beautiful eyes off of me…..Cum with me……now!"

In that moment the entire world, universe for that matter ceased to exist. The only thing that mattered to her was that moment of mutual nirvana, absolute tantric unification that solidified not only their bond from so many past lives shared together, but in this lifetime as well.

The energy was overwhelming so intoxicating that words did not exist. The strength of their bond so unexplainable that the universe itself couldn't have planned such a serendipitous circumstance, only pain endured through many lives that spanned continents, space and time.

Their energy so intertwined that their breath, heartbeat and reactions were identical and simultaneous.

"Mmmmmm" they both moaned in unison. "My beautiful Bella Luna." Master Jimi smiled contently. '

"My master, my king, my one true God."

Bella looked at him with endless adoration. Gripping her leash and pulling her in close one last time before rolling her over to his right side and embracing her closely. She laid on his chest feeling his heartbeat slow along with his breath. He then proceeded to utter a name a name that Bella recognized quite vividly.

"What did you just say Master?" Bella was in shock and awe instantly perked up and looked him in the eyes.

"It's been you! All along! After so many years why didn't you tell me!? Even online! Why didn't you tell me it was you Master?!" She was so surprised and in disbelief that he began to reach for his mask that was typically worn at all times.

"Does this look familiar?" Master Jimi laughed hysterically.

"It's been such a pleasure getting to know you in this lifetime and watching you from afar. Knowing when the time was right, I would strike; take you as my own once again. As I have so many times before."

Smiling and looking into her eyes, Bella was still in shock and awe smiling

"But how could you? When could you? It's impossible!" She exclaimed.

"Nothing is impossible my perfect concubine. Did I mention that I've also found the key to immortality?" Bella sat in amazement completely overwhelmed by master Jimi and all of his profound genius.

"Master I have so many questions." Master Jimi smiled and looked into her eyes; "Of course you do, always so persistent." Kissing her on the third eye gently, deeply, exchanging their beautiful energy once more.

"Rest now my precious pet, after all, we do have eternity, and you mustn't forget….. We are now one, mind, body and soul." Bella fell fast asleep sighing contently on his strong chest, never had she felt so free before, so incredibly alive.

Worship Me

WRITTEN BY DJ SIGNIFY

THERE she was. In her majestic, gothic castle. Dressed for the kill oh so sexy, and looking for a candidate to fit the needs of a Goddess. Looking down onto the outlay of the land. The army barracks, the miniature hovels built into the hills where the commoners lived. The colosseum she had setup for the weekend's death games and executions. The cemeteries, the livestock pens, blacksmith quarters and alchemist's den. All fit to serve a need and purpose intricately designed by a mastermind set to rule and conquer other lands. Expansion of territory and plundering of far off distant places with a thirst for taking their exotic goods, people and their very souls.

Her previous high servant and slave had failed in an attempt to keep an intruder from sneaking into the vastness of the lower dungeon area. She found out because she heard the man's screams. Being devoured by some beast spawned from whatever mother beast or abomination lurked there within. The thing was. She did not recently throw any such man down below. That's why she knew he must have snuck in. Slipped the key from her previous drunken high servant, to wander down below for a little snoop to see what just was down there.

For there were rumors throughout the land that there were literally caverns filled with precious jewels, gold, and ancient stones pillaged from other lands that delighted her wanton desire. Needless to say he did not find his fancy, for the instant he reached the bottom of the spiral stone stairwell he was greeted with a huge, bulging, oily muscular tentacle flying towards him at an incredible speed. Wrapping around his entire body within seconds and squeezing him first.

Instantly stopping his blood flow, strangling his innards and intestines up and down, some exiting his asshole like sausages, some flowing up his throat and out of his mouth. Choking on them, biting through them, spewing from his mouth letting out a loud gurglish

"GGGLLLLUUUGGG!!!"

Mixed screams she heard. Becoming both curious and excited by the idea of what caused such horror. His eyes popped from their sockets and the monster pulled him into its mouth to be slowly devoured alive. Then to be dissolved and digested amongst the acids and gastric juices to be dissolved to sludge, slowly to death.

The powerful woman was in search of a new high servant as the one who previously served her. Upon his begging, kneeling, crying pleas to be given another chance, she stood there on her throne, legs crossed; staring down at his pettiness and worthlessness unfazed. No emotion but a slight gleaning in your eyes at the thought of what she was going to do to him. She let this go on for an incredibly long time.

He asked, then screamed "Please Goddess.... *SAY SOMETHINGGGG!!!*"

Looking up at her with a horrified shocked expression. Sweating, heart beating so loud you could sense it ready to burst. Then she simply told him in a robotic voice; to lay down. He did so willingly, slowly he got up. He walked over and brought her black, thick leathered, intricately laced high heeled boots, with the four inch needle like heels;

down with blazing speed. Through the middle of his forehead, all the way through his head and into his brain.

The sounds of cracking skull followed by squished brain matter leaking out from the man now all over the floor. Seconds prior to his death she had cast a spell on his worthless existence, rendering his body paralyzed. Glued to the floor lifting her lovely wicked foot encased in her deadly boot from his brain slowly, wiping the brain matter off the spike onto his shirt. She slowly glided over to sit at the window and look down upon the land. With her black cat nearby she sat in serenity as the storm clouds thickened. Thinking. The powerful woman wrote two brief notes. One to each of the candidates she had been surveying at the death matches each weekend.

A place where man would be pit against man; or man vs animal. Even animal vs animal to use various weapons of her choice to kill each other all for her amusement. Sometimes the last man or animal standing was forced to fight in a free for all, leaving the last man or beast standing to claim the title of victory. Notes were sent by carrier snow owls she summoned from the mountains, and who were not seen after. There was a note on his doorstep written in beautiful violet/black calligraphy; demanding him to be in her quarters at midnight. Exactly midnight.

The powerful ruler made him and the other man kneel down before her as was the proper position to be in when being addressed to by someone of supreme status. She explained to them how she wanted someone to serve her.

A slave. Someone to serve as her personal bodyguard. Someone to provide the role of assassin when she needed an enemy snuffed out and was too bored or tired to get her own hands or mind bloody with a spell. She wanted someone for the pleasure of being an accomplice in a hit. Someone to massage and caress her lovely skin, to play chess with, to hunt with for the simple thrill; to be there as a servant to whatever desires she had in mind.

To feed you and do odd errands about the estate for you. As she spoke down to us of her requests; his strength, passion and desire only grew stronger. His head spun and he was shaking a bit knowing well then and there he was to win this battle to be granted such a high privilege of serving her in such honor. He couldn't wait to get my hands on him as she stood there, black lipstick, skin tight leather pants gleaming in the light. Her black deadly leather knee high boots, skin tight leather corset which was red but mostly black. Rumor had it that the reddish tint was from the blood of her enemies, and that she had some of their blood soaked into the leather as a keepsake. All who existed within her kingdom knew for certain that she kept a room full of enemies' skulls somewhere in the castles insides.

Amongst many other unfashionable jewels, treasures, talismans and oddities of immense value and power. Just to be on his knees there beneath her was intoxicating. He learned a lot subliminally about her in that speech that only made his intense passion grow more fiercely than ever before. To be given the grant to be amongst her in the future. An honor incomprehensible to people in the rest of the land.

Yes she had potential candidates fight to the death before but even the winners sometimes in those battles always disappeared shortly afterwards as they weren't held high enough for her standards; were often found long after sticking out of puddles of quicksand, drowned. Other times they ended up going through a meat grinding machine which she fed their squished meat to her dogs. But he knew just how she would want the battle, to wage on an utmost confidence in pleasing her desires.

He knew when she threw the dagger into the pit. The pit was located deep in the castle dungeons. It was a sandy bottom floored hell with circular surrounding stone walls, marked with blood, bone fragments, fingernails strewn here and there and stuck into the sides of the wall itself.

The sand was reddish tint. And it was hot. He and his opponent stood facing off against each other dressed only in loincloths hiding their private parts and yet they were both still soaked with sweat, bodies glistening in the light. He knew when the dagger was launched at them, that she had absolutely no interest in seeing it being used yet, and that what she really desired was to see an awe inducing yet excruciating battle. One full of brutality and struggle of moans and noise. The arena was thick with the smell of fresh blood and sweat. The air of nobility synchronized well with the endless martial arts tactic and strategic warfare on the utmost cunning cruel level; with the ultimate outcome being, death.

His victim made the first mistake of reaching for the dagger first. Permitting him this allowance to get there before him as planned. When he reached down, I planted my foot into the side of his head upon which there was a sickening crack. The sound of his temple bone crushing, sending his opponent's eyeball to come out of its socket silenced the roaring crowd. This sent his opponent into a rage, just as he had calculated. His fighter intelligence went out the window and he started throwing wild punches, which were easily sidestepped.

His thighs splintered in pain by endless kicks, he winced in pain each time the impact was felt. The sound of his kicks hitting his flesh only and over driving the fighter to kick harder, slowly crushing the blood vessels on the inner and outer portion of his thighs while sending the discoloration to black and blue throughout his limbs. Oh was he frustrated. His opponent couldn't connect and the fighter kept toying with him as he could have easily dropped him with a head kick or uppercut early in the battle. But wanting him to suffer and to die slowly was much more appealing.

The powerful woman was up there watching like a queen black widow peering into chaos supplementing itself in the middle of her vast strewn web with stone silence. But what the fighter sensed was delight as her cheeks reddened a bit. The fighter noticed her move a bit to get a closer look at what was happening. The fighter's poor, poor opponent started to sway as his leg had hardly any circulation left to hold him up. The fighter helped him down with a blast to this knee which was like kicking out a support from underneath a giant tower.

Down he went howling in pain as dust came up from his fall. It was the last time in his life he would be standing tall. The fighter quickly applied a stealthy leg and arm hold on him thereby positioning his body with his opponent's back to the ground and the fighter on top of him but with his back to his stomach. The fighter wrapped his legs around his upper torso and rib cage and his arms around his neck and head. He applied pressure slowly with his thighs squeezing tighter and tighter around his opponents ribs; like a boa constrictor on a hog. Each time his opponent inhaled the fighter tightened his squeeze further cutting off his airflow; with my arms choking his windpipe off and holding his head in place. He made low cries, and noises which resemble the prey in its last breaths.

"Ooooohhhhhh." He struggled.

Sweet, sweet struggle his opponent squirmed to try and break free but to no avail. The fighter actually started losing his grip with his legs because his torso was so slippery from the sweat and there was up and down movement, endless and endless defiant squirming.

The fighter began watching her as he held him. He saw that she now had her mouth open and she was unaware that her right hand had slipped to her pussy; a sign she was in quite the amazement at the desired effect she wanted, that was now taking place just below. The fighter had been hard as fuck for over an hour now. The constant up and down motion of him gaining and keeping a stronghold on his opponent's body while he tried to squirm free caused him to cum heavily. All over his back, the fighter spilled his seed, in which when his opponent felt it; left him crying in horror at such a violation to his manhood. But the fighter only grinned and felt quite satisfied. He noticed the man was finally near to losing consciousness, because his eyes were bugging out of his head from the choke hold that left him gasping for air.

The fighter released the hold and let out a barrage of punches onto his face over and over again, and that's when the blood started to flow. His left eyebrow let loose split and gushed blood. The nose breaking had quite the audible crack, and the final punch connected where he loosened his eye earlier; only this time his eye completely dislodged and hung out of his skull for all the world to see. The fighter had a crazy idea that the dislodged eyeball was watching her inducing a burst of laughter to echo manically off the stone colosseum.

The fighter simply stood up and went over, picking up the dagger he then sat on his back pinning him to the floor. He held his opponents hair and head back then he started to cry.

The fighter told his opponent whispering in his ear, "Sssssshhhhhhh."

The fighter then in a nonchalant demeanor started sawing at his throat with the dagger holding his head out as he convulsed; the blood spewing everywhere including all over the now victor. He watched as he bled out he let his head drop, raising the dagger over his head with both hands he brought it down with full force through the back of his skull and base of his spine. The tip going through his body and sticking into the floor.

It let off quite a cracking sound followed by the horrors of squishing skull and brain matter. Yet he was not completely dead as the blade must have set off a part of his brain processing in which he started asking him in a haunted dying robotic voice if he was his father. Repeating the troubling phrase slowly, over and over again. The fighter delivered the kill shot lifting his leg and driving his heel down and upwards smashing his nose bone into the center of his brain.

The fighter quickly looked up and saw her standing on the rim of the wall with her hands on her hips smiling wickedly in full. Her glowing smiled showing extreme pleasure and valor. He knew at that point she had found what she ever so desired. But he was by no means going to get ahead of himself. She made a come forth gesture with her index finger and he had to pinch himself to get moving. So overwhelmed with mixed emotions that he's pleased her that he nearly fainted.

He came to her and stood face to face with his new owner and queen. A very bold move to do even in light of the occurrences, looking into her eyes as she looked him over.

Then she put her arms out and said, "Carry me."

He took her in his arms and walked slowly back to her chamber. She showed no discomfort granted, he was still covered in blood and sweat. She clung tight pressing against him and Ooohhh the feel of her near exposed breast pressed against his heart; which pounded intensely. He laid her down on her bed and she told him directly that this was the one time for a very long time he would have the privilege to feel her so he'd better make it worthwhile.

She told him her feet hurt. So he ran his hands across the leather of your boots feeling the sleekness and smoothness of them while his heart raced. Relishing the thought that some of the highest decisions made on other people were made while she was standing in those boots. The brilliant lacing pattern so intricate he loved the thought of how long it would take to undo them. So tight. That they'd carried her through battlefields to examine the aftermath that her armies had caused and the blood she walked through. The throats and heads she stepped on and squished when she noticed an opponent was still alive. They were laced eloquently and precise up the back as well and I untied them slowly watching her laying there motionless still in shock and disbelief that this was happening.

He pulled her right boot off slowly and laid it down carefully at the end of the bed. He then put his lips to the bottom of her foot and kissed. He kissed every inch of her foot and toes then her calf. Running his tongue from toe under her foot up her heel to the soft spot behind her knee. He did the same with the other leg. Kissing oh so soft and wet. Then he massaged her where he'd kissed; firmly and gently depending on each part of her body catering to her every whim.

These hands had done horrible things. He then sat behind her, kneeling as he went to work on unlacing her corset slowly and carefully; taking quite care not to cause her any discomfort. He then lay the lacings to each side of her and applied his lips to the base of her spine near her ass. In the middle of her back he kissed her gently over and over; moving his kisses to the sides of her lower abdomen and up her back again. He ran his tongue up her spine licking her like a serpent.

He continued massaging her and licking her feet. Stroking her and caressing her soft skin, feeling her intense energy build. He wrapped his arms around her and just lied there with his head relaxed against her upper back as he started to feel her breasts. Kissing her neck firmly and stroking her hair, he heard his queen let off a soft moan of pleasure which made his heart dance and smile. She moved to her side both lying next to each other face down but staring into each other's eyes. They explored the depths and listened outside to the gusting wind as the sky went black; promising the storm of the century that was about to strike down. But it was warm the breeze soothed their naked bodies and the candles blew out, He then took her into his arms and slipped inside her. The pleasure shared lasting for what felt like eternity.

The Hunt

WRITTEN BY BELLADONNA

HIS heart racing, he darted through the trees hearing the yells of the others all around him. The crushing sound of leaves and branches beneath him as he raced faster and deeper into the woods knowing the hounds would soon be released and that she would be after him. The shadows of horns on his head surgically screwed into his skullcap, he found himself altered quite sadistically at the hands of a bloodthirsty psychopath.

"Here she comes!" The sounds echoed through the woods as the others bounded over trees, through cold iced winter waters in nothing but hooves bound and chained over their feet. Suede loincloths adorned their flesh cold from winters chill. Their breath heavy, the icy cloud increased with each rampant leap to get as far away from the manor as physically possible. For a chance at freedom from hell on earth.

"Oh God No!"

The screams filled the woods as one of the others was shot down. The bullet pierced his upper shoulder and he was instantly out. Her henchmen picked him up by his limbs adorned with hooves the perfect stag for her winter solstice sacrifice. Tonight was not a night for one, but many deaths. She enjoyed each galloping impact of her steed, riding her pussy wet, swollen and aching for the stag she would take to her dungeon tonight for her own personal alter. The dogs howled loudly barking in the direction that Joseph found himself. His heart racing, he ran swiftly into the wilderness.

Recalling every survival tactic he knew to outsmart this sick twisted bitch. His face still dripping from a recent forced operation his head throbbed from the drugs that coursed through his veins. His long muscular body perfectly sculpted able to endure all that she had to inflict and so much more began to falter. His body twitched from the cold, his heart burned in his chest barely able to breathe from the slicing air. His fingertips red and purple were barely felt along with the rest of his body. He felt her, he could sense she was gaining on him yet he refused to surrender, refused to not go down without the fight of his life.

He knew that water was the only way to detract scent, but without getting warm soon he'd surely die. He knew if she caught him that prolonged torture and death was soon to follow, that it was his only destiny, so he gambled. Russian roulette style to outwit this demented debauchee. He quickly and painfully submerged himself into water; this was extremely difficult with the water so cold that all he wanted to do was scream but he couldn't make a sound, utter a word, without her soon closing in on him. As he submerged he could hear the yells and screams grow less and less, fainter and softer until there were only one or two voices left. He knew she found them all, the other men that were captured outside her private estate. *Broken down car, hitchhiker, and wrong place at the wrong time.* They all found themselves in her grips, he forced himself knowing he'd soon be a mutilated corpse if he didn't try.

Fully submerged he leapt out of the water and began forcing himself up a nearby tree having fashioned numerous traps from earlier punishments out here of exposure and isolation. He knew that someday he would lead her here, and take advantage when she thought she knew every square inch of this huge fortress. He longed for this moment after many months of being jailed below in the estates dungeon cells, along with the others he wanted his revenge.

His time soon approached when he heard her horse galloping faster and faster. Closer and closer. He heard no more voices, he knew that she was looking for him. He knew that he was the only one that she hadn't caught, this infuriated and aroused her to no end. She was used to hearing the reports from her henchmen about Joseph, about his intelligent trickery, his clever charm that seduced men to speak intimately with him forgetting his status as a prisoner to dealing with three of her men killed brutally broken in pieces. They were found screaming and bleeding with only his bare bloody hands and a devious smile letting them know that nobody else was to blame.

"Tell that bitch I'm going to kill her with my bare hands!"

He'd scream at the other officers as they had to isolate him, enclosing him in a mummification straight jacket to prevent him from killing more. The others knew that Joseph would be the one to escape; they all knew they didn't have a chance. He trained them in secret and she later found out, knowing he was dangerous but aching for the thrill of the kill. As this moment approached she foolishly fell into his trap and he was more than glad to placate his revenge. He leapt from the tree, pulling a cord he'd fashioned from dried wood fibers that he slowly gathered over what seemed like years of growth, from when he was out here for punishment. Instantly her horse was tangled and snagged both front legs launching her to the ground the impact was hard he heard her whimpered curse and for the first time he saw the woman that kept him prisoner against his will for the past year.

He was shocked and mortified to see this vixen with pale translucent flesh, and piercing green blue eyes that swirled together in a hypnotic myriad of colors. So beautiful she was that he forgot for a moment all that she had done to him from afar. Her bounty of red curls spilled over her large, full, pale breasts adorned with bluish veins that pulsed and raced when she met his eyes for the first time. Instantly the fear set in knowing her gun had been flung two yards away and that he could kill her instantly. His eyes met hers and soon they filled with fire an anger that no hell could create, and inferno of hatred for this cunt that kept him caged like a beast with no explanation. He leaped at her with every ounce of strength he had left reaching for her thighs tearing at them like a wild beast. As she reached into her laced up knee high boot to pull out a hunting dagger, her anger matched his own and he now realized that this would be an equal fight to the death.

His body shaking as hypothermia set in, his lips blue and purple his muscles begin to tremble as she fought for her footing.

"You stupid whore. Why the fuck did you keep me locked up here?!'

He climbed up her torso and straddled her waist, her corseted breasts rampantly rising and falling as her breath grew heavier and faster in his near death fury. He realized it had been so long since he was inside a beautiful woman far too long. His body betrayed him and his cock began to rise. Moaning aloud he didn't care in that moment she looked, felt and smelled so divine her heavy thick black fur coat wrapped around her. He was mesmerized by this beautiful sadist. This woman of torture that physically altered his body and hunted him down like a wild beast. He was a dark creature and for a moment his primal instincts were the only focus. He leaned in close gripping her body, her red satin buttoned corset molded so tightly to her body that he could see her heart beating fast underneath. Burying his face into her chest and neck and smelling her perfumed skin and her fragrant locks. She moaned feeling his grip tighten and his cock bulging as hard as stone, aching... to cum.

Without warning she slammed him hard across the chest and shoulder and pinned him to the ground, taking her dagger and slicing his thigh he backhanded her hard against the face. He leaped to retrieve the dagger, she leaned back in the snow and planted her boot into his stomach and forced him down to the ground. Angry as hell he tried to fight but his body trembling it was useless, he knew he was going to die soon but still he refused to surrender. As she picked up the dagger his blood stained the fresh white snow, she licked it off from base to tip relishing in the heavy iron taste of a man's elixir. She approached him with a devious smile on her face and as she went to pin him down. He was ready for her; kicking her hard in the torso she yelped and tears of pain streamed down her face. His cock grew bigger and it was torture that he was not deep inside her warm flesh, already making her pay for her torment.

He crawled on top of her with the last strength he had and pinned her down. Straddling her each movement felt like an eternity. Each moment, each second a lifetime of agony. The cold had penetrated deep inside him yet he could feel the warm blood flooding his hard cock,

"You killed three of my men, you bastard. What am I to do with you?!'

He restrained her wrists behind her head,

"I don't think you're in any position to bargain right now."

The yells of her men filled the forests behind them at least a quarter of a mile away was her only help in the world and yet she still smiled and laughed wickedly in his face.

"If you really want to kill me sexy boy then do it. You have your dagger and there's another strapped on my inner thigh."

With a confused look on his face but one of intrigue he gripped tighter and she began to smile, "Mmm yes. That's right, do your worst."

He reached for the dagger and her breath hastened while her pulse quickened.

"Mmm Yes I love it when the pulse quickens before a kill."

He smiled and met her gaze with a lustful breath. He dragged the tip of the blade from the back of her ear down to her neck and chest. A faint line appeared and droplets of blood trickled from her pale white flesh. Kissing her neck and ravaging her with deep bites her moans of ecstasy grew stronger from beneath his grasp. He took the knife and slowly cut each of the five buttons down the center of her corset from breasts to stomach. Kissing and biting her he felt the warmth from her loins, knowing that she would soon bring him back to life. The final button was cut to reveal two large soft, warm breasts with beautiful pink areolas and pert pink nipples hard as tiny pebbles.

His cock dripping pre-cum all over Mistress Bella's lower abdomen.

"Ooo you are a very naughty boy, you're lucky you're on top at the moment or I'd surely punish you for that."

With a wicked smile of mischievousness she felt her riding pants being cut away, her arms released she could have reached over at any time and killed him with yet another dagger he hadn't found hidden above her round luscious ass.

"Well you're not on the top are you?"

He continued to cut her pants off to reveal the dagger she had mentioned earlier, he kissed her thighs and dragged his teeth to the knife and removed both knife and harness. Spreading her thighs he felt the warmth, he smelled her sweet scent and buried his face into her. Moans and soft muffled vulgarities were whispered to him. She was so horny, she hadn't felt a man in a very long time. She usually killed the ones she used and kept their bones for personal tokens. But with Joseph it would be different.

He sliced her underwear and they fell away to reveal a beautiful white pussy, with soft pink lips. Swollen like a ripe fresh piece of fruit, she gripped his hair,

"Uhh, Ohh I need you.....I want you inside me."

Worshipping her pussy with his tongue and lips kissing it, teasing it and watching her head dig back into the snow her breath so heavy and fast that is looked like a cloud of smoke was escaping her lips. Her body contorting and shuddering with each change in sensation gripping his hair and digging her nails into his shoulders;

"Oh God Yes! Joseph, Mmmm Yes!"

She pulled him close to her body and plunged his cock deep inside her, gripping his hips she fucked him from the bottom fast and hard, furiously hearing his moans as he looked deep into her eyes. Watching her inching her way closer and closer, without warning she slammed him on his back and threw his arms above his head, pulling out the hidden dagger. What she had behind her back was now pressed into his throat. She gripped his chest:

"Put your hands on my hips….Now! Or I'll slit your throat!"

He smiled wickedly and obeyed her commands, watching her breasts heaving as she ran her fingers through her hair and fucked his rock hard cock in circles. She furiously fucked him harder and faster her moans were met with his and he gripped hard onto her hips fucking her as roughly as he could. His strong arms furiously moving faster and faster, faster and faster. Deep inside her warm body, her flesh warmed him to the core, in this icy chill of frostbitten air. Biting his body less and less as their body heat increased into an explosive inferno of pleasure and pain. She took him deep inside her filling her completely fucking him hard as their bodies clenched together they looked deeply into each other's eyes knowing that they were both about to meet their climax.

"Beautiful Goddess," Joseph panted and moaned, "Please I beg of you let me cum!" With a wicked smile on her face Mistress Bella replied, "Cum inside me Joseph, cum inside me now!"

With a deep kiss he gripped her close and they both moaned into each other as they met their mutual release. Squirting all over his cock, gripping his body close and feeling his hands in her hair ravaging her neck biting her chest, "Ohhh Fuck! Yes!" she continued "Oh God Yes!"

She reached for the dagger and sliced his arm and chest he fell back into her coat completely spent. Drained to near death she licked his arm and chest and every drop of blood off of her dagger.

"Mmm Joseph I have so many wonderful things to show you." Mistress Bella lied on his chest pale legs wrapped around his strong thighs, red painted toes curled from such an explosive orgasm:

"You will enjoy being my slave Joseph and every moment of your existence will be worshipping and serving…Me."

With a wicked smile she closed her eyes knowing her men would find them soon. Licking the blood from his new body modification.

"What a good fuck toy my big stag is. What a good little cumslut you are for Mistress Bella." He smiled and shut his eyes whispering her name, "Mistress Bella," knowing that this was a world he never wanted to escape.

A Sick Scene

WRITTEN BY MASTER DARKEEL

CHAPTER 1: AWAKENING

THE moon was slung low in the night sky. Hidden almost completely by the dark luminous clouds. The sounds of the city rang from a distance, but to one young woman, the world was as empty as the chambers of a dead man's heart. As she woke from unconsciousness her head swam. She remembered sitting in the park working on her novel when everything went black. She had been drugged and now found herself bound to a chair in an empty room.

The room was dark, and appeared to be made of brick. A single window hung high on the wall across from her allowing just enough light to see the outline of a man in the doorway to her right. She could see nothing of the man except his figure, which was tall and muscular, and his eyes. Never before had she seen eyes like those. An emerald green, almost glowing.

"I see you have finally awoken my dear." The man said, his voice sounding foreign.

"I have been waiting for the chance when we would meet face to face."

"W-w-where am I?" Her voice squeaked out from behind her chattering teeth.

"Shhhh. My darling, do not ruin this by trying to ask questions.

Questions lead to answers, answers lead to understanding and understanding leads to courage." He cocked his head to look at her. "And you need to be as frightened as possible for this. It makes your blood pump harder." His eyes fixed on hers. "After all, you wanted this did you not?"

"I want to go home." Her voice almost nonexistent.

"Ahh, but you are home my dear." He stepped forward into the dim light of the window. He was a handsome man, tall, lean, with long flowing black hair hanging into his face on the sides. To her he looked almost like Johnny Depp, but a little older. One thing about his appearance she could not miss was his teeth. He had a two inch long fang on either side of his mouth. He smiled proudly displaying them for her.

"I suppose it is only fair to tell you who I am, seeing as you will be part of me forever. I am Arturo, the master vampire." As he leaned in she could smell the iron on his breath. "And you are to be my love." He gently brushed her cheek with his hand.

"No! I want to go home! Please." She cried.

"Stop your crying you little bitch!" He shouted, pulling her over by her hair. Her chair fell sideways pinning her left arm under her. Her head hit the ground causing her to lose consciousness once again.

Her eyes flickered open. She had been out for a while but still remembered where she was. She tried to pull free of her bonds but was unable. The leather strap was too tight. She rolled her throbbing head to the side at the sound of footsteps behind her. She was not able to see him but she felt him near.

"Ahhh, you are up again." He said, sitting her upright in her chair. "Oh, oh my. It seems you have hurt yourself." He ran his hand along her face and she could feel the crust from the dried blood on her cheek. "What a shame." Arturo leaned in licking the dried blood from her face.

"Mmmmm, you taste sweet my child." He leaned back and smiled. "Pure." His smile grew larger, his white fangs almost hypnotizing. "A virgin."

"Are you going to bite me?" She asked, fearing for her life.

"And then some. You think that nonsense on television is real? You think we just bite you? Sorry my sweet, it is much more fun than that!"

He reached out and set his hand on her chest. She could feel his strong fingers gripping her shirt. He closed his hand and pulled. Her shirt tore free effortlessly showing her black lace bra. Her heart pounded in her chest like a drum. As his hand returned to her chest he could feel her tense up.

"What's the matter? Not in the mood? How about a little music to help you get into it." With a wave of his hand she could hear the sound of a radio in the other room.

~*You let me violate you, you let me desecrate you, you let me penetrate you, you let me complicate you.*~

The music rang in her ears. His hand slid under her bra. His strong fingers squeezing her breast. He pulled her bra down below her breasts. Her nipples hardened as he worked them with his sharp fingernails. Flicking them back and forth they began to turn purple. He knelt at the foot of the chair placing his face into her cleavage.

She could feel his sharp teeth on her porcelain skin. He bit gently at her nipples flicking them with his tongue. He would blow across them making them swell. His hands slid up her thighs, rubbing against her warm crotch. She looked down into his emerald eyes as he tore away her jeans. His eyes showed centuries of pain and anguish. She was trapped in them as he rubbed her clit with his cold hand. She began to moisten at his touch.

He stood up in front of her; her chest heaving, her breath gasping. He cut the buttons from his black satin shirt with his razor like fingernail. As he dropped his shirt to the ground she was amazed at the artwork displayed. Across his solid abdomen was an upside down cross circled by a serpent, in the serpents mouth he held the earth. A tattoo of the sun graced his right pectoral and the moon his left, and above his heart was a tattoo of a shield. He stepped forward, reaching behind her and undoing the leather bond.

"You will behave, or I will pull your insides out and feed them to you. Understand?" He asked holding the leather strap in front of her.

"Yes." She answered.

"Excellent." He slid his razor sharp nail over his wrist spurting blood in small streams. He soaked the leather strap with his blood. She waited eagerly as he gagged her with it, tying it tight so she would be forced to taste it. Her teeth bit down into the strap and lines of blood streaked down her chin.

"Is that a smile?" He asked. She reached and put her hands on his belt pulling him towards her. Her fingers brushed across the front of his pants awakening what lies inside. She pulled his belt off with her right hand as she ran her left up his stomach to his chest. His muscles were rock solid almost like granite. Once she had his belt off, she reached into his pants and pulled free his massive cock. Hard it was every bit of eleven inches. She stroked it now with one hand, and rubbed his testicles through his leather pants with the other. She yanked down on his pants and he stepped out of them. She pulled him to her and placed his cock between her large tits. Pushing hard into them he looked into her wanting eyes. She bit down hard on her gag; squeezing blood out onto her chest. Her hands rubbed slowly as she lathered her tits and his cock with his blood. Once it was rubbed in, she reached back slowly and untied the strap. As it fell from her mouth she almost instantly missed the taste.

Arturo grabbed her by the hair hard.

"You will learn to crave me!" He shoved his stiff dick hard into her open mouth. She wrapped her lips around his giant poll. She tilted her head back allowing his bloody cock to enter her throat. With every gag she took him deeper until his balls rested on her chin. She lightly flicked at his sack with her tongue; he pulled out little by little just to slide back in. She slowly pulled her head back and removed him from her mouth to breath.

"You go until I tell you to stop whore!" He yelled smacking her across her face hard enough to make her fall onto her side. "Get up!" He pulled her up onto her feet. "I will show you what it means to take me in!" He turned her around and held himself against her back.

"Lift up your hair." He ordered. She did. He smells the base of her neck. "You will beg me." She can feel his cock between her cheeks. "You will beg me to fuck you!"
"Please."

"Louder"

"Please!"

"Louder!"

"PLEASE!"

"Good." He bends her at the waist. Rubbing her clit she begins to quake. He rubs her pussy juices on his cock and slides in towards her tight asshole.

"Fuck me!" She screams, grabbing his ass and pulling him into her. Her ass stretches to accommodate his huge tool. She feels her insides move as he pounds her ass, his balls bouncing off her pussy lips. He wraps the leather strap around her neck and uses it to pull himself deeper into her. Her moans fill the room. Soon pain turns to pleasure and she screams.

"Fuck me harder! Fuck me harder, master!" She screams as he bangs against her. He pulls the strap off her neck and folds it in half. He begins to spank her bare ass with it, welting her perfect skin. She feels him inside of her, pulsing. She pulls hard and spins around to face his cock.

"I want to make you cum!" She grabs his dick with one hand and his balls with the other. She moves her hand quickly up and down his shaft shooting his goo into her mouth.

"Mmmmmmm" She moaned.

"Now it is your turn." He said laying her on her back. With her legs spread he begins to tongue her soft lips. Moving in circles and in and out; it was as if his tongue was possessed. Her body bucked hard as she shoved her clit into his mouth. She screamed as she began to orgasm. He kissed along her inner thigh until he sank his fangs deep into her artery. She came hard! As he drained her she smiled.

"You are now one with me." He said, grinning through the blood that filled his face. Then he kissed her sharing the virgin blood with her.

PART 2: TRIBUTE

HUNGER awoke the young girl. Hunger not as any man had ever felt. No this was the hunger of a beast. Jess had been bound again. Her hands tied to a steel ring in the floor. The chain that bound her was eight feet long and allowed her to move around the entire cell she had been placed in. The walls were black with centuries of dried blood. Scratch marks adorned the walls, presumably from the fingers of unsuspecting guests.

Jess stood. The weight of her shackles forcing her to slouch. She leaned against the wrought iron door and placed hear head against the bars.

"Master! Master I am hungry!" Her cries echoed down the dark corridor. No answer came. "Master, can anyone hear me?" again the echo met no reply. Her stomach ached and her head pounded. She craved blood, and even more she craved torture. She could feel darkness growing in her as a child grows in a new mother. Hours past.

"You have been reborn." Arturo's voice came from the darkness. "You are his child now."

"Yes master! I serve only you." Jess agreed.

"You must learn girl that you only reply when prompted." The cell door swung open without him touching it. "Stand."

She stood. Her face looking pale. He circled her, observing her now frail look. "You look as though you are starving." He said. She did not reply. "Good. You are learning. And you will feed. You will pay tribute to the Great One by feeding on him. He is our master, master of all, and you will share in him." He grinned that awful, beautiful grin. "Understand?"

"Yes master." She said, the hunger gripping her.

"No. I am no longer your master. You will answer only to Darkeel. He is your master now. Take him, bite him, feed from him, and serve him." He squeezed her breast. Leaning, he whispered into her ear. "Be careful. He can be a little rough."

With that he left the cell. Few moments had past when the doorway was filled with another form.

"The virgin cunt." The voice sent chills into her body. The pain from the hunger was maddening, and his voice only served to make it worse. "Do you know who I am?" he entered.

"No." She said, not wanting to look directly at him. His open hand struck the side of her face sending her flying into the corner of the room. Her chain reached the end and she jolted to a stop. "You only respond when called whore! Understand whore!"

"Yes master, please feed me." She begged while raising her eyes to see him. He stood six feet six inches tall, his muscular body rippled under his loose satin shirt. His cropped blonde hair and chiseled facial features gave him the look of a pretty boy, but she believed different. His menacing blue eyes pierced the darkness, almost glowing. "Do you wish to live for eternity as my pet whore?"

"Yes master. I want nothing more." She said getting up on her knees. Her face burned from his slap, she ached to be tortured.

"Then if proven worthy you will." He said turning his back to her.

"No master, please don't leave me!" She pleaded. He spun quickly planting his large black boot into her gut. She buckled over her arms extending as she was thrown back and yanked by the chain at the same time. She shrieked in pain. His large hand wrapped around her neck lifting her effortlessly into the air. She was unable to breath.

"I told you not to speak unless I called you whore! Did you not understand that?!" He looked her in the eyes. She did not respond. "Good." He threw her to the ground. "I will return when I think you are ready." He left the cell, leaving the door open.

After hours of waiting he returned. He was carrying a body.

"You will feed first on this." He put the body down. It was a young Asian girl, maybe eighteen years old. The girl was gagged with a white rag and her hands and feet were bound with cords. "Wait until she wakes then feed. Understand whore?"

"Yes master. Very well, thank you." She smiled, fangs had slowly begun to form in her mouth. They were still very small but very sharp. This would make for a messy feeding.

"Good." He left the cell again, closing the door behind him.

Not long passed before the young girl began to stir. Jess jumped to her feet prepared to pounce. The girl jerked at the sound of the chain sliding across the floor.

"Who's there?" She said her lips quivering.

"Shhhhhh, relax. This will only hurt for a minute." Jess said drawing herself towards her prey.

"Who are you? What do you want? Where am I?" The girl was panicking. Jess could smell the endorphin level rise in the girl's body, the hunger grew.

"I am your release." Jess pulled the girl towards her. She pulled away at first then settled in almost accepting her fate. "I will set you free from mortality." Jess said as she poised to take the first bite.

"No!" Darkeels booming voice echoed hard off the walls startling both hunter and prey. "Give her a proper kill, she deserves at least that."

Jess looked at the girl. "What is your name girly?"

"What? Why?" The girl looked afraid.

"I want you to tell my master your name." Jess slid her hand up the girl's thigh.

"Ann." She replied as she tried to pull away.

"Ann huh? Well Ann I am Jess, and we are about to be very, very friendly."

"What do you mean?" Ann asked. Jess did not answer. She slid her fingers under Ann's skirt rubbing gently on her soft cotton panties. Ann let out a soft moan as her body went limp, giving herself completely to Jess.

"Is this what you want master?" Jess asked looking up at Darkeel. "Does this make you happy?"

He nodded rolling his fingers in a gesture to continue. Jess pulled Ann's skirt and panties off. She began to lick up her thigh to her nicely trimmed patch. Her tongue worked carefully around Ann's hole, rubbing her pussy between her lips, sucking gently. Ann pushed against Jess's face trying to grind her deeper into her eager hole. Jess slid two fingers into her tight cunt sending waves of heat up Ann's back.

She moaned harder this time. Jess fingered her quickly as she slid up her chest biting the buttons from her white shirt. Her large breasts fell freely once the shirt was opened. Jess bit softly at Ann's small brown areolas, flicking them gently with her tongue. Ann began to move in sync with Jess as she added a third finger. A small trickle of blood began to drip from Ann's bare breast. Jess sucked pulling as much of the sweet nectar as she could from the small wound. Ann arched coming to climax. Jess quickly moved to the neck striking the artery at the moment of orgasm. Ann screamed in pain then again in bliss. Jess continued to rub Ann's clit as she drank. Soon Ann closed her eyes. Jess turned towards her master.

"Was that to your liking master?" Her eyes eager for approval.

"Yes, it was good." He smiled showing his pearl white fangs.

"I am here to please you master." She smiled through her blood soaked face. He stepped forward and knelt to meet her face to face.

"Let me taste her on you." He ordered. She leaned in and kissed him. She could feel him puling the blood from her mouth as his fangs grew longer. His kiss was like eternity. She felt her soul move as he drew her deep. He kissed her as if he was unlocking every mystery she had ever pondered, as if he held the answer to her every question and knew all her deepest secrets. He kissed her and pushed her onto her back. He lifted his head and she gazed deep into his eyes. She saw centuries of torture and pain.

"You will be mine forever." He whispered as she felt him penetrate her. The wind was pulled from her lungs as his huge member pierced her for the first time. She bit down hard on her lip causing blood to spurt into her mouth. He pushed into her slowly at first but building speed quickly. Her pussy stretched to accommodate his gorging tool.

"Fuck me harder master, fuck me until I can no longer breathe!" He rammed harder, pushing her across the floor with every pump. He wrapped his massive arm around the back of her neck and pounded harder into her. "Yes! Fuck me master. Take me to your heaven!" She screamed. He thrust harder and harder pushing the air from her with each blast.

Her body seemed to wrap around him, her finger nails digging into his flesh tearing it out in ribbons. She came, but still he pounded. She came again. Her body went limp. She was no longer able to control her limbs. He lifted her head to his neck and pushed her face deep into his jugular until her fang punctured his thick skin.

Her mouth was filled instantly with the thick red liquid. He continued to fuck her. The blood in her mouth was the richest sweetest thing she had ever tasted. It tasted as if it had been blended together over a thousand years, from a million victims. She came spewing her juices all over his giant cock. He rammed hard and pulled out. He pulled her head back and she wrapped her lips around his pole and drew him in. Her teeth grazing the shaft as he pushed deeper into her face. He pulsed releasing his fluid into her. She swallowed a small grin forming around him. He pulled out.

"Thank you master." She said, falling back onto her side.

"Sleep now. For we have eternity to play." He said caressing her cheek. She fell quickly into a deep sleep.

Jess awoke with the sun lighting her face. She sat up and looked around. The park where she sat was emptying as the sun sat alone on the horizon. Her notebook computer had slid off her lap. She hit save and then the power button. She looked at her watch. She had been there asleep for almost three hours, yet she felt as if it had been weeks.

She gathered her things and stood up.

"What a weird dream." She said walking towards the path back to her house. She walked home whistling Nine Inch Nails, as a small trickle of blood ran down to her knee.

The End

The Final Release

Written by Belladonna

THE wrought iron gate shut firmly behind her. She looked down the dark alley and wondered if she was in the right place. The stench of garbage and putrid water clung to the midnight air and the glow of the full moon was the only source that lit her way. Brick walls that narrowed to a single door at the end of the alley were waiting for her. She passed homely beggars and junkies in frail forms. Fear grew inside of her by the second, but for some unknown reason she felt safe, untouchable.

She reached her cloak pocket and read the note she found earlier that evening under her doorway. Wondering what it all meant she continued her approach. At the end of the alley was a single stairwell to what appeared to be an abandoned building. But the towering man at the doors entrance hinted differently. The hood of her cloak covered everything but her hypnotic stare and blood red lips. She heard objection in the man's voice.

"Only members and guests allowed. Do you have an invitation?" He firmly asked.

She handed him the letter, his dark eyes widened as he read the signature on the note. Blood red letters that spelt out the name, *Darkeel.*

She didn't know what it meant but was eager to find out. He immediately gestured her in a terrified look that appeared on his face. But she chose to ignore what was meant to be a fatal warning.

She walked through the entrance and was surprised to see hundreds of bodies writhing on the dance floor, moving in unison to the thrashing's of industrial music. Absinthe intoxicated souls in animalistic states feeding off of each other's sexual energies while moving to the sounds of *Nine Inch Nails*. Pure amazement took over her thoughts, she'd never known of this place until tonight. Sitting at the bar all alone, a foxy bartender with blonde locks and every piece of visible flesh tattooed and pierced. The woman approached with smoky eyes and smeared lipstick;

"What'll It be doll?" A hint of New York in her voice.

"Nothing for me thanks. I'm meeting someone." The girl fluidly replied.

A cocky smile appeared on the bartenders face.

"Oh, yea? And who would that be?" the bartender asked.

"Darkeel." Jess sternly replied.

The girls face lost all emotion, she reached for Jess and gripped her jaw with her long painted fingernails. "Be careful." She whispered. Her hand dropped from her face, the woman bit her lip and left Jess entirely alone.

Jess slowly turned the barstool around and dropped the hood of her cloak to her shoulders. She lifted her eyes up to scan the room of lost souls. Their eyes meeting instantly. There he was across the dark room of writhing bodies, sitting on a couch all alone.

Dressed in all black from head to toe, the only thing of color on his body was those piercing blue eyes that read her soul completely. His smiled seemed to beckon her from across the way, for an instant she was too scared to move…to breathe. It was as if the room froze and they were the only two that existed. The sea of bodies seemed to dance without music, people seemed to speak without saying a word, and the only thing she was sure of was her blood coursing through her veins.

She stepped onto the floor, her boots not making a sound. An eerie silence filled her head as she made her way across the room. Bodies moved from her approach effortlessly without a word, without a touch. It seemed like eternity when she finally reached him. His leg placed on his knee at the ankle. His arms to the sides of him resting on the back of the crimson velvet couch. She timidly approached him, biting her bottom lip in anticipation. His smile was powerful and so was his voice.

"Ah, Lady Jess. Welcome."

He slowly stood to tower over her nearly a foot above her head. He reached for her hand and kissed it in a respectful gesture. Keeping his eyes locked on hers, the entire time.

"You must be Darkeel I presume." He smiled wickedly and leaned into her ear.

"That's Master Darkeel…Understand?" His voice startled her, her body stiffened.

"Yes Master." She gently replied.

"Good girl." He said with a grin.

He slyly gripped her by the waist under her cloak, "Come with me." He said.

She walked with him, their pace identical. Her breath grew quicker and so did her heartbeat. She'd never been this helpless in another person's grip before. They walked to a door at the end of the room that was guarded by two very intimidating men. They quickly opened the door with fear on their faces. She marveled in his power and continued her pace alongside him.

The door opened to reveal a long dark corridor that lead to another door. The red lights were dim she stuck closely to him, her arm wrapped around his strong back; her hand gripping his waist. He smiled at her in that mischievous way, piercing her soul and sending chills up her spine. He burst through the door forcing it open with his free hand. The door revealed a private garage with a single car in the room. A Porsche convertible, blood red. The top was down and the moon glowed down through the skylight to reveal the beauty of the car. He walked to the passenger side door and opened it for her.

"Get in!" his voice boomed and she quickly got into the car to hear the door slam shut.

She jumped and he laughed that wicked laugh. Fear struck her. Was she completely insane or would this be the night she'd always wanted? His footsteps echoed as he walked around the car. He jumped in stealthily and the ignition roared.

"Open the glove box." He demanded. Jess quickly did. A roll of duct tape and a cloth blindfold. She looked into his eyes with fearful questioning. He smiled.

"Put it on." Her hands shaking, she blindfolded herself tightly, the black cloth left her completely blind. She could only hear the power of his voice and the sound of his laugh. That laugh that sent chills up her spine. He leaned over and grabbed the duct tape from the glove box grazing her inner thighs with her fingertips, she moaned. He laughed and bound her wrists with the tape.

"Such a *pure* cunt. What a pleasure it will be to break you in." The radio turned on to reveal *Athamay's* "Caged." She bit her lip, how did he read her thoughts knowing this song made her weak? She heard the sound of the garage door open, he gripped her by the back of the neck and pulled her close to his lips and whispered into her ear; "You're all mine."

Her lip quivered and he quickly sped out of the garage and onto the street. She had no idea where they were going, all she could hear was the sounds of the city as she felt the roar of the engine. The pounding of *Athamay* coursed through her veins as he drove faster and faster into the night. What seemed like hours went by when they finally slowed down she felt the car turn into what felt like a driveway. A long driveway. She smelled fresh earth and trees, her heart pounded faster. The car finally stopped and she heard his door open; he shut it firmly. His boots stoically walking on the gravel to her side, he opened the door and ripped the duct tape off of her wrists. She moaned in pain as the tape ripped off the top layer of her skin.

"You know nothing of pain. Get out!" Darkeel's voice coursed through her body. She unbuckled herself as she heard her door open. Still blindfolded she was eager to ask questions but feared she'd reap the consequences of such actions. She cautiously stepped out of the car and stood. He pulled her towards his body. She could feel his rock hard member pressed against the part of her abdomen just above her pussy. She moaned, feeling his tool against her body. He slammed the door and turned her around, she felt him pressed against the back of her body. Completely blind and vulnerable to what would happen next, her thoughts were clouded with sex.

"Put your hands on the car!" He demanded, she was confused.

"Now!" He said.

She jumped and put her hands on the car door. He worked his hands all over her virgin body. Moaning with pleasure from his touch, feeling his hands travel from the back of her thighs, up her ass, around her hips and up her stomach and breasts. Trembling from his touch he pressed his body against hers. As his strong hands traveled down her shoulders, her arms and stopping to grip her hands.

"Meeting a complete stranger, and not bringing a single thing to protect yourself with? Not very smart." He said with a cruel tongue.

He flipped her over, her back forced against the car. He trailed his fingers from her lips to her stomach. She squirmed under his touch unable to control herself laughing once again.

"You like my touch, I've only begun." He spoke in her ear and her body went limp against his chest. He gripped her face in his hands and forced a kiss. She moaned feeling his hands slowly working the blindfold, his tongue seemed to taste her soul. He took the blindfold off and tossed it into the car. She opened her eyes to reveal Darkeel in front of her and what she saw behind him blew her mind.

A house of gigantic proportions, trees surrounded this enormous house, she saw the driveway they approached on. She couldn't see a house anywhere near this one, she looked around and realized she was completely, utterly alone. She could see gravestones on miles of property and wondered how he knew that she loved cemeteries so much. His own personal graveyard.

She wondered how many bodies were here but quickly got rid of the thought, refusing to think of such morbid things. Once again he gripped her firmly by the waist and pulled her closely to him. They walked towards the double doors of the mansion and he entered with ease. Such luxury appeared in this beautifully decorated home, velvet curtains everywhere and morbid artwork as far as the eye could see.

It was a home that was a perfect vision of *Tim Burton's* mind and every square inch was the most amazing thing she'd ever seen. Only things she'd seen in her dreams but never expected to see in reality. The doors shut firmly behind them and locked her into his world. A world that she'd never been in before and was scared to the core to see what it had in store for her. He removed her cloak and hung it on what appeared to be a meat hook suspended from a chain that fell from the ceiling. Her leather corset revealed her porcelain shoulders, her tight pants adorned with combat boots that firmly tied at the knees. She felt naked without her velvet red cloak.

"It's icy in here." She said hinting her vulnerability. He slapped her hard across the face she gasped in shock from pain, but mostly the action itself. She gripped her jaw to feel the swelling of what would later be the bruised imprint of a hand.

"Only speak when you are spoken too. That was your warning." Darkeel's face tightened.

A tear formed in her eye but she refused to cry, refused to show any sign of weakness even though he'd already found plenty of things to use against her. Too naïve to know that he'd watched her for years waiting for the final release. She looked behind him to a stairway that spiraled upwards to the second floor. The steps velvet, crimson and so was every piece of fabric in the house. All around her was the blood red color, which comforted her in the deepest pits of her heart.

"Follow me." His voice again startled her.

She followed him closely down the extravagant hallway, hearing his footsteps travel up each step. Her pulse quickened and her breath grew short.

"Quickly cunt. We have many things to do before sunrise."

She hurried her pace and reached the top of the spiral staircase. He stood waiting for her. She stood next to him with apprehension that evil grin appeared on his face once again her lip quivered. There were a set of double doors at the top of the stairs with marble and granite décor around the doorknobs and frame. She looked closely at the detail, they were women. Naked, writhing women in sexual positions orgasmic expressions on their faces of ecstasy and bliss. The doors had beautiful gothic crosses on them of marble and abalone. Such beauty and attention to detail.

"Rare to find a girl with taste." They both smiled and looked into each other's eyes.

"It's beautiful." She said with apprehension, preparing for the consequences of her statement.

He placed his strong hands on the doorknobs and pushed them open. The room was enormous and obviously *his* bedroom. A four poster canopy bed with black silk sheets and black curtains tied to each post. Floor to ceiling windows that revealed his private cemetery. Elegance everywhere, paintings by her favorite artists, ones that she'd dream to see at museums; but never expected to see here. She heard the roar of a sudden thunderstorm, the booming sounds of thunder and the pouring rain drenched the windows. Lightening lit the sky and illuminated the room to reveal racks, swings and harnesses. All things she'd desired in the darkest part of her mind was here, everything a girl that yearned for pain and pleasure could ever desire was in this very room.

Candles were everywhere they dimly lit the beauty around her. The fragrance of roses lingered in the air, lightning crackled again to reveal dozens of roses in red and black all over the room every piece of furniture was covered in petals. He wrapped his arms around her body and pressed his eager form against hers. She moaned, she'd waited for this touch her entire life and finally she had it wrapped around her. His touch drove her insane, her body was useless in his grip and she knew her mind was as well. He ran his fingers through her hair and laughed in her ear.

"You're all mine!" He pulled her head back by the hair and bit down hard on her neck.

"Yes Master!" She wailed in bliss.

Her moans competed with the thunder as she melted against his body. His touch was agonizing. She wanted more, he teased her with every kiss, every graze of his teeth and fingertips. All she wanted was to be his for eternity. He brushed her hair from her shoulders to reveal the top of her porcelain skin. He slowly unhooked her corset with each hook that came undone her pulse quickened faster and faster. Her breath grew shallow with each kiss that was placed on her neck. The final hook came undone as her corset fell to the floor. She gripped his hips pulling him closer to her, she yearned to feel his member against her half clothed flesh, and she relished the fact that he desired her. He slid his hands up her stomach and to her breasts, whispering words into her ears that she didn't recognize. Her lip quivered and her moans grew louder, he teased her nipples and trailed his kiss from her neck to her shoulders.

"Take off your boots." He commanded.

She bent over and pressed her ass against his loins. He moaned as she rubbed herself against him. She slowly untied the laces and kicked them off gripping her hips and rocking himself against her. She stood back up only to be dressed in pants now, his hands slid to her hips he pulled her pants down with stealth lingering at the back of her thighs kissing them with each inch of fabric. He removed them from her. Her pants reached her ankles and he could smell the aroma of sex on her. She stepped out of them. As he stood, he whispered to her:

"Now...turn around and remove your panties."

She slowly turned around, he sat on the edge of the bed now with a grin on his face. His breath quickened as he saw her, she stood there smiling at him sliding her hands through her hair and down her bare chest, slowly making her way down her stomach and to her red underwear. She slid her hands under the fabric and inched them down her hips. They fell from her thighs, she stepped out of them and stared deep into his eyes. She walked to him slowly with the swank of her hips his smile grew. She placed her hands on his knees and fell to hers, looking up to her towering master's eyes she waited for his command.

"Such a good slave." He spoke fluidly with a grin.

He reached towards one of his bed posts and grabbed a spiked collar. Tilting her head up, he fastened the collar around her neck. She bit her lip knowing now that she completely belonged to him. Her hands slid up his thighs, she felt his hunger and longed to be his victim. She placed her lips on his loins the only thing between her lips and his eager flesh was the fabric of his pants, which she was determined to remove; at all costs.

She gripped his thighs and as she slowly unzipped his pants with her teeth she felt him swell. His moans filled the room as he gripped the leash that was attached to her collar with one hand, and his other hand gripping her hair. Her nails sliding up his torso, she jerked on his pants hard and pulled them completely off. She massaged his hard cock with her fingertips as she slowly removed his boxers. She ripped at his shirt to reveal his chiseled body. He gripped her hair hard and tilted her head back gazing into her eyes.

Her breath quickened. She licked her lips and a grin appeared on his face. Her mouth opened completely, his cock hard, she gorged herself instantly on his tool. Forcing every inch down her throat she went faster and faster flicking her tongue all over his shaft and sucking hard at the tip he controlled the rhythm with his grip in her hair. She felt the need to gag but refused to stop until he came. She teased his balls with her fingertips and pressed his perineum. He moaned and grunted never had a girl sucked on him with such determination, he almost came when he pulled her head back.

"You're not pure!" He yelled. Shock appeared on her face, never had she been accused of not being the virgin that she was.

"Answer me!" He yelled.

"Master, I'm completely pure." She timidly replied.

He pulled her leash close to him giving her no means to run and slapped her hard again across the face.

"Do not lie to me!" He yelled.

"I've been with many cunts, both pure and used and nobody has your determination!" His voice echoed throughout the room, she nervously spoke.

"Master I swear to you on my life, that I'm as pure as the day I was born."

"Swear on your life… Are you sure you want to gamble with that?" Darkeel asked.

"Stand up whore!" He demanded.

Jess quickly rose to her feet and waited for his torture. He grabbed her by the neck and lifted her up, throwing her to the bed and quickly tying her limbs to each post. She shook in terror not knowing what would become of her. Tears formed in her eyes and streamed down her face. She was too scared to make a sound; his half torn shirt fell from his shoulders and he stood at the end of the bed. Crawling on top of her he kissed her neck and laughed that evil laugh once more that sent chills to her core. She shook in terror crying she couldn't help the tears.

"Please don't. Not like this." She begged.

He slapped her again, the bruises formed on her face two of what would be many that he planned to give her. He bit her hard on the chest, the pain took the air from her lungs and he continued to take control of her body and soul. He made her way down her stomach and slapped her pussy, she gasped in pleasure.

"We'll see if you're as pure as you say you are...Cunt!"

"Please Master...No!" She pleaded.

He kissed her swollen flesh and teased her cunt with his lips and tongue, she bucked wildly against him screaming his name in bliss. Her muscles tensed in sexual possession and she felt her blood quicken, her body stiffen; until she met her release. He climbed on top of her pulling her body up by her hips, he teased her entrance with her tip and as she caught her breath he rammed himself inside of her. Her screams of pain filled the room as he pounded away. Ripping her body and raping her mind, tears streamed down her face; but she wanted more. She ignored the pain as much as possible. They met their release together and he fell on top of her body.

"Now you know what it means to be broke in, my filthy cunt." He gripped her by the neck and spoke into her ear. The tears ran down her face as she caught her breath.

"Take me completely Master. I'm yours for eternity." She said.

"I know you better than you know yourself Master." She said heavy breathed.

A look of interest appeared on his face. No girl had ever dared say such things and he was eager to know what she meant. He gripped her face and demanded to know what she meant.

"Explain whore." He cruelly spoke.

Her lip quivered as she was determined to explain herself. Bound to the bed she knew she'd get what she longed for and knew she could grant him the one thing that no girl would willingly give him.

"I've watched you for years Master. Hoping that someday I would be the one that you longed for more than anyone else. I know the demons that haunt your soul, the reason why you find such peace in your cemetery. You yearn to bury your conquests there but have never found one that you wanted to keep here with you for eternity." Jess said.

"I'm the one you've searched for your entire life, the one girl that wants to be yours for eternity. I only needed you inside me once to know that I belonged to you. Like a victim belongs to her vamp, you've called to my soul for years and waited to find me. Here I am, yours for the taking. I want to be the one to wake your demons, the ones that you cage deep inside of you, thinking that nobody sees you for what you are. I do. I see you completely." Jess fluidly said.

A look of shock appeared on his face. Never had he run across a girl with what appeared to be such an interesting concept.

"Continue." Darkeel replied.

"You conquer girl's minds and bodies but still that isn't enough. You've always wanted more to take than a girls mind, body and soul, your conquests satisfy you but never completely. You want their lives. I want to be your first, take me completely. Release your demons that you have inside and take my life. Kill me, release the side of you that you've never revealed to anyone." Jess said.

He was speechless the one girl that knew him to the very core now knew his darkest secret. He sat up and straddled her vulnerable body. The darkness swirled inside him and his demons grew by the second. The grin of pure evil appeared on his face, he knew that she was the one he's been searching for his entire life. He gripped her neck and she smiled in anticipation.

"Do it!" She screamed.

He bucked inside her with such force, the entire time they held each other's gaze ramming harder and harder his hands around her neck. With each breath he gripped her neck tighter and tighter. Her breath grew shorter with each pump, she felt the breath of death approaching and she smiled one last time as they came together for what would be the very last time. He closed the eyes of her lifeless corpse and began to dress putting his pants on along with his trench coat. He stared at her lifeless body and smiled knowing that he was now complete. The one girl that released his caged self, releasing the terrifying demon locked away deep inside of him.

Lightning lit the room up to reveal the only girl he ever wanted. He walked to each limb and untied her. He carried her limp body outside. Each step he took to the cemetery was a step of release, he placed her body on the ground as he dug her grave. The rain poured down and he continued to shovel the fresh earth into a pile. Hours passed; finally her resting place was complete. He picked her up one last time, he kissed her lips and noticed the blue color of her flesh.

"The final release." He whispered in her ear. He placed her in the shallow grave under the giant oak tree and threw a single red rose on top of her body. He peered into the freshly dug hole looking at her face to see what appeared to be a smile. He grabbed the shovel and slowly threw dirt onto her corpse. Thunder continued to roar as he finished his dark task. Dripping wet he walked back to his house and made his way to his room completely satisfied with the nights end. He slept soundly that night unlike any other time he could recall. The next morning he awoke gazing out the windows to reveal under the giant oak tree, the freshly packed earth. What shocked him to the core was to see, what appeared to be an entire bush of wild red roses that bloomed overnight on her freshly dug grave.

"You're mine now, for eternity." Darkeel said as he sipped his coffee on the balcony of his mansion. He knew that she was the only one that was brave enough to release him; completely.

Solitary

WRITTEN BY BELLADONNA

SHE awoke from her drug induced slumber without sight or mobilization. Head aching, covered in sweat and consumed by fear. The side effects of the unknown substance coursing through her veins. She screams in an English accent.

"Where the fuck am I?!"

Pain. Silence. She cringed in agony, her head throbbing. Being blindfolded had its disadvantages. As she sat immobilized and clouded by darkness she pondered what got her here in the first place. She had no concept of time, if it was day or night, where she was now was a complete mystery and all she had was time to think.

The last thing she remembered was being in that club. A club filled with scantily clad women with an eternal thirst for sadistic torture, submission and blood. Donna always was a prized possession for all the truly sadist females living behind the veil of darkness. The absolute epitome of sex appeal and true masochism.

Her long raven locks of hair swaying from side to side as she felt the pounding of *Athamay* coursing through her soul. Her cat like eyes and mischievous grin oozing with thoughts of pain and torture. Torture for a tortured soul, she relished in that. If only she could find a Mistress that could fulfill her every depraved desire. The pounding continued all eyes were on Donna and her heaving breasts. As the music coursed through her body the vultures craved her fresh meat.

Preoccupied in her fantasies of lust and torture she didn't see the woman that had been watching her for years. Donna came into that club every night since she was old enough to hypnotize the employees with her sex appeal. She had always been able to keep all eyes on her even from an early age. With that said she never noticed the owner, and intoxicated in this atmosphere she had no idea that the owner was a woman. A woman that would have Donna for her taking when the urge for torture became too much. Too much for fantasy she needed fresh meat for the taking and Donna was the perfect specimen for her new personal endeavor.

She heard the creaking of what sounded like a very heavy, metal door. She screamed in frustration.

"Where the fuck am I?! And what the fuck is going on!"

She was immediately slapped hard across the face. The pain made her whimper like a small canine, disciplined like the little bitch that she was. Her face stung and her headache intensified. Her blindfold was removed to reveal a candle lit torture chamber. A figure clothed in black from head to toe removed her blindfold. She was shaking in utter fear. She began to open her mouth when the tall muscular figure put his index finger over his lips and gestured the sign of silence. She wisely decided to keep her mouth shut since she was in no position to be making demands. She began to look around. It was a tower room of some sort.

The room had no windows and was lit only by candle light. She was strapped spread eagle on her back and naked to a medical table. This table was meant for control. Every one of her joints had been tightly secured with leather straps, including her neck.

The only choice she had was to lie still and look around as much as her eyes would let her. Candle light never was good for seeing torture devices clearly if anything they made them more intimidating. Peering around the tower, she saw a table on her left with all sorts of medical tools, things she hadn't even seen in a surgeon's room. Things she did recognize such as scalpels and syringes covered in blood, and tools that looked so ancient and painful that she could only ponder with curiosity. Next to that was a St. Andrews Cross, black like her soul, covered in shards of glass, stainless steel spikes and razor blades, her heartbeat quickened and her clitoris throbbed.

Next to that was something that she thought would only reveal itself to her in her darkest depraved fantasies. A reproduction of Elizabeth Bathory's very own iron maiden, or was it a reproduction? She wasn't sure but her fear and lust intensified. The door of the medieval torture device was slightly cracked to reveal freshly sharpened spikes, and layers of blood coating the entire device. The entire place had scratch marks and blood that was left to dry as a lovely reminder of all of the girls that had been sacrificed in this very tower.

Within the confines of this tower was a giant wooden trunk, it looked ancient sitting next to the iron maiden with a clear glass pitcher of what looked to be fresh blood. Beside that was an offering of bread. A giant pentacle hung above that, she then realized it was an altar, and this tower room was an offering to the Goddess Lilith. There we're all sorts of interesting items on this altar, what appeared to be bones that used to be fingers. There we're feathers and crystals the pitcher of blood next to the loaf of freshly baked bread, all resting on a tapestry of red velvet.

A small slot on the door opened to reveal a pair of hypnotic eyes. The pare eyes in all their changing glory appeared to smile, smile in a very sinister way. The metal slot slammed shut and she could hear a female voice speaking with somebody. Feeling nauseous from the drugs she leaned over and began to vomit onto the stone floor. The door creaked slowly, painfully open. The metal door slammed with such force that it made a loud echo against the stone wall that made Miss Donna shudder. All she saw was darkness; she peered into it to see whom or what was going to enter, feeling scared in this vulnerable state. Silence. Complete silence. The sound of a pair of heels on stone, Donna was very fond of the sound, her body ached for it.

The sound of heels on the stone floor grew closer and closer, Donna's heartbeat quickened with each step. There was a beautiful cloaked woman in shades of black, crimson hair and crimson lips on porcelain white skin, her eyes put Donna in a trance, she hardly even noticed the vomit all over her face. Perky tits and a gloved hand were the first thing that grazed her naked flesh, Donna shuddered these eyes felt so familiar yet she could not place who they belonged to. The gloved hand grabbed her by her long locks and slammed her head against the table.

"You fucking bitch, I just had this place cleaned for your arrival, only a cunt would disgrace my tower with such filth."

Donna enraged not ever being completely out of control did the one thing she could still, she spat in the veiled woman's face.

"Fuck you." She said with a devilish grin and laughed that arrogant laugh.

Immediately the veiled woman forced her hand on Donna's lips. She leaned in so close that Donna could feel the woman's rage deep inside her.

"You will regret that you little cunt."

She slammed her head against the table and walked towards the table of surgical devices. Donna shrieked in pain, not from the blow of the table but that of the drugs coursing through her throbbing head. She began saying anything and everything she could possible, to anger the veiled woman; but of course nothing worked. The clank and clatter of metal was echoing throughout the room and Donna had no choice but to sit and wait. Wait to see what this mysterious woman had in store for her. The night was young and the torture hadn't even begun, she felt the hand of death inside the pit of her stomach. Donna knew something was going to happen but even her instinct couldn't have warned her enough. The veiled woman turned around her veil gone, the look in Donna's eyes was utter shock.

"You!'" She exclaimed but nothing followed.

The veiled woman smiled with complete and utter satisfaction with needle and steel thread in gloved hand.

"But of course my dear, I've had my eye on you ever since you walked in that cold foggy night years ago. Now I will show you what your true purpose is in life. Donna was your Christ given name, there is no Christ here to save you my dear. Heaven does not exist, just a twisted delusion created by greedy man to keep profit in his pocket."

She continued, "Hell is the realm that I belong to my little specimen and the reason why you are here is simple...fate. You will discover your purpose in this incarnation and I am here to show you your way. Welcome to the *Realm of Paradox* Slave Fate."

It all suddenly hit her in an overwhelming mass of memories. She remembered that intriguing rich woman at the club lingering near the bar. The women were all afraid of her and nobody ever questioned why she was there. She never danced, just watched, peering into the souls of those on the dance floor. Those too tainted by human poisons to even observe what was really going on.

"You were watching me!" Donna said in shock.

"Not watching my dear, hunting." She began to laugh.

"You will see my dear, in time."

Donna flashed back into her mind and remembered always being the center of attention, getting what she wanted with the bat of an eye. That night was different, she felt as if nobody wanted her anymore. Sitting at the bar frustrated, not caring about all of those that have worshiped her in the past, her only concern... she wanted more. The beautiful woman that worked behind the bar set down a glass of the most expensive Absinthe in the entire Country.

"This is from Mistress Belladonna."

Donna not caring who or where this Mistress was, greedily relished in the expensive mind-altering drink. She drank it quickly and felt a burst of deviousness. She went back to the dance floor, Unaware that this delicious glass of liquor was laced with a strong tranquilizer. The drug coursing through her veins as she danced, relishing in the fact that people were lusting for her. She began to stumble, the entire club began to look very odd, very frightening. She stumbled to the bathroom and leaned against the wall, out of nowhere appeared a very tall man, muscular with blonde hair, pretty boy features and gorgeous blue eyes dressed in a security uniform. He smiled an evil smile and picked her up. At the exact time Mistress Belladonna met his evil grin with hers and they both exited the club through separate doors. The music continued and so did all the women dancing in this hidden establishment.

Donna peered into the darkness speechless and stunned. She never saw it coming. She was abruptly pulled out of her drugged recollection to a loud noise. It was the door, it didn't creak this time it slammed hard against the tower wall. Donna jumped yet didn't move and inch. A towering figure appeared in the entrance, Donna's worst fears jumped into mind.

"Is he going to fuck me?!" The thoughts coursed through her head.

This was the worst fear of any woman that craved only female flesh. He stood an intimidating six foot four inches, with a hangman's hood. Piercing blue eyes we're the only thing that we're of color on this man shrouded in black. Long rubber butchers gloves adorned his massive hands and forearms. His skintight clothing revealed she was going to be ripped to pieces by his massive cock. He approached Mistress Belladonna with a presence that sent chills up Donna's spine. Discarding his hood, He firmly gripped the domina by the nape of her neck and forced a long kiss onto her mouth. She moaned in submissive ecstasy a side of her that was for his viewing pleasure only. To feel his satisfaction on her lips was all she needed. She did what she was told and he was satiated with her taste in victims. He peered into her eyes and formed a sinister grin.

"I've trained you well Belladonna. You found such a pretty piece of flesh." With these words appeared a smile of content on her face.

"Thank you Master Darkeel, I do what I can to please your cravings."

She was no longer Mistress with him here. She was and had always been his minion. The one that he molded with his ideals. The one that did his biddings upon request, stripped of morals and values. A slave in complete and utter submission, everything he ever wanted. Belladonna walked towards Donna with needle and steal thread. Donna's eyes grew wide in fear. She started to squirm as much as she could which wasn't much at all. With each step they took towards her Donna's fears grew, the evil that was in this tower was an evil that she was never prepared for.

"What are you going to do with that?!" Donna screamed at Belladonna

Master Darkeel immediately grabbed her face and forced her head to the table. She was completely immobile, they both laughed in sadistic tones. The tears poured out of her eyes and streamed down her alabaster flesh. Belladonna set the needle and wire on her bare chest. Her breaths were shallow and quick she grazed her cheek with her long red nails. Dragging them down her neck and tits she licked her lips and peered into her master's eyes. Her gaze traveled to his pants and lingered on his rock hard bulge.

"Mmm Master likes this Miss Donna and what Master Darkeel wants. I make sure he gets, do you understand?"

Trailing her fingers down her stomach to her pussy mound. Donna was furious enraged that a man would be pleasured by her body in anyway. She spit at Belladonna, the liquid hit her cheek and before Donna could say a word her face was jolted by the pain of a very hard slap across the face. Belladonna enraged wiped her cheek and grabbed the needle and wire."

"Hold the cunt down Master I will give her what she deserves."

Darkeel firmly held her head in place against the table, gripping her jaw to stay closed. Belladonna grabbed her lips harshly and pierced her bottom lip, then upper lip; at one side and began sewing her mouth shut. Donna's muffled screams of agony we're no match for the sadistic pair, trying to move was proven useless and her mouth was slowly, and painfully wired shut. Belladonna double stitched the cunt's mouth to make sure no more fluids would escape. Darkeel was pleased his hunger for sadism was long overdue and this is precisely what his soul craved.

"Very good my pet." A sinister grin spread across his face with a gleam of evil in his eyes.

He reached for the needle and thread. The stone floor echoed with his powerful steps as he approached the specimen's tits. Mistress Belladonna reached behind her on the medical table for a latex nurse's mask, black with a blood red cross on the front. She walked towards the specimen with a gleam of excitement and cruelty. Darkeel met her evil eyes with a smile reaching his long strong arms over and grazing her chin with his fingers.

"Clamp." Darkeel instructed Belladonna.

She grabbed a pair of long metal clamps and handed them to Master. Her long latex gloved fingers gripped Slave Fates nipple. He clamped down firmly and pierced the tender flesh, Donna whimpered. Belladonna firmly gripped her other tit and held it tight for her beloved Master. He forced the needle through and Donna's eyes rolled back in ecstasy. Belladonna adorned the holes with silver metal rings. Darkeel was pleased with the jewels and stood back and watched as his creation, his slave, Belladonna made her vicious fantasies come to fruition. She walked into the next room to a fireplace with red hot embers she reached for the shovel and took a small cauldron full of embers out, and with that a flaming red branding iron with a pentagram and inverted ankh in the center. She walked into the tower room and saw her Master and all his manly glory he was sitting in his favorite chair the chair that he always sat in to watch specimens tortured. Belladonna missed seeing that look in his eye that look of freedom and power that look that possessed his soul when he saw a woman in a vulnerable state. She set down the cauldron of red hot embers and the branding iron and seductively walked across the room to her god.

"It's been so long since I've held you in my mouth, I beg you give me the pleasure once again Master."

She dropped to her knees like the whore she was; the whore she was, only for him. Her gloved fingers unzipping his pants. His hard member of generous proportions was throbbing and begging for her mouth. His breath grew heavy and that look of pure lust resonated from within him. He slapped her hard across the face and gripped the back of her hair with a force that brought a shriek from Belladonna he slammed her mouth onto his firm cock and groaned in utter bliss. She furiously gagged on his cock pressing her lips hard around his engorged member and forcing it in and out of her mouth as fast as she could. Swiveling her mouth side to side tormenting every inch of his dick. Suckling on the aching head and looking him directly in the eye with a cock hungry smile on her face. Her long crimson nails gently held his balls close to his body. He grunted, his body jerked and his hand gripped harder onto the back of her head. With a gasp of air Belladonna said in utter submission.

"Fill me with your glory Master!"

Master Darkeel's eyes fluttered as he blew his massive load in her throat. She gagged and swallowed lustfully cleaning his cock with her mouth and tongue relishing in every drop of cum spilt. Darkeel's heart was beating fast, his breath heavy, he was satiated. She wiped her lips and looked down at a smear of cum on her hand, she looked her Master in the eye and licked up the mess with a smile.

"It is a privilege to serve you Master Darkeel."

Donna waited anxiously for what was to happen next she had her eye on the branding iron and cauldron of red hot pokers during the entire sexual act. Donna lied there, Stiff in fear. Mistress Belladonna dusted her knees off and picked up where she left off.

"Awww where we're we?"

"That's right I was about to brand you as my own." She smiled that deviant smile.

She grabbed a pair of steel tongs and held the embers over Donna's restrained head, lingering around her eyes. Donna shook in fear.

"I could blind you my dear, all it takes is one slip of the finger and you'll be in utter darkness until you're food for the worms."

Mistress Belladonna reached down under the table, a handle and crank appeared. She began to turn, Donna and the table began to rise, higher and higher with each notch on the wheel. Donna and the table suddenly stopped. Mistress Belladonna kept cranking the handle, Donna's legs began to separate. The farther and farther they separated and the more muffled screams of agony were echoed throughout the ominous tower. She was stretched so far that her legs we're straddled, the pain was smeared all over Donna's face her eyes watered and squinted and her thighs began to tremble.

"Now my dear we must remove this filthy hair. Only bitches have hair and I never experiment on bitches. Stay very still my dear or you will be in excruciating pain."

Mistress Belladonna picked up the tongs with the hot ember and began singing each section of pubic hair on Donna's pussy. Donna wide eyed and in utter fear was so nervous she held her breath the entire time. She set her head down and one of the hot embers fell right into her wet pink pussy. Instead of screaming she moaned in utter ecstasy it was the only thing that's touched her cunt all night, or day; she was unaware how long she'd been there. Time didn't exist anymore.

"Awww look Master, the cunt wants to be fucked like the whore she is."

Master Darkeel walked towards Donna on the table, the fear grew strong in her soul, she had foreseen what was about to happen ever since she laid eyes on him earlier that night. He walked in between her thighs grazing his fingers all over her body. She was disgusted, full of utter rage. She began to squirm as hard as she could, but it did no good, with each jerk the straps automatically got tighter and tighter. Darkeel was pleased, he'd take away the one thing she ever had complete and utter control of, who would have the privilege to fuck her.

Mistress Belladonna grabbed the hot embers and set them on Donna's new nipple rings, they began to heat up very quickly and the scalding temperature made Donna turn every shade of red, her face flushed with pain. Mistress Belladonna lingered on the other nipple the heat intensified right when she thought that she was going to pass out from pain. Darkeel's cock rammed into her tight pink pussy. She screamed, ripping her wire stitching the blood trickled down her lips. Darkeel pumped hard, dominating her from within, his throbbing cock stretched her pussy, the pussy that was pure to all males. He fucked furiously, the loud smacking of flesh on flesh filled the room and the hunger for forbidden fruit made Master Darkeel cum harder than he'd ever came before.

At that exact moment Belladonna ripped the wire thread from her lips, she screamed as blood squirted all over her and down her lips and chest. Mistress Belladonna's sinister laugh filled the tower room and Darkeel grunted in ecstasy.

"Broken in properly like a well-bred slut, that's precisely what you deserved."

Master Darkeel zipped up his pants and walked towards the table and grabbed a pair of sheers. As Donna lay there is anger and disgust he sheered her long raven locks off to within an inch from her skull. The long gorgeous strands of hair floated to the floor, Donna wept in disappointment. Her beauty was stripped from her. The one thing that she used to manipulate those around her into the puppets she always wanted. Mistress Belladonna began shaving her head bald, the tears flowed to the stone grout in the floor. The buzzing of an unknown machine came from the dark master's direction. Donna's head now smooth as the day she was born would now be adorned with a number, a number that would haunt her to her grave, a number that when she was intoxicated called to her darkest side. Master Darkeel began tattooing the phrase SF#666. This number made no sense to Donna when Mistress Belladonna showed it to her in a small hand mirror. Mistress Belladonna looked at her with a look of amazement.

"You don't know what this is my dear? It's your number, I've had many slaves that found their fate in *The Realm of Paradox*. You have by far been the darkest specimen I've ever found. With your ridiculous obsessions with Satan, 666 is the mark of the beast and you my dear are the closest thing to a beast that has ever graced my physical presence."

Donna speechless and racking her brain for every memory of her dark days, doing lines of coke and worshiping the dark prince. She never knew that her darkness would manifest into her demise. The table began to slowly drop towards the floor the clanking of the wheel was swift and the table bluntly stopped with a jolt. Mistress Belladonna grabbed a cattle prod nearby.

"Now my dear I'm going to untie you. Try anything and I will send pain through your flesh that will make you wish you'd never been born."

Master Darkeel and Mistress Belladonna began by untying each strap. Donna behaved and waited patiently for her release, or what she hoped for was a release from this hell. She lied still waiting for permission to leave the table.

"Stand up." Darkeel told her with a firm tone.

She stood with a glazed look of trauma in her eye, her neck restraint still in place it had a lovely O ring in the center of it. Master Darkeel chained her on a long metal leash. She stood there internally frustrated but concealing the rage in her soul with utter silence. She knew that if she didn't cooperate this would be her last mortal night. Quickly without Donna suspecting it, Mistress Belladonna grabbed the branding iron that was still hot from the fire and yelled.

"Hold her tight!"

Master Darkeel gripped her arms, Donna was shaking, the pain of searing flesh made her squeal loudly her ass was on fire. Mistress Belladonna confirmed that the deed was done properly with a satisfying look on her face and a smile to her Master. Darkeel gripped the leash and led Donna out of the tower room. Mistress Belladonna followed behind and shut the heavy metal door to the tower room. They descended down the small stairwell to what appeared to be a grand hall. There was a masquerade of some sort in progress, though this was no ball that Donna had ever witnessed. Master Darkeel and Belladonna led their pretty piece of flesh onto the stage, the entire room of people men, women all in black and eyes covered with decorative fetish masks. These individuals were of obvious high stature this room was lavished in royalties that no common person could ever own. Donna was led naked onto the podium she was humiliated never had she been in front of so many people stark naked and bleeding everywhere. The auctioneer's voice reached the back of the room on the microphone.

"Who wants to own this lovely piece of property?"

Donna couldn't believe what was happening she was being auctioned off, this wasn't a party it was a slave auction and she was the prized specimen.

"I've been informed that she's a feisty one that doesn't like the men. She's formally been broken in by Master Darkeel and his minion Belladonna, SF#666 adores pain, we will start the biddings at fifty thousand dollars!"

The auctioneer rambled at a fast pace and Donna tried running in fear but was jerked down to the ground by Master Darkeel and shocked by Belladonna. She quivered and dropped to her knees in submission. She heard the bids get higher and higher from the masked audience.

"I have a lot invested on you cunt, the only way you're leaving here; is with your new Owner."

Master Darkeel never lost money on his investments. The auctioneer slammed his gavel on the podium.

"Sold! To the lovely Mistress in the back for one hundred thousand American dollars." The lovely Mistress older and still radiant as ever walked towards Master Darkeel and handed him a briefcase full of money. She was a French aristocrat who was a descendant of Marquis De Sade a real sadistic type into all sorts of torture and edge play.

"Merci Master Darkeel." She said with a thick French accent. "I look forward to molding this one to my liking."

Master Darkeel gladly handed the leash to the lovely Mistress and smiled that cunning smile.

"You are most certainly welcome."

Master Darkeel and his slave and minion worked their way towards the exit, the night was crisp and cool, the moon was full and the stars peered through the hazing clouds of the night sky. They made their way to his Porsche. Oh how she loved riding next to him in his car it made her feel alive, like the world belonged to him and that she was so lucky to watch such a skilled, powerful man, manipulate it while making it his own. They drove towards the nightclub.

"The night is still young Master, you crave more darkness do you not?"

Master Darkeel smiled at her with those piercing blue eyes, they headed towards the club for their next victim.

"I thought you'd never ask." He grinned in satisfaction.

Belladonna returned his smile with hers as they made their way back to their club for the next specimen.

THE END...FOR NOW...

The Slaughterhouse Hills Hunter

WRITTEN BY BELLA BLOODLUST

CHAPTER 1:

BITTERSWEET CHANGE

IT was a cold, dark, rain soaked evening. The deep pools of her emerald sapphire fused eyes, peered out through the dark tint of the limousine window. Down the distant road that came closer with each moment arrived a hopeful opportunity; an opportunity to start over again. The bittersweet situation she found herself in was one she never imagined, her former fiancé seated next to her; unfortunately not of flesh and blood but in a small urn that bore his name. The tear stained her cheek and the weather outside matched the pain she felt within. Cold rain beat down hard onto the roof of the vehicle. As the sky darkened with clouds the clash of thunder gave her an uneasy feeling, stirring her soul in mysterious ways.

Trying to pull herself together to make a proper first impression with her gracious new employer, who provided her with a renewed purpose that seemed in this moment like just an illusion. She remembered looking down at her kitchen table months before seeing the bills accumulate, remembering the one thing that she was told by her former lover.

"If anything ever happens to me, don't mourn my loss, move on and take care of yourself."

As hard as that promise was to fulfill she granted his wishes. Among the many pieces of papers that urgently required payment lie the hopeless future she would soon have if she didn't have the courage to make a change. When out of nowhere after months of searching she was astonished to see in the classified ads of her paper an opportunity that seemed to call to her like no other. The ad read:

URGENTLY NEEDED:

Single father in search of maternal multi-tasking woman. Must be good with children, scheduling, errands and general house duties, as well as possessing skills in clerical and assisting a very busy, over extended man. Room and board plus salary. Needed immediately.

She now found herself in a car being chauffeured from the Denver Airport to what would soon be her new residence. She peered out into the dark sky and watched the rain fall wiping the tears from her cheek she smiled at the urn and said;

"I hope you know what you've gotten me into."

The driver then updated her on what currently goes on at Burnett Manor around seven o' clock. She hadn't eaten since before takeoff and she was pleased to hear that she'd be arriving just in time for dinner.

She cleared her throat, "Excuse me driver, can I ask you something?" He smiled. "First my name is James and as for your question, shoot." Her pearly smile glistened and her dimples shown just a bit,

"Nice to meet you James, I'm Jessica; I was wondering... *what is he like?*"

James smiled back enjoying her naive curiosity, "He's not as intimidating as his first impression, I assure you. He's a very nice guy and a lifelong friend of mine."

Jessica blushed trying to hide being caught off guard, she peered down;

"I feel embarrassed, I just assumed you worked for him as I'm about to."

James laughed, "Relax you have nothing to be embarrassed about." She met his eyes with a smile and sighed with relief as she peered back out the window.

They were much closer now she could feel it, the trees were many and the road was long. She could smell the earth, freshly watered; the intoxicating aroma danced inside her. She inhaled deeply and cracked the window to embrace the scents of pine and dirt as she started to day dream. She found herself pulled out of it by the grim cemetery that suddenly appeared to her left off in the distance.

With a perplexed look on her face she tried to hold back her curiosity she asked "James is *that* what I think it is?"

James knew instantly she was speaking of the cemetery. It was always a conversation starter for anybody new to Burnett Manor. Little did she know her new employer had quite the fascination with the macabre and the morbidity of what cemeteries infinitely represent in the psyche of the human mind.

James laughed and said "Yes it's a cemetery. I hope you're not afraid of living near one, as this one is owned by Mr. Burnett. He enjoys having one nearby it fuels his creativity." Jess digested the new information and as much as she tried she couldn't help but ask more questions about this alluring and mysterious new employer of theirs.

"So who exactly is buried out there? And what does he *need it for* creative wise?"

James was amused that the cemetery threw her off a bit. This reaction was something he very much enjoyed with new people, the reaction to living in a place with a cemetery right out back was not comforting to most people but to Jess that was a different story. She often visited cemeteries, a place of peace and solitude from the chaos of life and the living.

"As far as who exactly is buried there, we're not quite sure; it's a very old cemetery and many of the tombstones are practically demolished due to age. We have no clue how many people are in there and who all of them are, in fact. As far as creativity goes you'll have to ask Kyle about that."

James continued to drive and Jessica began to ponder what her new employer Kyle was like. The road continued to wind and turn farther and farther into complete solitude the car finally stopped and what appeared was one of the most beautiful and ominous looking mansions she'd ever seen before.

The cemetery in prominent focus, the rain had stopped and the clouds hovered above, she opened the door and took in the beauty of this place; a beauty unlike anything she'd ever seen before. She grabbed her former lover peered at his urn like they were his eyes and whispered to the container;

"To a new start."

She placed it in her purse and enjoyed what would be her new home. James checked his watch to see that he had plenty of time to give her the grand tour.

"It's now 6pm Jess, do you mind if I call you Jess?" James waited for her reply.

"Not at all. I prefer it actually." with that said, James continued to fill her in that they had plenty of time to walk the grounds and show her a room by room tour of this mysterious and somber place.

"Well, being that it's almost dark we better give you the outdoor tour first."

Jess opened the door of the car and placed her former lover and her purse inside and quickly shut the door to catch up with James who was already walking ahead towards the cemetery.

The fresh earth so pure and clean from the day's rainstorm permeated the air;

"Mmmm I love that smell." Jess couldn't help but say out loud.

"There is nothing better than the smell of earth after a rainstorm." James smiled as they approached the Iron Gate to the cemetery.

Fumbling with the chain that kept the gate closed he finally untangled it and opened one side of the gate to let her in. She ascended the hill to what appeared to be the most ornate and oldest of all the tombstones in the entire cemetery. Peering around and seeing the countless graves all around her, she closed her eyes and felt the kiss of the clean breeze on her neck, the energy here pierced deep inside her and a wealth of emotions and memories that were not her own appeared before her eyes. Little did James know that she was very perceptive of the dead and what secrets they whispered to her.

She heard voices telling her that she was in danger that this would be her last stop, the final destination in her journey of life;

"I hope you're right." She told the voices, "I don't care what happens, I no longer wish to travel anymore."

"There are many more bodies here than tombstones aren't there?"

James quite astonished and a bit alarmed as to how she would know that pretended as best as he could that he had no idea what she was talking about. What Jessica didn't know was that the many unmarked graves that were here were women that were formerly in her current position, former live-in's that suddenly vanished without a trace.

"There is much more to see Jess we must get going for now, you're more than welcome to come out here whenever you like, Kyle often does. It's a place he often visits for reflection and solitude."

If only she knew that the sadistic pleasures he felt deep in his demonic soul when he reflected in solitude all the victims he himself buried here, one could only imagine the horror James would feel if he knew the ultimate truth.

Years of victims piled up, one on top of the other, a morbid display of the dark side of human nature. Would she find this place as peaceful as he did? They descended the mound and exited the iron gate to her left. She saw the back of the house, she sensed lots of slaughtering had taken place here. The color red pierced her psychic intuition and she then asked James:

"What the hell did this place used to be?" James with a perplexed look asked her "What do you mean?" she hesitatingly replied.

Jess not trying to reveal too much of her gift said "It doesn't look like your typical house it has a very industrial quality to it." She kept peering in for more answers yet nothing came just pools of blood and the screams of animals.

"This used to be a slaughter house for cattle years ago, Kyle bought it and renovated it into the home that you're about to see." James said educating her on this morbid place's history.

Jess laughed thinking how devious that she was now going to live in a place where animals were slaughtered with no conscience. What a deliciously morbid place for her to end up, the filthy thoughts of her possibly being that prey caused her pretty pink pussy to swell, her clitoris throbbing at the thought of being sacrificed like cattle made her tremble exceedingly in delight.

"Is everything okay Jess?" James asked.

"Of course. I'm just a bit tired from the trip, and haven't had much to eat today, that's all."

Jess smiled and James realized that the tour of the house would have to wait as dinnertime was soon approaching and Kyle would want to meet his new property in the flesh.

"I've only spoken to him on the phone. James how does he know I'm the right candidate for the position?" James smiled almost grinned with a sinister smirk;

"Kyle is very good at knowing people just speaking with you on the phone, he just knows somehow. I honestly don't know how he does it, but he has this gift for knowing who will fit the mold he has and who doesn't. Apparently you fit quite nicely as he typically waits longer to hire new help. He hired you instantly which is something I have never seen him do before; obviously you have impressed him."

He continued, "In other words, you have nothing to worry about."

With that they approached the back door, "Oh wait what about my things? I need to go get them first." As Jess started to walk towards the car James interrupted;

"Not to worry Jess we have people that will bring your things to your room Kyle is as eager to meet you as you are to meet him, and dinner starts in fifteen minutes we haven't a moment to lose, let's go."

With a quick pace she followed James into what appeared to be a back entrance and coatroom for the hired help. She took her jacket off and hung it up to reveal her gorgeous porcelain skin, white as snow and soft as a newborn child's. Jess was dressed in a gorgeous form fitting long dress, delicate lace on her breasts only added to the blood red color that made her flawless skin glow.

"Wow your look amazing." James blushed, "I can't believe I just said that out loud." with a laugh Jess smiled and thanked him for the compliment.

"I hope I don't look too casual I'm just so used to living in California." He shook his head

"If it's one thing Kyle doesn't care about, it's uniforms." With that they entered the kitchen.

Quickly sliding her heels off, so used to being around diverse cultures that the ancient custom always followed her wherever she went. She delicately walked into the elaborate kitchen full of pots and pans hanging from the ceiling adorned with decadently ornate kitchen cabinets in a dark mahogany red that she always had a fetish for. The color instantly put her in a dark mysterious mood. Her soft hands gliding across the granite countertops dark black slabs of marbled granite streaked with white quartz, her absolute favorite.

"I have a feeling I'm going to like it here." With a coy smile, more of a smirk as thoughts went from professional to sexual, she smiled at James and he responded with an affirming grin.

"I'll go get Master Kyle, wait here." In the center of the kitchen was an island with three barstools covered in crushed emerald green velvet. She chose the right one as it was always a habit of hers if the seat was available. Waiting patiently for the Master of this exquisite manor to arrive Jess's eyes wandered around the room to see an array of plants and flowers that she'd never seen before.

James exiting out of the same entrance that he escorted Jess to in the kitchen; waited to make sure he was unseen before gently pressing a wooden panel that triggered a trap door to a secret staircase. Ascending up to the next floor, the dark stone steps lit only with the dim flickers of light every few feet. The cold stone spiraling up, James suddenly stopped at one particular stone with great importance. Pressing on the stone he watched it push open a false wall that appeared to be a lavish bookcase. The dark mahogany wood pried open to allow enough space for him to enter the secret office room of Master Kyle.

"She's waiting in the kitchen, I've fulfilled my obligations Sir. She looks forward to making your acquaintance."

With a dark sinister grin waiting for Master Kyle's response he watched the hand of his very powerful employer reach towards a cabinet on his ornate desk. A key that was always chained to his left wrist was used to open this hidden compartment; a small closed circuit television turned on with vivid color to reveal his newly hired employee.

"Mmm excellent." With a dark smirk of satisfaction he met James's eyes with satisfaction "She's perfect, exactly what I've been waiting for, you're free for the day James, I'll take it from here."

With an affirming nod and slight bow James exited the same way he entered and descended down the stairwell to yet another secret panel hidden by a small stone; a much different one than before. The faux wall opening in the hallway of the lavished home opened wide leading James to exit out the front door. Walking efficiently fast as he felt night approaching he knew something dark was in store for the fresh meat. Master Kyle's piercing blue eyes hypnotized by his new experiment watched as the girl absorbed every bit of imagery she could while waiting for him to make his formal introduction.

Examining her from the long thick curled red locks of hair that cascaded over her shoulders to the pale color of her soft supple skin trailing his eyes down her delicate neck, he found himself entranced. Her beautiful pale skin above her cleavage line, the part of a girl that was so easy to overpower with precisely enough strength. Her eyes curious and infatuated with her new surroundings never had he seen such a creature. The other girls quite bored with waiting for him to introduce himself, this one was different so enamored by the smallest of observations, this peaked Master Kyle's enthusiasm.

"Pretty girl, *where have you come from?*" Jess biting her lip with wicked thoughts running through her head.

"*Mmm I wonder what it would be like to be taken on such a firm countertop?*" trailing her fingers up her chest and throat, sweeping her long thick locks up into a loose pile of curls neatly secured by an ornate clip of golden leaves that made her appear Grecian. Moaning quietly under her breath, eyes closed and head tilted back as she thought of what this powerful man looked like. Whispering out loud, "It's been far too long since I've felt a powerful man." feeling her nipples harden she hissed deliciously.

Leaning closely to his private television Master Kyle met the screen with a wicked grin;

"Delicious girl… It will be *such a pleasure to break you in.*" laughing to himself and feeling his cock stir at the sight of this unbridled exhibitionism. He continued to watch and listen to her erotic confessions down below.

Jess' nails were quite defined for their length to most they appeared rather shapely and feminine but what few knew was that they were sharpened to a delicate rounded point that felt divine when drug properly on hot flesh. Tracing from behind her ears, down her neck and chest to that exquisite V of her lower neck she felt her skin rise in ecstasy and knew her panties were moist with her delicious peach scent aching to be used and abused for his pleasure. Dragging her nails down both her arms she moaned, instantly biting her lip hoping that she wasn't heard.

"Control yourself Jess for god's sake you're about to meet your new boss."

Kyle laughed out loud at the site of this delicious girl knowing in time he would do to her what he'd done to the others just like her. But with more thought, more force and much more contemplation. This one was different, she was a challenge, one to quench his thirst and fuel his intoxication for power and control. He was more than delighted to watch her, to observe the smallest movements; the signals she sent when she was aroused and weak. Completely incapable of controlling herself. The perfect time for him to glamour her with his power, his presence, his overwhelming strength and fleshly desires.

Watching her teeth clench down on her lower lip as the small wry smile formed at the corners. She reached for the golden vine once more as she let loose her crimson curls cascading over her shoulders. Shaking them from side to side to tame the wildness of the locks that were always as much out of control as she felt inside; just like her curls aching to be tamed by the right trainer. Dragging her fingers up the back of her head and twisting the curls into a beautiful bouquet before fastening the clip in for the last time, two wild strands of hair fell to the left side of her face;

"It's rather chilly in here." looking down at her hard nipples standing out pert and prominent under her thin crimson dress, "Betraying me again my flesh? Ceaselessly betraying me." She said with a smile.

Searching around remembering where she placed her jacket she walked back over to the hall, all the while Master Kyle leaned in close with a pleased smile on his face;

"Perhaps it's time for formal introductions."

The phrase left his full kissable lips with a wicked ring and a laugh that would inflict tension in even the cruelest of creatures. He continued to watch her from his private viewing room.

Jess reached up and pulled on her soft warm cardigan that made her appear so pristinely innocent she knew how it drove men wild. It pulled out a side of carnality that she genuinely enjoyed although she'd never truly admit it. Wrapping the soft peach colored cardigan around her shoulders delicately placing it just so to cover her aching nipples and to give her some sort of professional appearance. When she was to meet this incredible man, she wasn't certain, but she wanted to be ready for him.

Descending down from the hidden office Master Kyle waited for the appropriate timing to make his entrance. From beyond the living room from another mysterious door that lead hidden rooms to ones that were known by the public and help. Jess stared at the clock and took a deep stabilizing breath before the approaching footsteps from off in the distance of the next room were heard suddenly. Instantly Jess stood and smiled to see the most delicious man she had ever laid eyes upon approaching her with a warm smile and incredibly piercing eyes that made Jess's heart pound and her knees fall victim to tremble. She instantly thought and imagined herself in carnal throws of dark tormenting positions that brought a smile to her face.

"Hello, it's a pleasure to finally meet you Jess; you don't *mind* if I call you *Jess* do you?"

Extending his strong arm for a gentlemanly handshake she expected it to be hard and firm. She found that usually men with arms like these would leave cause to smile and bare the crushing blow that most desperate to showcase virility would display. She was pleasantly surprised when his eyes warm and engaging met hers with inviting embrace.

With a serene smile her melodic voice met back with;

"It is a pleasure to meet you too Mr. Burnett, I usually do prefer being called Jess I wonder, *how did you* know?"

"I've always had an intuition about these sorts of things." Kyle said with a smile;

"By the way Mr. Burnett will *not be necessary*, I've never been one for formalities just call me Kyle."

"Yes Kyle, Sir." She said with a mischievous smile, he reciprocated the same gesture and laughed to himself knowing full well she'd be calling him Sir, Master and many other formal titles that she had no inkling about in this moment.

"Now Jess can I get you anything? Dinner will be ready soon, the children are all taken care of for the evening and I will not need you services until Monday. So you have the rest of the week off, paid of course to settle in and find your way around my home."

"Do you have any coffee? The layovers and jetlag have drained me. Thank you very much for the extra time to get settled in, I truly appreciate the generous offer."

"You're welcome. If you need anything just let me know, it's a pleasure to have you here." With a warm smile, "Let me see what I can find, I'm not a coffee drinker myself, perhaps the kitchen staff will know better than I will."

Kyle continued searching around the staff kitchen looking through cabinets he finds the coffee maker and all the ingredients needed to make the perfect cup of pick me up. Unable to look away as he leaned down; Jess unable to help but stare directly at his ass, his large arm span and strong back. From head to toe she began molesting his entire body with her eyes, unable to control herself. She expected to work for some typical business man, middle aged, and fatherly presence, not anybody she'd ever be sexually attracted to. In her time of grief this is what she expected, but she was wrong. This virile man that stood before her was one of God's greatest temptations to women, she slightly moaned under her breath.

"Is everything okay?" Kyle keenly responded. A bit shocked not realizing she let that moan escape from her lips Jess quickly responded "Oh yes I'm fine, just getting used to making a big change in life."

Rolling her eyes to herself thinking how she appeared to be nothing more than a horny teenager she smiled and waited for her cup of coffee. Kyle continued with his search for everything needed, smiling to himself the entire time knowing her eyes were on him. He wore a form fitted shirt and tight jeans that showed off every muscle and every vein that pulsed through his body. Combat boots and a cologne that would make any woman's knees weak. He was a lethal combination. The perfect predator to any prey, and Jess didn't realize deep down in her soul, how badly she wanted to be caught.

"Now then while we wait for the coffee perhaps you will join me in the dining room? I know dinner will be brought in any moment from the main kitchen and cook had something special planned for your arrival... This way."

"There are two kitchens here? What luxury." Jess responded as Kyle laughed;

"Yes there is one for the family and the other for the staff. I find it's much easier when they feel that they have their own part of the house just to themselves. I'm not used to finding anything in their kitchen which is why it took me so long to find coffee, of all things."

"You didn't need to go through all that trouble for me, Kyle I would have gladly found it on my own." Jess replied.

"You worry too much Jess, follow me."

She walked behind him out through the staff kitchen door finding herself in a beautiful hallway, a tall opulent corridor of fine art and beautiful ornate furnishings. Crimson red tapestries on the walls, red draperies and lush Persian rugs on hardwood floor it truly was a site to behold. As they walked down part of the hallway the main kitchen appeared on the right, the staff was moving swiftly in tune with one another to finish the meal and have it ready to serve precisely at seven o' clock. A few feet further to the left was a grand dining room with a long mahogany table adorned with two exquisite thrones at each end. Upholstered with antique tapestries, chairs that seemed to line each side of the table for miles, beautiful ornate wooden furniture and fresh flowers adorning the very center of the table. There was only two place settings. Candles were lit and the entire room glowed softly and sensually beckoning both parties to sit down.

"Will the children be joining us?" Jess curiously asked. Kyle smiled knowing full well that she was quite pleased with the intimate setting.

"Not this evening, they've already had dinner, tonight is their night to do whatever they want, so they'll be busy playing games until it's time for them to sleep."

"Then it's just, you and I Kyle… Sir?" Jess tried at all costs to keep her smile as innocent in appearance as physically possible.

"Does that bother you?" Kyle asked waiting as long as he could while drawing out each word intensifying her anticipation.

"Not at all Sir, I just didn't expect the *royal* treatment." Jess smiled and continued to look around at the wonderful atmosphere.

Following him into the candle lit dining room, the end of the table was situated in an enclosed space. The candles warm and the light soft she sat down next to him, and her arousal increased. Watching every image of him, taking him into her mind. Wondering what these dark flashes were that she was not familiar with from anybody else she tried to read. She could hear the screams of women, feel the most intense lust arise within her. Coursing through her veins like a serpent seeking the sun, his eyes pierced into her psyche and she could sense that his guard was now up even though his outward facial expression gave no affirmation of it all. Jess had never had a problem reading people's minds or seeing their thoughts, memories and visions of what was yet to come.

Kyle was different, he was a locked iron door and Jess didn't have the key. She'd never felt so vulnerable before, always relying on these gifts was what kept her safe all these years. Even after they used it to try to kidnap her, take her from her family and use these gifts for dark intent she was always one step ahead of them knowing when and where they were at all times. With him his mind was a fortress of dark desires and thoughts she could sense, permeating from his firm flesh, like the thick scent of cologne that hung in the air whenever you were near him. Such an intoxicating aroma that cast a spell on Jess, unable to understand this feeling she was completely open. This was a dangerous energetic place to be, at least for her, for this is where he ruled; not only the world of man but the world of women and demons.

Kyle sat down after turning on a nearby stereo. Pouring forth melodic music in ambient tones beautiful beyond anything she'd ever heard before echoing off the stone walls of the room. Jess felt her energetic self fall into a dream like state of relaxation, hypnotized into a trance. Kyle was content knowing that she was now his for the taking. Her mind would be malleable for any question he desired answers to. The doors opened and the chef and kitchen staff brought out salads, soup and beverages. Jess distracted by the dance of service not realizing his predatory gaze upon her, thirsting for her. The blackest soul, craving her like a wolf hot on a sanguine scented trail. Kyle's menacing eyes, his smile so dark and sinister, and his cock rock hard. He could smell her perfume, his eyes trailing from that soft flesh behind her pale ear down to her collar bone and full alabaster breasts. He imagined her caged to the wall in seventeenth century iron shackles naked, cold, bleeding; tears streamed down her begging face...

"So Jess I'd like you to tell me more about yourself."

Jess no longer distracted by the formalities of dinner, turned and looked Kyle serenely in the eyes; he knew the music was helping to tease her into a subdued state. "What would you like to know?" she inquired with felinesque curiosity.

"What prompted you to respond to my ad?" Kyle said with a smile.

"I needed a change in my life, a second chance so to speak. Your ad was the only thing that made sense. So far I feel it's the best decision I could have made due to the circumstances I find myself in presently." She solemnly replied.

"What circumstances?" Kyle pried.

"I lost my fiancé a year ago and I promised him I wouldn't grieve his loss to the point where it prevented me from going on with my own. Your ad was the hope that I almost ran out of and now I find myself here dining with you, who I'm sure to be a brilliant man with an interesting story to tell, and surprised by my fortune." She said trying to hold back tears.

"I'm sorry excuse my tears it's been a year now, but it still feels like yesterday." She gently dabs beneath her eyes with her napkin as Kyle reaches his hand and places it gently and warmly over hers.

"I'm truly sorry for your loss. You never need to apologize for your tears, ever; is that understood?" Lifting her eyes to meet his she replied, "Yes Sir, Thank you."

"It's been only three years since I lost my wife. I wish I could tell you that in time the wound heals but if I did, I'd be lying. I sometimes still think she'll walk in the door at any moment, but remember the horrid reality shortly after, then realize I have to pull myself together again, for my children's sake." Kyle replied.

"I'm so sorry I had no idea, I just assumed that you were separated, or divorced." Jess took her free hand and placed it over Kyle's. The gesture was unexpected and took him by surprise; for a moment the darkness that had taken over since her death was softened and warmed for just an instant. Gripping her hands in his he said:

"Jess I want you to feel comfortable here, I want you to feel that my home is now your home too, is that understood?"

"Yes Sir." Jess smiled and replied.

His dark urges tormented his thoughts once more. To see this pretty girl with tears in her eyes while his cock was forced down her throat. Her whimpers and screams muffled by each tormenting inch of penetrating flesh. Blood coursing between her lips, making it impossible to breathe. His cock pressed firmly against his pants and it took every ounce of control he had in him to not rip her out of the chair by her hair and shred her dress with his cruel hands, tearing it apart. Forcing her legs open and raping her on the wooden table. Her arms held over her head with one hand while he molested her body with the other. Covering her mouth her muffled screams of pain, each thrust ripping her apart. Her blood soaking his cock as he took her as his filthy whore.

With a melancholy smile she continued to lose herself in the tones of the music and the decadent flavors of their meal. Each moment she let herself go in the music was a moment closely watched by him. How easily she fell into this planned melody, this music with overtones that were specifically designed to lull even the strongest of will and mind into a hypnotic, more impressionable trance.

"Mmm I don't know if it's the jetlag or the meal but I feel so relaxed now, so peaceful, I *really* needed this. Thank you." Jess said with a smile.

"You're welcome, I'm pleased you enjoy it here, are you ready to see your room?" Kyle said.

"Yes! I am!" Jess said with sudden excitement, Kyle laughed and Jess blushed slightly not realizing how boisterous she sounded. "This way." Kyle replied with amused sentiment.

They walked out of the dining room into the hallway, for what seemed like miles. Jess could see the service quarters, people on the staff coming to and from their boarded rooms and busying themselves with their daily tasks. They approached a staircase that lead both up and downstairs. What was even more curious to Jess was the fact that there was a rather large and ominous looking bookcase blocking anybody from ever going downstairs.

She reached deeply with her intuition trying to figure out what was hidden down there to hear the faint screams of tortured women, followed by the moans of ecstasy. She instantly saw Kyle in a way she surely wasn't prepared for.

"Is something wrong?" Kyle noticed that she sensed something odd about the bookshelves.

"Not at all, I guess I'm just exhausted, more so than I expected to be."

He felt violated for once in his life, it was a new unsettling feeling. Nobody has ever so much as glanced down those stairs for her to truly find interest and to see that look on her face as if she was already there, was shocking.

"May I ask you something Kyle?" His heart began to beat faster under his tight shirt, wondering if she could see it beating in his chest, he calmly replied.

"Yes, Jess ask me anything I'm an open book."

"I know that you've described to me that the upstairs is your private living quarters as well as a few extra rooms, but what is *downstairs?*" She knew she was playing with fire, she had no right to ask this question but couldn't help herself she wanted to know what those erotic images were, and she ached to know why she heard those sounds of pleasure and pain.

"Many years ago this house was a slaughterhouse. I bought it and renovated it into the home you see today. Unfortunately some of the more dangerous machinery couldn't be removed without completely destroying the house; so to keep my children safe I had this giant bookshelf placed here to keep everybody out." Kyle said. His heart raced but his darkside grew hungry for her even more. He was fond of this curious kitten, just waiting to be killed.

"Now my dear Jess, if you'll follow me, I'll show you to your wing of the house." Kyle replied.

"*I quite like the sound of that, my dear Jess*" she thought. He continued to walk ahead of her smiling, while reading her thoughts.

"I have my own wing? How big is this house?" Jess said.

Kyle laughed again out loud amused by her blatant honesty "At times it feels *endless*."

She followed him up the spiral staircase to walk up two flights of stairs. She saw many well-dressed business men coming in and out of doors talking things over with arms full of paperwork. The second floor was Kyle's office and business associates work space.

"I'd give you a tour of this floor but unless you're interested in seeing endless desks and office space there's not much to see. The children's rooms are also on this floor but I'll let them show you tomorrow when you meet them for breakfast." Kyle looked at Jess wondering just what was going on in that pretty little head of hers.

"I look forward to meeting them and helping them grow in any way I possibly can." Kyle smiled.

"Good. Then I chose the right woman for the job." Jess blushed her twinkling eyes fixated on Kyle's as he continued to lead her into his personal sanctuary.

"Now to the private part of the home, where I personally enjoy the most peace." Kyle said. Jess smiled listening intently and soaking up the beautiful atmosphere Kyle had a way of decorating every inch of this home with the exact amount of elegance without detracting from its natural allure. Oil paintings of his ancestors as large and vividly painted as those done by Goya for the royal family.

"Wow, I see a resemblance."

Jess said when staring at a painting of a man that looked identical to Kyle though from a period of at least two hundred years ago or more. With striking good looks just like him, she swore it was him in a past life as the likeness was far too uncanny.

"Who is that Kyle?" He stopped midway up the stairs, "He's a distant uncle. He was in the English royal family if I remember my facts correctly, not a very good man so I've been told." Kyle watched as her eyes were entranced with each painting.

"What a rich family history you have, it's rare that people know much about their lineage these days, most often it's long forgotten. Though I find it's crucial to know the past, if we're to grasp what the present currently dictates; who we are and now, further yet who we will become." The words slipped from her lips before she realized it.

"Now that is a philosophy you and I both live by." Kyle smiled and Jess met his grin with hers. As Kyle ascended the staircase it took every ounce of strength for Jess not to eye fuck him. Obviously she was ravenous, she hadn't felt a strong man inside her since after her fiancé died. Her body was starving for a beast to take her as his own, and Kyle was a beast that any prey would gladly sacrifice themselves too. Soon Jess would learn this lesson all too well.

They arrived at the third floor to a hallway that ended in two directions, to the right was Kyle's wing, he gestured;

"This is where you'll find me more than anywhere else in the entire house. My study, library and office are here as well as my bedroom. My greatest works and most enjoyed solitude happen here."

She smiled knowing she found a kindred spirit. To find another that loved books enough to sleep near them she knew she was finally home. He then gestured to the left side of the hallway to the rooms that were there.

"Follow me." She did as he requested and peered inside each room along the way with doors open. She saw a new office for her in another room, a dayroom for her to tend to the children, and at the end of the hallway was a beautifully ornate carved door; with gold filigree etched over mahogany wood. On either side of the door were two small tables with large vases full of fresh red roses.

"Red roses, they're my favorite." Jess said as she inhaled the sweet seductive aroma of the beautiful flowers.

"How did you know?" she looked at Kyle both pleased and surprised.

"As I've said before Jess, I have an intuition for these sort of things."

He smiled and opened the door to a lavishly large and ornately decorated bedroom. Antiques from centuries past were in ever part of the room. A full fireplace adorned with reading chair, blanket and table. A large four post canopy bed adorned with plush red velvet, curtains tied back to reveal a red velvet bedspread adorned once more with gold filigree.

"This is your room Jess, I hope you like it." Kyle stepped back and watched her as she absorbed every element of ambiance.

As she looked around at the walls of tapestries, oil paintings and furniture covered in vases or fresh red roses she almost cried;

"This is for me? This is the most beautiful room I've ever seen in my life." Jess smiled looking into the large mirror that hung over the fireplace as she took in all of the surrounding beauty. Kyle walked to the large walk-in closet and opened the door:

"This is your closet, and over here" he walked across the room "is your bathroom."

He opened yet another ornately decorated door, to reveal a sauna shower with marble tiles from floor to ceiling and a large Jacuzzi tub. The room was painted ruby red with gold accents all around the large mirrors and vanity just for her. Cabinets filled with the finest towels and bath essentials. She opened the bathroom closet door to find a large plush exquisitely red robe. She looked closer to see the lush fabric adorned with her initials in gold embroidery. Red roses were strewn across the counter tops and the back of the bathtub. She no longer has the resolve to hold back the tears.

"I'm so thankful. Honestly I don't have the words to express how much this means to me, I've never had anybody show so much generosity."

She turned away to wipe her tears and Kyle approached her turning her around by the shoulders and wrist, "Never hide your tears, they're absolutely beautiful."

She gasped as he took his right thumb and wiped the tears from under her eyes and held her close to him, wrapping his arms around her firmly and protectively he'd never encountered such a fragile, pure woman before. It drove his animal instincts insane, as he held her close smelling her fragrance and feeling her impossibly soft skin she melted into his chest burying her face into it, embracing his warm, strong arms wrapped around her body wishing that it wouldn't stop.

He kissed her on the forehead and told her,

"I want you to find happiness here, as much of it as you can; this is your home now."

Her freshly wiped eyes glistened as she looked up to him; "I never thought I could feel this safe again, and you are solely responsible for this feeling of comfort." She leaned into his chest and he hugged her close, "If there is anything else that you need, do not hesitate to ask Jess. I'm only down the hall and rarely do I sleep." As they both let go of this much needed embrace she smiled,

"Kyle, Thank you *so* much." She glowed.

"I know it's been a long travel and you're eager to get situated, enjoy your room, I have work to do as usual, but we'll speak again soon I'm sure." Kyle left the room and closed the door behind him. Smiling wickedly knowing in his heart of hearts that now he had her exactly where he wanted her.

With a twinkle in his devious eyes and a confident step added to his powerful stride he quickly vanished towards his wing in Burnett manor. As he passed by numerous antiques and bookshelves lined with every conceivable old book on endless subjects. He then firmly reached for a piece of ornate crown molding out in the open to any that passed by. But for his touch, and only *his* touch, would this seemingly innocent wall yield and reveal yet another entrance woven into this hidden staircase tower at the very center of this haunting place.

Chapter 2:

FORBIDDEN SUBMERSION

WITH each step he descended towards the secret room that James visited only hours before; alerting his ominous employer of the new flesh that arrived on silver platter ripe and ready for the taking. Kyle settled into his large inviting wingback chair. Itching to see what his pretty new property was up too now; reaching into his left cuff finding the small chain that dangled his personal key and private entrance into his own carnal circus where only he had front row seats. Once again reuniting the key with its wanton keyhole the cabinet on his large mahogany desk opened to again reveal the closed circuit color television that now skipped to an entirely new channel; one where Kyle's eyes could witness and watch every nuance, moment and voyeuristic desire as Jess settled into her private chambers.

With a gratified smile he poured himself a much needed drink and tuned in to see what this captivating creature would do next. What if any words would she mutter while she believed herself to be entirely alone? Slowly Kyle reached for an antiquated book, quite large and heavy, adorned in brown leather and gold leafing. As the spine cracked open to reveal pages of erotic scenarios involving rope, leather restraints and manacles with beautiful tear streaked faces of women crying in heavy makeup he perused each photo personally taken by him. He smiled reminiscing in his already rich collection of pretty pieces of flesh and longed to see if Jess would be the one he'd always hoped would find her way into his trap. Or if she like the rest will find good use in a much less desirable position within the scream filled dungeons of Burnett Manor. Only time and observations would display the truth, until then his cock stirred as he watched her slowly, seductively wandering around the room with an alluring smile that glowed as delicately as her skin.

Jess was in love with this room, and instantly found herself looking inside each and every drawer of her new dresser. Gorgeously built into the wall adorned with a mirror as tall and wide as the room itself. The nightstands held hidden gifts that she never expected. Trinkets, lotions, shampoos and conditioners all blood red with a personal note, gold lettered in Kyle's handwriting,

"Red is most certainly your color."

She instantly saw blood, *her* blood all over her own body, yet for once in her life it wasn't followed by screams, but by moans; echoing ecstasy bouncing off the dark charcoal insides of a very small, dark and dreary room.

"What does this mean?" Jess said aloud, the first words that Kyle heard her lips speak since he left her room.

"Yes, what *does* it mean my undeniably curious prey?"

He was used to the instant awe struck responses from past victims in regards to the decadent room that was now theirs. Never realizing the gorgeous surroundings were to distract them from a grim future, but never had he heard such words that provoked his heartbeat to rise and fall faster than he had ever recollected before than when they were uttered from her delicate pout.

Kyle was fascinated with the cogs and wheels of her powerful psychic mind turning and grinding to solve this case that she'd assigned herself since the moment she spoke to him on the phone; accepting the job and accepting her presently unknown death wish.

"Perhaps it will suffice to wander around later and see much more of this place than just the insides of this what I have to admit is a sexy fucking room."

As the words rolled off her lips with the greatest of ease, Kyle found himself laughing and smiling even more wickedly than he already had during this private boudoir show;

"Oh how I treasure the ferocity in you Jess, one of my greatest possessions; a woman who can, and *will* use her claws."

Wandering around and slowly opening the closet, awestruck by the organizational compartments and sheer size of it, quite easily it could've been another room. Putting away each and every piece of clothing, gently stashing her lingerie in the delicate silk lined drawers of her dresser she smiled never knowing that mere inches away behind that mirror was a private room.

A room that allowed Kyle to be ever so close to his future hunt, watching and appeasing his carnal desires as she wandered from the dresser into the bathroom. Never knowing that the mirror to the right along the wall used for dressing was in an addition, a two way mirror. A mirror that allowed Kyle to permeate the mind, and private chambers of Jess without her ever even knowing it.

"Mmm these cold Colorado nights will take some getting used to, perhaps it's time for a *long... hot bath.*"

With these words uttered Kyle stood up, his gorgeously broad shoulders reaching for a thick hunter green cashmere sweater. He put it on, grabbing his drink and abruptly locking his cabinet door with key in hand, gently tucking it into the cuff of his sleeve and exiting this private office of books; the shelves that housed them, and the only desk he ever truly enjoyed working from.

His calculated steps ascended what seemed like an entire floor but was only an optical illusion in this winding spiral passageway. His eyes penetrated a brick that had a gold key melded inside, with the mere power of his mind and desire for this private show for his eyes only; he instantly thought of her naked body writhing and moaning on every inch of his deliciously hard cock. Instantly the key glowed and Kyle smiled as the cracks between each bricked groove opened and separated. He gently nudged the sides of the openings and the brick revealed a doorway that lead right into a private study with windows directly into Jess's bedroom, bathroom and private world of ecstasy. A fire was already blazing in the hearth, where luscious Persian rugs filled the entirety of the quaint space.

Kyle tended to the fires and placed his glass on the side table next to his favorite chair and ottoman. Another room filled with books, this time one's from his favorite comics. A rich collection of provocative issues, the ones that were far too taboo or rare for most collector's to appreciate. As he kept his eyes focused on this gorgeous creature as she glided in and out of sight, she continued putting things away and finding her robe to wear after removing her clothes in the closet. Out of Kyle's prying eye's sight, to reappear seconds later with her luscious ass hugging the silk fabric so deliciously that a crease formed between it as she bent down to remove a small case filled with toys most certainly, for her pleasure.

"Mmm after spending the night having dinner with such an intriguing man, I'm sure I'll be in need of you tonight my darlings."

She opened her nightstand closest to the bed and near the bathroom. Jess filled the bottom drawer with every toy, device and instrument for pain infliction that Kyle had ever seen. As his eyes began to sparkle and his smile turned to a wry sinister satiation, he leaned in close and watched with eyes focused on her delicate neck waiting to see just what this little minx had in store for him next? His cock was hot and engorged, as he ached for her soft supple mouth. She had a way of playing with her labret piercing that really made him hungry for her, unlike any new toy he'd ever come into contact with before.

As his mind began to drift to many different games he wanted to play with and inflict into her, he heard the voice of a siren singing as she entered the bathroom and the hot water poured. Filling the tub and tossing in the delicate red rose petals that were now falling on the countertops from the stunning bouquets she created an alluring paradise.

"You let me go but you'll always belong to me. You belong to me... *You belong...* to me, though you've let me go... you'll always belong to me."

With each note of this mysterious song that escaped from between her silk lips, he found himself for the first moment in this lifetime that he could ever recall, completely entranced. Hypnotized and subdued into watching this melodic voice trail off as she wandered from plush bed to closet and finally to the longed for bathroom. She opened a small vile of *Rose Otto* her favorite scent for such an occasion and poured the heavenly scent into the filling tub. The fragrance danced in circles of rainbow color, and the room continued to fill with her signature scent. That delicate scent that already made his mouth water.

"Much better, now Aphrodite can embrace Poseidon's warm affections."

Gently pulling back her ginger curls and twisting them she delicately clipped them into place. Her face now resembling those classic ones found in the works of *Mucha.* As usual a few delicate curls fell from the clip to frame her face like an old world portrait, slowly dragging her talon like nails down her neck and décolletage she smiled and said;

"Too bad Kyle's not here right now…watching me." The words sent a carnal chill down his spine, *did she know? How could she even form such an idea?*

His breath stopped wondering if somehow, some bizarre way she'd figured all of this out. Instantly dismissing the idea from his mind, brushing it away like a buzzing fly with no concept of space. Impossible, even with her obvious gifts Kyle realized she hadn't yet had the time to explore his world to *really know* what he had in store.

She sinfully smiled in the mirror and giggled to herself, a mischievous sound that only made him want her even more than he already craved her. She looked deep into her own eyes smiling salaciously;

"Not even here for a day and you're already aching to fuck your boss, what a filthy little whore."

There was something so captivating about seeing a woman turning herself on with such filthy words, each articulated with such precision that his cock swelled with every pause. Every nuance and every word pressed between her lips, before spilling out effortlessly like the beads of oil now swimming around, and aching to caress her skin.

"Mmm I wonder what his hands feel like, what strength they have. I bet he could *tear me* into pieces…" her nipples hardened at the thought of being captured by this fascinating man. She began to moan and slowly caress her beautiful form, watching her hips and ass sway seductively under her crimson silk robe, drove Kyle absolutely insane. Reaching into his pants and releasing his heavy cock he began to tease and stroke the tip awakening his hunger. Never had he felt a hunger like this before. His eyes constricted and fixated on the prey he longed to chase into a field. He longed to devour her alive, before fucking her to death under the sun kissed spring. Hearing screams of terror soaked pleasure fading into deathly silence, as the snow melted away and she was the only piece of color for visual attainment.

Her hands slowly, seductively, sliding under her robe. Her flesh still out of sight except small glimpses of porcelain that slipped through the opening. The light dancing on a delicate form of legs, torso and streaks of breast. She started massaging her plump milky tits, moaning and slowly biting her bottom lip. She opened her eyes and smiled walking towards the bathtub, she turned towards the nozzle and placed the bottom of her foot delicately on the steps alongside of it. The perfect arches leading his eyes towards painted nails of blood red. They wandered up to her calf and thigh peeking out as her hands seductively sought to slide the collar of this robe off each shoulder effortlessly. The silk fell almost to the floor, but first clinging to her voluptuous ass before finally falling to the floor completely. Giggling again in that mischievous tone before watching her ascend the steps into the hot waiting pool for her body to bask in, he leaned in stroking his cock with fervor;

"Who *are you,* beguiling creature? Who *the fuck* are you?" As the hot water enveloped her cold flesh she moaned in bliss, leaning back she opened her eyes and said;

"Much Better" as she giggled that infectious laugh once more Kyle noticed the lights dimming without anyone there to adjust the dial.

"Now perhaps we can have a little fire to make this escape complete?" Her eyebrow raising in a cocky expression that fit her face as well as that robe fit her body.

That very instant the scented candles previously unlit all around the bathroom began to glow each with its own flickering flame. Kyle mystified, knew in that moment he'd finally met his match.

"Mmmm this water is perfect." Jess purred as she felt her body slowly submerge into the warm oil scented water dish. She found her feline self, uncurling her limbs fully for the first time since she stepped off that plane. Kyle reclined with his right leg extended forth in front of him and his left bracing the floor beneath him for what this sensual child of the night would do next. Looking menacingly through the two way mirror into her hauntingly gorgeous eyes, watching the pools of green meld with the streaks of blue swirling into each iris. For a moment his breath grew shallow as she stared directly into what felt like were his very own eyes.

Kyle's portentous stare penetrated beyond the glass deep within the core of her already aroused body, she felt him powerfully close. Intoxicated by such power and virility of will. She felt her body tingle and awaken, moaning without control she lost herself in the thought of being taken by him. She longed to feel his touch, his powerful grip that she could foresee easily turning her in whatever direction he desired to use her as he wished. Her nails instinctively sought out her soft porcelain flesh, tearing into her breasts she hissed as her lips parted her canine teeth glistened deliciously her tongue flicking at the top of her teeth, drawing in breath as streaks of blood appeared on her chest delicate drops falling into the water and turning the bath a lovely shade of pink.

"Ah there we are, now it's complete… without pain beauty cannot be captured." She muttered the words slowly, heavy with arousal and aching for release.

"Mmmm now where we're we?" Her hands trailed between her ample breasts her milky white skin blended in with the porcelain tub leaving her fingertips to guide Kyle's eyes to where she longed to feel him most. Looking deep into her own eyes in the mirrors reflection she imagined his eyes upon her, little did she know that the very spot she fixated on was where his eyes were always watching; from the other side of this erotic show just for Kyle's pleasure. His heavy booted leg propped up on the ottoman, to his right the table with his freshly poured drink, nestled beside a vial of silken fluid. His left leg dropping the heaviness of his boot hitting the ground for a moment, Jess seemed to look around as if she thought she heard something, but it was impossible, these walls were sound proofed; Kyle ensured that his privacy was eternally his own.

His strong hands manipulated the lubricant until his throbbing dick found its way sliding into his hands. His deep sigh of sexual contentment and relief was followed by his body sinking into the chair to leave his face hidden in the shadows except for his parted lips, strong jawline and glowing eyes. Jess maintained complete contact with her eyes in the mirror she wasn't sure why but felt compelled as if there was a strong magnetic pull behind this glass. She longed to torment her pussy without letting herself cum. Leaning her head back she reached for the end of the tub and pressing a button near the faucet smiling wickedly into her own reflection as the roaring jets turned on full blast. She moaned in pleasure her sinister smile was matched by Kyle's that now appeared out of the darkness as if everything he'd ever longed to attain in life was mere inches away from his menacing grasp.

Biting her lip she reached down below the water and started moaning in eager anticipation, knowing how these powerful jets will help her to release much needed tension built up over these past weeks. Fantasizing about what Kyle's delicious voice, would instruct her to do in every waking and sleeping moment of her life. She raised her legs up into the air, while simultaneously gripping the sides of the tub and repositioning herself.

He could now see her ripe plump ass pressed deep into the jets that were previously to her left side, her legs dangled magnificently as her toes curled and ankles gave way to pleasure she leaned back and her gorgeous J breasts burst forth in front of her. Pink areolas awakened and her tiny pert nipples, hard as two glistening rubies, just freshly polished. She gave way and instantly moaned, her body bucking under the hard penetrating jets.

Blasting her cunt and asshole so perfectly that her legs trembled and gave way sprawling out onto the side of the tub as her head fell back and she moaned. Kyle began stroking his cock rigorously watching her, taking in every soft curve, every ounce of beauty. Her lips parting and pressing together while she uttered his name.

"Kyle, take me…Oh God yes Kyle…make me your filthy little whore. I'll do whatever you want to earn the honor of feeling every single raw inch of your blazing hot cock inside of me…"

Her hands found their way into her hair tearing out the hairpin and pulling it back making it hurt as she uncontrollably bucked and writhed under the powerful jets, spewing hot water into every hole she ached for him to personally fill. Her breasts continued to swell engorging and heavy she gripped the sides of the tub.

Breathing heavy as her entire body contorted and tensed as her approaching climax was guaranteed to be a magnificent show. This was exactly what this ringleader had hoped for when he hired her for his private carnal circus. After seeing some striking images of her erotic modeling, that his private investigator dug up a week before she agreed to the position. Just one of many photos that lingered in his book of horrors and depraved female collection. Kyle's body tensed as the sounds of his hands pumping his cock were heard throughout the sound proofed room just beyond her mirror.

The delicious sound of juices and impact play, his moans turned to visceral grunts his body tensing as he watched Jess writhe without blinking, keeping his eyes upon her as if she was a dangerous creature that could kill him at any moment, never wanting to miss a second of this. She started shaking and writhing so hard that her body bucked her pussy mound against the spraying jets to hear her seductively scream;

"Oh God, I'm coming, Kyle I'm coming all over you…"

In that moment her pussy squirted and gushed spraying a geyser of freshly squeezed peach juice all over the side of the tub. Spraying the entire window and creating the sexiest rainstorm Kyle had ever seen with his own eyes. He came hard, grunting and squeezing as his abdomen clenched and his back stiffened. His ass firm and the heavy heeled boots of his feet digging into the carpet and ottoman as if he was clinging onto it for his very life.

"Oh fuck" grunting and moaning continued to fill the room as Jess kept moaning and writhing, falling back into the tub in glowing smiles and laughing salaciously. Heavy breathed and panting,

"Now…that's…better, *for now.*" She smiled again and Kyle joined in;

"What a lucky man I am, to now own a woman with an endless sex drive, one that can't be tamed."

Smiling he reached for the silken towel waiting for him on the table near his now empty glass. Cleaning himself up as Jess moaned and smiled. She relaxed before standing up and stepping out of the tub to reach for her soft crimson towel that was embroidered with her initials.

"Mr. Burnett Sir, you *really do,* know how to keep a woman."

Smiling she repinned her hair and Kyle stood up slowly stuffing his massive cock into his pants, zipping his jeans and smiling more contently than he had in ages so it seemed.

As he started to leave the room and wander back down most contently to his private office, he watched Jess apply her usual skin regimens, her perfume and other soft supple skin inducing lotions all over her body.

"It puts the lotion on its skin, or else it gets the hose again." She winked at herself in the mirror and Kyle chuckled;

"What a morbid sense of humor, who *are* you?" shaking his head transfixed he awaited her next move as she glided into the bedroom.

"Now that I've juiced this ripe summer peach…" smiling deviously she dropped her towel and placed it on the edge of the bed. Kyle was intrigued, repositioning his chair to stare into her bedroom from the built in dresser with the large mirror for Jess, and the window into her world for Kyle. She wandered into her only room that was entirely private to him, the staff of this home and the world; her closet.

Waiting eagerly his heart pounded wondering what she'd do next, minutes passed by and he started to worry. Had she found that panel to the back of her closet that lead to this private spiraling staircase, hidden between the walls and her room in Burnett Manor? As his mind started to race, she strolled out in high heels, latex gloves and wearing a waist cincher. The waist cincher made her supple breasts look almost cartoonish in their large size. Like two billowing whipped mounds of cream adorned with two strawberries; her nipples hardened. Placing two small alligator clips with adjoining chain onto each nipple, hissing violently when they were in place.

She then reached into her bottom drawer of her nightstand and pulled out a thick dildo ridged in structure, covered in prominent veins and an appetizing mushroom like tip that she longed to slide between her sticky lips.

"A nice ripe cock before bedtime will surely help me sleep well my first night, in this dark and haunting castle in the woods…*in the middle of nowhere, where no one can hear me scream.*"

Biting her lip Kyle was already in his chair watching her, much closer in proximity to her than he was before when she was in the tub. He could see her skin form goosebumps from the chill in the air and the contrast of latex on freshly washed skin. She slid onto the towel at the edge of the bed and spread her thighs, her heels digging into the wood panel on the side of the bed, giving her the position and footing needed to take a much needed pounding.

Hissing and tugging as she pulled on the nipple clamps, she yelled in a mix of pleasure and pain. She inserted this ripe cock in her tight little pussy. Her heels already digging into the wood, her back arching, Kyle leaned in to watch. His cock jerking, jumping and aching to watch with him, his eyes saw her dragging her nails down her torso, she started rubbing her pussy counterclockwise while simultaneously pumping her dildo slowly and deeply into her wet, silky folds. Her pink pussy swelling, continued to shine with every drop of sweet honey dew that formed on her full folds. She once again screamed his name as climax approached faster than only moments and rooms before. Kyle's grin was ear to ear watching as her body contorted, jerked, slammed up and down on the lush cushion's and blankets of her freshly made bed. Her lips parted slowly stuck together at first and parting from center to corners;

"Holy Fuck, I thought I was going to die, maybe next time." She smiled and waited for her legs to come back.

"What a sexy little fuck toy. I'm glad you're already making yourself at home Jess."

He stood up and left his chair in its newfound position. As she wandered into the closet and hastily returned in ruffled white cotton boy shorts, a soft ivory tank top and plush peach socks, she wrapped herself in a coffee colored robe and with heavy eyes found herself in between the inviting sheets of her four poster bed. She stared into the bathroom and smiled as the candles went out all at once. The room with its soft glow from a very dim light that was still on above she licked her lips and instantly the curtains at the foot of the bed fell closed to leave the sides open for Kyle to watch. He peered into her world watching this sorceress curl up into a feline as her kissable ass still peeked out from under the sheets, the rest of her body was encompassed in shades of crimson, blood red and gold, making her skin glow as she fell fast asleep.

"Mmmm wish you were here Mr. Burnett Sir." The timing nearly perfect as he smiled and left the room to descend back into his private office, that harbored his private collection of books and his favorite piece of equipment; that voyeuristic television for his prying, carnal eyes.

Jess moaned and sighed with utmost content, a deeply serene sound like the siren softly wailing after seducing an entire crew to throw themselves into choppy waters from sturdy shipside, to their imminent deaths. That same serene feeling Kyle was intoxicated by for what felt like centuries after he wrapped his strong hands firmly around a fresh kill. Kyle in amazement felt deeply content, as he intended to turn his latest employee into his most debilitated prey. Strong hands interlocked, as he sat in his wingback chair, each elbow firmly placed on his knee he sat with calculated focus, like a Wolf in haunted forest in the bleakest parts of winter. The hunger for flesh at its ultimate high for the lack of feasting that ensued for what viscerally felt like lifetimes. Electrocuted into place waiting for that exact moment when instinct overrode logic and reason to gorge on a hot, flowing blood feast until the whitest snow was covered in shades of red, crimson and pale pink. His sinister smile matched the dark hollow existence that illuminated in the twinkle of his devious eyes.

Once more having reached for the key within his left cuff the closed circuit television was still on, and Jess continued to sleep deeply. Her soft ample breasts swelling, rising and falling into one another underneath her soft sheer tank as she smiled sleeping deeper than she ever had before. She purred, her siren moans filling the bedroom with a serene, intoxicating sound that focused Kyle's mind as vividly as the smell of fresh blood. Her arms languidly wrapping themselves around her ribcage just beneath her breasts, her mounds swelled to what appeared to be three times their size in a series of moments.

Her ass still peeking out from underneath the sheets now slightly fell over the side of the bed, cascading forth into two luscious mounds of porcelain. Her long red hair surrounded her head in a crown of crimson curls. To some it resembled a river of sensuality, to Jess she always thought it looked as if someone had bludgeoned her nearly to death and the blood flooded forth around her in a crown of glory. She never quite knew why such thoughts came to her but as her eyes were heavily shut her soft lips parted and her tongue slowly flicking at her parted lips until the sheerest layer of honey glistened. As Kyle's eyes grew large once again his cock began to torment ceaselessly.

"Oh, dear Jess" Kyle groaned in agony, "This is going to be much harder than I ever thought."

The idea of violating her peaceful sleep right now in this instant with ravenous penetration, hearing her screams. Her tight pussy strangling his cock in fear and overwhelming pleasure, as she tried to claw herself free, before finally succumbing to everything she ever feared and desired more than life itself. It was usually easy to pace himself on fulfilling such cravings, but not this time. What has this beguiling woman done to him already with her exciting presence in his life, a new fire burned deep within the formerly dead chambers of Kyle's heart.

"What are you dreaming of? To see such bliss on that beautiful face, what curiosity you've evoked in me, show me what's in that enigmatic mind of yours?"

Jess's mind wandered to a place she longed to visit for years ever since she first started writing. As a mystical woman who was always haunted by the dead from dusk to twilight, those same spirits angered by her ability to slip through the powerful hands of death; time and time again sought to claim her for shadow walking out of death's infinite grip. She has the profound ability like a feral feline to return from the dead with additional lives in hand. For years this ability felt like a curse, but in places of profound power, and infinite inspiration, this energy naturally channeled through Jess's mind; body and soul until words flowed effortlessly onto paper from her tormented inner sanctum filled with dark fetishes and carnal cravings. Leaving even the vilest of sadist's in awe of such a salacious appetite.

In her dream she heard the sound of her heels slowly echoing off the tile floors and walls of *The Stanley Hotel.* She felt compelled to look behind her every so often and in that moment Kyle's awakened mind connected with her dreaming cauldron of mystery he was the presence she felt compelled to look behind and see with her very own eyes. He could hear her breath quicken, her gasps in her dreams nearly matched those that escaped her dreaming lips. Her blood red curls swept up to reveal her delicate neck, her shoulders were embraced by a long black trench coat that stopped right above the back of her thighs just below her ass. Her fishnet stockings lured his eyes to fall upon ankles adorned with black stilettos that continued to echo in the distance. While stopping briefly every so often to once more find his gaze, smiling composed once again. Her eyes meeting his she quickly alluded with her gaze to where she was going; upstairs to the room that matched the gold key that dangled from her right wrist, an ornate golden key just for Room 217.

The moment her elegant leg reached out for the first step towards the next floor, the echoes of heels turned to silence. As tile turned to sumptuous carpet, in an instant she was out of Kyle's line of sight yet he could smell her, feel her and almost taste her. The elevator doors opened with a bell that reminded Kyle of so many of his favorite horror flicks from eras long since passed. Out stepped a bell hop asking him if he'd like to be sent up to the next floor. He nodded in disagreeable affirmation and turned his predatory eyes intensely on the stairs, to see Jess smiling wickedly as her left hand found its way coursing through the top layers of her trench coat. He watched her hand finding, each delicate finger reaching for her throat, chin and lips in the most ravenous of gestures. Smiling flirtatiously she felt his eyes penetrating her throat, her right leg was placed over the bannister in a most convenient way, the shadows of the old stairwell kept her exposed pussy just out of sight to Kyle's fiery eyes.

Her right hand slowly teasing her ginger mound of wanton flesh, aching for his touch she let the key to Room 217 fall from her wrist. Watching as the key bounced from one step to another down to the lush carpet of hunter greens and vivid red. She slowly removed her leg from the bannister giving Kyle time to stop and watch the show. With one elegant turn towards the next floor her ass peaked out from beneath the bottom of the coat and for a moment Kyle was unable to move from such a delicious sight. His mouth parted in her dream in awe and arcane hunger, yet his waking self smiled wickedly amused by the fact that he could ever be so powerless even in the presence of such perfect prey. Something he'll keep in mind for future games of blood sport that were waiting for Jess, *just like all the others.* His mind reconnecting strongly with hers to reveal where she was taking him he focused on her dreams. Taking a moment to see her hands wandering across her clothed body underneath the sheets in her bedroom, from closed circuit television one last time before walking up the stairs, and up towards the second floor to the pair of legs that lured him into these wicked fantasies.

Kyle reached down to retrieve the key, he suddenly felt the coldness of the key within his waking hands, this was by far the most vivid mind meld he'd ever experienced with anyone before. As if he was stepping into her vivid dream, right into a film that was created for his body to experience as much as his eyes and ears. He smiled and laughed to himself for a moment;

"What are you? Talented creature of the astral plane."

His heavy boots appeared beneath him, she never saw him wear them before while awake, too imagine his exact boots that he was wearing this very night while watching her from every spiritual and physical plane in existence gave him the second feeling in a single evening of exposure. How was her mind this powerful, what had she endured in life to be this connected so early and for so long? Kyle thought he was the only one with this accelerated evolutionary ability. His broad shoulders repositioning with the rest of his body, now faced towards the top of the staircase. Feeling the bannister with his left hand the wood was smooth, cool and dry. He again smiled in awe an ode to her powers, to literally pull him into her world, never before had this taken place.

With each powerful step he made his ascent towards the top, seeing the infamous foreboding hallway found in one of his favorite films of all time. One of many that inspired him to write, create brilliant manuscripts that eventually turned into movies for one and all to thoroughly enjoy. The only light in this dark sepia toned hallway was flickering above her head at the end of the hallway. Kyle's pace quickened to match the pace of his blood coursing, pumping through his body, he wanted her; he could smell her sticky essence from here yet she was so far away.

"Oh, I see two can play at this game" he smiled knowing that some part of her was aware of the music that he played earlier in the evening at dinner, the music that lured her into an open state of exchange in communication. Even if she was still yet unaware, something inside her knew what he was capable of, this revelation was most amusing to Kyle. He continues to walk across the hallway, her body writhed with her back against the door she continued molesting herself in the public doorway. With each lumbering foot step past closed rooms on either side, her smell became stronger, more enticing, his very mouth was watering in wakened state. He could taste her aroma in his palate, as if he'd been tasting her for the past twelve hours uncontrollably gorging on such a sweet and endless feast.

She smiled wickedly reaching into her left pocket for an additional key, one she'd already requested, knowing Kyle would show up just in time as she accepted it from the front desk. You see she'd been dreaming of this day for far too long, he felt the slight resemblance of a dream like memory of seeing himself receive a phone call stating that a dear mentee, friend and business associate from his creative past would be stopping by. She would like a chance to catch up for dinner and a night cap before leaving town again for other business stops required for her current projects. That is how he found himself in this position in her dream sequence of intrigue.

How could she have possibly known that *The Stanley Hotel* was one of his absolute favorite places? How did she know that he'd met Stephen King there years ago? A personal literary hero of his, a man with the same temperament and mind for torture, one of many reasons why his friendship was treasured for all these years. As her red painted fingertips found the key within her pocket, she turned around and unbuckled her coat to reveal that she was wearing a black lace bra, a retro slip of black silk and embroidered lace. Her lips parting with heavy breath, the cranberry infused lips of hers separating slowly, with a sticky viscous that reminded Kyle just how hungry he was for her sweet dripping peach.

She held his gaze as he continued to approach, by the time he was only two doors away from hers she was able to get the key into the door and open it, abruptly shutting it behind her giving her just enough time to toss her coat on the bed and to pour two drinks before sitting down at the desk provided with her back to the door. Continuing where she left off writing, her laptop still open the curser left just as it was before retrieving the extra key from the concierge. To the left of her laptop on this wide cherry executive desk was an ashtray, barely smoking was the rest of her joint adorned by her gold kissed wooden cigarette extender. The melodic medicinal smoke filled her lungs, her blush lips exhaling it into the ether, she placed the extender onto the side of the astray continuing her story, right where she left off. She often found inspiration in the presence of this powerful plant, it aided in healing her body of its tortured past while freeing the mind to create worlds within worlds for all eternity.

The floor creaked, she could feel him approaching, hear his massive footsteps echoing off the walls of this haunted place. Her heart beat swiftly, she ached for this moment for far too long and never did she imagine it actually taking place just as she'd always dreamed of. The thick wood doorway felt heavy, all encompassing, as if his broad shoulders were already formidably behind her, hovering and waiting. Her fingers continued to type even though it felt as if the words were in no way connected to her in this moment, she could feel him inside of her, hear his voice whispering filthy suggestions to her that she wanted desperately to appease in every conceivable way. Finally his echoes turned to precise sounds which signaled to her skin to tremble and her thighs to quiver, she felt his hands hit her with each knock that impacted the solid door three, calculated times.

The blood rushed from her heart to her neck, her face flushed, she stopped typing to reach for her one final moment of composure inhaling the sweet nerve soothing elixir and exhaling, she heard his hands find the key with utmost urgency. The cool brass was vivid in Kyle's waking hands, his pulse quickened never had he felt so immersed in someone before. The key's weight felt in hand began to turn, and slowly the solid fortress revealed itself completely. The moment she heard the door unlock, the handle turn and Kyle walk through the precipice, she exhaled just to ensure breathing was continued. She could smell his scent, it wafted in on the breeze along with his dominant energy; calm, smooth, and precise as a freshly sharpened knife. She tried to find the courage to speak, to utter so many words she hoped her lust would provide. The bravery needed to address him with back turned in such a way, but all she could do was place her fingers back to the keyboard and breathe, in and agonizingly out.

Kyle's awakened mind and the part of him that was wandering into Jess' psyche smiled in unison, what absolute masochism she must relish in, to offer herself up to a hungry killer with such voracity. He slowly walked towards her a mere five steps and leaning over her shoulders. She could feel the heat coming off of his body, his scent became stronger and wafted through her palate to make her mouth water and her nipples harden as her skin began to tingle with electricity, sensing imminent danger. The floor creaked one last time before she could feel him standing right over her. Kyle stood there waiting for her to move, to speak, to watch her shoulders rise and fall along with her sumptuous breasts knowing full well that he was there feasting upon her with his carnal eyes. His hands slowly reached for the left side of the nape of her neck. Trailing his fingertips from the back of her ear down to the middle of her neck his hands firmly gripping her shoulders. Jess' body stiffened in urgency, feeling his strength was intimidating. Her heart pounded knowing she had absolutely no place to run. She had to face the beast inside, she wanted to invite him out, she ached to be possessed by him utterly and completely. Kyle leaned in smelling her, blowing a cool breeze across her neck, her skin shuddered, and the awakened Kyle whispered intently aloud so that the sound of his voice echoed and reverberated through space time and deep into her dreaming mind.

"Feel the breeze upon your neck and know that I am always with you." Jess began to stir from sleep, her body gasping just as her body gasped in this dreamscape interlude for psychopath lovers. His hands gripping her with fervor she couldn't help but swoon, a sigh of content escaped her dreaming lips. That long lost mystery of where that powerful energy was coming from for all these years was solved within moments finally at long last, he was in control. Before she could even begin to speak she heard his licentious voice beckoning her to follow his instructions;

"Touch yourself for me my pet, I want to watch those delicate fingers explore what is already *mine*." Without hesitation she sighed in bliss, her left hand gripping the front side of the desk while her head fell back glimpsing a vague impression of his wicked eyes. Watching, and waiting for his very own boudoir erotica to begin. Her index and middle finger slowly dragged each painted nail down the path between her cleavage, her pale skin instantly revealed raised red lines and small droplets of blood forming along the path to his sweet fountain of eternal euphoria. Her breath continued to quicken in pace, her heartbeat so strong he could see it pulsing, beating and throbbing in hypnotic rhythm in her, in that gorging artery in her neck.

The black silk slip agonizingly tight made it nearly impossible to slide her fingers underneath, watching her struggle to writhe and wriggle her fingers where he wanted them most. He smiled watching this tension in her body, this ferocious hunger that caused her limbs to fail her in agility, taking so much longer to find that warm, wet paradise that smelled of some mystical fruit during harvest season. Ripe, sweet and ready to be plucked and devoured endlessly. As her other hand found itself at the bottom of her slip forcing it over her luscious thighs the first of any sound besides his breathing that quickened pace in sequence with her racing heart, turned to moans of pleasure. He was enjoying himself, it felt so natural to be in this position, to show women that being treated like a filthy whore could feel oh, so fucking good.

Her fingers finally finding themselves nestled in her soft red velvet curls, the sweetest elixir wafted through the air as busy fingers found themselves teasing, tormenting and undulating in rhythms that she dreamed were Kyle's hungry, ravenous tongue. She moaned effortlessly unable to hold back, her filthy mouth opened and the first words she uttered were filled with liberation;

"Oh God yes this feels so, fucking, good." Kyle's grasp cinched in tightly as Jess swooning fell back even more, her thighs spreading so freely unable to stop this feeling of overwhelming pleasure that has seeped into every limb from her burning core.

"Taste yourself and describe it to me." His hands fell to her swelling breasts, she smiled at the wicked command, her busy fingers swirled into a hypnotic river of sweet ambrosia, moaning scandalously she laughed and plunged her fingers deep inside, pulling them out after fucking her warm tight cunt, instantly Kyle jolted her. Turning the chair around abruptly with her still inside of it, and slamming her thighs apart cruelly making her squeal in shock more than pain. Her blood red lips parted to indulge in the honey coated fingers of pure heaven, and in that moment Kyle unable to wait plunged his tongue deep inside her making her gasp as if she'd had her throat slit in a single swift annihilating moment of sudden death. His moans filled the room never had he tasted such a sweet otherworldly flavor before.

His awakened mouth was watering as he tried with all his concentration to not lose focus from this vivid dream world she'd created for him, but the hunger that in invoked deep within his hunting soul created such a difficult parallel. He could see her body bucking and writhing, her hands finding ways to recreate his tongue as best as she hoped for dream time's sake to convince herself that he was feasting upon her flesh like it was the last meal he'd ever have on this earth. He wanted to wander up his hidden passage way, and find himself opening that special door that lead right into her closet, how torturous this game had turned wishing he could ravage her from erotic sleep to waking ecstasy, knowing that it would turn into sheer nightmare. Once more he refused to allow this idea to take hold, he had far better plans for this rare breed of woman he found so captivating.

Jess's sleeping fingers found their way to her lips, Kyle found himself overwhelmed, with every sense intoxicated. Her taste so sweet and vivid in this powerful interlude that he felt drunk from just the taste of her. She bucked wildly unable to stay still for long his tongue penetrating her deep, teasing and tormenting her g-spot until she was unable to hold back, her body cumming so hard that an entire geyser of sweet juice erupted all over Kyle's lips. His mouth felt warm, sticky and wet in dream sequence and awakened state, leaving his rock hard cock so stiff that pleasure in this surreal conscious state turned to pain with little room for air let alone this erection that ached for Jess' tight warm inviting hole, displayed in a patch of summer honey dew. His firmly placed elbows lost their position on his knees as his hands fought to unzip his jeans. His cock bursting forth dripping with precum, he groaned in unison with the part of himself that was still devouring her pussy in her carnal dreamscape.

Each time he buried his face into her sweet little mound the more his cock raged craving to be inside her, every warm inviting part of her. Her hands furiously gripped his head, he could feel her nails dragging along his scalp, tearing at the back of his neck wanting more of him, and he felt enraptured in two worlds of pleasure. As the trickle of blood formed along the back of his neck and tense right shoulder, he felt the same beads form underneath his jacket. Her thighs grasping to close from the sheer build of pleasure about to burst forth once more in waves of satisfaction. She came once, twice, three times, four, harder and longer everlasting these feelings of pleasure continued to wash over her endlessly. She couldn't help but scream she never felt such visceral release before, it was excruciatingly painful, and all the while entirely satiating.

Kyle's wakened eyes looked at the screen before he could see the sheets between her thighs moisten with silk honey spun from the trembling limbs of his future concubine.

She surrendered to his explorative touch. Feeling his strong hands glide across her torso, dancing across her ribs and the undersides of each breast. Watching her head fall back in ecstasy, her mouth contorting and opening widely moaning his name;

"*Kyle*" without hesitation.

He gripped her firmly by her waist, embracing her with one fluid swoop of his arms. He stood her up out of the chair, while gripping just beneath each sumptuous ass check. Walking her towards the dresser with large sweeping mirror, reflecting her luscious hindquarters that overflowed, in his expansive grasp. He placed her with thighs wrapped around his strong legs onto the sturdy wood. Kissing her neck and gripping the delicate fold between each thigh and her sticky pussy he relished in every moan that was mixed with pleasure, pain and the fear of a swift beating heart that might ultimately stop beating.

Biting at her breasts, he slid each strap of her bra off of each shoulder. The silk felt like heaven. Slowly soothing her sexually tense body, and making her fall deep into an intoxicated trance space. Leaving her logic filled mind succumbing fully to this more than wanted submission. She felt his hands reaching behind her, his eyes watching her body tremble as he unfastened her bra. Kissing her face, her lips and chin he couldn't stop tasting her, feasting upon her soft sweet skin. She smelled of red roses in the dew kissed morning of springtime, layered in a rich scent that filled his mind with the ancient queens of empires from centuries long since passed.

With each moan she felt the hooks of her bra loosen delicately, her heavy breasts began to descend. The very moment the fabric left her body the chilled Colorado air bit at her nipples just long enough to harden before finding themselves in Kyle's warm mouth. His eyes devouring her beauty as his lips pressed against each nipple feeling them swell. Her gasps escaping each touch was wanted so badly for far too long. Her body could barely endure even the gentlest of touches. Even these intensely satisfying moments of pleasure were strung together between each nuance of vulnerable time that left her body hurting, aching, wanting for nothing in this world than to feel him inside of her. His moans of pleasure were felt as well as heard echoing through the wood paneled layers of this haunting hotel. She tasted as sweet as honey soaked in bourbon adorned with raspberries. He trailed down from her breasts tasting her skin, little beads of honey soaked sweat traveled down her stomach to her fragrant mound. Her mound that his hungry mouth craved to gorge himself on. His hands began to pull at her slip realizing it was skin tight for a very sinister reason. She began to laugh a little, smiling her eyes twinkling green, always green when she was hungry, blue when she was sad, but never could she imagine herself finding sadness in *his* enthralling presence.

"Oh you think that's funny do you?"

Kyle maintaining his observing gaze, waiting for her response. Biting her lips she leaned back gripping the dresser with her hands bracing herself for what may very well be brutal punishment, leaning down to match his provoking eyes she found herself mere inches from his face,

"I must admit, a little."

She attempted to lean back cockily bantering with his primal side in such a state would've been deadly for any other whore, but she wasn't just another fuck toy, there was something magnetic, powerful, enchanting about her, that felt combustible. He'd feel, her fire burning on his scorching skin all the way down to his soul tonight. Kyle violently reached for her neck standing her up and peering into her eyes, her heels no longer touching the floor. Now floating on the tips of her toes, her eyes bulged maintaining contact with his wondering, what would happen next?

"Ah, you want to play? *We'll play.*"

Her head swooning back her body languidly fell into his arms before she could gain her footing once more, she found herself flung forward at the foot of the four poster bed. She tried desperately to flee but he instantly overpowered her, pulling her footing out from beneath her she gripped the bed and heard him stand his heavy feet. Firmly planted his strong hands swiftly, effortlessly removing his belt, in that moment Jess's knees gripped the bedding and he shoved her ass down, grunting as if the wind had been knocked out of her, she began to cough. Feeling his hands wrapping her wrists together and then to the left corner of the bedpost, the buckle cinching into place leaving her completely immobile. As she kicked her body bucking trying to find liberation, Jess found herself captivated by Kyles luminescent blue eyes, She looked out the window to see the snow kissed covered mountain tops, endless forest of green fir's and pine shrouded by a veil of fog settling in, she realized that darkness soon approached and this night with her hunter was far from over.

"Now where were we? I believe the lady owes me a drink."

Leaning in kissing Jess on the cheek in an affirmation of adoration he walked over to the bar and pulled out a glass. Pouring himself a nightcap as promised in his original invitation to this mysterious meeting of the minds, Kyle sat down at the chair where Jess was just bleeding her soul onto paragraph after paragraph.

"Now then, you mentioned you wanted to turn your novel into a movie, but I see here you're not quite finished just yet."

With arms crossed and bound, Jess lying topless on her stomach with stockings, heels and black slip still on, she smiled turning her head over her right shoulder towards Kyle;

"Yes my publisher seems to think I need a bit more experience before I can finish this book and then hopefully hire you."

His awakened mind connecting with hers, "*She's a writer.*" Realizing that connection was one of many that inspired an instant fondness for Jess he smiled peering back into her dream; while Jess still slept peacefully now enraptured in her wildest dreams. Kyle seeing the fear in her eyes realizing that he was reading her roughly written work responded.

"I realize I'm putting you in a very *vulnerable position* right now, but this is the experience you need, do you trust me?" Jess laughing and biting her lip once more trying to suppress the urge to defy him with her charms;

"Are we speaking about these lovely bindings that you have me in? Or my soul that you're touching right now without permission?"

Kyle instantly leaned back slowly moving the liquid around in his glass delicately.

"You do want my help, that's why you brought me here? Or are you looking for experience?" Jess replied shyly;

"Both." Kyle smiled;

"Well it requires me to delve deep within that beautifully dark mind of yours to see what experience, *if any* that you're missing before I can even hopefully take on such a project. Am I understood?"

Jess turning red, never had she wanted to share her work with somebody before. But at the same time this visceral feeling of exposure left her nauseated at the fact that he held her entire being within the palms of his delicious hands, just mere feet away and there was nothing she could do to halt such an overwhelming violation. Kyle continued to read, each time his hand clicked down to the following page, Jess bit her lip, wondered and waited anxiously as drops of dew kept washing over her entire body and her fragrant cunt filled the room with the most appetizing scent for his carnal being. He was enraptured in her novel, reading it swiftly unable to stop;

"You make it awfully difficult concentrating with that delicious pussy of yours trailing under my nose, tormenting me to come back for more."

Kyle peered over his left shoulder to see her response, she smiled wickedly looking down and then away coyly playing like a fox with a starving hound in the thick woods of Sussex during hunting season. She crossed her right leg over her left at the ankle, arms still bound tightly above her making it difficult to find comfort. Kyle laughed at her comical, animated face and continued to read long into the night, taking a pad of paper nearby writing notes every so often.

"You're killing me." Jess said hours later as he couldn't stop reading. He stood and shut the curtains, Jess watched the brightest stars she's ever seen vanish behind them. The lights were suddenly on and the room was illuminated where Kyle was still fast at work. Jess started to grow tired, her eyes heavy she fell asleep hearing his hands every so often writing notes and clicking to the next series of pages in each chapter.

By three a.m. she awoke to the sound of Kyle gently closing her laptop. His drink long since finished along with a few glasses of ice water. Jess peered into his eyes fearful of what critique was about to come her way. He smiled with such ease that she felt his generous energy seeping over her body which was now ice cold and slightly shivering.

"You're a brilliant writer, it usually requires me much longer to read someone's work, and I can see a few areas that experience would suffice in nurturing your growth, not only as a writer but as a woman… as a sexually liberated woman."

Kyle stood from his chair, slowly removing his coat and placing it on the back of it, he stretched kicking his boots off and removing his socks tossing them across the room in various places. No longer needing to unbuckle his belt as it was already put to good use, keeping Jess immobile in illustrious restraint. Her eyes watching his silhouette unbuckling his jeans hearing the sounds of jeans being maneuvered over legs, knees and finally hitting the floor. His form so foreboding, an ominous presence for any woman who wasn't ready to be ravaged by the beast inside of this powerful and brilliant man.

Jess blushing kept watching as his boxer briefs continued sliding off his body, with utmost difficulty as his hard cock made it nearly impossible to remove them. She could smell his carnal scent lingering in the air, feel the heat of his blood coursing through his veins and radiating in steel furnace like certainty. Her skin ice cold, her fingers numb from lack of blood and clothing were pale, wishing she could warm them on his hot flesh. She wanted to say so many things to him, she had such a filthy mind to share but for some reason no words came to them now. She was too in awe of his power, she wanted to feel this power all over her body, roughly, without relent, even when fear and the desire to flee arose; she ached to be obliterated by his touch unable to find reason or logic behind this masochistic thrill. She waited as his shadow approached the lights were so dim, that only the nuances of his haunting facial expressions were seen beside his debilitating shadow.

As he crept slowly towards the foot of the bed where Jess's ankles delicately fell from. His hands removing each heel and gently placing them on the floor so easy that she couldn't even hear him, only feel the soft release of formerly bound feet. His knees placed on either side of her body slowly crawling on top of her, his arms reaching for her bindings. His weight and scent upon her, his cock hard and pressed firmly into the back of her pert slip shaped ass. Raging against the delicate fabric, feeling as if it would cut through it and fill her ass completely in a single thrust of hunger.

He leaned in releasing her wrists from the belt bindings, massaging them and rubbing the blood back into them, the burn intensely coursing back into each digit, his warm hands encompassing her delicate fingers bringing life back into them after hours of frozen stasis. Before she could feel comfort from such an attentive measure she felt his hands locking her back into her bindings, much firmer than before her arms stretched out entirely in front of her Kyle leaned down straddling her wrists with his grip now firmly resting on her body. Watching her beautiful face being shoved into the ornate fabric made him harder, seeing her embrace, such wanted torture was invigorating to a soul that was usually kept in deep slumber. Kept within a self-sustained hibernation ensuring those he loved were well nurtured and alive, while the darkness inside of him continued to surge starving, no matter what he fed it to keep it at bay.

His lips opened with calculated measure, "You will be silent, *that is if you can*, I want to see just how much restraint you're actually capable of. Is that clear?" Jess's face delicately pressed into the comforter red stained lips parting in utter subservience to his will.

"Yes my Lord." Unable to move, barely able to breathe Jess spoke clearly with unabashed desire. The arousal and near orgasm shuddering in her voice as she responded caused the intoxicating pheromones of both creatures of the night to radiate filling the room with musk's and floral scents making her lips, both pairs swell. She felt his body descending back to the floor, as his feet found themselves firmly planted. Jess found her present resting state take flight as Kyle's powerful hands gripped the top of her slip each hand on top of her hips, fluidly pulling it off in one solid motion. She was airborne for a moment her arms jerking her to stop as Kyle removed her slip.

Her ass spilling out beckoning for teeth, fingers, cock and whatever else Kyle could imagine. As the silk fabric made its way gracefully down each thigh, calf, ankle and foot it fell effortlessly to the floor on top of the pair of heels that were gently placed aside just moments before. She felt his hands reach for garter belt clips and stockings that danced down the back of each thigh. His fingers delicately working the fabric over his fingertips, each one falling to the floor, she felt his breath on the back of her legs, his lips kissing her ankles and heard his muffled groans. His boxers were painfully tight, she heard his hands effortlessly tearing his shirt off. Jess moaned wishing the mirror beside her revealed more than just a Godly shadow of a man possessed with power and capable of using it whenever he willed.

Kyle did his best to maintain his grip on reality, connecting with such a powerfully erotic mind was more than he'd ever endured in this existential state. Momentarily opening his eyes to see her arms above her head wrists placed firmly over one another, her soft silken breasts falling out of their covered paradise of silks, velvets and goose feather filled comforters. Her luscious, inviting thighs parting as her teeth bit down on her lips, he saw her left leg move down toes curling, *when did he have his cock out again?* Before he could keep his focus on his wakened state he found himself feeling those thighs between his as he straddled her naked bound body in that haunting hotel room. Seeing those blood red toes of hers curling in delight feeling his weight upon her.

"Shhhh" he whispered into her left ear, brushing away the hair from her cheek so her eyes were no longer blind to his full form. She could see every detail of him, down to the stubble on his jawline, to the lips that formed the words. Leaning in kissing her on her cheek, she felt him reach for her wrists, the clanking of metal on belt loops, she felt her shoulder blades release and the warmth flow once more to her fingertips. His strong hands warming her body, bringing it back to life. His hands massaged her arms and shoulders, brushing the hair from the back of her neck, he kissed her there and instantly Jess melted into ecstasy.

Kyle eased back now pressing his cock into the bottom of each lush over pour of hindquarter, groaning aloud she saw his mouth open, jaw clenching reminding her of the painful arousal that the infamous dark knight possessed. She felt her feline side building she couldn't be good for much longer even though she desperately tried. Instantly maneuvering herself underneath him she spun partially around the only part of her trapped was still under him;

"I don't recall asking you to face me!" gripping her wrists with one hand he smiled, wickedly throwing her leg up and instantaneously forcing himself inside of her while penetrating her mouth with his carnal kiss. Jess' moans of pleasure and shrieking pain escaped into him, she met his ravenous mauling with the most voracious howls. Unable to be silent, knowing that only a corpse stood a chance a midst such ecstasy. As no woman made of hot blood and salt drenched flesh could ever provide silence to unending bliss. As every inch of his gorging cock tearing, ripping and stretching her open with softest kisses, gentlest touch and sweetest embrace to overwhelm the body and leave her mind absolutely powerless.

"Oh God! Oh my fucking God!"

She screamed, tearing his flesh apart her nails clawing ceaselessly at his back. Causing him to plunge deeper, harder, faster and without a thought of concern, her moans of pleasure were met with groans of ecstasy;

"Here I cum, cum for me Jess, *cum with me Jess.*" In that moment Kyle opened his eyes and watched Jess on screen cumming for him her lips forming his name;

"Oh God, Kyle, I'm cumming for You, I'm cumming *with* you."

Her body jerking, her pink nipples as hard as rocks, he wished he could feel them in his mouth right now. His cock was jerking uncontrollably in the same haunting rhythm as Jess's body that couldn't currently stop moving. She was helpless in the throes of ecstasy, smiling and biting her lip and repeating his name over and over again.

"Kyle….Oh, God Kyle…"

He looked down and his sweater was covered in his glorious pleasure. He didn't even remember cumming he swore he just felt her pleasure overload him so vividly that he felt as if he'd came too. Smiling and looking down, and still watching his writhing astral slave calming her twitching limbs, he laughed and said;

"What am I fifteen again?"
Instantly removing his sweater and tossing it to the floor, realizing he needed to drop this in the laundry room for the maids to tend to along with the rest of the laundry for the week he found himself laughing. Watching Jess awaken smiling in such lust filled afterglow, like a new vampire who fed for the first time, she looked rejuvenated; full.

He realized how cold it was in his office without that sweater realizing there wasn't another one in here, Kyle found himself watching Jess one final moment seeing her lips part as she licked her fangs he was captivated by this alluring creature, to which he still had so many questions for his curiosity was finally peaked. Kyle entered the private corridor ascending to his public office on the third floor, his pleasure stained sweater in one hand he found himself at the very top of the stairs, a dead end to be perceived by deceived eyes but to the brilliant mind that built this place all it took was the well informed touch of his hands on a special brick that was stamped with the image of a small metal key. He touched it and slowly the wall moved forward and Kyle was standing in the hallway, completely dark, silent and so far the only one here. So far.

As Jess awoke to find herself hungry from such vivid dreams, she looked down to see herself disheveled, her smile turned to a laugh as she placed each of her breasts back into her soft ivory shirt where they belonged. She moved her porcelain tinged shorts back to the position they were when she first dressed for bed, finding her soft robe at the foot of her bed with her socks was amusing, she hastily put them on and took the candle lit on her side table and wandered off into the dark for the kitchen. Passing by the day room and her new office to the right that was yet to be organized to her creative and pragmatic standards she saw the light on in Kyle's office and slowly walked by looking back hoping he was too busy to notice her in these twilight hours. The grandfather clock struck midnight as she started to descend down the stairs to the first floor and hopefully operative staff kitchen. All the while Kyle was still ascending to his private exit the wall opening mere moments after Jess's curled locks gently descended down into the floor below in this mysterious and intricate home.

Chapter 3:

Scintillating Intermission

HE could smell her perfume, knowing she had just been here, gently pushing the wall back into place and feeling the drafted air cease, he reached to his right and opened his bedroom door, a striking gold with ornate bronze scroll work on the knob. As far as Jess was aware this door had been closed since before she arrived. Kyle slipped into his palace, a dark hunter green, adorned with touches of emerald and gold filigree, the four poster bed was unmade, yet the linens underneath perfectly positioned as if they were just laid into place. He didn't sleep much, he never really remembered a time in his life when sleep was present. From one haunting experience to surreal dream like state that left him with bloody hands in icy rivers and a complete inability to recall fully what had happened, sleep very rarely if ever visited Kyle. Beyond the glass window pane that overlooked the cemetery where so many of his treasured possessions now lie for as long as he decides to keep them there. Beyond the tapestries, heavy curtains and rearranged sheets sleep never visited the crypt keeper of Burnett Manor.

As Kyle closed the door behind him, the draft instantly doing the job for him without resistance. He turned towards his left where his dresser was, just next to it his laundry basket, instantly the pleasure stained sweater found its final destination. Peeling off the rest of his clothes he crawled into bed, his Superman sheets freshly washed and inviting him to find her, in his dreams this time. Kyle stared into his bathroom, wishing he'd had the energy to shower after such an exhausting night, but his new toy has drained his batteries for once, unlike all the others before her. Leaving his tormented eyes heavy, his dark and hungry beast drained of blood inside, turning inwards for a deep slumber and much needed carnal hibernation.

Jess made her way down to the first floor, the winding stair case slowing her usual feline stealth pace, saw a dim light on in the kitchen. Cinching her robe after catching the brisk chill of the mountain air on the back of her thighs, she peered into the doorway and wandered over to the fridge in what appeared to be a completely empty kitchen. After walking in a few steps she realized that this kitchen had hidden spaces, nuances between degrees that left everyone blind. From out of nowhere James was sitting there, on a barstool with a sandwich in front of him on a crisp and clean white saucer, he continued texting looking anxious well dressed in a leather jacket with his hair slicked back.

"Oh wow, I didn't see you there." Jess said suddenly unable to move, she laughed nervously shaking off her nerves.

"I didn't mean to startle you, I always come in here to relax after a busy night working for Kyle, not to mention the staff has a way of keeping my favorite things prepared, take a look, you'll see what I mean."

James waited and watched his eyes bright and his smile beaming. Jess slowly and unsurely walked towards the door,

"Is this some kind of trick?" she smiled that wicked little grin that implied she was already well in on his games. Jess opened the steel door and as the over lights helped illuminate a massive fridge filled with her favorite and hard to find treats, she sat there jaw dropped and wide eyed.

"Who is he?" She looked over at James as he started to laugh.

"I've been trying to figure that out since the moment I've met him, he's honestly beyond words." James continued texting as Jess reached for the chocolate cheesecake smothered in bloody strawberries.

"Nice choice, I have to admit it's sexy to see a woman indulge." James smiling, Jess began to laugh as she pulled up a barstool and sat in front of James,

"Thanks, I have to admit I've found in my experience that life is far too short not too; however that may be due to the fact that I've nearly died more times than I can probably count."

Her fork stabbing into a sizeable bite, her red lips parting taking in the bite, her mouth closing and teasing every morsel off the tip of the stainless steel device, her eyes rolling back revealing how fucking sexy she was when she came. Completely unbridled, without inhibition, utterly liberated.

"Really? What happens when near death becomes a part of life?" James asked with a calm, anxious, yet curious pry.

"Well I've found one obtains certain, how shall we say, *gifts.*"

James stiffened wondering where this conversation would lead, she's seen the signs of panic all before, she was used to it, by this time in her life she relished in it. It gave her a true sense of feeling alive. Being completely unabashed with who and what she was, no matter the dire consequence, her heart palpitated at the mere fact that she could be in danger, yet somehow again would find her way out of it, completely unscathed and more powerful and even more unstoppable than ever before. But those skills and special talents would be reviewed more intricately by another; that is when he chose to make his formal introduction. Jess's eyebrows arched in a beckoning way, her wry smile curling Cheshire like with each bite of her sumptuous cheesecake;

"Forgive me, I usually wake up ravenous when sleep visits me so creatively, so deeply, I find myself famished as if I'd worked for an entire week in a single evening's time, yet I have no explanation as to why I awaken in such a state." James smiled.

"You never answered the question, what do you mean by *gifts?*" Jess's intoxicating yet menacing eyes held James' gaze until she swallowed the final bite of much needed decadence.

"Let's just say I know there's plenty of bodies in that rather sizeable cemetery of his that are very *personal,* to him, *meaningful,* in ways that measure far beyond a mere ancestral attachment. As if he knew them all personally and treasures their presence here years later even if they are no longer by his side in physical form."

James was instantly dew stricken, beads of sweat formed on the sides of his face, trickling and forming into tiny globes of insignificant measure to most, but in these cold nights in the wilderness of the Rockies she knew that there was more to be investigated, discovered on the grounds and through many hidden passages that Jess started sensing were present ever since she arrived.

"There's no need for answers, clarification or even need for a response dear James, I assure you, I have no interest in giving up such an ample opportunity in life, to start over, fresh and anew once more. Kyle's secrets are safe with me, as I'm sure they are with you." Smiling his head overwhelmed, his mind swimming wondering what she meant by these vividly accurate yet cryptic phrases.

"So what do you have going on this evening? You are dressed for what I'd imagine to be a carnal adventure?" Jess said smiling getting up and opening the fridge again,

"I'm in paradise." She exclaimed reaching in and finding yet another treasured treat from her youth, a small jar etched with apple leaves containing the most delicious juice she'd enjoyed since before her mind could remember. As James messaged Kyle the information alluded in Jess's confession of abilities he then turned the conversation to his attire.

"Well if this gorgeous woman who I've been trying to meet with for weeks now confirms for tonight, I'll be on my way to Denver to enjoy something I've been looking forward too; she keeps indecisively changing the time, dating is the worst isn't it?" James replied.

"I have to admit I've never been one much for dating, I find that I usually find myself swept off my feet in the most peculiar of ways, for better or worse I'm afraid. But I prefer the adventure, the danger, the way my heart beats when I meet yet another monster on this planet and seeing if my light helps to illuminate his soul, or is it a light that he or she desires to stifle out." Jess smiled coyly pretending to be shy and unsure of such conversations all the while knowing that she was putting herself in a very precarious circumstance.

"But yet I do imagine that traditional dating like most courtship rituals isn't comfortable to say the least, maddening perhaps, and not even the slightest bit comfortable. That's also the magic of it all." Jess smiled, finishing her juice.

"Well as its Friday night and I have much to do before finding myself settled in before starting work Monday I wish you the best of luck tonight, here's hoping my crimson charm sends a bit of fortune your way for carnalities sake." Smiling and bidding James goodnight she sauntered out of the kitchen and back up the spiraling staircase, slowly ascending, taking her time she wanted to relish in this beautiful home that felt entirely possessing of her.

Feeling the soft fabric beneath her feet, Jess never realized that Kyle was awoken moments before by James' text stirred and unsettled, a feeling the lord of Burnett Manor wasn't used to feeling inside of him. A most formidable energy, it felt violent and chaotic, he preferred his smooth sense of control, as soft and supple as a finely poured bourbon aged for centuries in oak barrel. He relished in that sense of power he transfixed over all who came into contact with him even in the most trivial of ways. Kyle's eyes opened reading the lines of information

James sent through to his lord most loyally.

"Is that right? She *senses* a personal attachment to my treasures, well she is correct, though so were all those who now find themselves resting there instead of breathing still. She's fucking toying with me." His anger at feeling exposed left deep sleep on the back burn of twilight at least for now sleep would not visit Kyle tonight.

Jess continued to walk slowly up the stairs, feeling the room expanding, turning this spiraling staircase into a rotating walkway. Her eyes hypnotized by the twinkling of dim lights on crystal glass sparkling and refracting the scent of Kyle trailing to her dainty French nose. Her heartbeat slowing down and the walls suddenly looking fuzzy and dark she knew something was very different about this particular treat left just for her in the kitchen dimly lit inviting her in after such an exhausting evening. It was laced with a sedative, fortunately one Jess was quite familiar with, *Belladonna*.

She could taste the final note of atropine sweetness on her lips, how she'd grown accustomed to this taste. She remembered it from her many experiments with her private greenhouse and all the exotic and deadly plants that she was more than used to touching and ingesting even though for most this would be the final meal they ever enjoyed. Jess smiled realizing that this hallway grew dark due to her dilating eyes adjusting to the toxin now coursing through her veins, turning this hallway into a glittering tunnel of the night sky twinkling all around her silhouetted form that couldn't help but venture upstairs. Her sinfully relaxed limbs reaching out for the bannister, the solid wood felt soft, its polished pieces seductively leading her to the top floor, and back to her room where her swimming mind and full stomach belonged; gorged on pleasure, adventure and most of all mystery.

Kyle stealthily leaped from his bed his furious mind racing much too fast for him to focus on anything else but Jess. How was she able to penetrate his mind so vividly all the while he thought he was doing a perfectly good job of penetrating hers, but something stirred within him driving him mad;

Was she able to coax out other information about his past?

His darkside he felt was most well hidden from the world, except for those that ended up in their final resting place. Outside in the cemetery was the only place that ever truly brought Kyle any peace, the one space in time that all projects were finished and completed with complete absolution. His secrets safe with him and only him now and always, until this insatiable hot, yet vexing little bitch arrived this afternoon. Kyle grabbed his large, plush dark green terry cloth robe from the hook nearby his bed where it always rested and briskly walked towards the bathroom, closing the door nearly all the way, leaving the cracked door to let light escape just barely enough to give Jess's third eye quite the titillating show as she finally made it to the top of the stairwell.

Her dark hallway turning into a vertical strip of light and between that glowing light that appeared in her mind's eye was Kyle's glorious backside. The mirror in his room in this angle reflected his back and shoulders. Molested by hot water flowing down his broad shoulders and splashing off of every sharp pointed bone that pressed itself from under his hot flesh.

"Oh if only you knew my darling that sharing such sweet poison with me only enhances my gifts, if you wanted me to play victim you should've tried harder." Jess smiled and giggled softly knowing that she was the only one on this floor now besides her stimulating new boss.

Jess's psychic eye probed the light until the water flowed down to his waist and over each of his gorgeous cheeks. Each plump, firm piece of his ass just beckoning her to open the door, to peel off her clothes and to step into the shower with him hoping she'd be devoured by the big bad wolf. Kyle could feel her prying psychic eye, the back of his head tingling, in that moment he turned around and glared at her, holding the most powerful and penetrating gaze, in the last moment when Jess's heartbeat so quickly she thought it was going to burst, he smiled and the room went black.

Jess was mortified, stunned and even shaken by being caught so easily and so directly shown the door for her sentient violations. She forgot that in the sweet aftertaste of apples and atropine that her abilities though heightened in one way or another, weren't as easy to control when her inhibitions were lowered, leaving her ability to cloak her presence in such metaphysical exercises that were keenly natural to her soul.

"I can't fucking believe it, did he, did he *catch* me?" Jess's mind raced and finally for the first time since James' message found its way to his resting form did Kyle find peace. He felt her heart racing, her mind moving so fast that he felt as if she was going to break all of space and time in that single earth shattering moment of adrenaline. The faster her heart beat the more vividly she felt the toxin absorbing into her bloodstream, she realized she was outmatched until this dose wore off, *hours* from now…

Kyle laughed manically under his breath, his eyes closed with his smile so vividly serene. Each drop of hot water was relished, he had her right where he wanted her. Jess felt afraid, unable to make sense of it all, slowly weakened to make tonight much easier than he would've anticipated.

"I'm pleased you've enjoyed your apple juice Jess, is nostalgia one of your many weaknesses? You beautiful, sentimental girl. How I look forward to showing you your place here, *very soon* you curious little whore."

Kyle's soaking wet hair trickled beads of water down his hot flesh, his hands feverously washing every part of his gorgeous body with layers of bubbles. His hands struggling to stay focused to their task, he wanted to stroke his cock again, knowing that he connected with her so vividly, scaring her nearly to death. How he'd particularly relished in the animated face of his victims, their emotions contorting to match their tears of fear and sorrow of leaving soon after a life not yet fully lived.

"You will be my greatest masterpiece Jess, you've already proven to me with your abilities that you're perfect for the position, now let's see if you can be, *trained*."

Kyle smiled as the words freely fell from his supple lips. A wry smile of satisfaction appeared on his face as less and less bubbles appeared on his rippling body. His shoulders finally fell in a relaxed disposition, he felt at ease. The universe knew all too well and so did the darkness that burned within the heart and soul of this sadistic being, as night fell the world was eternally his to take.

Kyle reached for his towel, he wrapped it around his hips, slowly letting the steam clear from the bathroom mirror he looked into his eyes. Smiling wickedly, his hands slowly drying off every limb, reaching for the robe and wrapping himself up. He walked back into the room, reaching for his clothes for bed, throwing on a long sleeve shirt that clung to every delicious part of his chest and form. Dark blue and green tartan pajama pants and house shoes Kyle found himself lying on the bed unable to sleep, but this time not out of anger, but from sheer satisfaction. Finally he could find peace knowing that everything he'd always dreamed of had finally arrived at this point in his life. With his hands resting behind his head, and his legs crossed at the ankles he leaned back smiling on his pillow waiting for his curious new toy to get herself into further trouble so that he could have an excuse to execute her formal training regimen, finally, at long last.

Jess felt the need to wander back to her room for both safety and comfort, did he really catch her? Does he have the slightest inkling as to who she really is and what she's capable of? Or was this for once in her life beyond her grasping as of yet? Her head was swimming, she knew it wasn't wise to spike one's adrenaline after the sweet taste of atropine was introduced into the bloodstream, but never before had anyone ever caught her spying on their inner world before. She was haunted with fear, yet captivated by his power and all the while aroused in ways she'd never known before. What first began as mysterious opportunity to start over, now turned into a dark adventure that she never knew existed on this planet; beyond the twisted and deluded thoughts that filtered through her mind onto endless pages of her written work. So consumed with the possibility of being revealed, she didn't notice that she'd walked back to her private chambers. She felt the soft crimson fabric tease her face, slowly slinking down towards her neck. Now visibly throbbing quaking, and coursing more and more of that precious toxin to her swiftly beating heart. Naively luring the beast within Kyle's chest to make his first appearance in an even more elusive and to most quite *unsettling* way.

Chapter 4:
LANGUISHING INTRUSION

SHE felt the decadent poison flowing through her veins, pumping serenely into every corner of her capillaries. Her red blood cells dancing and slowly bumping into one another, her eyes felt heavy, her body felt as if she was floating in the hot bath that her skin felt just hours earlier. Caressing her body, sliding down slowly over every curve and supple piece of exposed skin. She swallowed feeling the muscles straining to form even the most basic of functions. She'd obviously had her fill for tonight, there was no way she could see herself moving an inch in her current state. Her eyes felt impossibly heavy, like two ancient stones unable to budge without the help of many hands guiding and sliding them back to reveal her sparkling jewel eyes. Each lid firmly in place, it felt as if she'd been blindfolded, for she could hear and almost taste the air in this palace room.

Her breath was shallow now, she wondered just how much he dosed her with, for any other they would've been long since out. Usually Kyle had to carry them back to their rooms on that first night, but as her strength impeded upon him the impression of pride and awe. He longed to take her back to bed tonight, but relished knowing that she was strong enough to do so entirely on her own. Her lips stained red from her now faded lipstick parted letting as much oxygen into her lungs as she could take in. She knew ways around the intoxicating touch of *Belladonna* along with many other potions he had ready to implement on his wanton prey.

Unbeknownst to her until now, was the fact that in the back of this rather large closet of hers that was still cracked slightly open, was a secret panel. Behind the layers of crimson and gold wallpaper, was a false wall, which after further investigation to only the most trained of eyes would reveal the thinnest escape of light, a crack no wider than a pinprick. Which trickled light in from the candlelit halls of the Lord of Burnett manor's private spiral staircase. Kyle could feel her energy weaken, he knew it wouldn't be much longer before she was asleep, in paralytic catharsis. He longed to smell her without fear or interruption, to feel her in his arms unable to move. To feel her pulse quicken as his fingertips pressed against her exposed neck. He effortlessly stood from his former position of comfort, eyes transfixed on what appeared to be an obsolete wall lamp fixture. Kyle smiled as his hands gently coaxed the ornate knob fixated at the bottom of the luminescent glow, and silently the wall clicked open. His attached nightstand gently moving forward, providing him just enough room to enter into his private path of exploration.

Descending a single floor, Kyle walked mere feet below where Jess's intoxicated head was still swimming, fighting in a calmed meditative state to stay awake just long enough to know what was going to happen next. With each step he approached underneath her the stone steps guiding him back up once more into the end of this spiral path, the candle light flickering softly as he knew it would be, she was so close to him, yet so far from the part of him that ached to capture her most. This was just a taste, of what feast soon waited for his hungry lips. He scanned her thoughts one last time before moving the secret panel forward, she was as silent as the grave, and even more beautiful in this light than he ever imagined she could be, than *any woman* could be. She kept her mind calm, peaceful, black and empty, alluding to her hunter that she was in fact a fresh kill, he continued to peer through the cracked closet door soaking up the scene of his sleeping beauty, never had he felt so attached to someone *so new* before.

This feeling inside left him peaceful within, like the wanted Spring that never came to melt away the darkness and bitter cold that beat within the chambers of this man's cruel, unyielding heart. He stood there watching, waiting to notice even the most subtle of nuances escaping her to reveal that she wasn't as subdued as he hoped she'd be in this moment. She was barely breathing, he loved bringing her so close to death already, just hours after arriving. She lied there captivatingly still, making the dark hunger in him grow. He felt his mouth water, the entire room started moving, she looked as if she was floating down a river of blood, her pale skin glowed in the candlelight, he didn't care if he was caught this time. He'd never been caught prior to this, it was worth the risk, even if it meant cutting this long sought after game extremely short if she did in fact, *wake up*.

The dark shadow of a demon stood in full height, towering over her a dark silhouette of six feet, four inches just watching over her. Smiling for the first time in decades it felt, Kyle examined the soft, supple and delicate folds of porcelain flesh that wrapped around this heavenly creature without the slightest hesitation. He couldn't take his eyes off of her.

"Where did you come from? Such a *ravishing creature*, where did you come from my pet?" He never felt so disarmed by such beauty before, he felt the benevolence of her soul permeating out, radiating as vividly as the sun on the highest mountain in Colorado on the clearest day. It was easy to dispose of wretched, vile little creatures, but to see beauty such as this, instantly hypnotized the hell hound inside to watch over her, to protect her, from *even himself*.

Jess continued to breathe softly, still unable to move even if she tried, she was grateful for this, she was never quite good at calming her biological functions for fear down. It wasn't easy for a woman who was raised on adrenaline to stifle such responses, she was grateful for the toxin still swimming inside of her. She knew it was the only thing that prevented death in this very moment, if he even knew she was cognitive he'd lose control. There really wasn't any gauge for knowing just what he'd do if she knew he was in here, and how he got in here in the first place. He couldn't risk losing so much of his world to another's *prying eyes*. Jess continued to slumber in front of her dark assailant, wondering what his true intentions were. She could feel his power, his strength, his dark presence was ominously expansive, and it felt as if he was generating all the power in the entire house from the center of his core. Kyle reached for her face, gently caressing her cheeks, studying the curve of her lips with his thumbs, he brushed the hair from her face, slowly sitting on her bedside, just watching her.

"You're so beautiful, I knew I should've killed you the moment you'd arrived, only a fool would continue to keep you around, it's dangerous to feel, and even more dangerous to keep those around me that provoke me to such feelings of content."

If her heart was able to it would've given her away, with its swift pounding, but still the poison subdued her. She floated in a surreal state of consistency, not something ever easily afforded to powerful sentient beings with a multitude of conflicting abilities, in fact it was something she'd been trying to achieve for years but still hadn't quite gotten the grasp of.

She felt the weight of him slowly leave, yet his footsteps continued around her room, he sat down on the other side of the bed and slowly lied back, resting his head back alongside the pillows. Jess could smell him, never had she imagined such a state of intimacy already with a man she just vividly masturbated too in fantasy a few hours before; to then falling asleep and finding him in her wildest dreams, playing them out in a way that convinced her that the dream world really was the only one true reality that she ever wanted to exist in. Without warning she moaned, she wasn't prepared for the wall of internal worlds and external worlds to shatter without warning, his eyes bulged open just moments after they closed. He thought to himself quickly;

"Did I not give her a strong enough dose?" He waited anxiously she smelled the air thick with his fear induced pheromones wafting through the breeze, as she continued to shallowly breathe he watched and waited for her to scream, to move for something explosive and unrelenting to happen, forcing his dreams to fade to black as he cleaned up yet another mess that wasn't intended, all for the sacrifice of a pretty face.

Not wanting to give herself away, she quickly focused her pulse elsewhere, down towards that sweet, moist little spot that started collecting dew the very moment his scent trailed across the air to subdue her much stronger than any poison ever could. His body now looming over hers, his dark shadow followed by the strength of two beautifully sculpted hands, wrapped delicately around her porcelain neck. His thumbs delicately moving her chin upwards, as if he sculpted her out of Roman marble. He traced her jawline, leaning in and inhaling her delicious floral scent, mixed with subtle tones of aroused flesh that reminded him of spiced strawberry honey.

He felt his heart beating fast, he wanted her so badly he could nearly taste her. His right thumb tracing that pulsing artery in her neck, coaxing the tip of his thumb into position he felt her heart slowly beating, like a whisper on the wind. She tried with all her concentration to cloak her mind, focusing on a stained glass window that blurred and contorted the shadows of white fading into black he thought it must've been the toxin moving through her body that caused this dreamless sleep. It'd been years since he slept, without waking to a world surrounded by his hands being covered in blood. It was the only dream world he knew, eventually driving him to recreating these horrific scenes in reality to coax his mind into submission. Providing deep sleep for weeks on end, recharging the missing pieces of a shattered soul that had seen far too much, too soon on this dark abyss of a planet, the tragic kingdom.

"I'm glad to see that little outburst wasn't intentional, I wouldn't want to have to get my hands dirty tonight."

He propped her head against the pillows and brushed the hair from her face, he couldn't help it, Kyle was absolutely captivated by her. Her ethereal skin was glowing and he wanted desperately to see what this porcelain canvas would look like stained blood red.

"I can't wait to see what you're truly made of you magnificent creature. I know you haven't even begun to show me what you're capable of. Time for me to find rest to further prepare for your wild, untamed mind." He gently kissed her on the forehead dotingly, leaving her bedside and standing at the foot of it to watch for any signs of fatality or more disconcerting, awareness. She didn't move a muscle changing her mental focus to pure black he scanned her waiting to hear fearful cries or fleeing ideas of escape, the usual responses from any prey in this certainly fatal position. Jess continued to sleep, not moving a muscle, an inch. No longer fearing but *knowing* with full certainty what he is truly capable of. He walked to her bedside and leaned in inhaling her scent, and smirking, as well as she tried to hide her awareness, that sweet spiced strawberry honey gave her entirely away.

He stood up with every fiber of strength with his controlled patience, he walked into her closet, ensuring to leave it cracked just as she'd left it before he arrived. He walked into his private stairwell, pulling the false panel abruptly behind him into place. Clicking silently back into its forged perception, he felt the fire inside his soul scorching him from the core and burning his insides. Bursting forth hot molten fire, he felt the primordial part of his brain click and his eyes instantly dilated. His adrenaline spiking he gripped his fists so firmly he slammed them into the stone wall, any other surface would've faltered, shattered and quaked the entire foundation but this former slaughter house stood firm and the blood once more trickled forth from his beautiful hands. He didn't remember walking back to his room only feeling the coursing blood pulsing through his body he trekked back into his room slamming the wall back making the nightstand shutter as the wall slammed into place. Jess could hear this in her room yet she was still unable to move. The house was still, silent as the grave, and she for the first time in her life she prayed that he believed her mental projection while fearing for the worst.

"Did she actually *think* I wouldn't fucking notice?" He slammed his hands down washing them rigorously in the sink, picking out pieces of concrete and groaning still furious while he doused them in alcohol and grabbed his towel. Barely drying his hands before slamming it to the ground.

"I chose that fucking poison for a reason, only the filthiest of whores could reveal herself."

She didn't realize that after his hands were on her, that her sweet pussy leaked sweet juice all over her panties, her soft shorts not safe from such a visceral release were now sticky, wet and her rich perfume carried revealing that toxic sleep wasn't captured, no woman could secrete with the high level of *Belladonna* now permeating every corner of her paralyzed form, *no woman* but *her.*

Her aching pussy gave her away, his anger rose from fearing that she was playing dead for her own safety, but in all earnest she just wanted to give him exactly what he desired. She wanted to play his game, his dark, twisted, sick and fatal game. She couldn't help herself, she was drawn to him like a moth to the flame. She felt alive in ways she'd always craved but never knew anybody was strong enough to provide. So many left her dark world years ago, not from the demise of her very own hands, but from the three ring fetish circus that grinded away in the twisted gears of her pretty little head. She'd always loved pain, ached for it, for the most part even more than pleasure, it was her body that forced her to indulge in such passionate satisfaction, driving her insane with lust, she found herself nearly fucking to death every slave, submissive and dominant that ever came her way. Being left with such a carnal hunger was almost too much to take. The weight of it was crushing, she wanted so badly to be toyed with, played with, tormented and even tortured on formal occasions. It was the only aspect of living that alleviated her constant thirst for sex, blood and torture.

Kyle saw a flash of this beautiful otherworldly creature in his head, she felt Jess pleading for his understanding, showing him fully where she came from, somehow, some dark and twisted way, this plant helped him see parts of her that she never showed to anybody anymore. She stood six feet, two inches, of course this was due to the seven inch spiked stiletto heels that her gorgeous feet wore. He saw a beautiful woman kneeling, completely naked, in collar looking up with tear stained eyes, mascara streaked down her face, her long straight black hair touching her waist cascading down her body like a river of death. He saw Jess step into frame and bend down grabbing the woman's face,

"Shhhh my pet, it's all over now, you've cleared your debts." She leaned her head into Jess's black latex gloved hand and she leaned in, her red curls spilling over her river of black. She kissed her on the cheek, her entire body was covered in black latex, her soft pale breasts bursting from the top.

As Kyle watched the girl continued to sob, the view of her back revealed strips of flesh torn off in perfect bullwhip execution. Jess placed her beloved blood stained whip on the wall, leaning over she reached for her favorite plant the beautiful *Belladonna,* her deadly children thrived best in her dungeon; little did Kyle know until now just how wise Jess was about such rare and exotic flora. Tucking her curls gently up into what appeared to be a rather mysterious mask or cowl of some sort, he watched from behind as she slowly stepped out of each heel. Dropping her to a mere five feet seven inches, he watched her slowly unzip and slither out of her latex dress, bending over and revealing in all her glorious possessions the most sumptuous ass. Her delicious peach opened just enough for him to see her full lips before she stood back up. Turning around, entirely naked she dropped to her knees, her crimson red lips filled this catwoman mask perfectly. Jess crawled on all fours to this naked, bleeding, sobbing woman and held her, drawing her towards her chest,

"Now tell me darling, how quickly do you want this to take place?" She began to lick her wounds, all the while looking back into what appeared to be oblivion or an empty, cold concrete room, but Kyle felt her eyes staring right into his. She smiled lapping up the blood;

"I don't care Mistress, just do it, I don't want to be here anymore, I can't handle it my love please kill me!" She sobbed and lied on the ground in her own puddle of life force.

"As you wish my darling, I hope you know that you, *will always* be my favorite."

She reached for what appeared to be a metal thimble, strategically placed nearby, she placed it on her index finger, now holding this nihilistic woman in her arms. Cradling her and soothing her, she buried her sobbing face into her sumptuous breasts, her tears softened and she swooned as her Mistress punctured her throat, holding her gaze watching her life gently fading away. She leaned forward and cried holding her close to her, rocking with her pale lifeless body buried in her breasts. Kyle realized in that moment she wanted so desperately to fill that void for destruction that his darkness conquered without thought or recompense. She took off her mask and gently set down the woman she loved her body blood stained red turned this former angelic canvas into a bloodstained demoness that he stood in awe of. She reached for her collar, and placed it around her neck. Tears streaming down her face, he could see the emptiness inside her, and she sat up on her knees and faced him with the most desperate plea, begging;

"Please, *teach* me."

The vision ended and Jess instantly passed out from exhaustion. She never realized that her favorite plant would cause such psychic burn out so swiftly but she had a much larger dose than she ever previously experimented with on her own. She partook of her potions before sessions with only her most trusted devotees, those that sought her out when this world became too much and the swift promise of eternal sleep was the only solace to their soul anymore. For the most part she enjoyed her work as an intoxicating old world mistress, as most of her clients wanted to explore and return in the future, it was only those that fell for her, deeply in love with her that eventually felt driven by passionate madness to deplete themselves to extinction long before they were intended to depart. They say that all beauty comes with a cost, Jess felt that this was hers. Being so powerful to captivate even those who attested to hating her, but also being so incredibly insatiable that she sucked the very will to live from the depths of the souls of those who ever claimed her heart, and earned their way into her bed.

Kyle felt all of his anger vanish instantly, once again this disarming ability of hers left him in a clarified state unlike ever before, and she had a way of sucking out the very poison inside him that usually left him incapable of maintaining control. Just moments before he thought he'd have to go out into the city, to his old hunting grounds and find a gullible bitch who was willing to risk her life with a ridiculously charming and incredibly sexy man. Just another addition to his collection of one time use toys. Jess's innate abilities absorbed all of Kyle's hunger for the kill, and he found himself in awe, smiling and shaking his head in disbelief.

"Right when I think I have you exactly where I want you, you somehow throw yet another obstacle in my path, *you*." As he curled up in his four poster bed that night he somehow managed to find deep and restful sleep, smiling knowing fully content that she wasn't done yet, not tonight, not ever, if he had anything to do with it, and he did.

Chapter 5:
A STUDY IN GOTHIC BLOOD

LYING in the same disheveled state that both atropine and her new hunter left her in, Jess slowly focused her mind to the microscopic world of her own cellular structure. Her eyes fixated on each toxin filled blood cell that was carrying this sweet poison through her body. She felt her healing abilities awaken, seeing electric green sparks of lightning glowing and connecting with each infected part of her body the potent elixir's great power wore off effortlessly in what seemed like just a few minutes. Jess smiled slowly cracking her eyes open to ensure she wasn't being watched too closely by the foreboding presence of her wanton captor. She realized this delicate exchange, this sadistic dance of sorts had to be strategic if she was going to survive. She wanted to earn her place in his world, no matter the darkness that existed deep beneath the confines of this house. She could hear their voices screaming in her mind, there were so many of them down there, an entire city it seemed. Those daunting and dangerous games would be explored another night when she wasn't concerned with passing out from paralytic poison that tried with all its chemical properties to subdue her for good, or at least fully for tonight. She slowly stretched and realized how aroused Kyle's ominous presence had made her;

"Oh fuck, I guess that is one experiment I have absolutely no test results for."

She was usually quite wise as to how certain herbs, plants and poisonous flowers affected the erogenous zones of the human body, in both males and females. As an intoxicating old world mistress of the underworld, only the most sordid creatures on this planet ever made their way to her dungeon doors to beg and plead with the dark apothecary eluding to their visceral desperation for torture, craving whatever elixir she had to inject into the darkness of night, into each of her sessions.

"Belladonna, you are a cruel mistress, giving me away to my hunter, makes me quite the vulnerable prey."

Jess reaching down to her soaking wet panties and sticky cotton shorts, she found herself moving her limbs to function and form the usual protocols required for limbs to move properly. Forcing herself to sit upright she moved her legs to fall effortlessly from the weight of toxic side effects alone towards the floor. Knowing yet another shower would be required before she was able to sleep or venture out once more before sunrise came. Jess slowly grabbed onto furniture, stabilizing her weakened limbs and finding her way once more to the bathroom, this time for a brief rinse.

The lights glowed as she turned them on, her face looked paler than usual, her eyes purple, displaying to her that he had given her quite a fatal dose, "You wicked, sadist." She smiled looking at herself in the mirror and checking her pulse, "Well at least that's back to normal, I'm sure I'll need another snack before my color comes back fully though."

Jess slipped her robe and soft cotton shirt off they fell to the floor and she smiled biting her lip as she struggled to peel off her sticky shorts and panties, still soaking wet with spiced honey. She reached her foot up to her hand and pulled her peach sock off and tossed it aside, switching legs and doing the same fluid movement with the other pocket of peach fabric covering her other foot, it soon found its place beside its partner in a soft pile of clothing now resting on the tile floor.

"Mmmm now where were we? I wonder if I'm all alone or do I have an audience tonight?"

Jess chuckled already fully aware that he was always watching, he'd been watching her for years now it seemed. She always felt his strange, alluring and intoxicating presence from time to time, never knowing who it belonged too. Why, it called to her so rampantly without explanation, beckoning her as to why she was compelled to find the answer to who or what radiated this salacious feeling of decadence inside her soul. She knew his eyes were watching her, in the kitchen when she arrived earlier this afternoon, in the bath when she couldn't help but ravish herself the way she hoped he would anytime now it seemed. She washed her body feeling the warm beads of fresh spring water sliding down her back and ass, teasing her thighs and swimming past her ankles to the drain below. She washed her delicate folds, teasing each one and ensuring that every drop of sticky honey vanished down the drain. She moaned feeling an overwhelming peace arrive within her soul. In this very moment Kyle was smiling sleeping peacefully, dreaming of the woman that constantly loved to frolic in the fresh waters, for the sheer pleasure of basking in the presence of his curious psychic eyes.

The water slowly turned off, her hands finally feeling like themselves again, the atropine wore off much swifter after a shower. Her inclinations to this powerful plant were right, she now hungered for something to satiate her calorie depletion. But what was available in this place that wasn't already tainted for her to sleep for eons waiting for the moment when he'd strike as her eyes opened for the first time after poisonous, dreamless sleep. She wandered into the closet, wrapped in her towel, reaching for another soft pair of shorts, this time dark brown. Needing yet another pair of dry panties for tonight she found a rather sensual white cotton thong to wear underneath. Jess wandered back into the bathroom finding her soft cotton shirt and putting it back on, it fell on top of her bountiful breasts, she had to then maneuver it around and over them for a proper fit. Wrapping herself in her coffee colored robe she reached down and slowly put her socks back on and walked back into her room.

Little did Kyle know how well equipped his new live in nanny really was. Reaching behind the nightstand she pulled out a very small black box. Opening it she reached in pulling out a few toxin test strips that she usually kept for testing purposes. To ensure she never provided a fatal dose to her clients of kink, unless that was their final request in life. For those who needed it most she gladly offered herself as their merciful angel of death. Slipping a few strips into her robes pocket, she was ready to go. She knew without vital sustenance she would only feel weaker in the morning and she had no intention of allowing Kyle to feel as if he had her cornered, at least not yet. Jess reached for the candle by her bedside and stared at the wick, instantly a small flame flickered into existence, smiling she said, "Now that's better."

Slowly walking towards the door, she took one last, *deep breath* before venturing back down towards the kitchen, for something to help her recuperate. As she made her way passed his wing and down below along the spiraling staircase she quietly made no sign of her presence. Once more wandering into the kitchen, this time entirely alone, so dark that the only light with her, was the candle that she carried in. She again found herself opening the fridge door and saw that her favorite items were now gone.

"How convenient." She said aloud.

Looking around she saw plenty of random items to make a meal with as well as a few labeled items for James that she trusted much more than anything else that was in here. She reached for a container of orange juice and opened it, she placed a tiny drop onto a strip that she reached for from her pocket and waited to see the results show that it was just juice, untainted juice. She remembered where James had shown her where the glasses were and reached for one. Filling the glass and devouring every last drop, she then reached for his leftovers, not having the time or patience to test everything in here that was available for consumption. She ravenously fed, his half eaten meal so delicious she didn't care to focus on what it was or how much of it was left to consume. She just remembered throwing the empty container into the trash and placing the now empty glass inside the sink, knowing the morning staff would tend to it. She didn't have to risk waking anyone up now, as it was creeping towards twilight, she only had a little time left to explore the one place that pulsed like the swift heartbeat of frail prey. His one sanctuary besides the cemetery that existed at Burnett Manor, *Kyle's... study.*

Jess stealthily moved up the spiraling stairwell, the twinkle of crystal now entirely absent in a room that was pitch black. She reached her hand out to feel the wooden bannister, her other was now doing its best to stop trembling making her only light source flicker in a most unsettling way. She took one more breath, exhaling with each step she ascended past the second floor, the offices still dimly lit, a handful of colleague's still busy working late into the twilight hours of early morning. No words or whispers, no movement, just the sound of typing, and phone buttons being pushed and redirected to other lines. Where these lines were, Jess hadn't the slightest clue. Her head still swimming she felt her body recalibrating, her curious feline eyes, sparkled green in the darkness of the upper floor. Knowing Kyle's bedroom door was only a few feet away she visualized herself completely invisible, and let the light lead her into his cracked and dimly lit library, the very heart and soul of the man who ruled this mysterious world. Her feet gently stepped towards the door reaching for the golden handle, slowly pushing it. The door didn't make a sound, she could tell it was recently greased, quite a calculated move as Jess had noticed every door in her wing was impossibly loud; ceaselessly screaming in sinful confession as to when and where she prowled around, in the middle of the night.

She smiled and felt the strongest energetic pull she'd ever felt in her life, as if the entire room moved forward, pulling her directly inside. She slowly closed the door leaving it cracked just enough for light to escape and for Kyle to feel her wandering soul. His usual anger at such rigorous exploration already faded to amusement, she was so, fucking curious. He couldn't wait until she started wandering downstairs, he thought it would take her months, like all the others, but at this rate, she was going to find herself in quite a horrifying predicament that Kyle had waiting for her, planned for Jess, for most of her adult life.

Her mind swam as she looked towards a book shelf that glowed to her eyes, sparkling like treasure in soft twilight. The stars twinkling just outside, a mountain adorned with thick trees, nearby a pond shimmered and reflected the full moon in all its pale glory. An entire top shelf covered in manuscripts and works in progress from what looked like over a thousand film concepts in the making. The shelf just below that captured her eye was filled with rare, arcane books of her favorite authors, some of which are even related to her, from Uncle George Byron and Aunt Mary Shelley, to Poe, Shakespeare, King, Koontz, Rice and so many others that invited daring readers to fall into a world of darkness. Where tragedy, fear and ecstasy, continued pushing them beyond the modern understanding of their times to somewhere far beyond this mundane plane of existence. Forcing those to feel the experiences of humanity flowing through their very veins and bleeding into their minds like liquid white fire, igniting a soul to dance, awaken, and *sacredly create*. She marveled at the array and endless selections, she could spend an entire year in this room alone, never leaving and still not absorb enough of the treasured possessions that Kyle had in this beautiful study. His reading chair was to her right, nestled under the window, a table nearby had a carafe of water with ice, realizing now that he'd probably be here soon. She tried to calm her excitement and set aside the rare and complete collection of her ascendant Lord

Byron's work as she climbed up onto the ladder reaching for a book that was handcrafted that stood out quite unlike all the rest.

As her ass swished towards the top of the ladder she reached for the book, not knowing that she wasn't alone, behind her were his peering eyes. Looking through the cracked door gazing at her curved flesh that peeked out just beneath her robe and soft shorts. He could smell her sweet spiced honey from here, how intoxicating it was to be near her. She made his mouth water, his cock instantly hard and eyes dilate, a predator always on the verge of his next kill. He watched, unblinking, waiting to see what she would do. He felt himself compelled to rip her to shreds the very moment she touched the book that now sat in the palm of her hands. As she opened the first page she realized it was a personal diary of Kyle's, not wanting to pry into this just yet she instantly reached and put it back on the shelf. Whispering aloud, "I hope he doesn't notice."

Jess said just loud enough for Kyle to hear, as she reached back to place the book on the shelf he opened the door and stood right behind her. Smelling her thighs and looking up beneath her soft terry cloth shorts, watching the delicate piece of cloth moisten between her legs, her scent was breathtaking. He wanted to taste her, he imagined that if he did, he wouldn't be able to stop until she died completely from sheer pleasure alone. At that very moment he grabbed the ladder and tossed it to the side abruptly, "I notice everything."

His voice sliced through the air like a knife cutting Jess just behind the Achilles tendons. Instantly she started to fall, the moment she could find the courage to scream Kyle's arms reached out and caught her. Gripping her close to his chest he leaned in, his carnal eyes matching the firm tone in his voice;

"Just exactly *what are you doing* in *my* study Jess, and at five in the morning, no less."

Blushing and biting her lip she couldn't help but be insanely aroused by the man holding her and scolding her for being a curious feline, out of her bed roaming around the castle far beyond her bedtime. Looking deep into his eyes and feeling powerless, she said:

"I didn't realize it was so late, I saw the door cracked and the light on and thought you were in here working and got swept away by your incredible collection."

Kyle slowly lowered Jess's legs down towards the ground, she stood staring up into his eyes. He towered over her by nearly a foot, his broad shoulders blocking her escape and his strong arms clenching in a way that made her wonder if she'd already gone too far, to the point of no return. Jess slowly backed towards the table and turned towards the book;

"This one for instance, is a collection of a distant relative of mine, one I've been searching for, for years with no luck as it's considered a prized antiquity." Kyle smiled;

"Are you telling me I have the pleasure of not only hiring but sharing a wing with a descendant of Lord Byron?" Jess instantly relieved continued forward;

"Yes, it's actually quite an amusing story, he was well known for his wine and orgy filled parties, it was how he became a father to so many bastard children during that era. He just so happened to invite over Mary Shelley, and well to avoid scandal their child was put into an orphanage and her lineage now ends with me. I've always wondered if it's why I'm a writer, if such things as these can really in fact be, *in the blood*, as they say."

She saw his eyes fill with wonder and amusement, he reached out towards her face gently caressing her left cheek, smiling longingly and deeply into her emerald filled ocean eyes.

"You continue to fascinate me, in the most surprising ways Jess, if you'd like too you're more than welcome to come in here and read this anytime." His hand fell to his side;

"Now if you don't mind beautiful, this is the time I find to write; you're more than welcome to stay and read if you'd like but I must remind you that silence is golden."

Kyle pulled out a chair and sat at the desk that had his laptop and current story waiting for him just as he left it the morning before, the words poured out of him effortlessly, as Jess cracked open the ancient book and delved into a world of wonder, from a mysterious branch in her own family tree. Hours went by and the pages turned slowly, gently as she read. Her eyes growing heavier as she felt herself trying not to fall asleep. She wanted to be near him, she could always feel his powerful magnetism even in this calm, flowing creative state. The sound of his hands pounding away at the keyboard swiftly turned into a passionate cadence. She felt herself swooning, the book resting in her lap she started to sleep, her head resting on the chair, her thigh propped up on the arm and her hands slowly finding their way to her breasts. She moaned softly, causing the rapid keystrokes to suddenly stop. Kyle smiled, his cock rock hard he felt her dreaming about him again.

"Your filthy little mind really fuels the creative fires, my pet." Laughing under his breath he felt her aroused energy flicking at his aura, inviting him to toy with her as he had been all night long.

He turned around and saw her hands roaming, teasing her nipples under her shirt, hardening them with each tormenting flick of the finger. She bit her bottom lip, moaning, her eyes contorting as her other hand found itself resting just inside her panties. Touching her soft wet folds, he was in paradise, his chair now facing her he watched her undulate. Her toes curling beneath her socks, her hand reaching towards her neck, the book now falling from her lap and towards the floor. Kyle reached out catching it to prevent her from waking up from this private show entirely debuted for his pleasure. Gripping her throat firmly she smiled and bit down on her lip once more before her lips parted and sweet ecstasy escaped them with one single word that made his heart rush.

As the blood pounded towards his cock and his eyes glowed, she whispered;

"Kyle."

Her body buckled and hips thrust and bucked uncontrollably, pulsing and pounding, she slowly caught her breath and smiled falling into a deep slumber. The sun began to rise and the coming light illuminated the office, Kyle closed the blinds dimming the provoking sun into serene golden bands that shimmered along the ceiling, realizing the house would soon be alive. The children would be up and the staff was already awake, he knew it was time to take her where she belonged. How he wished tonight that it would be his room but for now she required sleep in her own chambers, she would need plenty of rest today, such a curious pussy, how close she came to being just a strange smell in the cellar. I suppose what they say is true, fortune really does favor the bold.

Chapter 6:
MYSTERIOUS AWAKENING

JESS awoke to the sounds of children laughing, the sun peered into her window, she could tell by the angles of light streaking into the room that it was much later than she expected it to be. As she opened her eyes, her heart pounded;

"Oh god where am I?!"

She remembered falling asleep hearing the sounds of Kyle's fingers typing away on keyboards. It was still dark while she was reading through her ancestry in one of his most treasured possessions, so how did she find herself in bed now hours later? She heard a knock on the door. Kyle had seen her wake up just a few moments earlier from the inner chambers of the home, watching her eyes crack open staring at her glowing skin as it was kissed by the sunshine of early afternoon. He couldn't take his eyes off of her, especially now that he'd grown so close to her so quickly it seemed. For the most part it was easy to allude to such feelings for the sake of those who pined for him but Jess was unlike anyone he'd ever met before. She felt surreal, like a dream he always hoped existed in this world, but one much too good to be true, it had to be a trick of the light, there must be something about her, anything that would turn his affections towards his innate thirst for power, carnal hunger and control.

"Come in" her voice trailed like a song bird to the door. Kyle instantly found himself smiling before he even saw her face, well at least in person. He'd been watching her sleep for hours as he continued his work downstairs, in the silent subdued dungeons of the home, filled with screams that were only heard by the lord of Burnett Manor. Jess turned her head and watched this towering man approach her with the greatest of ease, so silent each step he took appeared effortless yet for a man of his stature it took a lot of skill to move so gracefully, with such stealth and ease. He was wearing a soft oatmeal colored sweater this morning, the texture alone made her want to open her sheets and crack a carnal smile before inviting him into bed for morning caresses. He was in jeans again with house shoes this time instead of those intimidating boots of his. Those boots she could feel on her head pressing into her skull while his voice boomed against the dark walls of brick rooms. It was profound the mere glimpses that flowed into her mind freely from his that revealed his true nature. She wondered if this ease of mind melding was due to the fact that he was comforted by her presence or aroused by it. Quite possibly both, it was impossible to tell with this remarkable man.

"I hope you slept well." Kyle said smiling,

"You definitely don't require beauty sleep, so rare to see such a beautiful woman fresh from the world of dreams." She blushed replying;

"Well I haven't quite made it out of bed *just* yet, how *did* I manage to get here Sir?"

"Well if I told you that, I'd have to kill you." He said as his dark eyes glowed and his grin turned mysteriously sinister. As Jess bit her lip waiting for more he continued with a taunting smile,

"You managed to fall asleep in my office as I worked until late this morning. For fear of leaving you to wake up alone, I thought it was best to carry you back to your chambers to slumber more peacefully."

"Wow" Jess smiled.

"I'm usually much more alert when it comes to being carried, or even noise in general. It just doesn't happen usually, I can't believe I didn't wake up, the flight and getting settled in must've exhausted me."

"Among other things." Kyle replied. Jess's mouth opened in awe, she didn't expect such boldness, and she thought he'd do his best to play the part of the coy, unknowing boss, perhaps she was getting to him?

Jess smiled blushing, as she started to laugh a bit and respond he instantly intercepted her thought already hearing it in her mind,

"When you're ready the children are downstairs waiting to meet you. I've asked them to play outside today instead of in their dayroom next door to your office. I didn't want them to wake you, I realize you needed the sleep after such a rigorous night." Kyle smiled his eyes twinkling and his right eyebrow lifting just so to inform her that he watched every nuance and detail of her long into the twilight hours before they were sharing his office together in such sensual ways.

"*Yes,* rigorous." Jess's eyes turned feline she matched his sensuality and watched him smile.

"I'm actually quite pleased you slept in this morning, it means we'll get to have breakfast together. The children usually eat much earlier than I prefer too, it'll be nice catching up before I'm locked away for the day in my office with my colleagues, there's a lot of chaos that goes into adapting your personal written work into a screenplay and film production company. But we'll discuss that some other time, I'm sure." Kyle started to leave.

"It's nearly Noon, would you like to meet me in the formal dining room at 1pm for breakfast? Or Brunch?" He smiled waiting patiently for her reply.

"It would be my sincerest pleasure, Sir." Jess leaned up in bed, her nipples hard, teasing his eyes he could see her long legs curling up, she rested on her blanket covered knees and smiled sincerely, counting the moments of eye contact between them as he started to leave.

"*1..2…3*" she counted in her mind, continuing her thoughts, "*I wonder just how long he plans to take.*"

"Good. I look forward to it Jess, prepare yourself for questions, my children are more curious about you than *even I* am."

Kyle left with that wicked grin that made her want to rip her clothes off and beg him to stay, to forego feasting on breakfast but to feast on her instead. The door closed, the golden doorknob locking into place, the clicking made her shudder. It was time to get ready and fast, an hour wasn't that long to get ready, at least this was just for brunch, not her ominous fate that awaited her in the world of Darkeel.

Jess instantly rushed to the shower tossing aside her sheets and running to the closet tearing at her clothes as quickly as possible. As she peeled her clothes off socks first, then chemise watching from his mind's eye Kyle could see every inch of her soft skin, white as snow, reminding him of the cold harsh winters of his youth where large families placated to little resources leaving him to survive in hellish ways; in ways that still haunted him to this very day.

He remembered the first time he saw a body like hers in youth, it was fresh after a blizzard and again Kyle and his siblings were sent into the darkness and pits of blustery hell itself to fetch more firewood to stay warm through the night. It was a dark March evening, he was alone with one torch telling his younger brothers to stay behind, knowing they'd never make it back in this wind chill. He marched towards the horizon near a patch of fallen dead trees that still harbored enough wood for winter, hopefully. He walked towards his usual spot, his eyelashes now icicles, his hands numb he saw it the palest snow after the storm hit late the night before, trickled drops of blood leading towards a trail. He wondered what wild animal had been hunted down and if it was still close by, or worse, *still eating*. He didn't carry a rifle like most, he preferred just what was needed for the task at hand, *an axe.*

His hand was ready, gripped hard on the axe even though he could barely feel it, he started marching towards the blood, as the puddles pooled towards a beautiful naked woman, lying there. Completely frozen with long locks of scarlet soaked in blood. Her face serenely sleeping, a wry smile on her face displayed on the corpses left Kyle for the first time with a serene feeling inside. Deep inside he felt that darkness of tormented youth sparked into existence, the thick energy permeated as his eyes continued to examine her body. He couldn't take his eyes off of her, the curve of her back, the way her torso flowed into her thick luscious hips. Never before had he laid eyes upon a naked woman before, he felt aroused and captivated by this clandestine moment frozen in time. Her thick legs were iced over and her knees and feet disappeared into the snowbank. Kyle started chopping, the woods were echoing with the sound of wood being torn apart. There wasn't much time before the next flurry of this storm came through he needed to get back with a piece large enough to burn through the night, but his eyes were transfixed on the porcelain back that was slowly disappearing under the snow. As the wind continued to scream, howl and swirl by slowly hiding what really happened here, between Kyle and this corpse who had opened Pandora's Box, and the one who left her there for him to discover in the first place.

Kyle was downstairs by now waiting for her, hoping to wash away the memories of both his tortured youth as well as the origins of his only way out. He never truly enjoyed killing, at least not those who didn't deserve it. But sometimes beautiful things are created from horrific nightmares, and all that is left is cleaning up the mess and picking up the pieces and trying to move forward.

Knowing that Darkeel was waiting again, *hungry*, fueling the fires and waiting to take his next victim. He was just too young to know just what was lurking in the forest that hellish night in March, one he always hoped he'd have long ago forgotten.

He soothingly took a breath watching his children playing in the yard, smiling, laughing and creating games that made him laugh and smile. *They were his light*, they illuminated his world and reminded him that life was truly worth enjoying; not just destroying. Even if the past crept in as often as it could to tear apart the world he worked so desperately to create for their sake as well as his. He knew it was the only way to ensure the tyrant within wouldn't burn the empire down and tear this world apart.

Suddenly he heard her voice within his head, her voice carrying clear as a bell, instantly taming his wandering mind, singing. Her sultry voice rich and melodic made him sigh in content. He felt her soothing energy washing over him like the hot shower she was in this very moment. He smiled wondering how much longer she'd be, she still had half an hour.

"I should've said 12:30, just to see her squirm." Kyle chuckled to himself feeling his cock twitch in his jeans, amused by his sadistic ways;

"Very soon dear Jess, you will be Mine."

Her hair was still perfect from the night before, between the silk sheets and the gentle, delicate way he positioned her into bed to sleep. She jumped out of the shower unclipping and tousling her hair onto her wet shoulders, she wandered to the window noticing the children playing outside below her.

"Oh God, I hope they can't see me." She tucked her towel under her arms tighter before trying to open the window. She cracked it and watched the steam escape.

"Ooo, she's up!" yelled the voice of a young girl,

"I wonder when we get to meet her?" another voice replied,

"I'm sure it won't be much longer, now let's go find him, he's hiding here somewhere." They continued wandering into the vines around the house calling out and searching for the dog.

Jess mindfully realized the time and knew she had only fifteen minutes to meet him in the dining room to make a lasting impression. She quickly applied her makeup, her eyelashes painted, lips and fresh glow she was ready for clothes now if only she could control her over aroused limbs, this delicate dance of sensuality and time would go over just swimmingly. She wandered into the closet reaching for her wedge peach shoes, putting on her skintight jeans before growing four inches, she always loved a man tall enough to wear heels with. She then reached for an emerald tank top, and the softest of her sweaters. Coffee colored angora, she set it on the bedside before positioning her day corseted breasts, and like a swollen soft melon patch they were ripe for the taking. Wrapping the soft fabric around her arms she felt the biting chill in the air.

"Brrr, I should've known better than to leave that bathroom window cracked, I'm definitely not in California anymore." She trotted in and couldn't help but notice how cold it was already. Looking down her red painted toes flirted well in these shoes;

"Alright ladies it's time to shine." She grabbed her book off the nightstand shut the door silently behind her, she loved being stealth it let her catch him off guard, he couldn't be so mysterious if she had the upper hand.

She walked downstairs, every so often a floorboard panel creaked and she smiled matching his in the dining room, he looked down at his watch. She had five minutes to spare and easily would make it at the requested time. Very impressive, as most took these informal meals as a sign of relaxed disposition, something Kyle detested and what usually provoked his former staff to vanish without a trace so much swifter than if they'd have minded or discovered formal etiquette.

He saw a glimpse of her, just her ass, in a pair of sinfully tight jeans.

"Dear god woman what are you trying to do to me, I'm glad I'm shackled to my desk after this, I need to decompress." Her heels made for a blunt, firm sound. She wandered into the doorway smiling shyly.

"Good Afternoon Sir." She smiled warmly holding in her hands a book, she was doing her best to hide the title or cover from his eyes. She approached him and without stopping himself like usual he asked,

"Is there any color you don't look beautiful in?" Kyle smiled and stood to pull out her chair.

"A man who realizes that formalities are exceedingly impressive." She blushed realizing she was more forward than usual.

"Forgive me Kyle, I don't mean to be so feisty, it must be this pure Colorado air, I haven't slept this well *in years* it seems."

"You never need to ask for forgiveness Jess, you're... *charming* to say the least. I better leave that for now." He laughed and Jess joined in unable to say anything knowing full well she'd be far too sassy and just opened the flood gate once more.

"How did you sleep this morning Sir?" Her elbow just off the table, she leaned on her right hand swooning, waiting for his reply.

"Not for long, but deeply. Thank you for asking, you're so unlike anybody I've ever met before Jess." Smiling with curiosity,

"What do you mean?" He took a deep breath and inhaled a peaceful state inside,

"With most people nurturing the world isn't a focus, children, animals, things in this world that are small, vulnerable and helpless without aid, but you, your healing energy is something I haven't stopped feeling since your plane landed. I find myself so serene in your presence, and the way you tend to my needs as well as my staff's and best friends already, yes I do know everything that goes on here as I'm sure you imagine." They both smiled and laughed.

"You're a captivating woman Jess, with a soul that glows like your beautiful skin." She smiled.

"Thank you Kyle, that means more to me than you'll ever know." Reaching for his hand she placed it over his, looking into his eyes.

"See I promised I'd stop flirting with you, but you make it so easy."

She smiled laughing,

"You're one to talk" she couldn't meet his eyes with hers when she blushed in such a way.

"Kyle?" Jess said;

"Could I ask you something and hopefully I won't find myself completely embarrassed." His eyebrows furrowed with curiosity, his pulse quickening for just a moment,

"Yes, of course, what is it?" Jess turned over the book she was hiding before and handing it to him;

"Could you sign it for me?" biting her lip he blushed;

"Wow I can't believe I'm the one who's too embarrassed to look into your eyes right now, I'd honestly love too, it's an honor to have another fan working for me, you and James that is. Plus I find fans seem to want to go to exceedingly creative heights to please me, I find it more than satisfying to say the least."

She handed him her pen smiling; Kyle penned a carnal inscription into the first edition of his very creation, smiling wickedly imagining her curious mind decoding it later all alone in her room.

"I never in my wildest dreams could've imagined that just last week I'd be working for one of my biggest inspirations as a writer." He noticed how old this copy was, he looked inside for the special mark that only he identified on first edition copies.

"How long have you had this? I didn't know any of my first editions existed anymore. What lengths did you go to, to get this?"

He was incredibly touched, he knew these were impossible to get there were only a crate left in the world the rest were destroyed in a warehouse fire, one he had set for the very reason of never wanting this particular issue released. It was the unabridged copy the one that shared far too much about his world, and she already had access to it.

"Well let's just say, if I told you that, I'd have to kill you." She smiled as his dark eyes penetrated hers, she felt that part of him pouring out, Jess could feel it trying to choke her, strangle the life from her, wanting her dead for making such idle threats. Kyle started laughing realizing that letting this energy silently out for too long would transform this brunch into a nightmare for her. Jess smiled, "I couldn't resist, with writers being so ready to kill." She winked and brunch arrived distracting them both from the tension ready to cut with a knife.

The kitchen staff arrived to dress the table with silverware, china and the usual glasses one would find in flute form for orange juice or mimosas. It gave them both just enough time to depart from penetrating gaze, before Jess knowing all too well that he was a bit riled up underneath the surface of calm, cool and collected. She lovingly caressed her book and opened the page, a strategically well written note in reverse was left with his signature. She smiled knowing she'd have time to decode it later as the staff instantly arrived with plates of galore, to peruse. For the next hour at least she found her eyes wandering to the window, watching the children play, laughing and screaming when their brother ran forth to capture them after hiding most undetected in the tall grass of mid-spring.

She relished viewing his world, his glorious creations right in front of her eyes, she knew they held such power within him. The true restraint of his darkness, at least in the public eye. They were his light, his paradise away from the visceral hunger that panged deep inside of him. In the very hellish pits of his insides, bubbling and hissing, and trying to remain calm to prevent explosion and sudden black that transmuted to red, the core of the energy inside that possessed him ever since he saw that woman naked, lying in the snow that cold winter day.

"Thank you Kyle, this is truly what I needed more than anything this morning, you've made one of your many fans more than elated. I look forward to reading the inscription tonight when I continue reading through this book for the thousandth time, but first I long to know so much more about you, and I can't wait to meet your children."

Jess said as she smiled, his sparkling blue eyes matching hers in this light, his smile curling slightly. He then watched her hands subconsciously reach for her womb, he'd recognized that same look of despair in his wife's face many, many years ago.

I wonder if this is where she came into darkness and watched the light escape. Kyle's mind bookmarked this for later.

"What would you like to know Jess, as I've mentioned before; I'm an open book." Kyle placed the cloth napkin on his lap, and watched Jess's hands match his in the same formal ritual before dining.

"Where did you come from? The origin stories I find are most fascinating and reveal the core of any beings primary focus in life whether they realize it or not, is all together another conversation."

Jess started deliciously indulging in her meal, savoring every sweet bite of fresh fruit, her supple lips excruciating torture for Kyle's cock, never could he imagine that she could eat so sensually, as if it was her final meal and yet the one she demanded was given to her each and every day as if she conquered empires to capture what she wanted in life. Never had he seen a woman eat with such passion, this just alluded to so many more of her talents that Kyle knew he had yet to see, well at least fully in person. It was just enough of a distraction to prevent him from flashing back to so many tormenting memories of a harsh, cruel and abusive childhood, an origin story no man should ever have to share, tell or desire too, if anything this world was his way of leaving all of that hell behind.

"As much as it would please me to invite you into such intimate details of my early life, I've found that often times the information shared is so heartbreaking to others and this morning it would darken this all too perfect meal shared; that I feel I'm already captivated by in your presence. For fear of ruining such a peaceful mood for the day for us both, do you mind if we save that discussion for another time?"

Jess was moved by the way Kyle so openly shared himself with her, she was powerfully drawn in, she could feel that his mind was doing this, opening her up to a preconceived trap, but she just couldn't defy curiosity anymore. She felt herself giving up inside, and wanting to relinquish all power and control to this incredible man, who has seen far too much for too long, and yet still somehow managed to retain the best parts of humanity inside of him in spite of it all.

Once more Jess found ways to incorporate subtle intimacy into what others would read as humanist and typical reactions. She visualized the subduing, soothing energy of the threefold twilight flame of love and adoration, knowing it would soothe whatever being that was attached to him all these years, to sleep and embrace her as his own. Reaching for his arm she adoringly embraced it with her hand, "Kyle it will be an honor to know that part of you someday, I value the time we have together until I've *earned* that place within your world. I understand all too well, and look forward to sharing with you my tale in exchange, of course being when the time is right."

He reached for her hand and comforted her with it, placing it gently on top of hers:

"Thank you Jess, I knew you'd understand." Kyle smiled matching her gaze of awe, in awe of his children, playing happily outside without a care in the world to show these two beings what it felt like to truly bathe in the light for a moment leaving behind all the darkness that brought them to this very moment in their star crossed exchange of darkness and ascension.

Chapter 7:
HAUNTING NOSTALGIA

BRUNCH turned into early afternoon, she didn't realize how much time had gone by. She saw the sun starting to set over the rolling hills of wild grass and flowers kissed in colors of gold, white, blue and green. It was nearly four o'clock, the food was long since eaten, glasses empty but the only thing that could be heard in this room from the servants down the hall was voices exchanging endless ideas. Laughter that echoed from the usually silent chambers of the lord of Burnett Manor's formal dining hall, covered in dust, without the usual events and enjoyment that his wife used to fill these halls with just a few years ago.

Precarious faces peered out from rooms in the fashion of both kitchen, cleaning and legal staff. Whispers were exchanged and eyes of wonder peering into the hallway that echoed the sounds of laughter from a powerful man who never made such noises before, not even when this house was filled with the sound of children and his wife. Even his dearest friend James who he'd known since childhood, an adoring fan of everything that Kyle conceived into notion; couldn't remember the last time, if ever that he heard his boss amused by anything quite like this before. He thought back hard discussing with a maid or two wondering if he'd ever invited any other women that worked for him into such a formal setting;

"None so far that I've ever known of," the words were the same from each and every member of the staff. Not a single one had ever shared such time and space with Kyle before, what was it about her that he found so inconceivably fascinating?

James already knew full well that she was unlike anybody he'd ever met before, knowing Kyle had a penchant for rare collections, he wondered if she would be his latest addition in the living breathing museum of unique creatures, resting just below this very floor. While the rest of those who dwelled here for work or for permanency found themselves completely oblivious in the routine life and daily errands that continued on from day to day with very little change. Each friend, colleague and staff member knew that he was more than strict with enforcing precisely what he wanted. They were used to his expectations for such rituals to be carried out in an effortless manner. His methods for gently scorning a person to cause them to transform any flaw into a shining representation of what he desired them to project to the outside world; as a true representation of what he'd always hoped to be was everything he lived for in the mundane aspects of his life, keeping his blades ever sharp and honed for the kill. Kyle knew in this moment that he was not alone on this dark path of hunger and panged carnality. The ink black existence of the abyss was calling. He needed to kill again, he wasn't ready for his latest employee to be prey, *not just yet.*

The children burst into the formal dining room, laughter, screams and giggles filled the room, Jess instantly changed her intimate demeanor with their father into a more stately form of professionalism. By their eyes she was the one tending to their nurturing and ease in life, in such a crucial time, the last thing she needed to do was to cause a wedge to grow between her and the children. They're the only ones truly keeping her stay here secure, so that she could further investigate the hollowed grounds of the freshly dug earth, to find what Kyle was hiding here. Buried beneath the crawl spaces, tombstones and layers of concrete that formed the house above this endless scene of horror and chaos, scattered to the winds in so many memories buried alive, still screaming, waiting for validation as to the endless purgatory waiting for them now infinitum, stuck between two worlds, and frightened never knowing if this pain would ever come to an end.

"Dad we can't wait any longer, you promised we'd meet her at two o' clock, it's almost four now!" Adie a rambunctiously dressed girl of eight wandered over and introduced herself, colorfully dressed with glasses and a smile she waved in a most relaxed disposition;

"Hi, I'm Adie, what's your name?" she asked most curiously as her older sister Tiffany a young woman of seventeen watched smiling and laughing, at Adie's curiosity and confidence.

"My name's Jessica, but I've always been keen towards Jess personally, I'll answer to either though." Smiling at Adie she continued,

"I love your outfit, so bold and colorful, it's quite perfect for spring." Adie smiled,

"Thank you" looking at her sister "See I told you I have style."

She wandered out of the room, still looking for her brother who'd now wandered off down the hall making animal noises, "It was nice to meet you!" Adie yelled as she ran out of the room.

"Hello, as I'm sure you know by now, I'm Tiffany, the eldest daughter." Tiffany said smiling, she was so demure yet free in spirit, and the devotion towards her family was obvious she could do nothing more than radiate her pride in being a part of such a world. It made Kyle glow, he was always grateful for her, her very entrance into this world was the first time he ever knew what the light was, his formal introduction to balance, easing the dark tension in his mind, she was always there to remind him that he was capable of self-control, even if it was excruciating at times to maintain.

"Your father tells me you have plans to travel before relocating in the fall for college, might I inquire as to where you plan to go? There are very few things in this world that I am more passionate about than traveling."

Instantly her smile turned upwards, she ran towards the other side of the table, instantly a plate was brought in from staff and she started to discuss her plans of traveling all over the country with her dearest friend from childhood and documenting the entire experience together and turning it into a short film. She was the creative apple of her father's eye, she really resonated well with him cerebrally matching his desires for filmography in ways that challenged even the notorious world renowned author to continue to reach for the stars. He wasn't quite ready to retire and watch his daughter subdue him with talent, not just yet. He'd rather wait until after she graduated to accept that like Sophia, she too would surpass him in ingenuity leaving him a proud but also challenged father. The epitome of Francis Ford Coppola.

She watched from the corner of her psychic eye seeing Adie sneaking up behind her preparing to interrupt this conversation of adventures and travel with hopefully a frightening shock to her newest caregiver and governess.

"Not so fast" Jess stopped and turned dead in her tracks towards Adie,
"I've caught you!" she instantly ran after her chasing her down the hallway, both Tiffany and Kyle laughed in unison never once for a moment expecting Jess to harness her inner child so effortlessly from such a cultured conversation.

The sounds of screams and laughter were heard as she tackled her to the floor in the living room laughing as Adie did her best to tickle Jess back.

"Oh god! You do not play fair, I'll remember this you wicked girl!"

They both continued to laugh and tickle one another until finally at long last a boy leaped over the couch screaming and roaring like a lion tackling Jess and Adie both. His name was Derek, a young boy of thirteen, his smile and blue eyes sparkled the very look of his father in his former youth. Jess finally at long last felt at home, in ways she never quite knew were possible until now, she realized that these beautiful children were now an added layer in complication.

"First you make me fall for you, then you let my heart glow after falling in love with your perfect children." Jess sighed contently, in a pile of laughing children, Kyle wandering down the hallway hoping not to interrupt. He smiled watching her play with his children in ways he'd long since forgotten how too, awakening a part of his mind and soul that he'd never been connected too before. Smiling wide his eyes glowing, leaning against the wall arms crossed in satisfaction.

"So I see you've met my son." Kyle's voice smoothly flowed towards her ears, as she smiled matching his she watched Tiffany leaning into her father's ear whispering, "Now I can leave for summer, knowing you're well taken care of. She's perfect Dad, truly I like her, *a lot."*

His eyes opened wide he wrapped his arms around his daughter hugging her close;

"Good, I like her too, and you've never said that before, about anybody I've ever hired previously." She smiled nodding in agreement, responding;

"I know, because none of them were her." Tiffany smiled at her father glowing.

"Alright children, show Jess the day room and if you'd like, your personal rooms as well. I'm sure she'll be checking in on you all from here on out in various places, make sure she's welcomed, settled in and informed about where everything is in each room please. I hate to run, but you know my schedule is insane now for the next few months until this movie is finished. I promise I'll take a break for dinner though, you have my word. See you at seven o' clock, this time in the living room I'll need to unwind after a long day of legal rhetoric and obstacles that need to be overcome. Jess this includes you I hope you understand that you are family now, regardless of employment I'd prefer you to join us as much as you desire too, that is, for intimate festivities. I do realize this might complicate things with the rest of the staff, but James is already discussing some new regimens I've had planned for years to implement; But until your arrival, it just wasn't realistic until now."

"Yes Sir, thank you for the ample details and I *sincerely* look forward to seeing you for dinner with the children later tonight, there's still so much for us to talk about, it'll take years."

She blushed smiling at him, watching his heart beat quickly pumping blood through his neck at an accelerated pace. His smile curled in a devious satisfaction he nodded in agreement and turned to walk upstairs watching this beautiful woman first captivating his thoughts, and now his heart, she was far too dangerous to keep so close, but he couldn't help himself, nobody had ever had such a powerful effect on him before, and his children? Absolutely never before. They all wanted to be near her, to know more about her. Her silk skin glowed radiant white in the sparkling light of the sun streaming in from the ceiling windows that illuminated the hallways on the upper floor each day as sunset approached.

Adie and Derek grabbed Jessica's hands and lead her upstairs to the dayroom, Tiffany followed shortly behind, hugging her father once more;

"Have a great day dad, I'm leaving soon, still need a few items before we take off for our trip, but I'll be here for dinner before my flight leaves, there will be plenty of time for goodbye's." She wandered off upstairs;

"Hey wait for me!" she yelled at her siblings who'd already opened the door and revealed to Jess just how treasured these children truly were, in a dayroom fit for royalty.

"Let's wait for your sister please, we don't have much time left with her over the coming weeks while she's traveling, best to make the most of it."

Kyle heard her words echo down the stairs as he entered his office a room filled with executives, waiting for him patiently;

"Gentlemen, apologies for the wait, it's been a busy weekend, a very, *very* busy weekend." The door shut as the trail of laughter started, men wondering just what wicked perversions he was up too, all never knowing the full stories, only the sexiest and noblest parts. The parts that painted him like the God he was in the public eye, even though Jess knew deep down a beast hibernating in wild disposition. Waiting for his next trap to catch the prey he longed to hunt down in the dead of night. Staking, waiting, just beneath the surface, to get out.

"Wow this room has literally everything." The mahogany door opened to a wall of Muntin windows, providing the feeling of freedom but also trapped within a world that soothed one to serenity. Lavished in the finest comforts, couches, and special chairs around the room centered in front of a home theater. The most impressive part was the red velvet curtain tinged with gold that parted with a remote control that Derek now held in his hands;

"That's just the start, Tiffany show her the library and loft I bet she never imagined just how much of a kid dad really is inside."

He smiled his eyes twinkling just like his fathers a certain darkness resonated within him that resembled his as well. A layered covert way of speaking, informing Jess that he was watching, aware of the fact that she was already enthralled with him. Leading her to more of his interests, watching and waiting to see what her reactions would be, and if they were not to his liking his father would promptly hear about it.

"Oh yes, this is by far my favorite place to relax besides my own room throughout the day, come here I'll show you."

They wandered up the narrow staircase and above was a loft the center rising towards the ceiling with a giant day bed. Adie had already found herself quite comfortable in, on either side of this day bed the narrow staircase lead to two built in mahogany shelves that stretched from floor to ceiling; requiring one to travel up three spirals of stairs to find the specific book she was looking to share,

"Here, I find this seems to hold special importance to those who desire to know more of where our family's history came from. The roots of who we are to every branch of the family tree are contained within this book." Jess took the copy entitled, *Burnett Genealogical Society*, opened to reveal a painted portrait of himself;

"Your father is rather dashing in this photo, who painted this for him?"

Tiffany looked down to her brother who smiled knowing full well they were waiting for such information to be revealed. A wonderful report that their father unbeknownst to them would be quite pleased to hear, as his thoughts were consumed with this enchanting woman. He hoped that soon she'd reveal that her mind was swimming like an endless ocean in the calm of a hurricane absorbed utterly in his world, with him completely in mind. It always pleased him to know that his prey was pondering of, swooning for and succumbing to his plans regardless of having to alter various back up plans for such a brilliant creature; he usually didn't have to rely on having his children to keep an eye on their new governess. But this time he was far too busy with work, pursuing dreams and transforming them into reality to keep his eyes on her in his private chambers deep within the center and heart of this illustrious home.

"So you find my father dashing, do you?" Tiffany caught Jess off guard she was too busy fantasizing about him in old world garb wondering what it would be like to make love to a King in his private bedchambers.

"Well to be honest any woman would be blind to consider your father anything but dashing, however this particular image conveys a regal energy that I have felt from him before we even met."

Tiffany impressed with such honesty waited for her to continue;

"You see my dear girl, I have a bit of a gift. One that usually haunts most with fear of reading minds, or knowing people far too well for how little time we've actually spent with one another. I like yourself come from a very long line of powerful, eccentric and especially skilled individuals, but they were in the healing and magical arts, I am one of the most powerful psychics in this part of the world left in my bloodline. It's what brought me here in the first place, I dreamt of this home long before I ever stepped foot into it and have since continued to question why I am even here, *truly here* in the first place." Jess continued;

"The universe has a profound way of dropping us off in places while we're on our way somewhere else, never realizing until much later that we're exactly where we're supposed to be. Where we were always meant to be but never knew quite where it was, it felt like a beautiful dream, too good to wake up from but one we tried to fall back asleep to venture into once more."

Tiffany smiled listening to such wisdom being shared;

"I'm sure this all sounds like nonsense but you'll see as we spend more time together just how heightened my powers are when I feel at ease around those I've grown fond of so quickly already." Smiling Jess saw her eyes sparkle and her mouth form a grin she looked up as Adie spoke;

"If you're Psychic, tell me what my favorite color is." She started hanging out of the day bed smiling most precociously, a child who had endured far more pain than her colorful aura could every convey. She was just lucky to be alive, beyond all else that came along with the unique health problems that she was born with.

"You a favorite color? Try *all* the colors." Jess smiled as Adie's face glowed and smiled she looked at her brother;

"She's good, can you teach me?" Adie asked curiously;

"I want to know how to read minds" she said excitedly.

"Well it's not quite reading minds for me, that gift isn't my strongest, if anything it's sort of like Pictionary, I *see* so for me specifically it's called the gift of sight, or clairvoyance, *clear sight* for that very reason, whatever image, smell, or feeling one has I can not only feel it myself but identify it sometimes before even they can."

Adie wandered down from the upper loft by golden ladder;

"Wow, that's so cool, so it's like using your imagination but better?" Jess smiled;

"Yes much like that, except the pictures don't come from me, they come from everywhere and everyone else, perhaps you and I can talk to your father about it sometime and we'll discuss classes. I do work with children you remind me of an Indigo, a child that's experienced more in their youth than most do in an entire lifetime, usually they endured near death like health issues when they were a child."

Tiffany and Derek looked at one another;

"Wow, now we're impressed, she was on an iron lung for most of her early childhood, she had a rare genetic disorder that came from my father's side of the family it nearly killed her, and well, I better not say this but you'll hear about it sooner or later, I'm sure; It's why we're so grateful you arrived, Dad won't admit it but he's scared he has the same gene and that it'll catch up with him later in life before he can manifest his dreams entirely." The eldest daughter of Burnett Manor confessed while Derek chimed in;

"Yea, it's why he works so hard, he's still running from the fate that Adie already beat in spite of the odds, I think dad just can't forgive himself for even having us in the first place, he feels responsible for it."

"Shh, don't say things like that, it's awful to think about" Tiffany chimed in trying to change the subject to better things;

"I know it's awful, but it's the truth, I just wish dad would forgive himself, it's not like he knew. Nobody could've known, the doctors barely knew, and it's not like Adie died, she's here, healthy and safe now, but we're still sort of trapped here in this room and on this mountain all the time, don't you want to leave?" Derek looked over to his older sister realizing she didn't have to answer, he already knew it;

"You know that's why I'm leaving tomorrow, for the next six weeks, I have to get off this mountain, there's an entire world out there, and I've never seen it before." Tiffany peered outside the windows watching the sunset and the long grass swaying in the winds, the trees on the horizon looked like shadows streaked in orange, yellow and gold.

"I just want to be somewhere that doesn't have a cemetery in the backyard, at least for a few weeks, Dad is such a creep sometimes, I know this place fuels his writing, his films and his creative processes, but I swear if I see another dead person wandering around out there under a full moon from my window I'm going to scream."

Jess descended back to the room wandering around to the cabinets opening them and seeing endless video games, movies and board games,

"Well you have me now, I can easily take care of ghosts, or anything else that's here, that comes slinking out of the bellows of this place." Jess said comforting her, wrapping her arms around her shoulders,

"Now is there anything else you need before you finish packing? I'd be glad to help in any way that I can." Tiffany smiled,

"Thanks Jess, I appreciate the help, but honestly I'm sure one more trip to Denver real quick before my plane leaves at midnight and I'll be set. I better get going though if I'm going to make it back before dinner."

With that she waved goodbye and wandered downstairs to the second floor. She approached the door and was about to knock, hearing her father's voice in serious discussion with his advisors she realized it just wasn't the time to interfere she reached into her pocket and quickly texted to him:

This is the first time in my life that I knew I could leave you all here without me for six weeks without worry. She's everything we've ever wanted and needed Dad, I

hope she sticks around longer than they usually do, not to mention she thinks you're dashing.

Leaving a winking emoji she sauntered to the staff kitchen and asked what was being prepared for dinner tonight grabbing the keys and a quick bite before her favorite chef kicked her out of the kitchen;

"It needs more spices." she said winking as she left;

"The nerve of that girl, I should beat her with a wooden spoon for sampling my cuisine before it's ready to be served."

The rest of the staff laughed and continued working, as the truck vanished into the sunset down the road towards the mile high city. Jess sat down with the children and her signed copy of her first edition book by D. Burnett, his dark tome that he'd hoped burned along with the rest of those unabridged copies. Hearing the sounds of the television beside her as her boss's son perused through channels, hearing Adie singing songs up in the loft while tending to origami she let her eyes focus, realizing before in the kitchen that the inscription was backwards, she was always good at decoding such games, covert communication was a skill of hers that few knew much about the powerful sentence left her motionless, unable to move or even breathe.

"You know where to find me, I've been waiting for your arrival, soon you will be Mine."

Sweet adrenaline coursed through her veins she looked down it was already six o' clock, she wanted to freshen up before it was time to eat. This message implored her to do so, to keep him ravenous, she wanted him hungry and ever ready for the kill.

"Well my darlings, as dinner is only an hour away, I'll ask that you both stay here until I return. Unless that is you have permission to go back to your rooms to prepare for dinner as well."

"I'll be back shortly." Jess waited for debates or inquiries Derek paused the movie he was watching;

"Dad doesn't mind if you're away from us, he just refuses to employ those who ignore us completely, we'll be fine and we'll be here when you're finished dressing up for Dad."

He smiled cheekily waiting for stern response and correction.

"Well I see I'm not the *only* psychic in this family now am I? Perhaps I'll have to keep my mind's eye on you as well."

Jess smiled and wandered off sharing that glow with Adie who waved and continued playing in her world of floating birds and paper butterflies. She exited the room and passed her office to the right, still entirely empty the curtains closed and the boxes she had flown in still packed to halfway up towards the ceiling.

"I know what tomorrow's plans are regardless of my plans for prowling late tonight." She allowed her self-designated chore to trail off, the thought preventing any ears from listening, she realized just how astute Derek was at peering into the abyss. She realized he had a touch of the same powerful gift his father has coursing through his brilliant, beautiful mind. He just hadn't fully harnessed it yet.

As she walked past her office to her right she entered her room and found it exactly as it was this morning when he'd woken her for brunch. Or it appeared that way, little did she know that he had time this morning before she woke to wander into her room again while she was sleeping this time to leave more cameras in devious places to explore her erotic body and passionate moans with much more intimate and vivid details. He wanted *all* of her. Each post on this four post bed was now covered in the tiniest, inconceivable cameras that now watched her as she wandered back into the shower. Never seeing that the small crack from the secret door to the center and heart of this manor home was still peering back at her. Shining still showing her the intricate layers of this mansion and the dark chambers that were locked away in iron chains in the mind of the Lord of Burnett Manor.

"She didn't say I couldn't text dad did she?" Derek smiled knowing full well that he did say he wouldn't leave the room until she returned from her shower and dressing for dinner.

"She's powerful dad, I've never felt another one like us before. She's so interconnected already, in ways no other has ever dared too, but there's something so beautiful about her, she's real. We've never been around a governess we can even stand before, but I like her dad, I really like her a lot. Even with the challenges of having to subdue my gift as you've taught me to do so for protection, she's worth the effort."

Kyle was just a floor below, he hadn't had the chance to read the text from his daughter yet, to find two waiting for him in just an hour. He feared that they'd already rendered their verdict, just another woman that was gushing in awe of his self-derived fortune, what he could offer her in the realms of fame, yet another pile of human garbage that masqueraded as a woman who cared for him and adored his children. He went from abrupt and brutal debates with lawyers about copyright laws and verifying that specific aspects of his film wouldn't be able to be viewed at least in this country due to censorship laws. He was on fire inside, ready to burst, he needed to kill. It had already been weeks too long, these added complications at home caused his time to stretch and his mind to break. He desperately needed to end something, annihilate and utterly destroy what someone else created.

The long table filled with faces in well fitted suits went silent and were utterly frozen in fear waiting for him to flip this entire table over as he'd done so many times before, defying both logic, physics and sheer human strength. Before he could unleash a long list of work to each well paid employees list to pursue into the early morning hours over the weekend; his phone buzzed and he read both texts and the rage instantly turned to calm, soothing smiles, he laughed and said;

"You know what gentlemen, never mind, take a paid week off, get some much needed sleep, then it's back to the grind we have to get things solid before the end of the month to ensure we don't waste money or worse, valuable production time."

Kyle wandered around and gripped the shoulders of each man sitting there,

"I want you each to bring me five solid ideas, no excuses I don't give a fuck how long you've worked for me, or if I just hired you this week, that's the assignment, got it?" The entire room agreed in unison;

"Yes." As they waited for him to finish replying to his son and daughter he said;

"You're all free to go now, see you Monday after next, 9am sharp, bring your ideas or don't show up, I'll be happy to hire somebody else." Briefcases and scurrying feet were heard before shuffling ensued by closing doors. He was once again silent, alone and smiling as he sat serenely in his chair.

"So she thinks I'm dashing," he chuckled to himself aloud, "I'll be sure to reminisce such insights over dinner tonight after the children leave for bed, and travel."

As he responded to his daughter;

"*Thank you for this, I've been more than concerned with filling this position ever since your mother left us. I hope she helps to fill the void, even though nobody can compare to your mother.*" Tiffany replied;

"*She never deserved us dad, she never wanted us, she was lucky if anything to have us.*"

Always hoping the same heartbreak was never bestowed upon her as it was as a core in his life. A mother who was distant, and eventually abandoned her family to find a new one, a shiny new one that she could pretend was perfect, even though she left behind priceless treasures.

"I'll be back soon for dinner, just had to get a few more things before my flight takes off." Tiffany responded quickly waiting for the red light to change green.

"Don't remind me." Kyle responded "It'll be impossible for me to let you go." He candidly shared with his daughter she smiled knowing how fortunate she was to have at least one parent who realized that she was the most incredible daughter any parent would be lucky to have, much less know. Kyle continued responding to Derek,

"My son, I am most pleased with your resourcefulness while I am busy. I do admit it's been most exhausting having to lower my abilities as well just to hide until she gets settled in. But I'm pleased for once we both agree, that having another gifted sentient in the house isn't a bad thing. Where is she now?" Kyle implored;

"She asked us to stay here while she freshened up for dinner, she should be back anytime now."

Kyle jumped to his feet and wandered to the back of the room, pressing his hands on a seemingly innocent side of the wall, his hand filled the entire brick perfectly and the wall slid open. He walked into his inner dwelling office, the one where all of his most private works and creations were documented. The endless novels that would surely provide legal teams without alibies, for all the gruesome crimes the infamous serial killer *Darkeel* or who local media knew him as *The Slaughterhouse Hills Hunter* was entirely responsible for.

The world never knowing that he lived just outside the city of Denver where all the crimes usually took place. Leaving him plenty of privacy to hunt, stalk and capture prey without a single man, woman or child ever knowing that this dashing neighbor of theirs was also the most notorious serial killer that the Rocky Mountains had ever seen in the last century. He sat down at his desk, his wrist jingling his special key. Turning the lock it clicked open, again the closed circuit television was showing his favorite show. His beautiful soon to be concubine, soaking wet, washing up and relishing in the hot water, knowing full well she'd soon be in his presence once more, hoping to leave her sensual marks all over his wild soul.

Chapter 8:

PRESUMPTUOUS ADVANCES

"MMMM after such a long day trying to convince morons without vision to let me play, this is just what I needed to unwind before dinner."

Kyle leaned back in his chair, his cock stirring, yet he just craved to watch, to let that tension build for tonight. A fresh grave was being dug right now outside by James for later this very evening in hallowed ground. A special anniversary of sorts, it was the night his dearly departed wife left this place, and found herself as one of many underneath the earth in the backyard cemetery. The children never knowing that when their mother decided to leave them all behind two years before, to start over again, with one of his best friends, that Kyle just refused to let her go. Instead keeping her there forever, reminding him each and every day that nobody could ever hurt him like this anymore. Realizing that all he had to do was find the perfect opportunity that he had planned for eons to ensure that they got exactly what they deserved. The white snow once more covered in blood, her naked body and long blonde hair stained red reminded him of that body in the forest when he was a child, he felt warm inside, his entire body soothed, he could feel her mind wandering towards him now.

She wandered from her closet wrapped in her silk robe towards the bathroom, picking up her first edition; now signed by one of her favorite authors and curiously let her fingers dance over the seemingly nonsensical letters; before smiling and laughing under her breath;

"Oh, I see what you're up too now, I should've known…"

As she held the book up into the mirror and read the inscription further; she nearly died.

When you, ravishing woman, can no longer take the hunger and feel your thirst tempting you further for a taste of my world…come to me.

Her pussy ached, her sigh desperate and pent up full of carnality she smiled and placed the book on her nightstand before adoringly kissing its cover. She walked towards the bathroom letting the silk robe slide off of her body in an ethereal and effortless way. Entering into the now steam filled pulsing hot shower she whispered aloud under the warm waterfall;

"Oh Kyle, I wish you were in here with me right now. Mmmmmm soon I hope… tonight I'm coming to get you."

Jess smiled and continued to rinse off, slowly turning off the shower and wringing her hair out, Kyle realized after peering into her mind that she already decoded the inscription that he'd penned into her first edition of his very own book of horrors.

"Shit, not tonight, any night but tonight. I need to kill, and I can't protect this fortress alone. Fuck what distraction will I need to leave, to prevent her from searching down below?"

His hard cock twitched and his mind wandered, peering down to his watch he realized it was just twenty five minutes until dinner would be ready. Standing up and exiting the room through the internal staircase that was entirely his own, he wandered up to his room opening it from the back and entering through the wall beside his bed. He instantly jumped into the shower realizing he had so little time to seduce her into staying around this evening, while he went into town to hunt some game. A nice trophy that ran in the wilderness on two legs, that wore lipstick and screamed until the bleeding finally stopped.

Jess tousled her curls letting them cascade down over her shoulders, gently spritzing her hair with a special perfume she'd made from several fragrant oils that she had in her collection. A subtle and intoxicating aroma that hypnotized anybody whose nose fell on such a heavenly scent.

She moisturized her face and applied the softest of glowing makeup, staining her lips with fresh cranberries she wandered into the closet to find her preferred flowing painted silk gown. It reminded her of the women on the stage in vaudeville shows during the 1920's, she always felt like a goddess when she wore this. She found a soft flowing shawl and warm socks to wear, her soft milky breasts ample, rising up and illuminating her brilliant face, she checked the time;

"With fifteen minutes to spare I think I'm for once in the clear."

Jess shook her hair out and watched the curls fluff to a lion's mane, she then wandered back into her closet to find her headdress, a simple jeweled piece that floated over her third eye, making the flow of psychic energy less potent; allowing her to enjoy dinner like a normal human being instead of one interrupted by so many otherworldly realms. The fire opal glowed, she applied a luscious layer of red lipstick and then noticed a streak of light trailing down her breasts, and instantly she turned towards the back right corner of her closet;

"What the hell?" she wandered close peering her eye into the light she saw a stone wall and flickering light, she heard a gasp and then without a word the door clicked shut completely. James had meant to shut it hours before but the draft of this inner chamber was always backfiring, yet another reason why Kyle was usually the only one inside of it, he never trusted anybody else fully to ensure that this inner sanctum was never penetrated.

"Well then, I see I don't have to go as far as I expected to find what I am looking for, or more specifically, who." Jess smiled wickedly;

"Here I thought I'd have to start in the cemetery, or the mausoleum, but there's secret passage ways all throughout this house, just waiting for me to enter, explore and to never return."

She turned off the light making it much easier to notice variations in this masquerade of a closet, she wandered to the bedroom door, taking one final look around to see if anything was out of place, new, different or missing. As she exited Derek was standing outside waiting;

"Have you seen my Dad?" he asked curiously, "He texted me to meet him up here but I haven't seen him." Jess looked around;

"I have a feeling he's probably downstairs in his office, or in his room getting ready for dinner too; where's Adie?" Derek pointed to the dayroom;

"She's still in there, watching TV now though on the couch." As Derek wandered downstairs, Kyle exited his bedroom, this time wearing his flannel pajamas and a long sleeve, skin tight shirt, showing off his ridiculously sexy shoulders, he was still towel drying his short wet hair,

"Well hello there, how are you this afternoon?"

Kyle wandered over to Jess hugging her and gently kissing her on the forehead. Blushing she found herself without words, Kyle instantly laughed;

"I didn't mean to catch you off guard, I'm just so relieved the day is over, my entire staff should be fired but I'd be a fool to go in alone this far into the process. I've given them a paid week off from the office to find inspiration wherever they can to solve these last few hang ups in the production process legally preventing us from shooting next month."

Jess grabbed his hand;

"Come here, sit down next to your daughter and let me take care of that stress. We have a few minutes before dinner is ready, and Derek wandered off downstairs looking for you a few minutes ago." Kyle sat down sighing contently;

"Your brother's right, I do spoil you, I forget I put the most comfortable couch in the entire house in this room just for you." He grabbed Adie and she laughed smiling;

"I love you Dad" she leaned in close watching television, Jess reached down rubbing his tense, broad shoulders;

"There, how's that? Prefer more pressure, or less?"

He melted into her hands, the healing vibrations of her deepest contentment poured down into his body, removing years of hardened pain that transformed his muscles into what felt like bones of iron and stone.

"Ugh, that is just perfect." His eyes rolled back into his head as he rested it on the back of the couch.

"I can't afford to give you a raise just yet, I'm sure the staff would consider it favoritism, especially after the first day, but you've definitely just reminded me for next quarter." Jess smiled;

"You're far too kind, you already pay me more than enough on salary, you're a generous employer it was one of many things that attracted me to this position for what I hope to be a lifetime career, in the first place." She kept massaging, moving her fingers up his neck and down into his back along his shoulders;

"While I continue to pursue both my own creative projects and academic work to hopefully get that degree I'm still presently working towards. To be able to provide what I know only I can for not only your life but for your children as well, is already a raise I kindly accept. An entire elevation and added richness in the overall fulfillment of my life." Jess continued and leaned into the ear that was separate from Adie's peripheral hearing;

"It is an honor to serve You, Darkeel."

Instantly his eyes opened staring into hers directly, the most visceral darkness about to burst forth strangling her in front of even this vessel's very own child. Jess matched his intense stare with a wicked grin and utter devotion, continuing her massage, gently coaxing the dark demon inside back into the waiting game.

Tick tock the hours slowly grinded by, he needed his fix, just a few more hours now and that little bitch is all mine. His mind howled into the dark ether, he could see that waitress he'd been stalking now for months, the one who always flirted with him whenever she saw him pull up in his red Porsche. Never paying a moment's notice to him when we showed up in less than casual attire in his truck. Ignoring him completely, as if he was entirely invisible, he knew she'd look so pretty buried beneath the layers of ice, earth and blood; another relished trophy in the private collection of Darkeel.

He bide his time as the family man until the clock struck midnight, for now he'd have to repress this urge to kill Jess, to instantly snuff the light out from within her, his strong hands entangled around her throat with unrelenting force; he'd already grown so fond of her. Even if she was more than bold, daring and downright suicidal with the way she decided to play this most delicate game of chess, a gruesome game of hunting for the kill, screams, and blood soaked certain death was waiting for another woman who Kyle had eyes for tonight.

Chapter 9:
UNEXPLORED TERRITORY

SHE heard the grandfather clock in the room chime precisely seven times, the tone announcing to them all that dinner was ready down below;

"Ooo, I'm hungry." Adie instantly turned the television off and burst up from the couch like a spring blossom from underneath winter's melting snow. Her colorful tutu's layered matching her vivid ribbons in her hair. She bound down the stairwell not realizing her brother was already waiting there, he remembered what his father said hours earlier about wanting a night in with his family; and a son with such similar nature and tendencies also enjoyed his distance and space away from others and even those closest to him. Derek leapt up from the couch tackling Adie and laughing as her screams were muffled by the pillows;

"No fair, I didn't get a chance to run." Adie said as she sat up fixing her hair. They both laughed and then headed towards the staff kitchen both waiting to see when dinner would be served.

Kyle still seated on the corner of the crimson sofa proceeded to beckon Jess to sit on the wooden ottoman mere inches in front of his penetrating eyes. With a wave of his hand she felt herself compelled to move. It was his will taking over now, she had no control over her thoughts, movements, and even the smallest movements in each limb were utterly his to conduct at will. Excruciating pain was coursing through her body now, she could feel the rage just beneath the surface, she was certain he would end her life here and now, there's plenty of ways to get rid of a body on the grounds of a former slaughter house. Jess pondered uncontrollably as if plucked from reality and set into the surreal ocean of madness, she floated over towards the table, her heart pounding incessantly she sat down feeling their knees touching. For the first time arousal was the farthest feeling from her body, fear the most intimate experience in her mind. His eyes severe, his adrenaline pumping, his peripheral vision saw the blood coursing through her body now, sending color to her breasts and cheeks that were usually pale white.

He had her right where he wanted her, but for the first time, this mere victim *knew Him*. She somehow managed to crack away the fortress of solitude; this brilliant and beautiful woman was able to see the darkness that dwelled within. Deep within knowing all too well the long list of crimes that were now collecting dust in the form of old newspaper clippings in his private room and dark sanctuary deep within the heart of Burnett Manor. Reaching for her chin and drawing her in close, she couldn't refuse his power, she was utterly submissive, for the very sake of her mortal life. She knew she'd more than crossed a line, she got sloppy, and let her emotions, her arrogance get the best of her, something that she never let happen before. She was ready for certain death, there was nothing she could do now but abide by his orders and to grasp the ideal that hope is still worth holding onto, even in this blood curdling moment between life and death.

"Fortunately for you that massage allowed my boiling blood to cool just slightly, or you would've been a strange smell in the cellar tonight. I'm still not quite sure what I should do with you now, I've never had to prepare for this situation before, *never*. Nobody thus far has ever figured out precisely *who I am*."

Kyle's foreboding gaze struck fear into the soul of Jessica deep within the pit of her stomach, she hoped that the vision in her mind's eye of just how she perceived him in all his glory would appease his desire to kill her. To inspire him to wait until the time was right if such a time ever came, this tale shared between two dark kindred spirits was nearly over before it even got started. He could see the desperation in her eyes as her pair of sparkling emerald sapphires transformed into pools. A single tear formed in the corner of her left eye, trailing down towards her cheek, kissing the corner of her downturned pout before soaking into her bottom lip. She smiled and giggled uncontrollably, just slightly forming the phrase to her lips;

"Mmmm, it takes a special hand to balance atropine so distinctly. Perhaps I'll show you sometime how to alchemically make it undetectable, for future victims that is of course."

Knowing full well that her usefulness was her ultimate skill in survival, at least in this monumental moment in their star crossed paths. His eyes narrowed in both irritation and curiosity;

"How could you even detect what was administered to you? I gave you such an insanely small dose, it usually takes months before I, can even notice its affect's on my projects."

His anger subsided, as his interest grew in her decadent codex of words and mind games he found himself compelled. He sat back into the couch with a wave of his hand a small light illuminated in the kitchen down below, alerting staff that they must take longer before serving dinner, Derek's eyes instantly saw this and his head instinctively looked up towards the ceiling thinking to himself;

"*She must've made a mistake, already? Not a good sign.*" he was always watching, forming timelines in his comic book loving mind and trying to decode what of any of it actually means, if anything at all.

He knew his father wasn't keen to keeping people around for long, especially after the way mother vanished all those years before, it was much easier to get rid of people before getting attached, it was his usual pattern. If anything they'd be saying goodbye to her by the weekend if his previous predictions were accurate in any measure. In that moment Jess felt the death grip subside inhaling and exhaling with great appreciation;

"Thank you Sir, if I may offer my sincerest apologies, I truly never meant to impulsively speak in such a way, I...I have just known you in a way for so long it seems, it's been impossible for me not to speak so freely sooner, but there just hasn't been an opportune time."

Scrambling for excuses to suffice and prevent herself from drastically shortening her own life, she hoped it would turn out better than she hoped for;

"And addressing me so intimately, more intimately than any living human being ever has before. Whispering in my ear as I hold my youngest child in my arms for her sake as well as mine, was the most opportune time?!"

Kyle's voice boomed the door shutting behind him with a gust of wind the moment his lips parted to speak,

"No, it was stupid, reckless, the failed impulsive response from the mouth of a fan that's adored you from afar for as long as I can remember, it's why I took this job Sir."

She continued, "I was absolutely compelled to work for you, to serve you and your needs in any conceivable way, I haven't stopped searching for you since I found this book. You've been my life's obsession. I have a degree in criminal anthropology and job offers from local law enforcement to find you and to bring you to justice, to hunt you down the way you hunt your victims down and still I took this job, *this job,* because I wanted to be *near* you."

Jess's large expressive eyes sharing the ultimate truth wrapped in insanity, the only authenticity she ever had to give, yet so many feared. To most the words always sounding far too insane to be remotely true, she waited for his ultimate verdict trying to slow the beads of sweat from traveling towards her breasts, her breath still quick to match her heartbeat, Kyle's face transformed from Darkeel's to his awe struck disposition. He reached for her face softly, tenderly;

"You came this far just to *know me?*"

His other hand reaching towards her face he leaned in and kissed her, he'd never before been so consumed by her, by any woman before. She knew him for his darkness and loved him completely still, putting even her own life at risk to find him. She could and should in her legal position make him the prize of her lifelong career as a psychic detective, but instead when she heard his voice that day on the telephone after answering his request in the paper for a new governess; she let go of every single one of those thoughts and burned all of her files and personal folders filled with scraps of information. Countless tidbits of paper trails and lengthy articles in the Denver Post about *The Slaughterhouse Hills Hunter,* she was the only one in the world besides him now that knew the identity of this calculated man. He was right here before her now, overwhelming her senses and reading her mind as his entire being melded into hers in that moment. In that decadent kiss, feelings of electricity flowing through her body, tingling and surging as if he was plugging her into direct current. The powerful flow of energy resonating within this *one man* was incredible, she felt as if they were floating underwater.

She opened her eyes and found herself straddling his lap, her painted silk dress cascading off of her shoulders along with her flowing red hair. She felt like she was on fire, his arms wrapping around her. Her body bucking uncontrollably under his touch, his hands gripping her upper back, her waist, her hips and cradling her head back as his lips found ways to ravage her neck, chest and luscious breasts;

"There's so much we have to talk about, Oh God how I wondered what it would feel like to have your hands upon me, those brutal hands to so many others, so ravenously passionate all over me, now; Oh God it's more than I can take."

Jess babbled uncontrollably she was overwhelmed feeling his hands grazing her outer thighs, gasping as his rock hard cock grinding against her pubic mound, she was so close to cumming it was surreal. His lips found their way to her stomach calming the overload in erotic energy coursing through his body into hers within the electrified layers of this intoxicating kiss.

"*Shh*, my darling there will be plenty of time for that, but for now, it's time you and I went down to have dinner with the children as we're already half an hour behind…"

Kyle interjected knowing what it meant to strangle such a seductive whore into submission, taking away her only escape from overwhelming fear caused by endless arousal; coursing through her pink parts and making her sticky pieces soaking wet with musk scented honey. Her eyes were so beautiful when they were filled with torture;

"Mmm already giving me a taste of what that pretty face looks like in such visceral torment. Good. No cunt has ever been so foolish in folly to address me so crudely and has yet somehow managed to *survive*."

Kyle's firm voice caused Jess to recoil into a delicate night shade plant, abruptly hit with the scorching summer sun. Her eyes unable to meet his with bashful blushing cheeks. With a wave of his hand the curtain opened once more to reveal Tiffany driving down the road towards the house;

"Ah, just as I expected, my daughter's here for dinner. Join me in the living room." Kyle said directing his sharp eyebrows towards her along with his outstretched hand. Jess reached slowly from the ottoman, up into his penetrating eyes;

"It is my sincerest pleasure to serve you, Kyle." Jess smiled extending her hand formally wiping away fear and self-loathing a trait that was strong within her when disappointing those she admired dearly was a part of the game. Her lips parted and she gasped ever so slightly;

"Good girl, already learning so quickly; you've impressed me thus Far." reaching for her face and guiding her eyes towards his;

"Truly you have inspired me, now try to keep that quaking pussy of yours under control; it's time to be a family." Jess swooned smiling ever so slightly.

"I'm famished, dinner as a family sounds divine."

She felt on cloud nine, descending back down to earth where the children were already waiting on the couch together, with dinner trays pulled up. Tiffany's tray still without her behind it, she came running in;

"I'm not late am I? I did everything I could to get through traffic, major road block some moron ran off the road drunk again." She texted her father as she heard the phone chime exactly as he descended down the stairs;

"Don't worry, we were late too, you're safe for now, dinner will be out in just a moment I'm sure of it."

Kyle winked at his eldest daughter while she made sarcastic faces at him;

"Ha, *very* funny dad, after all these years you think you'd come up with something better than the go-to serial killer bit, you're a writer after all."

She smirked knowing full well that he'd find amusement in her boldness he smiled at Jess;

"I guess it's true what they say, fortune does favor the bold."

He smiled with a sinister grin, while Jess's heart pounded she thought to herself;

"I can't believe they're completely oblivious and he's just so bold."

Her mind started to wander to sensual places, but was swiftly interrupted by his taunting voice in her head;

"I thought I told you to keep that ravenous cunt of yours on a short leash."

Her eyes widened and she smiled instantly responding;

"Oh God how long have you been able to do THAT!?"

Kyle instantly laughed out loud and told his daughter;

"You're a sass mouth."

She laughed with Adie and Derek and they asked him;

"What weird movie are we going to watch *this* time dad?" Adie's voice always the comic relief in any situation.

"Well we can go for a classic, or *what if* we let the newest member of our family pick something for tonight?" Derek instantly replied;

"I prefer that option, I'd rather see what her taste in movies is, that's a major requirement for the job, *especially* in this family." Tiffany added to this idea;

"He has a point dad." she smiled setting her phone on the table and waiting for Adie to chime in,

"Sounds good to me, what do you want to watch Jess?"

Kyle walked over towards the big screen television and pressed the wall where the crown molding formed into an image of the laughing and crying mask usually found in most theaters. The wall started to move forward and wrapped around to form an entertainment center where thousands of movies from every genre showed up, right before her very eyes. She instantly found the section titled *Classic Horror* and smiled; "That was incredible and the rare films you have here, some of which I've been trying to track down for years for my private collection, impeccable." She said aloud knowing Kyle was grateful for the interest and candor;

"Derek you were not kidding, this should be listed in the job description, I feel so underprepared."

Everybody laughed realizing her sarcasm was welcomed, "I have a question, before I hand your father my selection for the evening, have you seen all of these movies?" Tiffany replied,

"Dad has but we've been catching up since we were born, we still haven't watched them all especially that section."

Nodding and reaching out for one of her favorite vintage films from Vincent Price's collection. *House on Haunted Hill* was handed to her superior and he smiled nodding;

"I'm impressed, a rare classic, and one none of the children have watched I assure you. This is perfect." Jess smiled;

"I'm pleased to hear that, it's one of my favorites, Vincent Price is one of the godfathers of horror in that era, a true mad man."

She looked at the children and made strange and exaggerated faces, making Adie and Derek laugh and Tiffany smile, she hadn't remembered a time in her life that she'd ever truly seen her father smile. This is exactly who she needed to arrive, so that she could finally start over in the world, the captain of her own ship, guiding her heart to her wildest dreams wherever they may be. A regular *Alice: Through the Looking Glass.*

Jess was the missing link to so many pieces in a broken chain that sat here rusting for years. Before finally finding just what was missing all along, that feeling of home that so many often describe but just can't sum up in one word. It takes an entire being to fill a place with light after the darkness has overtaken it for so long. She was everything that Kyle wanted, desired or dreamed of, now curled up next to him on the couch while his other children on theirs were enthralled in this film. Enjoying the final dinner they'd be having for quite some time together, this was all he ever worked for in life, he finally had everything he'd ever truly wanted, in a dark unrelenting world a true place to call home.

Each dish that arrived was piping hot and especially made for each individuals ultimate cravings, the children were elated to see their favorites piled up high, while Kyle was most pleased to watch Jess's eyes open in awe again;

"How did you know that manicotti is my favorite?" He smiled;
"I have people, who look into such things for me." She smiled gratefully indulging,
"Ooo this is my favorite part!"

Jess said enthralled, for a moment she lost herself in this sweet existence in life, four pairs of eyes were watching intently and when that moment came where the first victim was about to die, she screamed and threw pillows at the children, causing them to scream even louder when the first character in this film was killed suddenly and brutally. Kyle burst out laughing;

"Ohhh, that was a good one, she scared you guys so bad." Jess laughing with him unable to breathe.
"I couldn't resist, it is the best part about having favorite films that no bodies ever heard of before."
He caught her eyes once more before they were transfixed to the screen and the children's face while the film continued;
"I couldn't agree more."

Kyle gently squeezed her hand, she gently squeezed back before letting go realizing that these children were more observant than most.

Derek and Tiffany's eyes meeting for a moment to confirm to one another that she was in fact staying around longer than a week, they smiled both knowing that it was exactly what the lord of Burnett Manor had longed for, a woman who could make him and his children feel at home.

Chapter 10:
HORROR STORIES

THE children were enthralled and Kyle was impressed with both her selection and the ease at which Jess fit into any situation. She seemed born to darkness much like himself, a by-product of survival, transforming even the most brilliant of lights in this world into dark lanterns tinged with agendas, and unnatural hungers that deviated the strongest will towards a path of unrelenting torment. First through self, then through transformation. He could see that part of her book in full light now more than he ever had before. He realized deep down that not only did Jess truly *need* him, but he needed her. This unnatural match felt more at ease in silence and conversation than with anyone ever before or after he assumed. A deep sentient connection, two gifted beings born from darkness and doing their best to create a moral compass and ethical guideline to adhere too, aiming for that small flickering light at the end of the tunnel that the past still holds in charcoal riddled destruction.

He realized he had to keep her alive, around and as close to him as possible for her sake more than his. The closer he'd find himself to her, in intimate ways he knew that Darkeel would awaken as well. Calling out and demanding empty trophies, disturbing the peace, silence and dawning of a new chapter that he relished even more, right now on this very night.

The final chapter of this gruesome tale was coming to an end. Jess smiled glowing, watching the children leaning forward, even Tiffany at her age with pillows in her arms gripping desperately not to scream. Watching the one behind it all reveal themselves as the mastermind, murderer and genius in this story. Kyle's eyes were watching her, they glowed, he didn't mind missing the ending to even this one of his favorite classic tales of horror. To watch her expression, it was as if he saw what it was like to truly live. He'd never been one who was fond of the early morning light, he usually preferred the darkness cloaking the layers of his personality that he never wanted to get out. It felt safer, to hide, even if it was from himself. But now, Kyle had never wanted so intensely before to know what it was like to bathe in golden sunlight. Gasps and screams were filled with claps and smiles;

"Wow that was really, *really* good. Now I see why Dad won't stop talking about Price and Hitchcock, suspense is an incredible art form in film." Derek said;

"Not to mention the writers." Jess chimed in;

"I've always personally found that era as well as the Gothic period to be so good at making you feel like you'll die on the edge of your seat waiting but not wanting to know what will happen next. The suspense is stifling, almost claustrophobic."

She mimicked being buried alive or strangled and the children started laughing, Kyle instantly saw her transported underground screaming and clawing for the surface, it hit him hard in his mind's eye, like a bus. He didn't know what it meant, was it something that had already happened to her? It did look like a younger but recent version of who she was now, or is this the future? Derek and Jess sensed his change in demeanor almost instantly;

"Are you okay?" they said in unison feeling each other's energetic link and then trying to pass over it to avoid drawing attention from the girls.

"Yes, I'm fine, I've just been working too hard and it's late, I'm sure

I'm just exhausted. Speaking of which it's almost nine thirty; shouldn't you be leaving soon Tiffany?"

She smiled somberly trying to keep the tears from welling from underneath her glasses,

"I didn't want to remind you."

He opened his arms and she walked towards him;

"Ugh! Sometimes I wish I came from a horrible place like you did when you were a child dad, it would make leaving so much easier." He hugged his daughter lovingly;

"*Shh*, it's okay you'll be back before you even feel like you've been gone long enough to miss us, I promise."

Kyle smiled and his daughter smiled back, she reached for her brother and sister and gave them a hug, her arm extending out towards Jess, she got up from her place on the couch and embraced her fully;

"You're going to have an incredible, life changing time, film it for us, we'll be there in spirit."

Jess smiled and gently kissed her on the forehead, realizing she was only a decade older than her and smiling at the distance as well as the closeness in years, half a generation behind her as her father was part of hers but beyond. She realized this place held a powerful space in this world in the realms of time. She kept feeling herself descending deep into the basement of this home, to which she was told there was no longer access too. As the eldest daughter of Burnett manor grabbed her coat, keys, and luggage, her father walked her out and placed all of her belongings in the truck. He got in the passenger side and waved to Jess in the window, she didn't realize he could see her watching.

"He see's everything." Derek replied while texting on his phone,

"I thought you would've realized that by now."

Jess smiled and turned around imagining an iron door covered in snakes, thorny briar patches kissed with wild red roses, her mind was now a fortress, she realized she'd been far too open with her shields ever since the stern altercation upstairs before dinner. Derek drew back in awe and realized that he had no understanding beyond simple energetic instinct to know just how incredibly dangerous she really was. Learning instantly never to cross her in such a way anymore, she demanded respect in her own natural inclination, a crucial warning for anybody that would come between her privacy and longevity in this mysterious and haunting place.

"I'm glad we have an understanding, I detected your abilities before even knowing about you, you can't imagine how much of an advantage that provides for me, I enjoy banter but playing with fire always results in burns."

Her eyebrow raised and Derek nodded in agreement, he realized he hadn't had a reason to dislike her until now, but it wasn't enough to bother father with just yet, he realized this wasn't a good time to interfere with him, in this delicate state with his sister leaving, quite possibly never to return. He was far too unnerved to be persuaded into such a conversation, no tonight the hunting ground was calling. He couldn't wait much longer, as soon as he dropped her off, he'd go into town and find reasons to do his biddings, already informing the house and staff that he wouldn't be back until well after midnight, he wanted to make sure to watch her flight take off before returning home.

Chapter 11:
Dual Nature

TIFFANY waved goodbye before entering the Denver International Airport. Kyle smiled knowing she'd be on her way to greater opportunities in life, as they parted ways he realized that he has one waiting at a bar nearby. She'd be working the late shift and getting off in less than an hour, the perfect amount of time it would take to cut her loose in the wilderness and watch her run naked in the snow, before *The Slaughterhouse Hills Hunter* struck again.

As he drove down the road towards *The Church* he smiled knowing that soon he wouldn't have to worry about unleashing sheer hell within around the delicate neck of that beautiful red head who was curled up near his bedroom right now. All the while reading her copy of his first edition yet again, for the thousandth time biting her lip and stroking the spine re-reading the inscription left for her by the man she saw as a living, breathing God. As soon as this hunger for blood was satiated there'd be no reason why Kyle couldn't finally have his cake and eat it too. A sumptuous strawberry was waiting for him at home, waiting to be feasted upon by the glorious King that deserved such an honor, to rejuvenate his life force in the endless warm oceans of her golden twilight paradise. To bask in her glorious light, fawning for his affections and adoring every part of his being, dark and light, inside and out. That warm feeling crept away and was replaced by the cold visceral bite of Darkeel.

"It's time to show that fucking cunt, just what she's been missing." Reaching for a bag of tools and hunting gear, made of black leather and worn from many, many years of use. A blood stained axe, rope, arrows and bow, a bowie knife and a pair of bunny ears with a little white cotton tail. He smiled relishing in the darkness that was in the air tonight;

"It's good to be home."

Darkeel peered into the eyes of the vessel that was currently on loan;

"Don't worry Kyle, I'll leave the pretty red head alone, for now, tonight that little blonde whore is going to die."

His boot clad foot pressed into the pedal, he was conscious inside, this exchange wasn't without his permission, in fact he enjoyed sitting back from time to time and letting somebody else take this drive, he'd grown so detached from the thrill of it anymore.

Something about tonight was different, just thinking about her in the back of his mind made all of these years alone hunting down strangers he'd built familiarity with seem empty, pointless. Suddenly he imagined hunting her down, how the blood coursed through his veins, directly to his cock, warming him down to his thighs.

"She'd make such a delicious bunny, Mmm to hunt her down, arrow by arrow, just to turn her into rabbit stew."

Darkeel pulled back and directed his eyes towards the rear view mirror once more;

"Hey, fucker, we have other plans tonight, get your head in it, or I'll change my mind about that little whore back at the house, remember you do sleep sometimes, I never do."

Kyle's voice came through firmly;

"Touch her and I'll fucking destroy you."

There was no response, just silence, the wheels creaking in the cold snow covered night, the wind howling through the cracked windows of the truck as he sped towards *The Church*. He didn't want to catch her well dressed in the bar tonight, he knew what time she got off. He'd fucked her a few times behind that bar outside against his Porsche, never letting her inside, never bringing her home, and never letting such a greed fueled harpy near him. Just amusing himself with a piece of meat, before hunting her down like the animal she was, one that needed to be disposed of, in the dark twilight hours in the cemetery, where a freshly dug grave awaited. Now's his chance after weeks of stalking to finally make things right. The demon of Burnett Manor would come home tonight with a fresh kill, whether Kyle liked it or not.

He pulled up and it started to snow, the former temple transformed into a night life sanctuary for all the local ghouls and boys who just never quite fit in anywhere just right. The creak of his axle's stopped as he turned the lights down low, he waited and watched, and silently the red lights shimmered on the snow reminding him of her imminent doom that would be waiting as soon as she found herself outside again. Kyle's mind trailed back home, he wanted to see her, know what she was doing, he felt her energy rising and swooning, was it his words? That delicious provocation masked in sadism, just waiting for her curiosity to be peaked enough to find him. He was impressed to see that she hadn't wandered around, at least just yet. She was far too busy pleasuring that sweet pussy of hers, bucking so hard against the palm of her hand, her fingers deep inside her fresh fruit salad. The juices squirting forth from her, moans muttered into crimson pillows now forming to the shape of her face, leaving lip prints dragged into the fibers of the fabric, she lifted up and said his name;

"Kyle."

Just doing so caused her to gush uncontrollably, she couldn't help herself.

"Mmm, I leave you home for a few hours, and you can't stop fucking yourself while reading my book? Already becoming my favorite, the other girls aren't going to like this very much."

Kyle said aloud smiling. His mood instantly shifted, his eyes dilated, his pheromones peaked; there she was, exiting the building from the staff entrance in the back. That shallow bitch who always found him so amusing when he was driving his Porsche, and well dressed for a business meeting with a creative associate. He always returned the same night after in the truck he was waiting in right now. Wearing his casual clothes, she walked by ignoring him, a few times even being blatantly rude to find herself snuggled up with the finest dressed man at the bar. Kyle never liked fake people. These walking mannequins who never knew how to connect, or if they did only did so through greed or lust.

He didn't mind using them, especially in bed. Realizing that he would be the last fuck they'd ever have was an honor in his eyes. Tonight would be different though, he never hungered for flesh on the night of a kill, in fact the only thing he craved was watching warm pools of fresh blood flow forth onto the whitest of snow. Seeing the light slowly dimming in their eyes, smiling serenely as he felt the warmth leave their corpses in the snow. Happily watching as deer, wolves and other animals approach to take parts away to scatter these bitches to the wind. Reminding him just how much he hated fake people, how he relished in the process of exterminating them, and knowing that he was the only person in this world that knew where they actually were. The ironic part is nobody ever seemed to come looking for them in the first place. They were the true expendable's in this world, nobody every missed awful people.

He'd killed dozens over the years, never once seeing a missing person's report in the paper or even on the news. Though Kyle was often much too busy to focus on such trivialities in mundane existence, his brilliant mind had much better things to focus on these days. Beyond recreating the same horror show that he found as a child, and tried on for size for the very first time when his wife decided that she'd leave that night, with another man. The entire world thought she'd died due to illness, it was still the golden story painted on a canvas of lies that held together the very fabric of his entire empire. The image of a widowed man, left with children, heartbroken and discarded to heal, provides the catalyst a city needs to invite such a mysterious man into so many circles of commerce without ever even asking for origin stories. His hypnotic presence never beckoned those types of questions anymore and if they arrived he knew exactly what to do with those who desired to pry.

It was a delicate game that Kyle played all these years, strategically disappearing towards the hunting grounds, while the rest of his empire was far too busy to ask questions or even notice anything out of the ordinary for the previous twenty years. He made it look effortless even though it was his extrasensory gifts that enabled such a reality in his world. He was able to manipulate much more than just minds and shallow minded whores into wandering into the jowls of death with no return. He could bend, stretch and even slow down time in temporal spheres around him expanding as far as he desired. Where others wouldn't notice a thing, those he hunted felt ripped down by gravity unable to move, desperately trying to flee the arrows and axe of *The Slaughterhouse Hills Hunter.*

Holly's heels clanked loudly along the parking lot, announcing quite clearly to Kyle and to the rest of the world just where she was located.

Fortunately for Darkeel the entire parking lot was bare, a wall of cars leading his dark energy towards the one he desired to kill. The horny teenagers that usually stayed outside were nowhere to be found in this frost bitten night, the club was closed up, the music was loud and even security waited inside. She cursed and tried to unlock her door, she was already drunk from the shots she'd been stealing all night. She managed to get the keys into the door, just as the sound of boots slowly emerged from out of nowhere, she saw his shadow behind her in the window, a tall hooded figure.

"Alright asshole, I'm not interested, I only date rich guys, and you look like a fisherman, so fuck off!" She started to get into her car, he slowly pulled back his hood, leaning into her dashboard and yanking out the ignition wires underneath the steering wheel, leaning just enough for her to see his face;

"What's the matter sweetie? Not interested unless I have my Porsche?" His smile transformed into a demonic face that leered back towards hers with such visceral aggression.

Holly's eyes bulged in shock, he mouth dropped open and before she knew she could scream, her eyes started to blur and she felt like she couldn't move. Atropine might not have been strong enough for a skilled psychotic gardener with a fetish for exotic and wildly toxic plants such as Jess or Belladonna. But for this woman a drop or two on the door handle will do just fine, he didn't expect this delicate toxin to work so effortlessly but then again he thought his good looks wouldn't cause such a stir in this venomous viper. Unaware of such things like that of adrenaline pumping hard causing the mixture along with several shots of alcohol, to stir the girls blood into a paralytic fervor. She slumped down wheezing softly as if she was in a coma, her eyes glassy staring at him haunted by the fact that she couldn't recognize this man to save her life.

Kyle took her keys and threw them in the trash, leaving her door unlocked but shut. He pretended to help her lovingly to his truck;

"Don't worry sweetheart we'll get you home, I told you not to drink that much, top shelf bourbon really gets to you, and so does being a greedy little cunt."

He smiled tossing her into the floorboard of his truck, her eyes now resting on the bag beneath her paralyzed frame not fully comprehending just precisely what those tools were for. She started to scream unable to move her voice muffled sounding like a kitten who was sprayed in the snow with ice cold water. The axe fell out and the tips of the poisoned arrows peered out as well,

"I *knew* you'd ruin my Easter surprise; are you cold? You're trembling *just like a rabbit.*"

Kyle laughed manically as the bunny ears fell out onto the floorboard, she started to cry realizing for once in her life how fucking stupid she was for using people and throwing them away for all these years, this is where it got her, in the fucking floorboard of a sadistic killer, a man she'd been so cruel too on countless occasions never realizing that he has two very different, sides to him. The worst part no matter how hard she tried, she couldn't remember him, either version of him; the creaking continued in the axles underneath the snow packed floorboards, time was fleeting, tonight Holly was going to die.

Jess with Kyle's book set on her nightstand smiled feeling his energy disconnect from hers for the first time since she heard his voice on the phone weeks ago. She smiled conscious to the fact that in her years and many lifetimes crafting her art in Tantra that anyone resonating in a human body could only endure either sexual energy or primal energy. As no physical body could create both simultaneously without imploding into the subconscious realm and destroying the personality into a mutated spiritual being. That magnetic pull he had over her was lifted now that his other self had risen from the inner dungeons and cold, stone cellars of his heart.

"I knew you couldn't handle that much of my succubus energy and still focus on hunting tonight, you made your choice, and I'm *more* than satiated. *Time to shroud myself in psychic silence and go on a little hunt of my own.*"

She pulled the bedding back and walked towards her closet, leaning down towards the floor in an inconspicuous place was a black steamer trunk with golden locks, she reached down opening it and pulled out her black tactical cat suit, boots and night vision goggles.

The screaming wouldn't stop tonight, she'd never heard it quite this intensely before, maybe they knew he was gone, and were trying to escape. Jess had to figure out who or what the fuck was downstairs, her mind couldn't focus on swooning anymore. She felt a deep pull, a psychic connection that ran deeply flashing back to a previous time in her life when she had never imagined herself ever being happier.

Those years she spent across the ocean with Sara, the one that went missing when she left late at night to run a quick errand before returning home to her beloved Mistress. Instead still missing, Jess still searching and following her cries across the globe to find her, to bring her home to the woman that loves her more than life itself. She knew when she'd gone searching for her that night hours after Sara went missing that a torn piece of cloth with a single drop of blood was the only piece of evidence she had to search for her in regards to her beautiful pet. This very piece of fabric and the DNA results that revealed the identity of *The Slaughterhouse Hills Hunter* was the only information she had to follow, to pursue to this very moment in her rigged closet with secret tunnel light creeping in. Hoping to find her and to hold her close wishing that she wasn't already buried six feet underground in Kyle's beloved cemetery.

Jess traveled back from nostalgia and lost dreams to present reality, wiping a tear from her face before pulling on the rest of her cat suit and hood, before lacing up her boots and turning out the lights. Putting her goggles on exactly as she saw fit she smiled as they turned on, the entire bedroom was illuminated in layers of green; she noticed another crack of light creeping in, not from the closet this time but from the bottom corner of her panoramic mirror. She tried her best to peer into the peeling corner realizing now fully that it was in fact a two way mirror, she then wandered into the bathroom smiling wickedly and searching for any clues. After nearly twenty minutes she found a small pinprick along the wall of mirrors behind her, the ones she relished staring into her own eyes while touching her sweet peach with Kyle's powerful image in mind.

"You weren't joking when you said you see *everything*, were you Sir?" she smiled realizing that the two way mirror in her bedroom extended into and throughout this entire wall in her bathroom. An entire room was behind there. Floor to ceiling exposed, the largest movie screen a director, producer and film creator could ever hope to find carnal muses for creative processes, or to help this big bad wolf's mouth to water while watching his eventual prey washing his next meal.

She wanted so badly for these goggles to have the ability to peer through walls, she had to figure out how to access this room behind her mirrored voyeur cage. If anybody else had done this to her she'd be livid, *ready to kill*. But in this moment she found herself absolutely soaking wet, the mere thought that he'd seen countless shows of her truest desires for him already. She was more than thrilled to find new and countless ways to share that torture with him, her entire wing was a silver screen slaughterhouse and she was the livestock being watched; monitored and waiting to be hunted down and devoured long into the night.

She peered into the snow, beyond the cemetery and over the cold frost bitten Colorado hills. Jess felt her spirit leaping onto the bitter cold and floating towards him out in the wilderness what felt so very far away, was only forty five minutes from home. She saw the truck climbing over hills, dark, desolate snow covered hills in the middle of nowhere. Jess saw the truck slowing down as it approached a frozen pond surrounded by trees. Feeling him stirring deep within his body trying to reach out to her and to reconnect even in this dark and devious time, the moment she saw the back of his head she realized a pair of feet were being drug out from the floorboard of the truck. Still with color, they were alive for now, instantly she saw darkness, a huge iron door and the light snuffed out. Darkeel was aware of her penetrating advances, and instantly shut her out of Kyle's mind. Tonight it was his territory, and he wanted to share this moment with Kyle, just like the first time all those years ago when the darkness leapt into him as he swooned for bloodstained locks and pale frozen skin in the middle of the harshest winter he ever remembered as a child.

"It's now or never, I can't gauge when Kyle will return after the hunt, I can only plead desperately for his compassion, I have to find her, he must understand."

Jess murmured to herself trying to hold her composure she knew if she focused on the tragedy and heartbreak the long, cold lonely nights searching and roaming all over the back alleys of Europe asking anybody who'd engage her in eye contact if they'd seen her. None of them had, and if they did meet her, they never would've forgotten her. She was eternally unforgettable, leaving Jess with so many restless nights wondering just what happened to her when she was returning home from a late night shift at the local dungeons.

Jess repositioned the night goggles one last time, knowing that the children were fast asleep in bed, and that only staff members' still wandering downstairs two floors below would soon be off to bed for their next much needed day off. She realized that she'd need the hall lights to dim or she'd soon be as blind as a bat in broad daylight. She imagined the hallway and all of the lights along their wooden paths. Inhaling she felt the light being snuffed out, her golden handled door opening slowly, she leaned out to see if anybody was around, nobody was there. She knew this would be an additional challenge once she descended down to the second floor, where Derek and Adie slept soundly, or at least she slept soundly. Jess knew that psychic cloaking wasn't the easiest part of her gifts to utilize, it was a gift in youth but one that became more and more difficult to use with age.

Already memorizing each and every creaky floorboard she slinked out of the hallway and towards Kyle's bedroom knowing that he might sense her more abruptly if she entered into his dungeon down below, she started slowly. She loved to prowl the way she fucked, with sensuality, slow, brooding torment in the form of seduction, easing her body down into a state of primal force. Her eyes started to slit, appearing quite feline along with her fangs that grew pointed on nights like these, she removed her goggles;

"I guess these are useless now." She placed them in her belt ensuring they wouldn't fall out, one more look over the bannister before trying his door for the first time.

Nobody was there, the only remnant of life throughout Burnett manor was the twinkling lights that reflected from the dangling crystals on the chandelier. She walked over to his bedroom, seeing that his private study and personal office were cracked open, she knew by psychic searches in the past that this place was just a collection of his most treasured literary possessions, nothing more, nothing less. Still extraordinary to her and to anybody who loved the written word in its most prestigious form, but this wasn't where she needed to be tonight. His room called to her as if there was something there waiting to point her in the right direction. She ached to find her love and to ravage her out back in the cemetery where Sara loved being taken most, reminding herself to live fully when death is always around us.

She slinked like catwoman coated in skin tight latex, her fluid movements towards his room were otherworldly. Jess possessed a preternatural rhythm inside her that would haunt any man or woman's dreams. Slowly making her way towards his door, she'd never ventured to this side of the upper floor before, she couldn't gauge where these floorboards would creak. Slowly but surely she inched forward step by agonizing step, her breath still, she felt his energy near, even though she was so far cut off from him right now.

"I wonder if he's watching me right now? Filming the show."

Jess looked around wondering if any bugs would be detected she had a special way of sensing them out even though it was said to be impossible by any modern human's understanding. She reached for the door and felt it turn, instantly she was overwhelmed with his scent, she could see the dark green and rich browns surrounding her on all sides. She felt as if she was at King Henry VIII's royal country estate, she read about the endless nights of passion that were spent in such a room, this one made her ache for Kyle in ways she never knew were possible. His room was inviting, his scent lingered in her delicate upturned nose the entire time she was there. Wandering around doing her best not to be captivated in a trance, she reached for the walls and started moving anything she could to find out where this private entrance to below was hiding.

While bending down near his nightstand she didn't realize her goggles fell from her waist, falling to lush carpet without a sound she found absolutely nothing. Even his journal near his bedside was a menagerie of short hand notes; only the gatekeeper to his mind could make sense out of it. Jess put it back exactly as she found it, never realizing she'd been sitting on his bed, in his favorite spot the entire time. When she rose her luscious ass left a very sightly mark on his bedside one untainted by the darkness, and would lead her to her ultimate demise when later *The Slaughterhouse Hills Hunter* had every reason to lock her up beneath the earth and throw away the key.

Jess started to meditate seeing if she could sense where Kyle was now, what had he done to that girl from the bar? She couldn't sense anything only the pitch biting black of the cold dark ether, chilling her to the core. She felt as cold as a corpse in the snow after a blizzard, she could tell she was sensing the terror in this woman right now, she didn't have time to save her though, she had to choose and her senses told her that she had to go down below, she had to figure out a way inside this house, into the very pits of hell itself; even if it was the death of her.

"She's in my fucking room, its impulsive actions like this that make me wonder if she truly does want to die."

Kyle said aloud now dragging Holly's body out into the woods, still alive, heavily hog tied with rope, wearing bunny ears with her mascara streaking black drops into the freshly powdered snow. She was sobbing endlessly;

"Quiet you little bitch."

Kyle backhanded her across the face, temporarily knocking her out cold, her teeth biting into and leaving her white cloth gag stained in red, the blood flowing from her lips. Darkeel chimed in viscerally speaking to Kyle in his mind;

"*We're almost there, not much further.*" His eyes shimmered with a horrifying glow;

"I know." Kyle said; "Tonight this little bitch is all mine. You get to watch." An endless howling cackle echoed deep inside his skull.

Holly started to stir, Jess felt her heartbeat quicken suddenly. She'd tuned into his location but not by melding into him as per her usual method thus far. She saw him through the eyes of the victim. The blur of snow washed over her vision, making it nearly impossible to see his entire face with either eye all at once. Just shadows, the shape of his formidable jawline, his glowing eyes raging with such hunger, she felt her body deadweight being carried and slung back and forth towards the woods. She could see the tops of trees everywhere above her, the snow below, curled up in a severe hog tie position, Jess could only feel her face, slowly growing colder by the second. She knew this girl hadn't had much time left, she could feel her pulse weakening from the sheer cold alone. It was hell beautifully decorated in endless white, the wind was brutal cutting through the clothing of this shallow bartender's body, Holly kept sobbing and Jess felt tears welling up in her own eyes realizing that this girl would soon die.

"I'm sorry I can't get to you all, tonight I have to find her if she's still alive."

"Now, where were we? Ah, yes, Rabbit Season begins today and I've been waiting for far too long to hunt you down and bury you beneath the crawlspace in my house."

Kyle slowly dropped her into the fresh powdery snow, she didn't flinch at the cold, and she was already frozen solid. Holly instantly screamed through her gag and Kyle smiled wickedly;

"You should've had some decency, but instead you only ever provided me with respect when I was dressed in an expensive suit, driving my Porsche for business." He continued;

"It's cunts like you who boil my blood, Mmm tonight's going to be a beautiful night."

Kyle smiled hearing the ecstasy of his darkside rally on in continued celebration. He placed the bag in the snow just behind him and untied her, lifting her up and waiting for her to stand he shoved her forward in the direction he desired her to run;

"Now run, run for your fucking life, so far only a dozen have escaped perhaps you'll be one of the lucky ones."

He smiled and started watching as she got up and struggled to stand, doing her best to run without feeling her feet. Instantly collapsing forward, face first into the snow before immediately trying again. He laughed and continued to pull out his bow and arrow, she gave him plenty of time to tie his axe to his belt before aiming for her back and shooting; missing her by mere inches on her left shoulder on purpose, he loved to hear them scream. Holly saw it land and struggled to dig herself up, sobbing, screaming and crying she knew they were miles away from the city, in the middle of nowhere during the night of a snowstorm, she wouldn't make it out alive, she knew she was going to die here tonight. She ran forward making it to the trees, Darkeel was pleased to see her wandering right into Kyle's trap.

"She's almost there, she's made it farther than the last one did, and I can't wait to feel her life bleed out."

Kyle's mind felt warm and serene, an ocean of peace expanded into a heightened sense of calculation. He saw the ears bouncing around between the trees, His mind teleported and he saw her from the front. Holly was tearing off the rest of the ropes that were still tightly wrapped around her waist, she tossed the bunny ears down hoping they'd distract him and she started to run towards the North hoping she'd lose him. Somehow she'd find help, she knew she had to keep going, his boots were near.

"Ah there you are, many have tried that way, but the gorge will stop you if I don't get a chance too first."

Kyle smiled walking into the woods after her hood over his head, his jawline and sinister smile the only thing visible. His boots made powerful tracks in the snow leading only the fools to hell as no creature would be out tonight, just the madmen who thrive in darkness. He wandered closer knowing she'd soon realize she was trapped, hearing her screams and shudders from a distance alerting him to her exact location. He watched her blonde hair moving frantically off in the distance, she was too low to shoot. He slowly stalked a rock nearby crawling up the backside of it and positioning himself on top, she was shivering, holding her arms, and leaning against a tree, looking over the gorge and sobbing, tears running down her neck she knew there was no way out.

He stood there watching, his bow drawn and arrow aimed for a paralyzing shot, he let go and watched it sail through the trees and into her right shoulder all the way down to the bone. She screamed and the blood flowed down her back, He took aim and fired another, this time landing it directly into her right thigh, she was hobbled she fell down and waited, she saw him over her right shoulder, and she started to cry even louder;

"If a single drop of those tears ever mattered, they're useless now."

Kyle's boots approaching were heard along with the steady pace of his steps, the same ones that lead her out into the woods in the first place. Pounding and grittily stomping into the snow with such stealth calculating movements, she watched him as he untied his axe and continued to approach her;

"What the fuck did I ever do to you?! Why are you doing this to me?!"

Holly exclaimed with utter terror in her eyes, her voice raspy, forming the words as best as she could. The axe instantly hit her in the chest, severing her pulmonary artery she instantly bled out he leaned in close placing his boot on her tits and prying the tool from her body;

"Because I take pleasure in the annihilation of beautiful things, especially those pretending to be beautiful. You were a dead fish, public sex should never be boring."

He pulled his hood off and watched her eyes bulge realizing exactly who he was. With the last breath in her body, choking on the river that flowed down her chest, pussy and thighs, he wiped her hair away from her face;

"Ah. Now that's better." He slammed her head down so that gravity would paint the masterpiece he wanted to see tonight in full moonlight.

"Mmm," Kyle moaned as he felt the darkness inside him subside the blood flowed and pooled down her neck leaking into her hair, making this pale corpse fire red, the only color that ever brought him peace such as this.

"Are you satiated now? Or shall we return home to the dungeons? I have a feeling we'll have fresh meat waiting if she's as intelligent as I've suspected she is up to this point, I better prepare the room Its going to be a very long night."

Jess knew he was finished, she felt the pangs of fear in her heart realizing this girl was dead;

"The only thing I can count on after this long of a hiatus is, that he's had his fill for tonight, hopefully… or I am fucking screwed."

In this storm it would take at least three hours before he'd be back, she did her best to leave his room exactly as it was and left the upper floor as swiftly as a feline in the night. She bounded down the bannister sliding off at the first floor and wandering down past the formal dining room and the bookcase that was never to be moved.

"There has to be a way to get in, I know this is the way he's entombed this place brick by brick, but there just has to be a way inside."

She reached into the books and pulled them forward, pressing her fingertips around wondering if she'd find a secret passage or door into this part of the house. Still nothing. There wasn't a way downstairs at least not from out here. He sealed this place up like a tomb. Jess's mind instantly flashed to a woman screaming bloody murder shackled inside a mausoleum, the full moonlight above casting the only illumination in this dark desolate place. Was she outside right now? Or was this yet another tortured victim who wandered ceaselessly across the grounds of the cemetery out back never finding peace, never knowing where she was or the final outcome of her own demise.

"The closet." Jess said aloud quietly under her breath, "Why didn't I think of it sooner?"

She shook her head realizing the simplicity of this search for entrance down below was right inside her private chambers this entire time. She knew there had to be countless ways inside but none thus far had she accidentally stumbled upon. She knew she had to go back to where she started. Creeping slowly down the hallway, it was utter silence, the darkness was everywhere, so thick in this distant place, far removed from big cities and light pollution this manor slowly formed and turned into a haunted house weaving it's shroud of mystery over her in every step a new layer of magic was revealed to her soul even if her mind was not yet ready to accept it. Not wanting to disturb the children on the second floor she climbed the bannister all the way to the upper floor, her fangs retracted and her eyes dilated back to their normal ink black state each sparkling one doing their best to see, she visualized the candles burning in the hallway and instantly the light started to illuminate the corridor beyond her office and towards her room. She noticed the children's dayroom was ajar, she instantly scanned the room for a presence, but none came forward.

"Let's hope it's the usual moans and creaks of a settling house that opened the door, I haven't much more time before he returns."

Jess entered her room and shut the door without a sound, she practically ran to the closet door and opened it wide, and instantly shutting the door behind her she was ravenous in this state. She did her best to ensure her talon like nails didn't' shred the wallpaper to find the opening, she placed her fingers on top of the panel and started to feel down the side, so far nothing allowed her to penetrate this secret entrance. The tears formed in her eyes, tears of frustration, of fear, of sheer anger that she knew for some haunting reason she had to get inside, even at the risk of her own demise. She could see her face still, hear her cries, her voice calling out for her;

"Mistress, please, I know you can feel me, I'm still alive. I hope you find me; before it's too late."

Sara's voice trembled in the biting air down below. It was all the psychic strength she needed, she recalled an ancient spell from the Egyptians that opened the passageways of any building so long as the sorceress using it was utilizing the incantation for noble purposes.

In this incredible case it was just what Jess needed to open the door; to retrieve an eternally invaluable piece of property that was stolen from her years before in the dead of night.

She felt her back sliding down towards the floor where the wood paneling was, her fingers reaching towards the wood she visualized the symbols needed to transform earth into air and to use that current to flow through this panel in the wall. As soon as she opened her eyes the door creaked open, she saw no light this time, but quickly visualized it and instantly the secret passage was illuminated softly with light trailing all the way down to the middle of nowhere. Jess stood up and wiped the tears from her face;

"I'm coming for you darling, I promised I'd never let you go."

She sent this message to Sara and felt it hit her instantly, she knew she wasn't too far now, she was closer than she ever could imagine, all this time. Her talons growing to reach between the wood and concrete paneling and to pry open this doorway, it took every bit of strength in her physical body to move this. She realized it must've been set up on a very ornate system to open so effortlessly for him as it did that night. When he came inside her room, dreaming and adoring, watching and waiting to see if she'd awaken to her destiny.

"Ugh!"

Kyle yelled driving back in the snow, his bag of tools long since packed up, his foot hitting the gas, hoping acceleration would ensure she felt his anger coursing through his being.

"She's prying the fucking door open in her goddamn room!"

"It's impossible, there's no way a mere mortal woman could ever open this door without powers beyond our understanding."

Kyle continued out loud feeling the dark energy of Darkeel swimming around.

"What are we going to do to her Boss?"

She saw his eyes over the steering wheel, his penetrating eyes flashing with that devilish grin that terrified her soul to the core, followed by his voice;

"You've been a very, *very bad girl* Jess, looks like you'll make it into my little collection after all."

Kyle's voice boomed in her psyche as she felt the air escape her lungs. Gasping her body shuddered and slammed against the wall at the very top step of the entrance. He continued;

"I know you can hear me Jess, I know everything there is to know about you, even your extrasensory abilities. I see all, don't you remember our little chat? I'm never too busy to correct a mistake, *never.*"

Kyle's voice stopped echoing in her mind, she instantly sent back a message, "I'm *so sorry,* I just hope you'll grant me the courtesy of sharing my final words with you before you bury me out back."

Jess's voice was torn, he could feel the self-loathing in her energy, hear the sadness in her voice, he knew there was something missing, a crucial piece to this puzzle of impulsive and suicidal actions. For the first time he was moved, his anger culled inside, even the usual taunting's of Darkeel's constant interruptions were as silent as the grave.

As his boot pressed firmly into the gas pedal, the truck roared and he sped forth towards home long into the silence and chill of the night. This feeling of invasion was more than unsettling, it was maddening to a man like Kyle, and the only hard limit he possessed in life was being at ease when those he never suspected breached the intricate security of his entire world. The blood rushed to his neck, he could feel the pulsing and beating of his heart in his throat, knowing every secret he ever kept was now being explored without his control, without the ability to gauge somebody into this world, he knew they'd be overwhelmed by the sights waiting for them down below.

"You were fucking *perfect.* Why did you have to ruin it?!"

He yelled, taking the wild turns and bends of these roads far too fast in this weather, but still he prevailed speeding closer and closer towards his home mere miles away, it would only be twenty minutes or so more before his headlights would be winding down the dirt gravel path towards Burnett Manor.

"Please forgive me, Oh God I can't wait anymore, I have to know if she's down here."

Jess focused her powers and the lights illuminated each step echoed, towards her descent to hell, on her way down she noticed every so often intricate stones with symbols upon them. Each more unique and defying understanding with symbols and archaic imagery that spoke to the soul, the very core of the man who created this passageway by hand. Realizing she didn't have much time, she continued forward and down, deeper and deeper into the jowls of the ravenous creature waiting for her below. In that moment Kyle's foot let off the gas pedal and he started to relax;

"At least she's focused on other things tonight, I'd have no choice but to kill her if she found my office, she can't find what's gathered in there, no one can. You're safe for now my pet, but not for fucking long."

His mind continued to chatter with a sentence that resonated through the trees and over the hills hitting Jess in the pit of her stomach as she heard his voice firmly state:

"I'll bend you until you break, tonight your formal training begins."

Chapter 12:
NOCTURNAL PULSE

"THERE'S not much time, I have to do this."

Jess continued faster, her pace quickening her steps formerly silent now echoing deep down into the chambers of this dark underworld. She heard the screams of torture, followed by the sounds of sheer unbridled ecstasy, which instantly jolted back to amplified sounds of terror. The empathic sensations were overwhelming, she felt herself shocked, burned, electrocuted and fucked simultaneously. She heard the wailing cries and fleeting screams of angry outbursts filling the room below;

"Oh god, No, he's coming back, Shhh, Shut the fuck up before he kills us all!"

Jess froze, the entire hallway grew expanding beyond her peripheral view and blacking out her sight. She knew that voice, she heard those pleas so many times in her dungeon back home across the sea, it couldn't be, it just couldn't be... was it really her?

Finally at long last her boots struck the basement floor, what she saw defied the dark dreams of Mistress Bella's carnal heart, her ultimate dream dungeon. The entrance was closely guarded with a small desk, just above covered in closed circuit televisions that were wired on every floor. In every corner of every room above and inside this dungeon paradise that her sadistic heart had hoped she'd create for herself someday. Each row of closed circuit TV's were categorized to match the floors of this impossibly intricate mansion.

The top row was entirely of Jess's room, there were too many cameras to count. Kyle truly had seen, heard and known *absolutely everything*. Her mind was overwhelmed realizing all this time she thought she had a chance to beat him at his own game, never imagining that he was decades, even centuries beyond her mind and foresight's capabilities. Her eyes wandered down to the next row of televisions, one in his private study upstairs, and a few in each office, to keep his eye on employees along with their complaints that they never cared to share with him at weekly board meetings. The next row following was the entire first floor of the house, from kitchen, formal dining room, the living room and random kitchens for both staff and family. Her eyes trailing down to the final row, each one with a special word under, elaborating to their best qualities. In a single word defining them and their entire being in a single role for kink. Each television screen showing the very women she heard all this time from above, from sensual moans that she saw on screen now, to tortured faces wincing in pain.

Her eyes danced over them, they were just behind her, beyond this very first cage's stone wall barrier. All she had to do was step inside and the entire room would scream or fall to silence. Realizing that he wasn't coming, not yet at least, tonight some preternatural creature arrived to silence their fears while introducing entirely new more horrifying ones in the process. The oddest screen without a woman inside was labeled *Masterpiece*. If Jess only knew what it meant, she had no idea, only a haunting feeling that she was running out of time.

She sat down wondering what she was going to do, and worse, what Kyle was going to do to her?! The chair beckoned her to rest and wait for the judge, jury and executioner to arrive home. He wasn't far now, she felt his rage, his power, his thirst for balancing the scales, she knew he wouldn't be kind, not tonight, tonight of all nights this was the one she would have to put up a fight, wondering and hoping if it wouldn't be for her life. As her mind continued to invoke fear into her being as well as his dominant rage that coursed through the snow like kryptonite, her eyes fell upon the screen of a woman with long black hair, completely naked and dangling on a cross. Severely injured and covered in deep bleeding lacerations, her eyes welled up with tears she wondered if he'd be back to finish what he started. As her head fell back onto the cross the light in the cage illuminated her face entirely;

"Sara…" Jess whispered in complete and utter shock, she inched her way towards the cage right behind her the wall that was keeping her presence private from the others imprisoned here, her eyes sparkling she peered around and placed her latex clad hands around the bars.

She peered inside quietly clicking her tongue to the top of her mouth, Sara smiled and did her best not to cry but the tears welled up inside her and poured forth from her face;

"Oh my Goddess. You found me!" She wept and cried;

"I swore I was going to die here, I've seen others give up and disappear, never to be seen again, but I knew you'd come for me my love, please get me out of here!" Jess smiled;

"*Shhh my darling*, soon we'll be together again, I wish I could break you out and flee this place tonight, but unfortunately things just aren't that easy, not anymore. I'll explain later, *please* you have to trust me." Sara screamed in anger;

"What do you mean Mistress?! I've been here since I left that night, defying your wishes and wondering if you'd come find me and I woke up here! I can't take it anymore, let me out! Please Mistress *please*, I beg of you, help me! You don't know what he's like, I've never feared anyone but you before."

"My beautiful Sara, I wish I had the time to explain, he'll be here any minute now, *Shhh*, please my pet, you must be quiet. If the others hear you we'll both be slaughtered tonight, just hang on, I'm here, it'll only be a little longer, I promise you, on my life."

Jess looked her deep into her eyes trying not to cry;
"Don't play games Mistress, let me out before it's too late."

Jess didn't realize how powerful Kyle truly was, if she'd only listen to the pleas of her screaming concubine that was stolen in the night clear across the other side of the world. Kyle had a profound ability to bend, shape and reform time, instantly taking away those additional twenty minutes Jess had to prepare, she thought she felt his car coming over the final hill, as the headlights smeared in blood penetrated red into the kitchen windows. She saw exactly what Kyle and Darkeel wanted her to see, a ploy a comforting trap to keep her mind busy while Sara continued to beg for her release.

He was already upstairs, picking up the pair of goggles that fell to the floor without Jess's knowledge, he was crouching down and inhaling her scent from his sheets. Her sumptuous ass formed into the layers of fabric, as he dangled the goggles from his right forefinger he reached up and pulled on the sconce above his nightstand. The wall instantly moving forward he wandered deep inside;

"Lights," the candles fumed on and the tunnel glowed in vivid light. His boots started plummeting below each one a bit louder than before. He could hear their voices already, from the usual screams and sounds of torture to this delicate, beautiful and appeasing conversation shared between Jess and one of his prized possessions.

Who is she talking to? Or better yet, *why?* Kyle pondered doing his best to figure out what the hell she was doing down here in the first place. His bag of tools still over his shoulder he descended to the basement's dungeon floor and set his ominous boots silently upon them.

He was still wearing his hooded coat, his eyes shielded from her view, only his lips and jawline revealing an inkling of his identity and only to those who'd ever seen his face to begin with. He stared at her across the room watching her speak to Sara the one he referred to as *Untamable* and watched this interlude between Jess and his unfinished project unfold;

"How is it that you know this woman who I brought back one night on vacation?"

His mind now turning, cogs and wheels moving and grinding towards answers, but thus far one could not be formulated. This was far too bizarre of a mystery for even Kyle, for the first time Darkeel was silent. As much in wonder of this adventurous creature who was completely absorbed in calming down her lover, hoping she's gained her silence before she expected him to enter the way she came down here. Her head looking to her right fearing he'd be there standing over her, ready to kill. Or worse, to keep her here forever in such a visceral state, she'd lose her mind, she'd endured long term torture before in similar circumstances and she vowed she'd never find herself in a cage again, not unwillingly at least.

As he stood there hearing these two share such sweet intimate exchanges, he was compelled to keep Sara alive; at least for now he finally had incentive to tame her into submission. The others were so willing, at least after the third month had passed, but she was nearly at twenty and she vowed to submit to no man or woman besides *Mistress Belladonna*. The words never made much sense to him, he just thought it was due to her preference for women versus men that made this path to bliss so difficult for her instead of easing her into such a well-kept life for as long as they lasted.

In a single gust of wind that Kyle channeled from his core and sent rushing down the dungeon towards Jess instantly alarming her senses and provoking her survival instincts to do exactly what he wanted her to do. She looked over to her left, her eyes so big that he could see them vividly from across the dungeon. As soon as she looked he pulled his head back and his right arm extended out in front of him;

Sleep.

She heard his voice say inside her head and instantly Jess fell into a comatose state, floating in the air above where she was just standing, her hood falling back and her red hair plummeting down in waves of fire. Her eyes were closed and she appeared as if she was floating underwater in stasis,

"What did you do to her?! Nooooooooo! I'll fucking kill you!"

Sara screamed and with her last ounce of strength tore off the leather restraints holding her wrist to the cross, "You can't take her away from me, not again!" her screams echoed filling the room.

A profound gesture of love but not strong enough to free her from these bindings, or even from this cage; all she could do was watch as her beloved floated away in frozen stasis out of sight, in the direction that all of the previous women in cages vanished, never to be seen or heard from again.

Chapter 13:
PENDULOUS INQUISITION

THE smell of iron was thick in the cold night air, in the distance, screams were heard yet echoed through layers of stone. As she awoke to a dark room the only feeling that was tangible was the cold steel table beneath her body, and the tight feeling of restriction that she felt across her latex clad torso, wrists, ankles, legs and neck. Her entire body was locked delicately into place, yet the firmness of each leather strap ensured she'd never move an inch without *His* permission.

"I believe these are yours." Kyle's voice trailed from the corner of the room, she couldn't see his face just an ominous figure sitting in the shadows with his lips parted, curled in a devious state, he'd waited centuries it felt for this moment, how she knew so little of what was waiting for her tonight, and how long this plan of his had been implemented. As Jess tried to look around to see where she was, she noticed a flickering light above her head, the twinkling of antique slaughterhouse equipment, her nipples were instantly erect under her skin tight latex cat suit.

"You really are a rare breed of woman Jess, it never ceases to amaze me what invokes passion in your dark soul, most women would scream for their life in this moment, but you?"
He stood walking towards her, watching her pussy mound swell at the mere thought of his touch, his presence was already more than

overwhelming to the senses.

"You're perpetually wet for torture." He leaned in close smelling her scent escaping from between her legs;

"I find that when one knows who one's captor is, it's much easier to find arousal, dear God! What are you going to do to me?"

Jess bit her bottom lip looking up into the darkness seeing that these antiquated slaughterhouse devices were now constructed into a crude guillotine. Rusted the only glimmer of its presence now residing in the one inch of metal blade that was still shiny, and stained *blood red.*

"Please don't kill Sara, she's my world, and quite literally everything that I've ever built in it." Jess started to cry, continuing on;

"I realize I have absolutely no place to request anything from you, tonight or any night after this, if those even exist anymore, but *please* Kyle, I beg of you, don't kill my girl." Kyle's hands reached for Jess's face, softly brushing the tears from her eyes and looking deep into them;

"As usual you captivate me with your boldness, tell me your story. I want to know of the woman who created the untamable cunt who's endured and survived more torture over the past ten months now than any other creature that I've captured on my hunts before. Perhaps your tale will buy you yet another night in this world of mine, but first."

Kyle smiled wickedly, dropping his hood and revealing his face, his piercing eyes penetrated deeply into her soul, she felt his warmth pooling into her chest and radiating throughout her body.

He reached for the zipper of her cat suit and slowly unzipped her, watching her luscious breasts spill forth towards the center, two ripe melons, her nipples were painfully hard now causing her to hiss aloud;

"First you're going to tell me how you discovered who *I really am.* Then if I like what I hear I'll let you finish the rest of your little tale."

Kyle slowly touched his hands from her bellybutton up through the center of her breasts, gently teasing the soft, warm skin that ached for him more than he ached to torture beautiful women to the very brink of ecstasy and existence. As his warm hands wrapped around the bottom of each full breast teasing the nerves along her rib cage, she tremored in pleasure moaning, unable to keep quiet any longer, this had been the longest week of her life. Kyle started to laugh deviously, as his curious eyes waited to see what this sex kitten would do next to find comfort in even the strangest of circumstances.

"If you skip even a nuance of details, I'll keep your pretty little head as a trophy on my mantle, with the rest of them to remember you by, though with your talents it would be a pity."

Jess's lip began to quiver uncontrollably Kyle's cock grew hard instantly the smell of her adrenaline fueled pheromones were intoxicating, as Jess's eyes finally got used to this impenetrable darkness in the dungeons below she noticed a dozen faces eternally frozen in states of sheer terror, some of which had been freshly mounted on the wall, how did he have the time for such taxidermy experiments with human corpses? Some of these faces were ancient, how long had he been doing this? Or worse was this a family trade? A lineage of fiends, mad doctors and psychopaths?

"So you don't know everything there is to know about me just yet?" Kyle laughed wickedly;

Fuck, and here I thought the audience of mutilated heads was going to be distracting, but my captor can read minds, bend the universe to his will, and for some insane reason has made a part of me ache for him in ways words cannot begin to express. Her mind chattered ceaselessly.

Kyle walked around Jess's head looking down at her face, studying her expressions, and waiting for her to gather her strength and courageously open up her soul, spilling forth all of her life's greatest secrets and many of his as well.

"There will be plenty of time for pillow talk later my pet, now your captor desires an origin story, more specifically, *mine*." Kyle's hands waved effortlessly in pace with his boots. As he wandered around the other side of the table teasing her liquid skin with his fingertips.

"Better get started, the clock is ticking you have until sunrise to convince me that you deserve to be here for another day."

Jess gathered her courage and with one final tear, her ruby lips parted and out forth spilled every detail Kyle had ever wondered about, alone, in the snow when his victim's cries could be heard thousands of miles away. Across the oceans of space and time, to a small village in Romania where Sara and Jess slept. Naked in each other's arms, together and waiting for that time of night when Sara would once again wander the streets to prowl and seduce any man or woman she desired to take advantage of financially for the night. Bringing home her treasures to her Mistress and tending to her passion that burned long into the twilight hours.

"It all started with the blood kissed snow, screams and waking up ice cold in Sara's arms, it's how I found her years before, following the echoes of psychic energy linking me to her, for years we kept crossing paths in the most inopportune ways until finally she was mine, *all mine*."

Kyle realized that this story was interlaced with his, not separate entirely, but linked in a much larger web that depicted the truest nature of Jess in all her authentic glory. As a lover of monsters and the darkness, a being of light that shone like a flame to the ravenous moth's that ached to feel warm again, never once before knowing the light. It was in her nature to embrace those mysteries in life that most feared as manifestations of death incarnate.

As he walked towards the corner of the interrogation room, he sat back down on his usual stool, his left leg crossed at the knee, his fingertips pressed together most ominously as his wicked grin held firm. The shadows on this dark place kept him in the shades of grey and black that encompassed this tower room, the only visual presence was his smile, at least for now he was intrigued. *Better keep talking if I'm going to make it out of here alive.* Jess's mind rattled.

"I met Sara when she was dating one of Europe's most powerful crime syndicate bosses. I never met him, but I was hired privately at the time by a family who was hoping to relocate their missing son. A young man that started working for the Romanian Mafia was Intel for our local agency, sadly he was also a good friend of mine and it wasn't like him to miss a chance to report to headquarters so they sent me in as a busy distraction. Booking me as a traveling brothel madam with a penchant for the finer things in life, a way to elevate their business to the next financial tier, that's when my entire world changed, the moment I saw her in the bar that night it was over. I'd never wanted something more in my entire life. She was perfection in flesh form, and even worse, she was, *she is so fucking brilliant.*" Jess smiled nostalgically, doing her best to remember every detail of that night.

"Continue," Kyle nodded still staring at her full breasts, still stuck heaving forward out of her latex cat suit, her arms, legs and neck still deliciously restrained into place on the cold steel slab.

"I wanted more than anything to know what she tasted like, to feel her writhing body on top of mine begging for more. To hear her laugh, to know her completely, that's all I wanted after that moment, I left my old life working for a special ops task force as a psychic detective, and disappeared without a trace. At least as far as they know. She was a shattered being, one who thrived on the darkness of others until I walked into that tavern late that October night."

Kyle smiled and rolled his fingers, the tear that started to flow down Jess's eyes were now floating before her and towards him in the air, weightless drops of her pure soul. He caught them in his fingers as his jaw lifted, his lips parted once more;

"You're beautiful when you cry Jess, possibly even more so than in your natural state." Her cheeks blushed she felt the hot rush flowing towards her neck and pumping color into her breasts,

"Mmm, such a whore for even the slightest of compliments, tell me how a creature like yourself with all her rare experiences in life could even muster such color on pale flesh?" Jess started to buck against the table;

"This is too much, it hurts to share such pain, it's too deep, I feel my heart exploding, I can't let you see that side of me, not yet, there's nothing left to say, I...I can't." Her cries echoed and her tears flowed freely, she couldn't say another word.

"Show me."

Kyle's voice firmly pried inside the intimate layers of her mind, a rush of images from her tortured youth, neglected and left alone to survive without any normal structure in a child's life. Jess started to scream her head felt like it was being crushed and pulled in a thousand directions simultaneously.

Her body started jerking and tremoring violently, she did her best to tear herself out of the bindings around her wrists, still his mind searched deeper into her deviant soul. An entire lifetime flashed before his eyes, images of her traveling the world and capturing those just like him and turning them into the proper authorities to serve life sentences and to endure being hunted, slaughtered and killed in sadistic death penalty ceremonies. Her heart rate spiked and he could see her feline side shifting into her now rampant physical form. Her eyes slit, her teeth grew sharp and long, her fangs were so beautiful, he wondered what it would be like to watch her feed with such carnality, would she spill a drop? Perhaps siphon off just a taste from her intoxicated devotees? Or would she tear them to shreds drinking ravenously soaking up every single drop? He had nearly a dozen girls waiting just below, and one wild, untamable cunt who was formally trained, owned and still devoted to die for the woman that lies on this very table. Her mind raped for information, and Darkeel finding plenty of space to call home in his latest victim's soul.

"You're... so deep."

Jess gasped and shuddered her eyes shut tight, tears streaming down her face as his mind searched through her images in latex, with women on their knees begging for another moment in her glorious presence. He saw the dark boudoir chambers of wood, lush reds and golds, they truly were her colors, He knew it wasn't just a hunch. He heard her voice chiming in;

"You haven't paid your fee, you have until Midnight. If I don't receive payment in full by then, Sara will know where to find you, she's so hungry tonight, I wouldn't fuck with me, if I were you."

A woman's voice continued to cry, shaking with every word, in a foreign tongue that Kyle did not recognize that he assumed to be Romanian.

He knew that this dark creature now resting on his interrogation room slab was far darker than she'd ever let on.

"She was my succubus, Kyle and I her Mistress in feline form, I'm not proud of what I did to feed her desires, but she had to eat, and I could never say no to her. It's funny really, she reminds me of you. I can never say no to you either, even now as you know me more intimately than any other soul on this planet, I realize the power you have over me is eternal, and I'll do anything for you, *anything.*" Jess stammered;

"But, please Kyle, Master Darkeel I beseech you to spare her life and return her to me, I'll be forever in your debt. I'll never leave and I'll serve your desires in any conceivable way I can. Even those I'm not proud of, you have my word. You own me completely."

Jess awaited for her judge, jury and executioner to take his position, hoping that the last bargaining chip she possessed in life, her very soul would be enough for him. Her eyes stared into the dark tower room seeing the many stuffed faces of victims along the wall in horrified states, watching the guillotine above shining in the light. She knew her fate would be decided soon whether she was ready to embrace it fully in acceptance or not. Kyle had all the power, every card was in his hand, he always managed to find himself in this profound position in life, wondering which path to take, which ax to watch fall, ultimately deciding his future and imminent doom if the decision at hand wasn't as wisely chosen as he'd previously envisioned. Kyle without a word raised his hand and reached for a lever on the wall, a red handle tip that was soaked in the endless layers of blood from many former victims alluded to Jess that in this final moment of her life that she wouldn't even hear him speak.

She screamed and watched as the blade started rushing towards her head, the glistening metal shone in full glory and she knew what terror felt like to the very pit and core of her dark sadomasochistic being. Without being able in what she thought would be her imminent doom she shrieked those three little words that no killer ever imagined would escape from beyond the parted lips of his next victim...

"I love You Kyle!"

Her lips gasped and her eyes shut so hard that she instantly saw black, she knew this was it, everything she'd ever worked towards was gone in this single solitary moment in space and time. Everything she'd ever wanted was about to consume her and return her to the void.

Suddenly without notice the entire table fell to the floor and the guillotine stopped, firmly jerked and dangling on chain, Kyle's hand in that final moment shoved the lever into the wall activating an emergency mechanism that transformed this final pit stop into the most exhilarating haunted house ride that she'd ever experienced in her entire life. Without warning the tears of fear escaped as sounds of laughter and joy at the profound experience of simply being alive. Kyle was overwhelmed by her words, her reaction, he realized he'd interrogated her too severely, but he couldn't help it. He had to know what her story was, where she came from, how the fuck she discovered who he was to the very core of his being, to the darkest, most private secret passageways and hidden chambers in this dead man's heart. The table slowly rose back to its original position, the guillotine now rising back to the ceiling hidden by the cloak of darkness that kept it out of sight, except for those poor souls who never passed Kyle's test.

As Jess's tears continued to flow along with the sounds of her desperate sobbing, she felt the leather bindings around her neck release, followed by the ones around her waist, wrists, legs and ankles.

Her soft breasts were still swaying and bouncing with every inhalation and desperate gasp for air that escaped her soft petal lips, before she could open her eyes, she felt his hands gently touching her face and wiping away the tears;

"*Shhh*, my beautiful concubine, I've waited for you for so long, let me show you."

His lips softly kissing each and every tear from her eyes, cheeks and lips, she watched through tear stained glass windows, his hands reach for a locket that was resting on the wall along with so many other pieces of parchment that were hundreds of years old. Instantly the images flowed to her mind's eye, Jess could see Kyle dressed in another time, place, he was just as handsome then as he was now. In this vision Jess saw from her own eyes a hand reaching out, it was her hand, grasping Kyle's and wandering around Chicago in the early nineteen hundreds. Suddenly she watched as the scenery changed and so did the clothing on Kyle's body, it turned into armor, the busy streets behind them suddenly changed into an endless meadow and her hand was still in his. Looking down she saw her clothes, medieval in time period, possibly the fourteen hundreds or earlier. She heard the sound of children laughing, *their* children. She felt happiness pour into her soul realizing now that the same children that ran around downstairs laughing and playing games in the same precocious ways, were remnants of the ones they shared together as a family eons, centuries and many lifetimes ago. The endless joy continued to pour into her soul like warm sunshine on the first day of spring. Kyle leaned forward looking deep into Jess's eyes;

"I still have more to show you." The images continue to fill her mind, suddenly showing the origins of Darkeel, the frozen corpse in the snow covered in blood, a childhood filled with poverty, desperation, cruelty and neglect. She saw Kyle's tiny child form being beaten by the hands of those who should've loved him unconditionally, leaving him outside to survive the harsh cold winters of Colorado, never knowing if this would be his final hours on this earth, alone, starving and without a lumen of light to illuminate the darkness that continued to swallow him whole. She saw him shivering in the cold, dark winter night, she heard the voice reaching out from the abyss, trying to keep him alive, forcing him to stay strong and encouraging him to hunt; kill and to thrive in this hellish wilderness that would never be tamed by a human soul. Only that of a demons, a dark god in flesh form, beating forth the heart in the chest of this young man that craved to hunt prey that was much more beautiful than the local rabbits, foxes and other small game. He craved the glory of capturing women and owning their souls, a sacred collection that continued to haunt him long into his life, bringing Jess to that final moment when Sara was snatched away from her and she was left for dead.

He saw his boots in the snow wandering off behind her as she prowled the usual streets, collecting and settling debts and bribing new tourists and travelers to spend a night with her and Mistress Belladonna, to find release in the oldest form of ecstasy. Never knowing that the man she propositioned that night in the tavern, was waiting for her all along, examining her for weeks now in layers of clothing, each night removing a single piece wondering if he'd ever catch her eye. It was the final night he planned to stay in town for a hunt on vacation. She just so happened to walk down the street precisely at the right moment, he was on his way back home and Sara was weak for a tall man with broad shoulders she just couldn't resist his charms.

"Hello there stranger, need something warm tonight?"

She leaned against the brick wall, smoking her cigarette and opening her floor length black fur coat to show off her luscious thighs and full breasts adorned in leather. Kyle approached her and leaned against the wall;

"Do you mind? It's been a long week and I'm leaving town, very soon actually."

Sara shrugged and handed him the cigarette, never realizing that his gloved fingers were laced in atropine, gently touching the filter, he pretended to take a drag, exhaling the cold air on hot breath, she took it back and started to inhale, suddenly realizing that this wasn't what she expected from her favorite brand.

"What the fuck, did you? *Oh no.*"

She felt her legs buckle, her knees tremble and give out and she knew he'd poisoned her, her Mistress was a keeper of exotic plants, ones that created special toxins to easily subdue those who refused to pay their fees on time. Never to be seen again after the snow fell in the night when they suddenly vanished, she never had to clean up the mess, the wolves usually took care of that for her, it was a perk of living in such a dark place in this world, just a few miles south from Vlad Tepes' final resting place.

In the vision Jess watched from behind as Kyle slowly walked Sara towards the forest, seeing her stumble she looked drunk, any local who would've usually been out at that time of night knew Sara never drank, but this was the only night in history so it seemed that she was entirely alone; a single soul never knowing that Darkeel lead her to her future cage, one without her beloved Mistress in tow. Before she blacked out Sara knew that the only chance she had was to leave something behind, hoping that her Goddess would find it, a brass locket holding a photo of them in loving embrace, Sara on top of her Mistresses lap with a smile as glorious as the sun. Jess's face adoringly looking up to her darling whore, embracing her and holding her close the epitome of dark love intertwined. The other side of the locket was empty, it bothered Jess she wanted to fill it with the perfect image but nothing ever felt or looked right.

"I have something for you, I'm pretty sure it belongs to you." Kyle dangled the locket above her head and instantly Jess smiled;

"Where did you find this?! I searched through the snow all morning, I followed your foot tracks as far as I could before the snow covered them completely. I found the impression of this in her tracks as you two left the village, but I couldn't find this anywhere!"

Jess sat up on the table instantly forgetting her entire ordeal in this dreadful chamber thus far in a single moment she was enthralled with this piece of jewelry that she bought for Sara right after they first met. As she opened it up she was speechless to see a very old photo, it was of Kyle and Jess in a previous life, and before them three beautiful children, all of which looked identical to the ones he had right now downstairs.

"I...I, really don't know what to say." Jess stared in awe of this portrait that she knew was of a lifetime shared with him eons ago, that she couldn't' recall presently in this moment.

"How is this possible?" Jess looked up and Kyle pulled his hood back and smiled looking into her eyes with his piecing blue ones;

"We have a lifetime to share with one another, you've always been mine Jess, I recognized you the moment I saw your face but I didn't want to admit it could be you. I wasn't ready to let go of yet another woman I thought was you. It's the only reason why I have so many bodies piled up on these grounds and many others."

Jess leaned in kissing him, wrapping her arms around him, she felt his hands embracing her face, wrapping around her body and gripping her waist, then hips.

"Show me, won't you, please show me. I want to remember what it's like to be your world, to be your everything."

She leaned back, her breasts heaving up towards his face. He crawled on top of her and pushed her firmly to the table and started biting, kissing, suckling and teasing her exposed nipples with his tongue. His hands furiously unzipping her cat suit, all the way down and beneath her wet pink parts. She gasped as his big strong hands pulled the shiny fabric from underneath her ass exposing every bit of hot flesh that was soaking wet and covered in honey. She watched his hooded cloak drop to the floor and his arms throwing off layers of dark sweaters until his torso was glistening and shining in the dark twinkling light of the guillotines reflection.

His body was moving rapidly, and his breath was building a rampant cadence of carnality that filled his soul. He wanted to devour her here tonight, to tear her into two with his glorious cock. He'd never been so desperate to feel her wrapped around him, roughly slipping into her tight warm, wet little hole, her hands effortlessly unbuckling his belt and ripping open his pants. His cock was bursting forth, the girth alone made her hiss and tremble.

"Oh god, how is that big cock going to fit inside this tight little pussy?"

She looked up into his eyes, ravenous, desperate to see what his answer would be. As he pulled his cock out of his skintight boxers he teased her clit and traced his cock around the edges and openings of her tight wet little hole.

"Oh you'll see… even if it kills you, you're going to take every fucking inch I have to give you my little whore."

With that final word he shoved his magnificent cock inside of her, and she yelled, shuddering and groaning in pain and pleasure. His back was tense and his arms were firmly fixated on her wrists, holding her down with one hand the other gently caressing her face, touching her lips, softly placing the fallen hair from her face behind her ear. The entire steel table was bucking and shuddering, Kyle's voice groaned and echoed as Jess couldn't stop feeling overwhelming pleasure rolling and coursing through her body, limbs and tits in endless orgasms. She came hard and squirted already just as he entered her;

"Oh God Kyle, Master Darkeel" she gasped,
"I can't stop cumming, Oh my God!"

She felt him pounding into her slowly at first, deep with each mind blowing pump she buckled under pleasure deeper and deeper into the intoxicating ocean of ecstasy.

"You will be fucked, every morning, every afternoon and long into the night until you no longer crave her, you are mine. You always have been and you will be for eternity, I'll never let you go…"

He whispered into her ear:

"Not this time."

His lips pressing against hers, his tongue forcing hers to open she took him into her mouth aching and moaning, gasping and screaming as she kept squirting and gushing her sweet honey all over his balls. The soaking wet waterfall echoed on the steel beneath and resonated on the concrete floor below.

He gripped her by the hair and looked into her eyes:

"Are you ready to feel your master's hot cum exploding inside of you?"

Jess moaned in ecstasy feeling her next climax approaching as his cock swelled exploding inside of her.

"Oh God yes please, cum inside me, I want to cum with you master!"

In that moment he groaned, his release was met with sounds of moaning, yelling and shrieking ecstasy from Jess in that final moment he wrapped her legs around him and thrust deep inside her one final time. Knocking the wind out of her Kyle slammed her body down on the table, gripping her tits and shooting his hot load inside of her filling her up and watching as her body tremored, shuddered, jerked and twitched uncontrollably. Each time he plunged himself inside her, he left her nipples a little harder than they were just seconds before. Jess blushingly smiled at Kyle as he stayed deep inside her after he came.

"Welcome home Jess, I've missed you" she embraced him smiling;

"I always wondered why I dreamt of your face, and for so long I felt you watching me sleep, I can't believe it's really you, after all these years."

Jess continued to examine his face as if she was seeing it for the first time in her life, in every conceivable life they ever shared together over the past few centuries.

"How will I explain all of this to Sara?"

Jess inquired realizing her questions were futile, there was no way that she could be near Sara in such a way anymore, not if she was going to keep her alive, not if she was to maintain her place here at Burnett Manor without notice, blending into a beautiful world as she always dreamed of.

"Leave that to me." Kyle slowly pulled out of Jess's sweet little peach and exclaimed;

"Dear God I thought you were going to tear it off. I've never felt such a tight pussy before, I'd swear you were a virgin if I didn't already know better."

Jess laughed blushing;

"Well I have had dreams about you for years now, decades even, all that adrenaline fueled fear really makes me tense." Kyle smiled and laughed;

"Come here, you're too fucking gorgeous for your own good."

Pulling her chin upwards and kissing her once more, Jess swooned and moaned, cooing in bliss, savoring every nuance of this perfect kiss, it was nearly sunrise and she knew she'd have to go upstairs once more to tend to the needs of his children, *their* children.

"You have worn me out entirely, and that was after an already grueling night hunting Holly in the snow." Kyle warmly spoke;

"Would you like to take a long hot shower with me before we crawl into bed and play house again?"

Jess instantly melted at the thought, after being bound to a cold firm, steel table all night long, at the hands of a serial killer, a long hot shower is just what she needed before everything in her life finally fell into place.

Chapter 14:
LUSTFUL INSTRUCTION

"I want to watch you." Kyle's voice instructed Jess;

"Do it slowly for me."

His words seducing her once again to adorn her soft, luscious white flesh with liquid skin, slowly each delicate foot pointed intuitively catching the end of the latex stocking, sliding into each one of her toes pre-molded positions. She watched Kyle leaning against the table behind him, the one with so many rusted torture devices, layers of dried blood painted and splattered on each tool, her eyes were glowing with curiosity;

"Will you promise me one thing my eternal Master?"

She looked deep into his eyes wondering what his response would be, if he'd curiously play this game even if just to appease the aroused state it often left her in, during trivial conversations.

"Perhaps…" Kyle's voice baited her in once more to confess her deepest passions.

"Promise me you'll show me how you use those lovely devices someday? Even if the images come from our shared mind melding connection, in a flow of visceral memories that warm the blood and torment the mind."

Jess smiled wickedly as she continued to smooth the latex cat suit up her quivering thighs, sore and slightly bruised now from the leather restraints. Kyle laughed in utter amusement;

"You'll have plenty of time to earn such priceless information, such a *fan* of my work."

He gripped her by the back of the hair pressing her ass back towards the cold steel table, she hissed in bliss and torment, the contrast between the fires that pooled into her soft wet folds was striking, the chill licked her ass like ice, sending shock waves throughout her body, leaving her shuddering in his arms.

"Get dressed, whore." He smiled watching her bite her lip;

"Yes Master."

Jess continued by pulling the latex over each of her luscious mounds, watching them fall into place was like watching gourmet chocolate being wrapped by hand, it was glorious.

Reaching her feline limbs into each sleeve, she pulled the latex up and over her shoulders, gently tucking in her red curls down below before leaning over the table and slowly zipping up from underneath, her fingers reaching back as far as they could unable by mere inches to grasp the zipper just above her tailbone.

"Mmm let me help you with that."

Kyle leaned forward zipping her up, watching her teeth bite down into her lip, as their fingers touched. He exchanged a long look with her making her maintain eye contact, knowing her heart was pounding swiftly, he could feel it in her fingertips. She slowly continued zipping up her cat suit, watching as he squatted behind her, his firm hands traveling up the back of her thighs, making her moan and leak sweet honey once more, she couldn't help it, she was always soaking wet, whenever he was near her.

"Mmm what a fucking whore, you can't even stay dry for a moment can you?" Kyle beckoned for answers from his shuddering concubine, now intoxicated with Stockholm syndrome.

"Mmm, not with you around Sir, I can barely respond I'm so wet right now."

Jess stammered trying her best to form the words unable to convey meaning behind them, just grasping onto each and every syllable she could cling too. His presence was overwhelming to the senses, she couldn't focus anymore, she could just feel him swimming around inside of her head, flowing into her body and shaking her soul to awaken to its most primal state of existence.

Her hands mysteriously sought out the zipper, easing it forward and up her body, reaching her luscious breasts, she turned around looking down into his eyes as he smiled. Her breasts spilling forth, she slowly tucked them into her cat suit zipping the latex firmly into place at the neck, her nipples were hard and this time Kyle was the one biting his lip. She smiled and flipped her hood over her curls, tucking them in and leaning forward, her breasts gently caressing Kyle's face as she reached for her goggles on the table;

"I believe these are mine."

Winking at him confidently, she placed them over her head and positioned them on top of her hood, realizing the need for night vision wasn't necessary now that she'd received the private tour of his dungeons, to ascend above for a decadent shower in his room and to later curl up in his arms for restful sleep that had never visited her soul before in this lifetime.

Without a word Kyle started to unlock the gate of the interrogation room. Jess noticed the small gold key on his wrist, she never noticed it before, but the bracelet it fell from was always fixed to his arm. Since the moment they met she noticed it there, she thought it was just a leather band that most men wore. He opened the gate and started to walk forward;

"Perhaps I should leave you here for the night, without a shower, a punishment for speaking to one of my treasured possessions." Kyle's darkness was felt in her body, she shuddered at the thought of sleeping here alone tonight, waiting for him until God knows when.

"If that is what Master feels I deserve I graciously accept your punishment, and will leave you filled with pride at your return. I know you want me to be a good girl, even if it's just for show."

Jess said as she walked towards the bars, feeling the cold iron between her hands, she gently stroked them looking into his eyes, her nipples hard, he leaned near the caged interrogation room, teasing her nipples;

"You couldn't be good if you wanted to, it's what I love most about you." Opening the gate he reached into the room and grabbed her by the elbow yanking her towards him.

"But it's a detriment, you'll see, I know you better than you know yourself Jess."

She looked up into his eyes feeling guilty, she knew he could read her like a book, before her eyes could well up and the words spilled out he gently shushed her;

"I already know my pet, follow me." As she turned left he shut the door behind her, the lights faded to pure darkness, and his hand reached for hers;

"This way, stay close to me."

Kyle smiled, he loved for once in his life to not be the only one ascending to the bedroom above from the perilous pits down below in his dungeon headquarters. As they ascended she saw the closed circuit televisions, each one depicting his eleven treasured possessions and one empty cage, her eyes fell upon a blonde woman with long legs, hung in the air and being sprayed with water, all of which was funneled to the floor and recycled to continue spraying her from head to toe.

Her wrists and ankles bound in metal shackles, she continued to sob wondering why she was here in the first place. Her skin pale blue, Kyle rested his eyes on her she felt the workings of his mind seamlessly flowing to their final destination;

"A bit longer and she'll be ready for the hunt." He smiled;

"I've named her *Frostbite*, I plan to keep her here until December, when the first frost arrives. I'll sedate her, and leave her in the woods nearby, until then she's being conditioned to tolerate extreme amounts of cold, I want to hunt her for hours, so many freeze to death so swiftly during blizzard season. It really kills all the fun."

She continued to receive endless amounts of ice cold water on her flesh, her trembling continued and she screamed her voice echoing through the stone rooms below.

"She held out an entire hour longer today than I expected her too. She's almost ready, a sheep for the slaughter, she deserves a break, at least until tomorrow morning." Kyle smiled and Jess looked in awe, in wonder of what other creatures he kept down here preparing for hunting season, and endless other projects that Kyle desired to adventure into.

"You mentioned that there were nearly a dozen down here. Do these screens show the others as well?"

Jess curiously watched this screaming girl dangling in pale blue tones, her finger tips touching the screen as if she were real, wanting to mold, shape and form her to Mistress Bella's ultimate desires. He saw the wonder and awe in her eyes, the look of intrigue, she was hooked, and Kyle could see the lust for blood in her eyes.

"Oh teach me your ways Sir, my dark and haunting Master, make me like you, and pull out the darkness that's already there inside of me. Please I beg you, make me a tool for your darkest dreams, I've never felt more at home in all of my lives."

She continued to caress the screen, she was enamored with his creations, she'd always wanted a place just like this, she and Sara spoke about it every night that they met. A private dungeon torture chamber and pleasure palace that existed in the shadows, filled with the screams and cries of victims that would never again see the light of day. How ironic that she nearly got everything she ever wanted, but now she was bound to a crucifix, covered in blood with deep lacerations, scarring her perfect body and leaving her soul angry with vengeance.

"I'll *show* you the others later before bed, I've already informed James to take the children to the zoo with their friends today, so we'll be alone to recuperate after such a visceral night together."

Kyle continued walking towards his secret entrance to his bedroom, each heavy step upwards toward the light, left Jess feeling torn between two worlds, she wanted nothing more than to break Sara out of her prison and cage, but her heart and cunt belonged to him. There was nothing she could or ever would do now again without his permission. She knew her place in the world, she finally found it, and nobody not even the former love of her life could interfere with such a bond; shared between lovers of darkness for lifetimes. Jess knew he had her right where he wanted her, half way between paradise and hell, waiting anxiously to see just what would happen next.

She walked up the stairs, passing by lights that illuminated as they approached. Her hand never once leaving his, she could feel how pleased he was to share this with somebody finally at long last. She smiled feeling at home, knowing this is where she always wanted to be. Suddenly without warning he stopped and she bumped into him, laughing and then wrapping her arms around his waist and reaching up towards his chest. She smiled waiting for him, he reached for a small glowing green emerald that started to glow, he gently teased and caressed it, rubbing it slowly and smiling, feeling his concubine's hands stiffen in aroused state. Jess watched as the stone wall slowly moved forward with the softest sound escaping, a whistle of wind that sung on the breeze kissing her neck and reminding her of his power over all.

"I'd say welcome but I already noticed earlier that you made yourself quite at home."

Kyle couldn't help but play with her, to fuck her pretty little mind the way he loved fucking her beautiful body. Blushing Jess buried her face into his back and tried to find a nice shade of pale to return too before he could take notice.

Jess giggled thinking of various phrases to tease him with before she heard his voice inside of her head again, whispering boldly;

"You're lucky curiosity didn't *kill* the cat..." startled she laughed out loud, his mouth closing his laughter could be heard in the back of his throat. He loved how quickly she moved when she knew she was in the presence of danger, it was going to be fun chasing her in the snow, capturing her and bringing her back home, time and time again. A fresh kill that would never die, too intelligent to dismember and scatter to the winds on the wild hungry moors of the back woods on Colorado nights.

She felt his tall body stepping forward gracefully, his sheer size was always impressive to Jess, and she felt so delicate, fragile and feminine in the presence of such height. Her arms loosened as she followed closely behind, her breath returning to a calmed state of cadence. He turned around in the dark, pulling Jess towards his tall, strong body, instantly the wall behind her started to close and he effortlessly pushed her against it. Kissing her deeply and passionately feeling her heart beat swiftly, watching her eyes close ravaged by him completely. He fell deep inside of her soul, swimming endlessly in the warm pools of her consciousness, his entire body warmed and he started to unzip her, slowly peeling the latex off of her shoulders and watching as her body slinked out of each limb's special cavern. She moaned feeling how smoothly he explored her aching body. Her muscles were sore and his hands were silk, caressing the layers of liquid flesh over the round curves of her supple ass. He leaned down unzipping beneath her once more, looking up into her eyes smiling;

"Rest your hands on my shoulders," he instructed to her mildly, his voice seducing her slowly into a restful state of being.

Jess leaned forward and placed her hands on his broad, firm shoulders. Her luscious breasts swaying like two ripe melons freshly harvested on a hot summer's day were captivating. He felt each one brushing against his face as he peeled off the cat suit, down her thighs and calves, lingering at her ankles watching each foot delicately escaping its wanted bondage. Her breath was heavy, her wild untamable red curls were sticky and the air filled with her sweet and inviting scent.

Kyle slowly stood and began to kick off each of his boots, his face was glowing. He could see exactly how she saw him. From her eyes, a living breathing god incarnate, a powerful being of mystery and intrigue that she desired to worship in every possible and conceivable way. She stared at him as if he was one of those rare beings in the world who walked the shadows in the guise of men who were truly gods in flesh form.

He slowly peeled his sweater off, she watched his body reveal itself.

Finding herself hypnotized by the movement of his finger, interlacing and undoing his belt in a single moment. The clanking of the belt tormented her heart, causing nipples to show and chills of ecstasy to form all over her body before his very eyes. His bulging cock was pressed firmly against his body by his tight boxer briefs, and she couldn't help but gasp and urgently bite her lip as she watched him pulling the fabric over his pert muscular ass and down his strong thighs. Stepping out of them, his dick still standing as tall as he towered over her every bit of six and a half feet tall.

Kyle reached for her face slowly drawing her close, kissing her deeply and holding her in his arms. Embracing her completely, kissing her face and smiling into her eyes, he took her hand and walked into the bathroom, the lights began to illuminate suddenly;

"Very impressive my pet, you'll have to show me just how you do that, fire was never one of my strongest areas in the shadow arts."

Jess glowed in the candlelight smiling fascinated with his humility, "I didn't even realize I was doing it, it's sort of intuitive for me, instinctual to simply *turn on the lights,* one must be part of it."

He sighed contently under his breath walking forward he reached into the shower turning on the hot water and waiting for the steam to form.

"That's a beautiful understanding of a concept that to this day still very much eludes me, both spiritually and metaphysically. For the most part the light that is filled in this home is channeled through the laughter of my children, they are my light, and now so are you. I do my best to provide shelter for such beauty in this world, even if I feel that deep down I don't possess such a state inside of me, at least not anymore."

Jess smiled feeling touched to the core of her being in regards to such a confession. She felt so intrinsically connected to Kyle, the fibers of their beings were woven into a much larger tapestry that was rarely noticed in the world except by those who called themselves dreamers, lovers and inspired the muses to dance.

"Then we are your light, when darkness is surrounded by the flickers of candle flame in the night, darkness coexists in unity with the light, a symbiotic way of survival. It's why Sara named me *Belladonna* in the first place. A beautiful woman will always bring out a shimmer of light in even the darkest of places in this world, including the hearts of dead men's souls."

She smiled recounting this moment in her life, sharing with him the very pieces that formed together like a jigsaw puzzle depicting her in her truest form.

"Together with your children, we are your light source, and you the moth to our flame, always drawn by the alluring light that escapes your soul. To keep you warm under the pale moonlight, providing solace for pieces of you that you never knew could be whole."

Jess smiled sharing this beautiful moment with Kyle, knowing that he could see her completely as she was inside, idealistic of course, a foolish dreamer perhaps, but with the purest intent to heal and to provide shelter for monsters when everybody else desired to hunt them down into extinction on cold winter nights.

He leaned in kissing her deeply, the steam enveloped the entire bathroom and Kyle whispered into her ear,
"I love you Jess, even when we're eons and miles apart, you were the one that sparked into existence a part of me I didn't realize was ever there. I know words rarely escape my lips, solitude in expression has been a reliable penchant in life when I feel I've grown too close to someone to quickly. But you have always embraced me completely, just as I am, no more, no less." He continued between kisses;

"You beautiful, magnificent woman, come with me, I want to wash away the fear, the tears and past, you belong to me now. I relish taking care of the parts of your soul that you've never before revealed to any one until now."

A sparkling tear rolled down her check, Kyle kissed it away smiling and leading her into the hot shower, she walked underneath the rushing flow of water, her wild locks of red curls sleek and straight cascading like blood down her pale back, he was utterly intoxicated by her.

Her scent traveled up from between her thighs catching him unexpectedly, causing his fangs to sharpen, his hunger to grow and his cock to twitch in eager anticipation;

"Mmm let me get my fill of you Jess, I haven't had nearly enough just yet."

As her head was back she felt his hands on her thighs, parting them gently and burying his face between them, tasting her sweet honey soaked cunt and aching for that glorious ass of hers. She washed gasping as she felt his tongue sliding around between the folds of her hot flesh, as her beautiful crack was rinsed clean, he turned her around;

"Place your hands on the wall my beautiful whore, I'm not through with you yet."

With one moment of focus she felt his face burying into her ass and forcing it to spread, his tongue ravenously tasted her salty delicate folds, leaving her bucking wildly, moaning with tits pressed against cool tiles. She couldn't stop shuddering, his tongue was wild, and deep, penetrating her asshole and tormenting that delicate nerve that caused her to squirt effortlessly. Her body bucking hard against his face, she came hard;

"Oh God, forgive me for not asking permission, your wicked

tongue forced such accolades to spill forth from my lips in praise, I've never came that hard in my fucking life! Oh Kyle!"

Her nails digging into the wall, her face pressed firmly nearby, lips parted and panting she wasn't ready for a man who hadn't provided a safe word before, she knew if his cock entered her right now, she'd surely die; again…

Jess's face was pressed against the cool tiles, the water rushing down her backside, his tongue still deep inside of her luscious ass. She never knew such pleasure like this before, she felt every blood cell in her body heating up and exploding in ecstasy. She swooned and undulated against Kyle's face as he continued to moan and groan searching every inch of her soft pink crevasse. She felt his strong hands traveling up the back of her thighs, gripping her ass and spreading it wide, before squeezing it together, wrapping her soft lush cheeks around his face. Kyle's lips slowly inched upwards kissing the very top of her ass and sending chills radiating throughout the bottom of her spine, leaving the small of her back trembling under his lips. His hands slowly maneuvered up her back towards her neck, delicately holding her in position, she felt his engorged cock digging into the top of her ass, pressing deeply between her cheeks. His hands slowly traveled down her shoulders and each forearm to her wrists, holding them firmly into place as Jess's hands spread wide now gripping the tile, aching for his instructions.

"Spread those beautiful thighs of yours, and hold on tight." Kyle smiled wickedly as he whispered into her left ear, her right check pressed against the cold tiles, her eyes closed as she swooned waiting to see how he'd violate her body next. Making her crave the dark feeling of being hunted in the snow like a wild animal on their final night. She felt his cock dragging down her ass crack and teasing the gaping hole that waited for him, leaking sweet honey all over the floor of the shower, her scent floating on the hot steam brought out the beast inside. He swiveled the tip of his cock inside of her sweet pussy, before she could finish asking between gasps and moans;

"What's my safe word Master?"

Kyle plunged himself deep inside of her, groaning in pain and pleasure, never had he felt a pussy so tight, strangling the breath from him. With every inch that carved itself inside of her like a hot knife through chilled butter, his body shuddered. His legs started to give out and he gripped her waist towards him, pulling her up and slamming her down onto his cock.

"There is no safe word for you tonight, as of now you're in formal training."

Before she could say a word, her gasps echoed off the shower walls and he swiftly pulled out. Teasing the opening of her ass with her warm honey, he slowly stretched her ass open enough to slide deep within. Filling her up in one fluid motion, she cried out in pain and pleasure;

"Oh my God! You'll be the death of me."

Jess reached behind and gripped Kyle's hips; pulling him inside deeper and deeper, her ass was hungry, ravenous for his girth.

She wanted to feel him completely, to wonder and count between breaths and skipping heart beats if this was the moment of sheer ecstatic pleasure and pain that she would die on his glorious cock.

"Oh yes, Kyle" she gasped;

"Take it, break me in as your virgin whore, I've waited so long for this night." He kissed her neck, moaning and whispering into her ears;

"God you're *so fucking tight*."

Before he could control his tormented cock, he felt himself filling her up. His cock twitching so violently inside of her, she came hard, squirting hot juices all over his balls, sending her warmth dripping down the front of his thighs. Her body shuddered uncontrollably, as did Kyle's; still deep inside of her. They shook and moaned in satisfaction, he started to laugh as he held her close, embracing her body as it tried to breathe at a normal pace.

"That ass, is most certainly *mine.*"

Kyle kissed her on the cheek, down her neck and shoulders and slowly pulled out, moaning in unison their bodies trembled uncontrollably, his fingers interlacing with hers as they still gripped the tile firmly. Slowly his hands started to wash his cock, reaching forward he soothed the hot parts of her flesh with gentle caresses. Washing her felt surreal, he heard her moan and shudder, never knowing whether she was in pain or pleasure was exhilarating. She felt him rinse off, opening her eyes she watched him rinse her off under the rushing water, turning her around slowly and enveloping her in his broad shoulders and his protective embrace she swooned, feeling herself falling asleep as she stood in his arms. She heard his hands reach for the faucet, turning the water off, he reached over the top of the shower for her towel, delicately drying her off, he loved that intoxicated look in a woman's eyes. Never had he seen a face filled with such satiated glow.

"It astounds me that you continue to look more and more beautiful than I ever imagined a woman ever could. Each time my eyes fall upon your face, I'm left speechless and in awe of your mystery."

Kyle kissed each and every drop of water with his gentle caresses from Jess's body, the dark green towel wrapped around her body, she stood there watching as he reached for his and wrapped it around his waist. She couldn't help but moan aloud under her breath, he smiled and laughed realizing just how infatuated with him she'd always be. She started to blush realizing he'd heard her, she exited the shower hoping to hide her crimson stained cheeks, he walked up behind her hugging her and kissing her neck again;

"It's almost sunrise my pet, come lie with your Master until sleep visits us both long into the night." Kyle and Jess floated to bed on an overdose of pleasure endorphins.

He reached forward throwing back the sheets, Jess instantly crawled into bed and sighed contently at the level of comfort she felt swelling up inside of her. Kyle crawled in behind her, his body curling up around hers, his arms wrapped around her, kissing her face and whispering into her ear;

"Welcome home Jess, sweet dreams, I know for once in this life I'll finally sleep like the dead now that you're in my arms at long last."

Jess turned over and wrapped her arms around him, her face now resting on his chest, she could hear his heartbeat beating slowly, and the dark rhythmic chant of Darkeel could be felt writhing deep within the chambers of this dead man's heart.

"Sleep well my king, may flights of demons carry your soul to a dark and restful slumber."

His hands reaching for her face, caressing it gently, Kyle leaned forward kissing her once more on the forehead before falling into the deepest sleep he'd ever experienced before. For once in his life, everything was exactly how he wanted it to be, and the devil inside of his heart, felt at peace too, in ways he never knew would fulfil or satisfy him. Finally at long last he had a companion who craved the taste of iron on her lips as much as he craved the smell of it on his hunting knife. He couldn't wait to watch her kill for the first time, well at least the first time in front of anybody else's eyes. For there would be plenty of time to hunt but for now the twilight hours transformed into sunrise and *The Slaughterhouse Hills Hunter* was slumbering deep within the dark dream world of his mind, undisturbed, silent and for once; at one with the light.

Chapter 15:
VELVET CIRCUS

THE sounds of children laughing were heard in late afternoon, outside and down below. Adie was saying hilarious things to Derek, as he chased her across the fields, the former green grass now turning to golden hues tinged in browns. Jess awoke a bit startled, Kyle's arms still wrapped around her, his eyes cracking open;

"No need to be startled, it's just the children, James brought them back from the zoo an hour ago, sounds like they had a lot of fun."

As he continued his hands waved and effortlessly the curtains opened in the bathroom lighting up the room just enough to see his smiling face.

"How did you sleep last night my pet?" He looked deep into her eyes waiting for response;

"Magnificently, I don't think I moved once the entire time." Jess suddenly realizing her place in his bed;

"Should I sneak out through the tunnel and back into my room? I wouldn't want the children wondering where I've been all day." Kyle laughed and smiled;

"James informed them that you'd be sick today and probably wouldn't be down until late tonight for a private supper to recuperate alone to avoid getting the rest of the house sick, in other words it's been taken care of." With that sentence she felt herself melt back into his soothing embrace;

"Now that's much better isn't it?" Kyle continued smiling;

"Oh I could get used to this, I'll never want to leave these sheets if you keep spoiling me this way."

Jess leaning forward kissing Kyle on the lips, she felt the need to satisfy him, and to shudder with pleasure all over his gorgeous body, ever since she arrived she wanted to ride him, to straddle his cock and to impale herself on every inch of his thick, warm shaft.

"Take what you want, or have you already forgotten I can read you like a book that I wrote the very pages too?" Jess smiled as the hunger inside of her grew, the darkness started to rise within him.

"Show me why writhing little whores call you Mistress Bella."

Kyle sat back, his cock rock hard, his arms resting underneath his head like a stoic God in Greek literature. Her very own Dionysus, beckoning the whore inside of her to give way to her urgent need for wine and ecstasy. Without hesitation she licked her lips and crawled on top of him, straddling his hard cock she slowly licked her lips, tormenting him into a painful state of erection. Her hands slowly reaching underneath her ass and teasing his tip on the soaking wet clit or her that throbbed incessantly, leaving her g-spot pounding, filling with liquid fire, her left hand reaching forth and bracing herself on his chest. She plunged herself down on top of him, cumming hard already and buckling wildly on top of his dick, in a possessed undulation that left him groaning at the sheer strength and utter intensity of her hot loins.

"You always wanted a front row seat to a three ring circus, where the show is made entirely for you? Let me take you there tonight. I'll be your mistress of ceremonies, guiding you to the ultimate fantasy world with every dream you've ever dreamt of from dark to passionate, satiated in one mind shattering orgasm."

Every word was intensely phrased while she stared deep into his eyes, his hands no longer able to stay in their god like restful state, he was overwhelmed with her power, her mind opened and he saw every dark memory in her lifetime. Each victim that begged her after years of caging and confinement to please kill them, release them from this incessant pleasure torture, not one more orgasm would they endure without taking their own life. A true succubus she always broke them into pieces, leaving their former selves obliterated by their newfound addiction to release. Transforming even the most delicate of flowers into ravenous harpies clawing and feasting on sin in ways that would horrify even the darkest of souls on this earth, *all except one.*

Her tits bounced gloriously as her hips bucked wildly her body stiffened and leaned back, she looked like she was riding a serpentine God, Kyle's voice was booming, the sounds of his ecstasy echoing off the walls of this sound proofed bedroom paradise.

"Oh my fucking hell, squeezing every last drop…" he groaned in bliss, "out of me will you?!"

With that final phrase he heard his voice falter and lose itself in her screams and moans of siren ecstasy. Her body swooned and gripping his chest hard she fell forward, her body throwing her from his cock and leaving her body jerking and shuddering while she giggled in ecstasy. His hands reached forward his fingers finding her sweet cunt and fucking it slowly, then roughly, so hard she thought she'd black out. Her voice screamed and her body continued to move against the volition of her very will. A fountain of juices exploded forth from her pussy, soaking Kyle's chest, cock and face. As her legs trembled and her toes curled her nipples hard, her long locks of red curls fell over the side of the bed as she tried to catch her breath.

"You will be the death of me." Kyle said out of breath and gasping for the normal rhythm to return, Jess laughed,

"You took the words right from between my lips." Smiling wickedly she gently caressed her pussy in front of him and watched as the bath tub turned on, Kyle said glowing;

"Join me." Jess swiftly responded "Yes, of course." Kyle's eyes glowed and his lips parted once more;

"That wasn't a question." He started laughing wickedly,

"I can't wait to have more fun with you. Later of course, the night belongs to us."

After a long soak together in the bathtub, limbs entwined, Jess found herself kissing him goodbye one more time passionately before sneaking across the hallway to her own bedroom, where she planned to have soup, crackers and soda sent up to appear as sick as she was; to the children at least. Keeping up appearances in such a fragile circumstance was of utmost importance to her, especially if she was going to figure out how to release Sara, to let her wild, untamable soul finally roam free across the hills of Burnett Manor and ultimately unbeknownst to Jess, her ill-fated destiny.

Chapter 16:
CHERISHED PENUMBRA

AS Jess lied back on her luxurious bed, she felt the panging in her chest, the beating of her heart, shrouded in guilt wondering if her precious Sara was alive, well, or even okay. She imagined her state of being to be ravenous, filled with anger, she knew her lust for blood and revenge, especially when it came to keeping her from the one being in this entire world; that ever had her eating out of the palm of her hand. The layers of somber sadness began to fill Jess with a void so deep it pained her to feel happiness, even though this is always where she truly wanted to be. She just never realized it until now. Kyle was everything she'd ever longed for in life, a man who could keep her, would keep her and would capture her if she ever tried to escape. The ultimate fetish for any victim that pined for a dark being that inflicted ownership to the deepest layers of her deviant mind. She knew that night when she met Sara that her life would never again be the same, a parting of the ways from her morals, ethics and very soul, to taste a forbidden piece of fruit that beguiled her in beauty the moment her eyes fell upon her glowing face.

Before her mind could wander too quickly she heard a knock at the door, the sound echoed from a height that revealed just who was knocking at her chamber door.

"Do you think she's awake? Alive?" Adie said with exaggerated terror, making ridiculous faces at her brother Derek,

"I don't know I guess we'll find out."

He knocked louder hoping to hear a response but moments later Jess smiled and played dead, knowing their curiosity would get the best of them. The door slowly creaked and cracked open, she heard the softest footsteps heading towards her bed, she did her best to appear as if she wasn't breathing anymore, waiting for them to inch their way closer in the darkness of the room.

"I don't know if we should be in here." Adie whispered in apprehension, her brother brave kept walking forward wondering if there was still life in this body that lied frozen on the bed, he could barely make out the silhouette of her form before Jess instantly leaped from the bed grabbing Adie and tossing her to the bed with her as she fell;

"Intruder alert! It's an ambush!" screaming wildly Derek ran from the room as Adie's voice continued to carry down the hallway to Kyle's door, instantly he burst from behind it and ran towards the sound of his daughter's terrified voice, to suddenly hear it transform into hysterical giggles;

"Oh no! Not that, anything but that!" Adie laughed uncontrollably as Jess continued to tickle her.

"That'll teach you to adventure into the unknown without permission," she exclaimed laughing in unison waiting for Derek to return and hesitantly enter the room wondering what would happen next.

"How are you feeling?" He inquired.

"Mostly exhausted, but after this delicious soup that chef sent up, I'll be back to my usual self again by this evening, I assure you." Jess smiled looking up at Kyle, he then turned towards Derek and Adie and reinstated the by-laws of Burnett Manor.

"You know you're not allowed in anyone's room without permission, next time you'll be punished, you're lucky Jess isn't alarmed by your intrusion, or we'd be having an entirely different conversation right now." Derek chimed in;

"Sorry Dad, it won't happen again."

Kyle looked down into his eyes with firm guidance.

"Good." He continued;

"Now then, I believe there was some sort of creature attacking your sister?" before she could run he grabbed her from the bed and started tickling Adie, she screamed bloody murder at the top of her lungs. Derek laughed at his sisters misfortune, Jess ensured he never felt left out, she reached forward grabbing him and tickling him to the floor beside his sister;

"Thought you could get away with it, didn't you, well not this time!" She continued to tickle Kyle's son, as he watched her laughing and smiling he realized he'd never seen that look in her eye before. She was the missing puzzle piece he'd always been searching for in life, and now she was finally home.

Chapter 17:

SEDUCTIVE INTERLUDE

AS dusk turned to night fall, the smells of delicious meals being finely crafted for each family member's unique palate could be smelled throughout the entire first floor of the house. The children continued to play upstairs in their day room as well as downstairs below searching through movies to watch that night after dinner upstairs before bed. Jess wandered around the very first room she entered just over a week ago, the private kitchenette that nobody ever seemed to use. She found herself sitting down on the barstool, wondering just where the hidden eyes that were lurking in every corner were watching from in this very moment. She bit her lip wondering when he'd be down from his office for dinner.

Kyle was in his private chambers, deep within the bowels of Burnett Manor. He could feel her arousal pulling at him, gently clawing and biting at him like a playful feline who wanted trouble but only as much as they could take. His fingers delicately fondled through the layers of newspaper depicting his career as a tormented monster, stalking the night in the bitter cold, slaughtering naked women like sheep during the harvest season. He felt his left wrist tingle with warmth, it felt just like her in those moments when she couldn't help but swoon in his arms. Intuitively reaching his hand forward and unlocking the cabinet in his desk, he watched her in the kitchen again, reminded of the moment he first fell for her, swiftly and without regret. He'd never been so calm, collected and calculated in matters of the heart, but just as Jess pined for a taste of Sara that night in the bar ages ago now it seemed. Kyle couldn't help but to try to get his fill of this satiating creature, wanting her just as viscerally as he did the moment James sat her on that barstool as she trembled waiting to meet her new boss for the very first time.

Jess peered towards the direction of a vase in the corner, she knew he was watching her from there, her nipples instantly hardened, pressing violently against her bra, dragging the delicate pink beads towards the brink of honey soaked lingerie. She slowly let her hair down, gently touching her neck and dragging fingertips down her neck to her décolleté,

"I need you."

She mouthed to the camera, his dark focus turned towards relished delight, as he smiled and laughed under his breath appeased by her constant want of him he said aloud;

"After dinner my pet, first we feast."

She continued to drag her nails down around and under her breasts. Beneath his view under the counter, she bit her lip, smiling, he knew she was teasing her soft red curls, before suddenly plunging her lips around her delicate fingers, savoring every sweet drop that she had to taste. Winking at him and giggling wickedly, she knew what she was doing to him, she always knew, nothing made her happier than to torment one who could tear her to pieces in a single possession of carnality.

"You fucking whore, I'm going to have to train you faster than I expected."

Kyle turned off the television, locking up the cabinet in his desk, rolling the top of his secretary down before locking it completely. He never left anything to chance, it's the only reason why Kyle never, failed at anything in life, ever. He was always prepared, with the foresight of Nostradamus he made his way out and down below towards the kitchen where Jess was sitting now, tempting him out of his dark cave and into the warm light of tonight's escapades.

Before she could finish pinning her red curls back into place on top of her head she realized she felt his energy, he was standing right behind her, towering over her, she suddenly felt his lips mere inches away from her neck;

"Provoking the hunger of a killer is such a dangerous game to play my wanton whore, next time you initiate such hunger inside me, I'll keep you chained to the wall downstairs next to your beloved for an entire week." The thought made her shudder and fall back into his strong form.

"Mmm, you sure make it difficult not to provoke you in such a manner my Lord, but I'll do my best to restrain these incessant urges that I find myself intoxicated by, in your presence."

Jess blushing, knowing her cockiness would only lead to blood stained cheeks later when he had the chance to get ahold of her in the way he desired most. Firmly without mercy, until he was finished and satisfied beyond his fill.

"I look forward to hearing more about the rest of your treasured possessions, there's still nine names that elude me." Kyle leaned down kissing her on the forehead,

"Later my darling, dinner with the children first and as soon as they're settled in watching a movie, we'll retire to the formal dining room together and all of the questions you seek will finally be answered."

He brushed the hair from her face and smiled, lovingly keeping his gaze connected to hers, he felt at peace, after years of masquerading as a man who wanted it all, he finally possessed it.

Chapter 18:
GRITTY ORIGINS

DINNER was served precisely at seven o'clock. Never late not even for a moment, the formal dining room was set and ready for the family to enjoy. The children ran to their favorite places, in the middle of the long table, leaving Kyle at his usual place at the head of the table, with Jess just to his right. Adie sat next to her father and Derek sat a few spaces down seemingly by himself. The food was hot, each plate offering exactly what they wanted. Jess never had a life so easy, effortless; it provided such space inside of her to daydream, fantasize and find curiosity that just wouldn't ease in the mind of this insatiable feline. She always wanted to know more about everything in life, to be intoxicated with wisdom and personal journeys was all she ever wanted to keep as her own. The way others hoarded money and possessions, Jess found solace in stories and dark creatures of the night.

"May I ask you a question about your passion for film Kyle?" Jess inquired as they all devoured their meals accordingly;

"Yes of course, as I've mentioned to you before I'm an open book." He smirked and she smiled;

"What created such a path in life? So many love film but very rarely do they take that passion and transform it into something real or tangible. Something one can touch and experience time and time again." Derek chimed in;

"They always start with the difficult questions first" as he looked at his father, Kyle smiled and sighed in ambiguity.

"I did promise to share more of my life even, though the origins are bleak it does paint a broader picture as to who I am today." Jess responded;

"I never desire to bring discomfort to you or the children, if you'd like we can save that for another time?" she smiled and continued to feast,

"No, it's fine, origin stories aren't supposed to be beautiful, at least not for superheroes." Kyle continued;

"I was one of nine, the second to youngest in the family, I wasn't really paid much attention too, due to poverty and very little resources, life wasn't easy, and it was a struggle just to endure it every day. My step father owned a video store, and that is where I found my solace, my love of film, books, and the art of storytelling." Jess smiled;

"Wow, the second to youngest in a family of.... nearly a dozen... What a challenging way to navigate the world at such a young age. I understand all too well, where wisdom is often received as pain at an early age, that road in life is less traveled and never easy." She smiled appreciative of his honesty,

"Thank you for providing a glimpse into your magnificent world, to know that you've created so much from such humble beginnings, it's incredibly inspiring."

Jess waited and watched as the children continued to eat, after such a long day of playing wicked games, they weren't much up for speaking, just enjoying the conversation shared between their new governess and their father, realizing that this was the first time in years that this giant mansion felt anything like a home.

"What about you Jess? Where did such an intriguing woman come from?" Kyle prodded curiously, he smiled intent on allowing her to understand the feeling of being put on the spot in what felt like a spotlight to a man with so many dark secrets.

"I was an only child of two adult children. To capture the type of childhood I had all one would need do is read *Matilda by Roald Dahl.* A life lived entirely alone, teaching myself the things in life that most had others to teach them in kind, patient and generous ways. I have to admit I often dreamed of better ways to arrive and grow in this world in my youth, but in spite of it all I embrace the brilliant mind that I possess now from such hardships in life. The worst experiences in life can either make us or break us if we allow it too, I've always been a fan of rebirth stories. It's why I strive to be one, to inspire others to reach far beyond their wildest dreams."

Kyle smiled and Adie perked up;

"*Matilda* is one of my favorite books, did you have a *Miss Honey* too?" Jess smiled,

"I was fortunate enough in life to have many beautiful people fill that position for me, I wouldn't change it for the world, it's what provided courage within me to explore and is ultimately why I'm here eating dinner with you tonight."

Kyle was in a serene state of awe, watching his concubine nurture, love and foster growth and wonder into the heart and soul of his youngest daughter brought fulfillment to the deepest parts of his being.

Derek usually somber, detached and doing his best to stay away from the intimate settings of family life, found himself smiling, and even moving closer, sitting next to his sister to be a part of this conversation. It was the first time since their mother mysteriously vanished, never to be seen again, that his children were loved, engaged both lively and curious to know more about their father and this new woman in all of their lives. Before they knew it plates were empty and glasses were in need of refilling.

"How about we go upstairs to your wing tonight and relax on the couch, watch a movie and get ready for bed?" He asked his children waiting for reply. Both mouths still full and chewing, but smiling in affirmation at the wonderful idea, and ultimate way to ease into the night.

"Whose turn is it this time Dad?" Derek asked eagerly waiting for his response.

"Jess was added to the rotation last time, and I believe Adie gave up her turn for her, so it's her choice tonight."

As she heard the news her eyes grew two sizes and the giggles started. She did her best to finish the meal before fleeing to the movie theater library and searching through the films as they continued to roll by. Derek ran after her;

"Hey wait for me! I have to reach it for you." He laughed and started to wander out of the formal dining room behind her.

"Set up the room, and text me when you're both ready, don't forget your snacks if you want any." Kyle told his son before he vanished into the hallway.

"Yes Dad." Derek yelled back before running after his sister.

"It'll only be twenty minutes before both of them are passed out on the couch, asleep to the movie Adie chose. After that we'll return here and I'll introduce you to the rest of my treasured possessions. To ensure their formal training isn't compromised, you'll have to watch them from closed circuit television screen. As I usually do."

Kyle snapped his fingers and the gorgeous ornate oil painting that rested above his head on the wall, started to move, the panel sliding sideways into what appeared to be the frame of the wall itself;

"As I've said before, I am always watching."

His eyebrow raised as she watched, twelve screens, all but one filled with women in precarious situations, being tortured within an inch of their lives, the final screen still empty, just a cage, nobody inside of it, just waiting, haunting Jess deep down to the core. Was this cage for her? Would this be her final resting place if she freed Sara from her proverbial bondage? Each time she felt that answers would swiftly arrive, she realized that she was possessed with even more questions that she had previously before.

His world was an endless mystery, one she knew would consume her before she knew it. She just didn't realize how very little time she actually had left. As this feeling of dread filled her soul, she watched the panel slide back into place, Kyle reached for her hand;

"It's time my darling, we'll be back here again before you know it." With an ascending gesture to rise, she floated up and wandered towards the door of the dining room.

"I feel so naked around you, always watching with your penetrating eyes." Jess said smiling,

"You are eternally naked in my presence, exposed completely mind, body and soul. Never forget that, it will be your undoing." Kyle gripped her shoulders firmly, ensuring Jess got the message;

"Understood Sir." Her mind melded with his, realizing that she was destined for death if she ever put thought to action towards setting Sara free, how was she able to endure this much longer? Being torn between two worlds was never her cup of tea, in fact it felt like scalding water thrown in her face and scorching down her melting thighs. There had to be a way around this, somehow some inconceivable way, she had to convince him to release Sara to her, before it was too late.

Chapter 19:
DREADFUL DESCENT

JESS followed Kyle upstairs. It felt like such a complete head change from the floors below, within the dark inner workings of Burnett Manor. As they ascended she felt herself swooning in a dreamlike state, he reached back for her hand;

"I'm sure you won't mind the little addition to your glass tonight, can't risk you running off before your formal training is concluded."

Kyle smiled wickedly she felt his lips curl in that dark debilitating way that left her frozen in his touch.

"The only question I still have is how did you find out my secret? Even Sara doesn't know the full details…"

As the atropine penetrated deep into her blood stream she felt her eyes dilate, taking as much crystal reflecting light that she could as she wandered upstairs.

"Later my pet, now we have a movie to watch." Kyle watched her slowly rise to the final step, now standing beside him a bit tipsy, his hands reaching forward and drawing her slowly towards him.

"I see the children have started without us, a good sign."

The door slowly opened without a touch, Kyle's powerful mind left it floating silently on a breeze without notice or disturbance. The television continued to play quite loudly but the children were already fast asleep. Adie curled up in the corner her face smooshed into the cracks of her arms, her head still facing the general direction of the TV as if she did her best to stay awake to no avail. Derek was reclined in the center of the couch, his back towards the entrance, his head resting gently on the back of it, his eyes closed, and breath heavy, he fell swiftly into a deep sleep.

Leaning forward she reached for an afghan that was on the back of the couch, gently kissing Kyle's son on the top of the head she covered him up and wandered to the back of the couch where Adie was now sleeping sound. She noticed she was curled up like a puppy, probably cold but not enough to wake her, not just yet at least. Searching around, her eyes caught Kyle's hand gesturing towards the blanket now lying over a rocking chair in the corner of the room. Jess leaned forward and brushed the hair from Adie's cheeks, "Sweet dreams."

Kissing her on the cheek she wrapped the blanket around her and watched her entire body relax and ease into comfort. Jess walked back to Kyle and instantly embraced him;

"You needn't use any method or mean to keep me here, your children are doing that entirely on their own."

A tear formed in her eyes, she quickly tried to hide her face, Kyle's arms were wrapped around her he grabbed for her face and gently pulled her gaze towards him.

"You never have to hide your pain, *I know.*"

He showed the array of memories that she thought she'd hidden even from herself, the night Sara found her leaving the bar, a man in the alley reached forward in the dark plunging a knife deep into Jess's stomach, he saw from her point of view the blood pouring forth to stain the brilliant white snow, blood red, that's when she came outside, with a single word an entire band of men surrounded him and beat him to death right before Jess's trembling eyes. Sara leaned forward and looked inside her coat, checking to see how bad the bleeding was, and that's when she saw it, a badge from a private government agency, she knew if they saw this that the blood loss would be the least of Jess's problems.

She tore it from her belt and wiped the blood off as quickly as she could. Sara stood up in her boots and fur coat and walked towards the man now convulsing on the ground covered in his own blood. She reached down into what appeared to be his coat pocket and pulled the badge from her gloved hands and yelled at her men in Romanian. Before she could finish her sentence the man was dragged off screaming, and Jess watched the snow fall above, each flake falling to her cheek.

"Don't worry, I'm here, you're safe with me." Sara's voice was the last thing she heard before it faded to black. Jess tried to hold back her tears but they poured freely from her face in front of Kyle's eyes, now sobbing, no pain expelled just silent tears as her mind replayed that nearly fatal night. Where she fell for a woman who saved her life when she should've executed her for self-preservation. She woke in the hospital to the sounds of doctors telling her bluntly in English, that she lost the child and would never carry one again. The same tears fell from her face then as they did this very night.

Sara held her hand firmly, "Don't listen to them, they told me I'd die the last time I was in this dreadful fucking place, and where am I now? Still alive." Sara kept brushing the hair from Jess's face, softly smiling;

"The color has returned to your face, you were awfully pale in the snow, I'm glad we got you here in time." Jess looked deep into her eyes;

"You know I'm here to find you, why did you save my life?" Sara smiled,

"What can I say, I've always been a sucker for red heads, I couldn't think straight after you walked into the bar tonight. I usually prefer men, but there is something otherworldly about *you*, that I long to understand." Jess smiled wickedly knowing she had her right where she wanted her;

"Kiss me..." Sara laughed Jess leaned forward looking deep into her eyes, captivating her with her intoxicating gaze, Sara leaned forward her heart racing, her lips parting, Jess leaned in once more;

"Kiss me, or I'll die."

In that moment their lips touched and she was transported back into Kyle's arms. Her tears soaking his sweater, his lips kissing away the pain, soaking up every tear that now stained her delicate cheeks.

"I'm sorry that you feel so exposed tonight, but there's parts of you that have a way of hiding, not only from myself, but most importantly, from you."

He started to walk her out of the children's day room, gently the door glided shut behind them, not waking the two sleeping on the other side.

"If you'd like some time to decompress before we meet downstairs, I completely understand."

Kyle held her close in the hallway right in front of her door, brushing the hair from the front of her face and kissing her forehead.

"I know what it means to lose a child, the pain cannot be healed, but over time it can be carried." Jess smiled,

"The worst part is I didn't even know I was pregnant, I was always told it was impossible. One night with an agent I ran into on a mission and my entire life was changed, and changed again the night I met her." He leaned forward holding her face,

"To see you with my children, to watch you nurture them, to see you heal, and to observe as you help each one of them as they grow, you can still be a mother, Jess, I never imagined that you'd fit right into my world, in every conceivable and inconceivable way." He leaned in and whispered into her ear;

"You're meant to be here, I always dreamed of you, but never knew you could possibly exist, from your hair that flows like waves of fire, to your melodic laugh. Everything I've ever wanted is inside of you, and it constantly spills forth from you effortlessly. All the good that still exists in the world, showered upon each of my most treasured possessions, every moment since you've been here, this entire realm has awakened to a twilight with promise for tomorrow." He continued,

"You've given me reasons to breathe, stretch my limbs and indulge in the beauty of life. I hope you realize just how essential you are here, this house is just a house without you, but with you, it feels like home."

His face pulled back and he held her gaze. Lovingly, he leaned down and her arms wrapped around his shoulders. She kissed him with every bit of golden twilight that existed in her soul. He felt warm and full, the way a victim feels after being left out in the cold, bleeding to be brought inside with a fresh transfusion. She embodied every aspect of his life that was always prone to suffer. In the sweetest taste of her lips, she swooned and moaned softly feeling herself floating in an ocean of his darkness, his carnality, his passion and ferocity. She'd never felt more safe in all of her lives, even though his strong hands could strangle the light and life right out of her in a single fatal moment. Her pain formed into mischief and she smiled deviously into his eyes;

"You mentioned *treasured possessions*... I'd love to view the entirety of your Masterpiece Sir." Jess's eyes sparkled;

"Follow me." He walked across the hallway past the stairs Jess was intrigued;

"I said follow me, so *curious*." Kyle said, instantly her face flushed red and she bit her lip in anticipation. He wandered towards a panel near the bookshelf and instantly a wall moved back and to the side;

"This way and hurry before the wall shuts, it's only timed for one body at a time." She leaped into the corridor behind him and the wall swiftly locked into place behind them.

"Where are we going?" Jess inquired once more.

Instantly Kyle grabbed her and threw her against the wall firmly, his hands dragging all over her ass, he reared his strong, wide hands back and spanked her severely. Each blow came down harder than the other and Jess screamed under her breath, keeping the noise within her chest and never letting it escape her lips. Her hands instinctively above her head, on the wall, praying for the moment his hands would stop, soothe each ass cheek that was now a blaze in a fire of rage, when he watched her knees give out from beneath her, he caught her swiftly with his freehand and whispered into her ear;

"Perhaps I didn't speak *clearly* enough, I didn't say ask a million questions, I said to *follow me*." Kyle laughed,

"Mmmm, I can feel your nerves shaking, such a low tolerance for pain, it's going to be such a thrill breaking you in."

Jess instantly moaned in fear, in want of asking yet another question. She quickly realized her anxious nature would get her even more lashings as she bit into her lip, drawing blood that rushed down the outside of her mouth and down her chin, dripping onto her soft milky breasts. Kyle noticed this wound in the soft light of candelabra. He could smell the iron in the air;

"Let me taste you my child, Mmm so sweet. Even your blood tastes like forbidden fruit, though nothing rivals that pussy...nor...that ass." Kyle watched her eyes get big and glow, before her cheeks flushed crimson.

"Such an enigmatic woman, for one with your experiences in life, to still *blush*, to put it lightly, it's divine."

Her blood stained his face, yet he left it there to dry.

"Now let's try this again, *Follow Me.*"

Kyle descended towards the first floor down the tunnel path, knowing exactly how many steps it would take to reach the level where the private entrance to the formal dining room was.

Jess was enamored with the endless complexities of this manor home, it seemed even more endless on the inside than it did on every single one of the public floors combined. As they made their way below she watched him reach for a stone in the wall that had the etchings of a golden goblet resembling the Holy Grail. His fingers traced the outline of the symbol the wall moved and out they walked into the formal dining room. From the wall in the back, completely bare, it now made sense why no art was ever on this massive space. Jess exited the wall quickly watching it lock behind her;

"Wow." Kyle smiled, "Now that you know how swiftly I get around, did someone mention *treasured possessions?*"

Chapter 20:
TREASURED POSSESSIONS

JESS walked towards the table, to her usual spot, Kyle sat on his throne. Watching his fingers she noticed the door shut gently behind them, locking firmly into place.

"Always keeping me on a short leash, I like that in a man."

Instantly he laughed and she watched him smile as the panel on the beautiful art behind him, slowly moved to the side again. Revealing twelve screens, each one within, containing a caged woman in various stages of torture. It was hard to see her beloved still restrained to a crucifix; though she had to peruse more closely, she was consistently quite taken by Sara's gorgeous body. Her full breasts that hung pertly in the air, her nipples hard, she was smiling; she noticed that an IV was administered into her left arm, firmly taped into place. Jess continued smiling and examining her body seeing how plump and swollen her pussy was, she knew Sara was more at home here than she'd ever been anywhere else on this earth. She peered closer;

"Ooo, such a sticky little whore, you always were my absolute favorite creature to torture."

A Cheshire cat like grin formed across her face generously, she started tracing her fingers hungrily down her torso, Sara moved in bliss as if she felt her very fingertips on her hot aching flesh.

"Speaking of torture the images I'm seeing of you two together right now pulled from your beautiful mind leaves me speechless."

Kyle leaned back in his chair, the regal disposition of a glorious monarch;

"I couldn't imagine watching the live show."

He smiled catching Jess's eyes instantly her response came;

"Perhaps you won't have too." Her hips subtly swayed from side to side as her free hand started invading her soft warm lips, parting them slowly and teasing her lip ring she continued;

"If you think I'm sweet, you should taste us together."

She winked at Kyle and returned her gaze to the screen, still playing with Sara's energy.

"Mmm, still responding to my touch, after all this time, such a devoted slave."

Jess continued to tease her body on the screen, tapping into her energy frequency and electrocuting her nipples and clit from afar;

"Do you think she'd let me set foot near her after over a year of torture under my cruel hands?"

Kyle replied with dark wisdom that revealed the ultimate ending to a love story that was forged in blood ages ago deep in the Carpathian Mountains.

"If I wasn't around, she'd do her best to tear you apart limb from limb, *but* with me around to keep her calm, sedated and in line…who's to say how well she can adapt to even the most drastic of circumstances? She probably thinks you've killed me, but then again the way her body moves for her Mistress tells me she knows I'm still, *very much alive.*"

Jess demonstrated her powers over Sara teasing the energies and magnetically pulling pleasure to parts of her blood that caused her body to quake.

"Oh fuck Mistress, I feel you, coursing in my blood, tempting my pussy to squirt hot juices for you, my tits to leak sweet milk, I knew you'd be too good for him to destroy. Oh Mistress."

Sara's head swooned back and her tits formed beads of milk as her thighs shined down to her knees in her sweet, sticky juices. She soon fell fast asleep, whatever it was in the IV was making her heal swiftly but sedated her so deeply that she barely moved even as the rest of the dungeon was filled with pain, torture and shuddered screams.

"Master? May I implore as to what is inside that IV?" Kyle laughed;

"Her lacerations were too deep, she was going to get an infection, which usually I would've used to my advantage to subdue her into submission. However after recalling that she was your entire world here, and now that you are now my entire world. I felt that keeping you two close would help to make this complicated transition, easier." He continued;

"The antibiotics will accelerate her healing process and keep her alive, once you've finished your formal training she'll be waiting for you."

As the epiphany hit with full force, she realized now who that first empty cage was waiting for downstairs below, in the very pits of hell, the dark dungeon of *The Slaughterhouse Hills Hunter*. Jess looked over towards Kyle;

"That empty cage… is for me."

As his eyebrow raised in affirmation she suddenly felt sheer terror penetrating to the deepest parts of her body. The screens continued to show ten strange women being tortured to the very last breath of their life, and now Sara resting serenely, sleeping deeper than she had in nearly a year.

"Yes, and I take great care of those I value, which is why *Untamable Sara* is still alive tonight, she means the world to you, and now she means the world to me." Jess smiled her eyes sparkling, glowing bright.

"When do we get started?"

Jess was eager to find herself reborn in the world of Darkeel. His laughter dark and satisfied, echoed throughout the formal dining room.

"Fucking lord, you're perfect for me." He smiled;

"If only the rest downstairs were as eager to serve as you are, they wouldn't be in cages now, and they too would be upstairs roaming free."

With a smile and a nod of satisfaction he beckoned Jess to the table, she walked towards him and spread her thighs across his lap, and he pulled her close kissing her firmly and pulling her back by her hair. Her body arched, her breasts in his face, she felt his beard brushing against her torso, his lips exploring her body and kissing every curve as he traveled towards her neck. His strong hands holding the small of her back, gripping her ass and gently holding her shoulder blades watching her buck in ecstasy under his precise touch.

"First I'll introduce you to my treasured possessions, then we'll plan for this grueling phase in your evolution. Six weeks should be plenty of time to prepare, and to form a backstory as to why you'll be on extended business vacation for me, even though the kids will be here without you in the meantime."

His head floated from side to side, waiting to find the perfect formula to execute over the coming weeks.

"Introduce me to your girls, Master I want to know everything that your brilliant mind has created in your world."

Jess held his face closely, he gripped her ass and picked her up, placing her on the table and smiling pleased with her curiosity. He stood and walked towards the giant panel of twelve closed circuit television screens and initiated a formal introduction.

He pressed on a button near the screens and watched as the girl in cage number two, jumped. She was still being sprayed with water and her face was covered in streaks of long golden blonde hair. She shivered as her skin turned blue and her body jerked from the biting cold. Her blue lips formed and chattered violently as the chains holding her above kept her swaying with the motions of the water that kept spraying her body in every direction.

His modulated voice came over the loud speaker and boomed;

"What is your name?" Kyle's voice transformed into the cruel cadenced tongue of Darkeel's. The girls eyes were covered in layers of hair, she did her best to form the words even though her body was failing her in this moment.

"Frrr…ossss..t Bi….te." she exclaimed as articulately as she could muster. He pressed the button again;

"What is your purpose in this world?" Kyle's voice echoed into her chamber room.

"To serve you as prey on cold winter nights." She started to cry and her tears froze as they fell to her cheek.

"Mmm she's almost ready, and to think we still have nine months before hunting season arrives." Jess implored,

"How long has she been here? I'm guessing a few weeks?" Kyle forgetting for a moment who she was and the power of her deductions skills;

"Very good Jess, Impressive. She arrived just a week before you got here, though the way she arrived wasn't entirely the same."

He smiled and she saw his mind, the way he stalked this girl in the cold of night, watching her walk slowly home on back roads in haunting darkness, dressed entirely too impractical for the weather. She watched as he asked her if she wanted a ride home, she declined stating she'd always liked the cold. Before she could continue to deny his advances she felt herself fall down and the entire world fade to black. She'd been hit with a small dart in the neck, tranquilizer with just enough to knock her out, nothing more, nothing less. She watched as the girl awoke from her point of view in this torture chamber down below, never quite knowing who brought her here or how exactly she was going to make it out alive. Jess nodded in an affirming manner.

"I realized that you never quite follow a pattern, what causes you to vary your methods?" She was intrigued by the gentleness of this hunt, compared to the vicious night terror that she saw in Holly's demise just nights prior.

"She was kind, so I showed her a final gesture of kindness." He revealed a part of the puzzle to his soul and his dark carnal legacy that now resonated deeply in the heart of his dark and beloved companion.

He continued his display of pride as he shared with Jess his deepest darkest secrets. Kyle continued revealing to her fully what it was like to live inside his nebulous mind. He took a step towards the second monitor, within lied yet another cage where treasured possession number three was waiting. Strapped to an inclined wall of steel and clipped all over her entire body were the painful alligator clips that Mistress Bella was inclined to use towards her unruly slaves that required additional pain to incentivize the ideal of submission as their way of life.

She saw as the girl grimaced her mouth eventually opening to a shrieking sound of pain, her body jolted by the electricity that Kyle had coursing through her veins in a sequence of rhythmic patterns that caused any intuitive to lose their mind in a mad existence of electrical shocks that could never be estimated to arrive at any consistent time. Jess looked curiously at the brunette who was being shaken, rattled and moved into contorted positions along this metal board, her eyebrows furrowed in confusion, Kyle waited to see Jess' ruby red lips form into another curious question;

"Does that build up her endurance for arrows? I'd imagine the pain to be quite similar when one is running for their life in the cold bite of night."

His look of concern transformed to a look of sheer pride;

"How well you know the limitations and strengths of the human body, that is the precise reason why I've conditioned her this way, she'll be able to keep running even when she's wearing a fresh set of angel wings that I've provided for her. They say that flying is the most exhilarating experience in life for those of us meant to walk on the ground, which is why I've given her the name *Dove*."

As she heard her name she saw images flooding her mind of being stalked in the autumn season, seeing the leaves change watching them fall to the earth. No snow on the ground this time, no, just a girl naked. Screaming, tearing through the woods as fast as she can, being hit between tree lines again and again until her entire body was trembling covered in arrows that appeared like wings in the golden hour of sunrise. With one fatal shot hurtling towards her the sight of her leaping off that cliff where Holly tried to flee was breathtaking, she knew that down below awaited her ultimate demise, yet she embraced it willingly to escape being recaptured by the only predator in the woods that any creature ever had to fear, *The Slaughterhouse Hills Hunter* was still alive and well.

"By September she'll be ready for the kill…" Jess trailed off aloud, Kyle wandered towards her kissing her and reaching for her face in surprise;
"There's so much I don't know about you yet, you never told me

you were a hunter." Jess smiled kissing his hand affectionately;

"We have a lifetime, to share such secrets with one another my King."

She looked deeply into his eyes, and relished in this feeling of finally being understood in this world, for her darkness and her light, all balance ever sought was experienced in this single exchange between dark lovers in the night. Sharing a secret and kindred passion of torture, pleasure and the most dangerous game alive.

Kyle walked back to the wall of monitors, a petite but curvaceous woman with dark skin, as black as night appeared. Her entire body was suspended in the air, nude and conflicted by the darkness that she now lived in for over a year. Her hearing was heightened as well as her sense of touch, even the smallest gust of wind from an old drafty house such as this startled her to her very core. She couldn't differentiate any longer between touch, smell and sound, an overwhelming existence fueled by internal hallucinations was all she experienced any more. Her legs and arms were locked into what appeared to be cast like metal casings. Her pussy was exposed and stuffed with a thick, engorged dildo that was attached to a metal box. Jess recognized this beautiful mechanism, it was what she used on Sara for weeks before she decided she no longer desired men, only women that could yield a cock better than she ever imagined.

The slow pumps of the machine in and out of her dripping cunt provided a thick viscous fluid to pump forth from this woman's deliciously dark, supple pussy. She watched as the woman swooned again, moaning with her head back, her eyes still closed, her long hair pulled back into a low pony tail, keeping her face exposed to all the elements down below.

Jess watched as she reached her face towards the left, to a tube that pumped fluids into her body, to sustain her while she made the most delicious looking honey one could ever crave.

With one final body shaking orgasm she passed out and Kyle

instantly pressed the button waking her once more to her conscious state;

"That was exhilarating to watch, number three, what's your name?" his modulated voice inquired sternly to which her reply smoothly came;

"Thank you Master, you've always called me Honey." His forefinger released the button and Jess stood up and rested her ass on the table, spreading her thighs;

"Mmm Master, that was fun to watch, I bet she'll lure some larger game your way with a pussy that sweet." Jess started touching her soaking wet peach, and Kyle smiled walking towards her;

"Yes, she'll be ready just in time to join Dove on one of my favorite hunts of the year. I plan to fuck her pussy with my gloved hands while she's bound to a tree, as soon as her sweet juices draw the Black Bears in this area, I'll let them destroy her in front of me before I take them down one by one and bring them home for my collection; along with her pretty little head. You remember the empty spaces in the interrogation chambers, I still don't have a full collection. She'll do nicely don't you think?" Jess smiled;

"Yes, and I have to admit, the mere thought of coming with you, just to watch, or better yet, to help you tie her down and glove fuck her myself, Mmmm words cannot begin to express how wet all of this is making me."

Jess began tossing her red locks aside and fanning her face, now flushed, she was hungry for Kyle to take her here and now, she couldn't get her fill of him, not now, not ever.

She always wanted to feel that visceral nature of his rise up from the depths of hell, to claim her as his writhing succubus. She ached to feel all of her holes filled up completely with his glorious cock, she hungered for little else in this world, than the perfect balance of pain and pleasure provided from a man who was strong enough to deny his urges to slaughter her even though he was capable of that and so much more.

"Keep touching yourself for me."

Kyle instructed as his bulging cock pressed against his jeans. He walked towards the next monitor to a tall buxom red head, with thick thighs and tits that made any man or woman ache to feel them between their lips.

She was in the corner of the room, her neck adorned with a rather medieval weighted collar, a long heavy chain was attached to the center of her neck, it lead to a short leash of chain that was affixed in the bottom of this cellar room. Next to her was wooden standing stocks and in front of that was a machine that instantly made Jess squirt;

"Mmm a pussy and nipple milking machine. A man after my own heart, did you capture this one just for me before you planned my arrival?"

The room had various sex toys all waiting for her to use whenever she pleased, a table in the opposite end of the room had various foods and beverages, all of which would provide extra calories to produce the sweet nectar and juices that Kyle knew Jess craved so much as Mistress Bella.

"Well I did have to experiment with her at first to ensure I could handle your mutually shared affliction."

As his smile widened, Jess began to blush,

"How, how did you? How did you *know*?"

She was in shock, it wasn't easy to locate her medical records, and to find that she was diagnosed as a nymphomaniac by former standards even though the new term for such an affliction was called persistent genital arousal disorder. She was always shy to share such information with anyone, even lovers, it usually lead to fear of her being insatiable.

Which was partially true, she just needed to feel herself used completely like a whore, and as often as physically possible by those she fell for.

"Needless to say it's one of your endlessly charming qualities, a woman who has a prescription to fuck her brains out like a paid whore." Kyle and Jess watched as she started to stand;

"Ah yes, she'll perform nicely for us in just a moment, like you she needs her fill at certain times each day or she'll lose her mind. She's even brilliant like yourself, an intellectual, it's why I've decided not to hunt her, but to give her to you as a pet project after you've finished training."

Jess smiled glowing, she'd never been given such a gift like this before, a sex hungry slave that enjoyed serving in such a state.

"How long has she been here?" Jess asked wondering how long she'd had to fuck herself into ecstasy as her only duty in life.

"Only a month or so, I stole her from a traveling burlesque show, sometime around Valentine's Day; who knew she'd have so many other fascinating facets to her personality."

When Jess' lips began to part once more, in awe of this woman's eagerness to shackle herself in and to feel her tits pumped full of milk before each tube, administered into glass and bottled on the ground below. She didn't notice that she'd squirted at the exact same time as this woman did writhing in her cage as the machine pumped and pumped, her body shuddering and gushing gallons of fluid below her. Soaking the stone floors and leaving other girls to moan and beg for her to cum again, it sounded so beautiful, especially in comparison to the horrific screams heard from others nearby.

"Mmm, a mess inspired by *Scarlet*, I knew she'd be perfect for you."

"Scarlet, after my brothel back home, or at least my former home in Romania." Jess smiled;

"You really have done you research, but it boggles the mind as to how much you know about me, that most could never find out even if they desired to in a state of vengeance."

She was in awe of his ability to tap into her for so long, for so many years, from so far away. It must've been their past life ties, she always felt his mysterious energy in life from time to time, she just never quite knew who or what it was, always blaming it on exhaustion, or the interference of so many people in busy spaces. A cluster fuck of confusion for any psychic and empath. It was easy to cross wires in those places, no wonder she could never see him fully, even now she felt he held so many secrets, and was weighted with such mystery that she found him to be eternally perplexing, like a cryptic cipher she longed to decipher every nuance his soul desired to share.

"I'd like very much for you to feel free enough to recreate your world alongside mine. *The Scarlet Gardens* shouldn't vanish just because you're no longer on that side of the world, you're welcome to rebuild here. No matter how long it takes, I want you to have a place to release your dark side, without consequence or fear of abduction." He winked smiling wickedly;

"You are the devil. They said it'd be a buxom red head, but I've always believed it would be a man so charming and so fucking gorgeous that nothing could be denied, even the recreations of a world I promised to say goodbye too ever since Sara disappeared. How quickly life changes and provides understanding to former philosophies in such enigmatic ways."

She continued to share her various reasoning's and logical assessments of the universe as a whole.

"I always wondered if I was a Lilith or an Aphrodite, perhaps Lilith really is the one who rules here deep inside, the twisted darkness fueled by carnal impulses, all I've ever wanted in life from dark to light, you serve up to me on a golden altar of seduction and pure unbridled ecstasy."

She continued;

"I'd be a fool to accept or deny what you have to offer, but I've always given into the urgings of the flesh, you have me wrapped around your finger. Right where you've always wanted me."

Jess smiled approaching her climax ready to cum, waiting for Kyle's delicious voice to chime in, pushing her over the threshold and forcing her body off the cliff of ecstasy, plunging deep down she felt her body quiver and shake.

"Oh God, Kyle, my incredible Master, please I beg of you let me cum." Her face was stuck in horrified state waiting for his words to escape and provide the catharsis needed to end this torment inside.

"Cum for me, my beautiful pet whore, cum for me again you filthy cumslut."

As the sentence ended so did the torment. Jess felt it building inside of her as soon as she saw the images of tortured girls on closed circuit television screens. She wailed in bliss, her thighs quaking open, her toes curling and her heels arching into the chair cushions of the table, she fell back as her body writhed against her control. Her sweet peach squirting all over the rug below, hearing the liquid soak into the layers of thick fabric was alluring. Kyle moaned happily, he felt drunk from her bodies intoxicating scent;

"That's a good sex kitten, you make your master proud witnessing such hunger inside of you. You'll need it to survive around here."

He smiled watching her regain her bodies' usual serene movements. She stood up and wandered over towards Kyle embracing him. As she hugged his body she watched him reach for the button once more, their eyes both affixed towards cell number five. Jess wondered what would be waiting there for her fresh eyes to see for the very first time. Her reactions were so animated, she looked just like the classic female archetype in all of Kyle's favorite movies, revealing her fragility in her aghast response. Eyes widened and her lips parted in sheer horror, was this a body lying on the ground, a corpse that didn't survive training? As her face and upper body peered closer, moving forward unknowingly, a natural response to darkness in the eyes of those who usually walked in the light.

There she was, a luscious feast to behold, a thick Swedish girl with long thick golden hair. Her breasts adorned her chest like two ripe pears waiting to be tasted. Her pussy was swollen already well used, her left hand wandered south, examining the lush curls that were nestled between her milk maid thighs. Kyle watched in eager anticipation as Jess ached for this woman, she wanted to be there, brushing the hair from her face and tasting her breasts while every drop of blood was slowly pulled from her body by needle. She looked so weak, as Jess's nipples hardened at such a gloriously wicked sight, the lights flickered in her cell, waking her to a mild state of consciousness.

"I can see how thrilling my horror show is to you, welcome to *The Silver Screen Slaughterhouse,* you are the only one to have ever laid eyes upon this before."

She smiled her eyes still fixed to the screen as if she couldn't blink. She felt compelled to watch every nuance of this delicious torture, a sweet nightmare to satiate the darkness that lied dormant in her soul. Something deep inside of her that she always tried to run away from, hide and suppress, but now in full epiphany she realized exactly who indeed she was, a killer. No different than Kyle, Darkeel, whomever truly reigned and ruled inside this man's soul, they both feasted for lust and blood and nothing in this world would stop them from indulging in every sick twisted fantasy that they craved more than ever again seeing the light of day.

His strong, glorious hands once more reaching forward to press this button, his modulated voice boomed across the loudspeaker echoing against the stone wall in these dark and dreary chambers.

"Whore, what is your name?"

The shaking blonde uttered a word that she formed with her lips in a most peculiar way, not understanding the reference, just stating what she was told to say so many times before while surviving the most severe beatings inflicted upon her naked flesh by Darkeel himself.

"Bambi."

Her eyes closed once more as a tear streaked down her face, the blood once more returning back to her body after being pulled, cleaned out and reintroduced through a plasma machine nearby.

"When I found her she was a trained Olympic Athlete, a track runner for the Swedish team. She craved gold medals more than life itself, it was the only Achilles' heel that she possessed. Late night runs made her an easy target, she was so strong, her muscles so healthy, that bleeding her out was the only way to make her submit." Kyle stated the facts, continuing on with his formal introductions, each treasured possession more beautiful and exotic than the previous one in my collection.

"She'll be perfect for deer hunting season, especially in late August, I assume you'll want to use arrows to hunt down such a fast and beautiful piece of game?" Jess looked up into his eyes smiling deviously.

"Deer hunting season is from late August to December, it depends on how well she's trained by then, and perhaps I won't be the only one to hunt her?"

Kyle said with a cunning grin and fierce devilish eyes. Jess gasped at the thought of being beside him, bow and arrow in hand, waiting for his signal before launching them high into the air. Her eyes witnessing them fall swiftly to piece the skin of the gorgeous game that was imported all the way from Sweden.

"Speechless." His grin widened into a carnal smile, he realized that he's plucked a dark chord that lies deep within the soul of this hauntingly beautiful woman.

"I confess, I'm used to a much slower method, one that leaves my victims swooning in bliss before they perish. This brutal, cruel blow has such a richer taste than that of poison." Her eyebrows curled and she winked cracking a smile.

Before Kyle could respond he noticed once again her eyes being drawn to the screens, this time to a stunning woman who appeared to be Colombian. Her long thick brown hair cascaded down her naked breasts all the way down to her waist. She was tied to the rack, her legs and arms being strenuously pulled in separate directions, her face contorting in pain as her body shuddered and sweat profusely. Jess was compelled to understand the reasoning behind this form of conditioning but before her lips could even utter a single word Kyle's voice intervened;

"Sometimes I prefer a swift and brutal kill, one who can barely move yet can watch in horror as their own demise approaches in full totality."

As the victim continued to strain and arch her back, hoping for even the smallest mercy in the form of centimeters, she started to cry and her luscious full tits hardened, from the stress of enduring such torment, not from pleasure but that of pain.

"I also should add that she was an infamous black widow when I came across her in Brazil, she'd already killed three *good* men, and was celebrating over a table of the finest liquor available. I thought she'd look better mounted on my wall instead."

He leaned forward his eyes narrowing into two devious black holes, she started to scream; she could feel his presence again inside of her,

"Just fucking kill me already!" her voice trailed through the air on a breeze, echoing into Jess's mind as vividly as it came across the speaker.

"What is your name?!" Kyle yelled furiously he knew this bitch would never submit, never for a single moment would this dark whore let any man feel superior to her, even while shackled on the rack.

"Reaper, Sir."

She responded, mumbling profanities in her native tongue, as Kyle waited for her to pause he continued to interrogate her;

"What is your ultimate purpose in this world?"

She started to cry, the rack pulled tighter and her limbs felt as if they were going to snap. Her ligaments already stretched far beyond their capacity, she hadn't felt anything below her elbows in weeks it seemed.

"To suffer. To die a glorious death by your hands whenever you ultimately desire."

Just repeating these words were enough to make her face contort as if she was being pumped full of poison, her body started to shake, her wrists and ankles started to quiver uncontrollably; without notice the light went out above her, in cell number seven, she didn't make a sound. She just lied there, stretched across the wooden rack like animal hide tanning in the sun during Indian summer.

"What we sew, so shall we reap." Jess's words had never been truer, she wasn't the only one who was waiting to meet their ultimate demise.

The next monitor was now displaying action, a woman who was continuously submerged into a tank of water, only to be pulled out right before she passed out. Her body was frail, she'd been here for ages it seemed, her long black hair covered her face. The petite size of her frame would indicate that she was Japanese, but in this state it was hard to tell. Her body was wrapped in a straightjacket her legs dangling, her entire body wrapped in a cage of chains. She gasped for air wondering if this would be the last time she could capture it completely. There was a morbidly elegant dance that was displayed here, her pale skin moved serenely up and down in and out of the tank, her swanlike neck exposed, elongated, just like her legs. She wasn't blue like Frostbite, no, she was warm, her flesh red hot and the water below steaming off of her, making it difficult for her to focus, concentrate or even see. The water splashed loudly, echoing off the floors, slapping it away vividly while the screams of other treasured possessions continued to scream throughout the dungeon floors.

"I have special plans for this one, she's of hearty stalk, one who can be hunted anytime throughout the year, there's a beautiful lake nearby that I'd love to show her, that is for the very last time. Strangling her underneath the running waters by her swan like neck. It isn't often that I enjoy such a kill, but for her I'll make an exception."

Kyle shared this information as Jess saw into his mind's eye, witnessing the very same frozen lake that that mysterious blonde from his youth was found; soaked in blood, naked and left to the wilderness to dispose of. She realized how important tradition was to a man like this, recreating his origins time and time again was a pattern that transformed him into the monster that stalked the hills of Colorado, wrapped around a dark demon that clung to his soul that was shrouded in cruelty in the guise of a well-respected man. As the woman was freed once more from her oceanic submergence, she gasped and choked while Kyle's voice addressed her formally over loudspeaker;

"Tell me your name."
Her almond shaped eyes peered out from her soaking wet locks of hair;
"The name you've given this sacrifice is *Swan*. I am at your disposal."

She long since accepted her fate here in his world, she'd been here the longest, her soul conditioned to this routine of torture, a strict regimen that altered the mind and willpower of any one who found themselves in Darkeel's Lair.

"That is all." Kyle's voice articulated his appreciation to her, she was the most well trained trophy he'd ever previously had, *besides Jess.*

Kyle's eyes left cell number eight to purvey the beguiled look on his new concubine's pretty face.

"I see you have a fetish for red heads, even more so than myself it seems, a woman after my red blooded heart."

Jess bit her lip hearing the tormenting words spill forth from his lips. As her eyes looked into cell number nine she saw a glorious vision of art in female form, a living, breathing Venus di Milo. Her long red hair cascaded down past her ass, her body was athletic, her tits full and supple, with vivid shades of red and brown interlaced in a blaze of color across her pale chest. She was clearly Italian, her nose was classic to the region, her luscious thighs and full hips made Jess moan aloud;

"Mmmm, you do know what I like."

Jess hypnotized continued watching this woman as she prepared to take a bath in a very small tub of water. Her chambers were simple but without the usual torture devices, instead she was left with magnificently carved wooden dildos, native to her country and to her wanton sex drive.

Her full lips forming into a feline smile, this smile all too recognizable to a sex kitten like Jess, "Mmm she's hungry, waiting to be used rough and put away wet." She didn't realize her filthy whore thoughts were escaping her lips;

"Is that right? Tell me more." Kyle's voice instructed as his eyebrow raised in sheer delight.

"It's the same look I get in my eye when only a thick cock will do, aching to be filled completely, the feeling of being so full you couldn't possibly take another inch without bursting."

Her eyebrow raised mischievously she could see his cock so rigid and thick, bulging and pressing against his jeans.

"You're making me hard." Kyle started to slowly unzip, his lips groaning in discomfort, he needed to release the wild beast inside, Jess brought it out of him so vividly.

"I want you to place your hands on the wall, just below her monitor."

Jess approached the wall and did just as she was told, she loved taking orders and executing them as swiftly as her owner desired. Watching as pride poured across his face relishing in such a well-trained toy, eager to serve. Kyle's belt buckle jingled as it hit the ground, he leaned in close brushing away the hair from Jess' face and whispering into her ear,

"Spread your legs, and watch *Crimson's* show while I tear you apart."

As she gasped from his words, sheer torment wrapped in intoxicating ecstasy, she felt his cock stabbing deeply into her, stretching her lips apart and gouging a hole, carving his shape into her belly, she moaned aloud, her nails digging into the wall as she took him in completely. Kyle pulled her head back by the hair, kissing that one place on her neck that made her squirt against her will. She bucked wildly, his voice groaned and moaned, he'd never felt such a tight cunt gripping his cock so viscerally before. He felt every drop of blood coursing into his shaft, flooding towards the tip, her orgasms only made her peach tighter, even in the endless flow of juices, Kyle felt youth restored once more, ready to cum long before he ever intended.

He held back, his hands gripping her hips and rushing up her ribs to her full breasts that were swaying and slapping down hard with every brutal blow and pump of his hips. Thrusting deep, harder and faster with each moment that went by. She looked at the monitor watching Crimson's body shudder as she stuffed two dildos inside of her, one in her ass the other in her pussy, as she came in that moment, her long red locks flowed wildly down her face. Her lips and nose parting the waves of red in two, she squirt sweet juices across the screen into the corner of her stone cell chamber, soaking the red velvet fabric and pillows that lined the center of the floor, a makeshift bed for a slave to pleasure herself. The stimulus was too much for Jess to take;

"Oh god she squirted and I can't stop, fuck me master, take me to your paradise, I want to feel you explode!"

Her moans loudly echoed and in that moment she felt his body tense, his back arch and his cock swell two more inches around and in length, it felt as if she was being lifted off of his body by the sheer magnificent force of his cum, exploding inside of her she reached back gripping his shoulders and neck and kissing the side of his face;

"Oh God, Jess." Kyle buried his face into her neck, kissing her endlessly.

"So fucking tight."

He continued to stammer as his rapid breath rose and fell, Crimson was long since spent, curled up in the corner, still shuddering as her thighs trembled and forced more liquid honey from her supple shaved mound. Her fingers still deep inside her slutty little holes, biting her lips in utter desperation wishing somebody would use her long into the night, *the way whores craved most.*

Jess still trembling from such a violent intrusion, her limbs did their best to leap and contort causing her to brace herself against the wall, pressing her cheek to the damask surface of the wall paper. Relishing in having to catch her breath to whisper in stammers aloud;

"Thank you master, for such sublime ecstasy."

Her lips slowly formed each word to articulate how vividly she swam in pleasure, warm and endless like fountains of blood surrounding her in a tide of carnality, she lost herself in his energy. Felt her swooning and giving way to more beautiful feelings in darkness, a serene existence that left her out of body until she felt his strong hands once more. Reaching forth to stabilize himself as he caught his breath Kyle stood behind her still slowly slipping himself from her warm inviting pussy. Never wanting to leave.

He bent down and slowly pulled her panties up over her thighs and ass, kissing her lower back and standing up, pulling his jeans up, Jess could hear the belt buckle, she felt angst set in, she always felt so empty when thighs parted and hard cocks vanished once more from inside her. The feeling of being filled to the brim with a prick as hard as iron was what she truly lived for, the rest of life's moments were layered fleeting adventures and memories that made her ache for pleasure and affection. She sighed and he felt the sadness well up within her soul.

"You will feel me inside you again, my pet, very soon, I promise you'll be begging for me to pull out, this I promise you."

Kyle smiled wickedly knowing what it means to feel that disconnect and remorse after releasing such ecstasy, intertwined the world seems to lack in existence, but once every drop was spilled the sad return to reality was a harsh blow to any artist, creative mind or those who pined for pleasure like air filling their lungs after drowning.

"I have one more remarkable creature to introduce you too before you've seen my entire collection of treasured possessions."

Kyle spoke directly into her left ear, the wind escaping left chills on Jess's neck, trailing down her naked shoulders and causing her nipples to harden once more.

"Your voice does wicked things to me, I'd do anything just to hear you speak, even over the most trivial of points." Jess smiled her feline brows rising and arching in unison with her back.

Kyle laughed aloud, "Flattery will get you nowhere with me, nice try though," she continued her wry seduction;

"Who said I was flattering you?" she smiled cockily;

"Perhaps a fetish for auralism is to blame, your tone is so intoxicating." Kyle gripped Jess underneath the rib cage and stood her upright directly in front of her, her face naturally focused on the screens before them.

"I can show you a tone that you wouldn't be able to find ways to make those thighs drip before me profusely, if you'd like?" Jess's eyes widened and bulged;

"As much as I understand and appreciate that side of you, I'd prefer to stay in your good graces, that place in your world provides even the smallest chance of survival. Now who is this final victim that will soon find her resting place out back?"

Jess knew she crossed the line, it wasn't easy to dance with the devil and not feel the scorching flamed tongue that coincided with such a beast. She was never good at being entirely good, it felt so much better to be bad, to feel that visceral impact left in marks by those that craved to inflict pain as much as she enjoyed relishing in their darkness as a porcelain sacrifice.

Kyle's fingers reached forth to press the button, "Vicious Cunt, what is your name?"

Jess peered forward horrified by the level of torture that this one woman had endured thus far, she was covered in bruises, her face still healing in its blackened state. Her hair was long, sleek an endless river of black and silver intertwined in each lock. Her face was frozen in a state of anger she sat up on a silver panel with shackles on her wrists and ankles, the burn marks displayed on each limb radiated from the center of the metal it was obvious to Jess that she was wired for a strong electrical current. One that should've killed her many times over by now, but for some reason she was still here refusing to speak even with this level of encouragement in the bellows of the dungeons down below.

Her eyes shimmered in silver and peered intently at the corner of the gritty stone room where both camera and two way speaker were mounted, she spit at it as best as she could with very little liquid to share, a gesture of obvious malcontent towards the monster keeping her here against her will.

"She hasn't said a single word since I captured her last year in late July. I found her wandering along the highway, I could tell she was baiting drivers to stop and invite her in before it was too late for them to realize who or what she was."

Kyle stared frustrated into the cell watching her eyes connect with his and smiling wickedly, she knew what was about to happen, she didn't care, to deny him of information was her sweetest reward in her current hell. Before Jess could blink an eye, the body of the preternatural woman before her eyes started jolting, convulsing and bucking wildly on the table. Her screams filled the room, echoing off the chambers and corridors down the hallway, the other girls covered their ears in unison, the ones unable, screaming aloud hoping the sounds would eventually stop.

"She's a Dryad, quite possibly a very distant cousin of mine. Our families were scattered to the South of France where the bloodlines eventually died off, but this is why her eyes change color, do they remind you of someone's?" Jess peered up into Kyle's eyes;

"But, your eyes were green this morning, and now their gray." She smiled and waited for him to remember;

"But when I looked into them while I was inside of you earlier, they were blue?!" Kyle's eyes widened at this revelation;

"Are you telling me that you and this woman are descendants of some sort of mythical creatures that lived in the woods killing people who wandered into their territories?" Jess smiled;

"Well something like that." She continued to share her lineage with him, expanding upon the eight families that traveled to that region to hide from the rest of the blue bloods that feared them for their psychic gifts and abilities to avoid war, famine, poverty and revolution. They were procured from the Kings and Queens of nations worldwide to predict their success or failures in future wars and strategic implementations of the time.

"I know this might be unorthodox, but if she's related to me, she'll feel my presence, and she and I can communicate through a very old language that is still prominent in my psyche to this day, would you like me to address her in that tongue master?" Kyle was overwhelmed with such information;

"I could turn this entire scenario into my next screenplay, you have my permission to address her and request that she share her name even if it's an alias. It's been almost a year and this woman, time and time again survives the trials I put her through during the formal training process."

Jess smiled and reached for the button, knowing that this woman could hear her, but Sara might be able to overhear her voice as well, knowing she's still alive, still here, hoping she could sense her presence beyond her current drug induced state of unconsciousness and sudden pitch black.

Her red painted index finger reached slowly for the button, she closed her eyes and channeled the information for the correct dialect for this specific creatures tongue;

"What is your name?"

She spoke in a phrasing that Kyle was astounded by, it sounded foreign, ancient and boggled his mind that this beautiful creature could speak so articulately. The woman's eyes changed from gray to blue, she started to cry and her lips parted in awe of hearing those words that no other human being had uttered for over two centuries. Her melodic cadence arose from her soul;

"My name is Lady Gray, I am the last of my kind, please release me." Jess smiled and the tears welled up in her eyes;

"I apologize profusely for the tears, it's just overwhelming for those of us left, to hear the language that after we crossover from earth will be completely extinct."

Her hands unconsciously reached towards the screen, brushing the woman's face, she could see she felt her even though Jess was two floors above and distantly watching her from a closed circuit television screen, the woman trembled and muttered once more;

"Thank you, whoever you are, your kindness is golden." Before Jess could say another word, the woman passed out and Kyle grabbed her finger before she could mutter back to her anymore.

"What did she say?" Kyle asked intently;

"She said her name is *Lady Gray,* she begs to be released as she is the last of her kind, and she thanked me for my kindness which in this moment is worth more than its weight in gold to her." Kyle pondered;

"What does she mean, the last of her kind?" Jess's head dropped solemnly;

"The reason why our families eventually vanished from the face of this earth is that the women in our clans are barren, at least those of us who are filled with the magic of the Dryad's."

"She is the last of her family, without the ability to provide offspring, after she is gone her entire lineage will die alongside her. It's funny really, ironic in fact, the only reason our families ever came into existence is due to dwelling in the woods nearby that were filled with dark demons that captured members of each of our families, keeping them hostage in dwellings very similar to these."

Jess' fingers reached out and trailed along the images of stone walls on picture screen;

"It's quite possibly why she feels such disdain, and clings to her strength and courage in adamant refusal of responding to you in kind. She feels you're a physical representation of why she, I and those rare few left in other families cannot bear children, and feel the weight of the world on our shoulders as we watch our entire family bloodlines die before our very eyes. To submit to your will would be to agree to the damage caused to our families eons ago before we were ever born. She's loyal to the core of her being to who she is, so breaking her in will be nearly impossible. It would be easier to wipe out her entire family tree than to convince her to adhere to a new order and way of life."

Jess rose her head and her eyes were blue, they always changed to this color when sadness enveloped her soul. She did her best to pull the tears back into her eyes. Kyle reached forward kissing her tear stained cheek;

"I told you, crying is never something to apologize for, or to hide your emotions from me. This reaches down to the depths of your soul, and challenges me to find new and interesting ways to train this former enigma and to transform her into the fox she's intended to be for gray fox season next year." Jess's tears stained his shirt;

"I know you can't let her go, that death is her ultimate surrender, it just kills a part of my soul, that one of my distant kin will find their grave soon here at Burnett Manor." Kyle lifted his head and Jess's as well, loosening his embrace to ensure eye contact would be maintained throughout this entire statement;

"Attachment is the hardest part of our human selves to break, detachment isn't an easy solution, but continuing your formal training is the only answer. The night is ours, I'll have you in bed by sunrise, but for now, follow me."

"Master Kyle?" Jess asked in sheer curiosity, waiting for his inquiring response;

"Yes, what is it?" Jess realized he was impatient with her questions right now, his mind was heavily fixated on actions, and giving orders and watching his concubine follow through without pause.

"Forgive me for the interruption but where is treasured possession eleven?"

Kyle smiled as he pressed the art panel it instantly slid back into place, revealing the ornate flowers in oil paint that were usually displayed in the formal dining room. As he walked over to the wall pressing and teasing the crown molding in the most conspicuous of ways he waited for the wall to slowly move open providing them the space and time needed to descend to the dungeons down below.

"Sometimes they don't possess the fortitude it takes to make it through formal training. Unfortunately some are denied the thrill of being hunted down by me." She knew he was covering up something much darker, that didn't feel past, but foreboding in the pit of her stomach.

Kyle's eyes got his point across, no more questions, following directions was the only way she'd survive this ordeal. As they descended to the bowels below she watched the torches illuminate the spiraling stone staircase that took them down into the earth. Deep into the crust, far away from light, and sound or man's reality; to his world below, the one he created years ago with the incessantly nagging force of Darkeel.

His hands reaching into his pocket, Kyle clicked a button on a small device that put all of his treasured possessions instantly to sleep, the dungeons were left as silent as the grave. Kyle and Jess descended into the dungeon floor, to the mirrored entrance of where Jess broke in a few nights prior. She could hear the wind howling between the cracks in each stone, yet this room was eerily quiet, she felt fear rise up within her soul like never before.

Oh god, that cage is for me, keeping me alive just to torture me later?

Jess's heart beat swiftly in her chest, she knew imminent doom awaited her now, just like the others who were captured here. Prisoners to a man who wanted their heads mounted on walls high above the ceiling to remind them where their ultimate place in this world truly was. Kyle continued to walk forward towards the empty cell that waited, Jess stopped a few feet behind him, her legs unable to move anymore in death march. She saw all of the girls fast asleep, in a coma like state of submission.

"I said *follow me*."

Kyle's hands moved swiftly and the cage door opened, the iron bars strongly supported by the layers of brick, stone and mortar solidifying this room into a state of permanence overwhelming the body and mind. She couldn't move, Jess was frozen, she couldn't endure this level of training, she knew her body would break, and her mind would cease to find logic or reason as her thirst for survival would reveal to her the worst sides of her preternatural self.

"Let me make this easier on you."

Without warning Jess floated into the air, unable to move her body. Slowly floating into the open cell that waited for her now, a single tear flowing forth from her right eye as she heard the iron bars close behind her. Seeing Kyle's face now streaked between shadows, darkness and an iron jaw, keeping her here for as long as he pleased. Her red locks bounced as her body floated to the floor, she was lying on cold stone, a single velvet red blanket to keep her company this night. No food, no water, not even a light source were present, just the remnants of shadows and a wicked smile worn ear to ear on Kyle's face.

"You belong to me now, my beautiful *Bella*; the poisonous flower that lulls even the darkest of killers to sweet serenity." His voice bantered within her mind;

"You will always be mine."

In that moment she saw his eyes change to a menacing shade of dark red, she heard the voice of Darkeel beating forth from the blood pumping in his chest, his wicked tongue had a powerful cadence that left Jess mortified. She grabbed the blanket and pulled it close to her body, before she felt each thread of her clothing tearing, ripping off and fleeing towards the corner of the cellar in an ornate pile of destruction. His boots echoed as he disappeared into darkness. The sounds of keys and sinister laughter echoing in her mind even though with his gifts, there was no need for such things. All the while toying with her while she sat there waiting, hoping that she wasn't the final victim being prepared for the most dangerous game of all; but she wasn't sure now in this moment just who she was dealing with anymore.

Was she the fallen victim of Kyle Burnett the world renowned author that she clamored for throughout most of her life? Or was the only ruler of this home the core of evil and darkness? Was she fooled all this time? Could it be?

Perhaps Darkeel was the only being who rested and resided as the complicated soul of *The Slaughterhouse Hills Hunter.* Jess started to fall asleep, until she heard those beautiful words muttered from the voice of her beloved Sara;

"Mistress? Is, is that you?" Sara said in her drug induced state, but Jess knew better than to respond, at least just yet. Even in the midst of this emotional torture, she realized that he was still here, watching, testing and waiting to see if she would be kept alive for eternity by his side. Or would she find ways to add herself to his hunting list for the sake of true undying affection?

Chapter 21:
ABSOLUTE CONTROL

JESS could feel his eyes penetrating through her flesh like the dawning sunrise to a newly turned vampire. The last thing she wanted in this dark and haunting place was to be the reason why Sara rebelled against her captor, leaving him without a choice; breaking her for good and leaving her in the virgin snow a kin to the bundles of hand cut red cedar that was stockpiled outside his bedroom window. Seeing the leaching colors of tree elixir flowing in eternal reminder of just how delicate of a game she was playing, and not only with her own life; But for the life of the first creature of the night in this entire world of darkness to ever capture her heart and to show her the origins of love exchanged ad infinitum. She wanted to whisper words of encouragement to Sara, but she knew they'd falter her survival instincts to peak towards a corrupt idea of escape, one that *The Slaughterhouse Hills Hunter* would never allow, even on his more generous of days would he watch his world crumble at the vindictive hands of a victim that was ripe for the slaughter.

"Shhh my darling, sleep deeply and serenely, quiet your love fool mind for just a little longer...I promise I'll never leave you behind again no matter what the consequence."

Jess sent her thoughts to Sara's soul instantly penetrating the deepest parts of her pleasure starved mind. Hearing her voice swoon in content as she felt her mind wander into the dream world, leaving her breathing in a rhythmic cadence that signaled to Sara's mistress that she was now in the deepest sleep you could possibly enter in such a deluded state. Jess lied on the cold stone floor, her back and body wrapped in thick layer of crimson velvet she smiled coyly up into the corner that she felt his eyes were watching her from. The camera zoomed in, and she felt her body shudder realizing how close she was to everything she ever longed for in this world. Jess's lips slowly parted to reveal a tongue that wouldn't stop tracing the delicate folds of her luscious pout, parting them and pressing them together in a maddening show of seduction. They broke apart again in a slow sticky procession that reminded Kyle of the delicious honey that endlessly flowed from between her legs.

He was already nestled in for the night in the central tower office of his home, tending to the formal planning of his next hunt, the closed circuit television monitoring the only cage his eyes ever desired to pry into anymore. His soul felt satiated in every conceivable way, he was still waiting for the moment to make it's ugly appearance that all of this and more with Jess was too good to be true, but he knew deep down in the pit and pendulum of his dark beating heart that she was everything he'd ever dreamt of in this world. He could never fathom even for the slightest moment that quite possibly a girl like this could exist that matched his darkened soul so seamlessly.

She smiled, it unnerved him in the most arousing way how even in complete darkness her gorgeous glowing green eyes could transfix upon the exact spot where his eyes connected to hers through closed circuit television screen.

"You will be my greatest masterpiece, a living sacrifice who never has to be hunted, but instead desires to hunt alongside me; the final procession towards the completion of your formal training awaits."

Kyle pulled out maps of remote locations nearby searching for the perfect way to train Jess in the arts of slaughter, "The gorge will be magnificent this time of year."

Kyle's words transformed into his penetrating thoughts, Darkeel was alive and well, waiting for the kill, he felt the two halves of his whole being melding together in harmony for the first time in his life, he never felt so free, and the inspiration flowed long into the night. As he continued to make calculated and precise notes ensuring not a single trap would be out of place. He watched his crimson goddess lean back, back arched, breasts bare and full, each snow covered mountain adorned with a perfect pink mound that shuddered beautifully under the bucking of her hips. He couldn't see her pink parts, just the pale river of legs flowing beautifully out of blood red velvet, a true Countess Bathory if he ever saw one in wanton flesh. Her flowing red locks dripped over her shoulders, melodically dancing in tune to her orgasmic release that left her lips biting firmly, her fangs shining bright in the dead of night, to suddenly hear all of his comatose victims moaning in unison as if they felt the quaking shudders of her explosive pleasure, he'd never witnessed anything quite like it before.

"You never cease to amaze me, my relentlessly magical whore; so strong your lust for pleasure that the entire world shudders alongside you in ecstasy."

Kyle's heart quickened and his lungs filled with air, watching her lip ring fall in surrender against her bottom lip was torture to his cock that was all the while sleeping until now.

"It's fortunate that you've taken a liking to your cage my pet, without such restraints how can any man get any work done with a succubus like you around inspiring such ferocious hunger in the pits of my soul?"

He smiled as he watched her fall back onto the cold stone floor, the blanket wrapped around her in a beautiful sight, her eyes closed. Her face as innocent as a seraphim's; how incredible she was in all her glory, sleeping soundly in the hollow's of a dungeon, more peacefully than a child in mother's adoring embrace.

"Sleep my blood obsessed, lust filled concubine, our world awaits you sooner than you can imagine."

Kyle reached for the closed circuit monitor and turned it off, he knew she'd be asleep until early morning when he'd wake her from her peaceful state, to ravage her mind, body and soul in her bedchambers before slipping away through the back panel of her closet wall; to find his way into his room once more; to capture his sleep in dark, heavy and for the first time in life collected in a profound contentment that his heart never knew existed before.

The dawn of early morning light streaked through the cracks and masked windows of the dungeon below, in the bellowing pit of the darkened soul that was Burnett Manor, a menagerie of living animals awaited to see what would take place in this pleasure palace and torture chamber.

Jess felt the warmth of sunlight streaking across her face, cracking open her right eye in this early dawn was painful to say the least. Searing down beyond the fibers of her nerve endings she felt the visceral attack of the sun upon her serene resting place, instantly provoking her to turn her head from the wall to the cage opening that kept her just feet away from the woman she loved. Sara was still fast asleep, once this realization had penetrated her consciousness completely her heart and breathing returned to normal. It didn't matter how deep of a drug induced state Kyle left her in, there was no possible way that she wouldn't awaken to the presence of her mistress, seeing her caged before her eyes would torture her to self-destruction; leaving a wake of chaos in the midst of *The Slaughterhouse Hills Hunter's* world. A crime that would come with the ultimate price a punishment she couldn't bear to contemplate. She swiftly covered her face in a way that made her appear to be dead, hoping that if Sara awoke she wouldn't find this scene out of the ordinary in a hellish place that she'd been held hostage in for far too long to know anymore; leaving her in a cage that slowly became her entire world.

Kyle's eyes after countless hours of planning dark ideations in the middle of the night, realized just how late it had become, he didn't usually allow time to slip away from him in such a way, but this formal ceremony and eternal invitation into his world forevermore wasn't something he took lightly, in fact it was a dream that he never imagined could find its way into reality.

"Time to collect my prized possession, the day is young and all of night's dark plans has left my body hungry for the dream world."

He descended down the stairwell corridor into the private entrance of his dungeons, chains rattling as each victim sensed his presence. He quickly snapped his fingers and each one instantly passed out as he walked by. With each boot firmly placed on the floor, Jess felt his energy growing in carnal hunger, the tendrils of thirst that beguiled her flesh to tingle, and surge instantly electrified inside her body causing quivering up her spine and over her breasts leaving her nipples pert with desire for his lips and greedy, ravaging hands. Kyle menacingly approached cage twelve, peering into Sara's mind seeing that she sensed him through the sedatives that were working their way into her body, helping to ensure her survival.

His mind spewed forth the dark feelings of vengeance he had for an untamable woman:

"You should consider yourself lucky, if it wasn't for her, I'd have slaughtered you years ago, a worthless waste of time and resources; your beauty doesn't hide the fact that you'll never surrender. A broken toy that I cannot fix for vice or sport. We'll see just how long you can endure this before you lose control, it's only a matter

of time."

He saw Sara's mind swirl with anger, rage and felt her coursing fury like fire in his cock before ravaging his victims for the first time.

"Mmm, I do love the fire in you, no wonder she can't let you go."

As Kyle pulled his hands away from the bars, his hooded cloak still hiding most of his face, everything but his lips, he turned around and took three ominous steps towards his prized possession, with a wave of his hand the cage unlocked and the door creaked open, "How did you sleep my love?"

His face was glowing, his eyes radiantly fixed on his beloved property. Jess's head slowly moved to reveal her eyes peering from the velvet blanket, slowly pulling the fabric down her face she smiled in a measure of contentment that no man had ever seen before this moment in her life;

"Like the dead." Her words resonated through his body in waves and oceans of pleasure, she slowly wrapped herself in the lush fabric and waited for his next command.

"I'm pleased to hear it, come with me my darling, it's time for bed."

Jess rose to her feet and Kyle leaned forward grabbing her by the waist and pulling her towards him, she felt his raging cock as his lips pressed ravenously against hers;

"I'd float you to my room in an instant if I hadn't been up all night working, forgetting to eat or sleep as I often do, will have to recharge first before further magick can adorn you the way I feel you deserve."

She lovingly wrapped her hands around his neck and stood on tiptoe smiling into his eyes. Her skin glowed and illuminated his world turning the lights on in a fog of penetrating black, his lips formed the smile of satisfaction and he began to walk Jess up to her bedroom, to show her paradise. As the light grew and began to fill the dungeon room below, it streaked across the caged cell walls painting her naked body in black bars that left Kyle speechless. All he ever wanted was in his very hands and words would never tell in vivid enough detail how complete his life at long last finally felt.

Jess followed Kyle out of the cell as she turned around swaddled in red velvet and gently locked the cage door behind her. In that moment she heard the words that she longed to hear for years but never in this moment of cruel timing, "Mistress? Is…is that you?"

Sara whispered, Jess could feel her eyes upon her, turning around would be sudden death for them both, she knew she'd recognize her and lose her sanity trying to flee her bonds and cage to be near her presence once more. Kyle's eyes widened in shock, there was no conceivable way for this woman to be conscious right now. As he stood between them, his ominous and grand form shrouded Jess in the only barrier to prevent Sara from seeing her right now, she reached forward shrouding herself within the folds of Master Darkeel's cloak. He felt her tears well up onto his chest, staining the shirt he had on and soaking it completely under the parts that held her eyes shut to shield the pain of abandoning the one she loved, even for this life saving moment.

He hugged her, covering her body completely, leaving Jess one final moment to peer through the folds and to see her beloved's face for just a moment before she suddenly fell back asleep muttering to herself aloud;

"I know you're here, I know you'll never leave me like this, I love you…"

As she fell back into her drug induced coma, Jess couldn't hold back her tears or emotional wailing anymore, this was just too much to bare. She suddenly broke out of his arms unexpectedly and ran towards the bars reaching through her fingers just inches away from Sara's torso;

"Forgive me Master for I have sinned, I've fallen in love with a beautiful woman and I can't let her go!"

Her blanket fell to the floor and Kyle grabbed her by the waist as she kicked and screamed hoping deep down somewhere that Sara wouldn't wake up but knowing all too well that there was no possible way she wouldn't stir to such a horrific scream echoing through the dungeon walls.

Kyle yelled in a rage of fury that should've annihilated any desire to rebel within the depths of Jess's soul, but she couldn't leave her like this, not for a moment longer;

"Come with me now, or I'll leave you both here to die, there's a better way than this you tempestuous cunt."

His voice was followed with grunts, visceral growls and sounds of sheer indignant angst never second guessing his prized possession until now;

"You've put me in quite the difficult situation and all while I was planning your formal initiation ceremony, perhaps you'll have to wait. I cannot risk losing my entire empire due to impatience."

He lifted Jess and carried her over his shoulders as her body shuddered and shivered naked and covered in tears, "Agggh! You've set my plans back for at least six months, because of this mistake one of those down below will now die, to ensure I don't sacrifice you instead!"

Each booming step up the stairs felt more horrific than the first descent down into this world that Jess explored hastily just weeks before in full cover of night.

"I'm sorry, my lord I'm so, so sorry. I've spent a lifetime cutting myself away from emotion, to find no matter what I do it's all consuming with the ones I love, please, *please* forgive me. I'll do whatever it takes to keep Sara alive."

Kyle opened the panel into her closet and walked Jess through to her bedroom, throwing her down hard onto the bed and grabbing her wrists and forcing them to the sheets;

"You will learn to silence your soul if it's the last thing I ever fucking teach you. Don't make a sound or I'll fucking slaughter you right here and now."

In that instant Jess nodded now in full understanding of her existence ensuring he understood that she was fully compliant. His cock plunged deep inside her, fucking her hatefully with a visceral pounding she never quite felt before from anyone on this planet.

"Need I remind you who you're dealing with my darling? I am Master Darkeel the dark demon of Royal Gorge who is known by the mark I have left upon this world as *The Slaughterhouse Hills Hunter!*"

In that quaking moment he came hard and fully, tears rolled down Jess's face as her orgasm was milked out of her tight pussy with his final stammering pump, stabbing her to death on his long, thick knife Kyle fell forward kissing her face, her tear stained cheeks and whispering to her, one hand gripping her wrists above her head, the other below gently caressing her breasts;

"It'll all be over soon, surrender to me and you'll have everything you've ever wanted and more I promise you this, but only if you surrender."

Her face caressed his like that of a well satiated feline after months of being left in heat, as he trailed his fingers down her chest and stomach towards her shapely thighs he kissed her passionately on the lips and whispered;

"Sleep, you need your rest, and so do I."

Her eyes shut gently and she slept deeper than she'd ever realized was possible, not hearing the sound of his boots wandering out of her closet and into the tunnel towards his imminent resting place. Jess was out cold, intoxicated by the overwhelming carnal paradise that was now the core of her existence, from the dawn of early sunrise into the dead of night, she was his prized possession and nothing did she crave more in this life than to finally feel home, at long last.

Chapter 22:
EPHEMERAL SATIATION

THE beast inside kept pounding, waiting to hunt. Coursing within the soul of Kyle's flesh, he was livid, knowing full well that he knew Jess's good nature far beyond even her own understanding of herself. He knew it wouldn't be long until she faltered, until she saw the killer instinct in his eyes when he had to take her out, had to place his hands around the neck of this beautiful woman after the arrows filled her porcelain flesh once she tried to flee.

It was only a matter of time, as he lied upon the top of his bed, hand resting in a folded state on his built chest. His entire body slumbering soundly with his piercing eyes wide open and glowing with a hunger for vengeance. He could hear the sounds from the cages below, somebody was moving around, he could feel it in his gut as to who was stupid enough to try to escape, no rest for the wicked. Oh well a penchant for blood staining untainted snow was soon to take place far sooner than he had planned, and without his new huntress by his side. She wasn't ready, not like he expected her to be, love was a mysterious concoction of poison that paid no mind nor reason to the dark thickets of a woman's complex inner workings. Overgrown with ivy endlessly turning one practical path into complete and utter insanity, he wouldn't force her to put herself in such a disastrous situation. He knew she would fail the test, anyone with a soul wouldn't be able to comply with the circumstances that were the mere glimpses of paradise and release that Darkeel craved and that Kyle endured for peace.

The chains were clanking floors below and no rest would visit this demon tonight, before he knew it Kyle's body found itself standing outside of Sara's cell with hooded cloak. He was unable to realize in this exhaustive fugue state what exactly he was doing, before he knew it the untamable whore's cell was unlocked, the rest of the captives left in shock as they watched *The Slaughterhouse Hills Hunter* release the first and only victim from the gates of hell that would ever escape his clutches on this very night.

Sara stood there speechless for the first time in her life, she'd tried escaping many times before and found it hopeless with his eyes always watching, seeing her every move, unable to hide any weapon she tried to make that would help her to flee this forsaken place.

"Why would you just let me go? This makes no sense whatsoever unless my Mistress really is here, I've barely escaped men like you before and still they try to hunt me down across the world to snuff out my light, what game is this? Where is she? Please tell me, it's worth dying just to see her, one last time."

Sara bravely stated as she watched this foreboding figure smile in surprise by her boldness, no wonder Jess had fallen for such a woman. She was kept here for so long she didn't even realize how or where she'd been taken, yet to strike such words of inquiry to a man who could crush her neck with a single clutching from his hand. She somehow managed to challenge his authority even when he was releasing her, giving her the only freedom anyone could ever hope for after such a dark experience in captivity.

Without saying a word Master Darkeel raised his palm from floor to ceiling and Sara effortlessly floated. As she gasped in awe of his supreme power she heard his voice enter her mind, in full stereo surround sound his demonic cadence whispering to her,

"It is only because you realize her true worth and that you're willing to sacrifice everything for her, that I'll give you one final chance to say goodbye."

The tears streamed down her face as she said over and over again mouthing the words *Thank you* she heard his voice once more whispered instructions, "Follow me, I'll take you to your mistress and my beloved concubine."

Sara was in shock she barely remembered where her clothes were, or if she even had clothes in the first place. In an instant Master Darkeel's wry smile was followed by his left hand snapping intently, in a single moment every woman that was awake and hiding in their cell was fast asleep, as his voice serenely stated aloud;

"Now, that's much better, and this should suffice for now, I can't imagine you'll be needing much more after you see her."

In that moment the dark ominous shadow that had tormented Sara's mind, body and soul for what seemed like eternity wrapped her lovingly in his hooded cloak. Revealing his tall stature, his glowing eyes, his gorgeously chiseled jaw and a comforting smile of ease that left her legs trembling, realizing this man who ravaged her before was glorious when seen in entirety, it is no wonder her beloved fell victim to surrender and submission again in this life. Sara was already imagining herself on her knees begging her mistress for a taste of his delicious cock. Master Darkeel smiled;

"I spent so many months exhausting myself trying to break you in, and all it took was knowing you'd see your precious Bella soon again, and you're melting in the palm of my hands. I should've hired her ages ago, would've made my job far easier."

Sara was bewildered and vexed, she still wanted to kill this man with her bare hands, but was intoxicated by his charm, his devilish good looks and she could sense that her love would only give herself over to someone like him if she wanted to completely.

"Now, Follow me."

He snapped his fingers and walked up the stairwell that lead to the closet of his beloved, he knew she'd still be sleeping, he already had dinner sent up to her to ensure that she's be waking up exactly when he wanted her too. A special surprise for the woman he loved and adored, hoping it would bridge the gap in affection needed to persuade her towards his way of thinking. Deep down he knew her time with Sara was limited, there was no way she'd stay here willingly after all that he'd put her through. At dawn's early light she would try to convince her beloved mistress to escape, and Kyle, Darkeel would have no choice. It would be time to say goodbye to this beautiful creature of the night, to ensure his owned property would stay close by to tend to his will and honor his household with her glorious presence; waiting to adorn his flesh with hers whenever and wherever he declared. Kyle's boots wandered up the stone steps, the lights illuminating before their arrival.

"Your castle is so beautiful Sir, forgive me for my former transgressions, I truly had no idea that you were such a complex individual. I assumed you were just a heartless killer and no more, but the details in this place show a great care that stems from a profound soul and I must confess I find myself beguiled by this entire situation."

She pulled the cloak around her and Kyle stopped and turned from the step he was on towards Sara to look deep into her eyes;

"I am just a heartless killer, but even those of us who love to hunt can appreciate the finer things in life."

He gently touched her jawline and watched her tremble in sheer terror, knowing she was completely vulnerable to his will, she realized that she would never be safe around this man. A master who felt she was unable to be tamed, trained and properly broke in, would usually dispose of such a vexing creature, even she was guilty of such crimes in her former days as *Mistress Sara of Hamburg*.

As the approached what to Sara appeared to be a dead end she trembled and silently let the tears flow, was this just another trap? What if he had many tunnels that he led captives too beyond the interrogation room, what if this room was worse?

What if this room was filled with torture devices that she could not endure that would ultimately kill her once and for all?! Before she could even think of fleeing Kyle opened the door with the use of his telepathy, silently whispering to the house what the secret password was that entered him into Jess's bedroom, Darkeel's voice whispered, *Paradise* in his mind's eye and the closet door cracked open to reveal to Kyle his beautiful Jess.

Still sleeping soundly, dinner had not yet arrived, he fingered to Sara to follow him into the dark, whispering into her mind;

"Silence is golden, she's still asleep and I want to surprise her, come this way and walk slowly, quietly…Silent as the grave."

She nodded in full understanding, wiping the tears from her cheeks waiting to follow him into a room of clothes? She realized now that this was the back of her closet, she smelled her scent on her clothing, saw her favorite scarves hanging from the rafters in a way that only she did, unlike any other woman she'd ever met. She smiled and whispered in her mind's eye;

"Thank you so much, Thank you."

Kyle reached for her hand and gently squeezed it in affirmation of her gratitude. As they exited the closet it took every ounce of strength for Sara not to run over to her beloved mistress and to leap into her arms, kissing her all over and never letting go, but instead she was shuffled past the mirror where she saw herself for the first time in almost a year, her hair so long and ragged from never being washed, she was covered in layers of soot, dirt and drudgery from her life in the dungeon below.

"I thought you'd want to shower first, before you kiss your mistress again for the first time in almost two years."

Sara smiled as best as she could manage, but she was shocked that she didn't recognize her own face, who was this woman in the mirror? A pale reflection of her former self, what torture had left her face with such a sad expression, no wonder she couldn't see herself anymore. The sadness of being taken from her beloved settled into the layers of her soul far deeper than she ever imagined.

As Kyle reached for the dimmer light, he slowly illuminated the shower and bathtub providing just enough light to show Sara that her beautiful Bella was sleeping soundly, her face was glowing, radiant and full of light, she was happier than she'd ever seen her before, at least without her arms wrapped lovingly around her in carnal worship.

"She's so beautiful, isn't she? The only woman who's ever captured me or my heart."

Sara looked into Kyle's eyes lovingly as he responded, "The water is warm, your sleeping beauty will awaken shortly after you've finished. I'll make sure of it."

He smiled as he watched her saunter into the bathroom, seeing Bella's trinkets and photos of her and Kyle really put things into perspective. She realized that she finally had everything she ever wanted in life, a pleasure palace and torture chamber. She then wondered where if anywhere she might fit into all of this. As the hooded cloak slid to the floor and Sara stepped out of it, she opened the shower door and swooned at the sight of organic beauty products that she wanted to slather all over her body but more so on that of her mistresses. With a contented sigh the door closed and she whispered softly, Kyle's mind overhearing from the bedroom;

"This is paradise lost."

Chapter 23:

PRETERNATURAL OASIS

JESS awoke to the sound of hair being washed in the shower, the door was almost entirely closed and steam was slowly peering out in billowing clouds that kissed the crimson lips of her bedroom ceiling.

"Mmm, what time is it?"

She leaned forward to see her clock that read; seven o'clock. As she rolled over onto her back and stretched, there he was. He'd pulled a chair from where Jess had no idea and was sitting there with a single red rose and a smile of dark carnality that matched the sinful glow of his wicked eyes. Dressed in jeans, his boots still on and that tight dark green sweater that made her purr at the mere sight of him, she vocally swooned as he bit his lip;

"Are you back for seconds? I thought I fed your demons well, long into the Afternoon."

Jess coyly wrapped her sheets over her naked body and rolled forward towards him, his hand reaching forward with the rose and delicately dragging it across her arm and neck;

"I have a very special surprise for you. She's in the shower as we speak." Jess's eyebrows raised and she inquired curiously;

"Really? A surprise? A beautiful woman perhaps, showering just for me? You really do know how to spoil me."

Kyle watched her eyes curiouser and curiouser; her mental cogs and wheels still turning, trying to deduce just where he found this little strumpet to bring home tonight.

"No, it can't be? Can it?"

Speechless she saw her form washing in her mind's eye, a single crystalline tear streaked down her right cheek and fell to soak the silk sheets below.

"Is it Sara?"

Jess waited for any form of confirmation to take place, in gesture or verbal form. She hung onto this moment with heartbreaking anticipation, but before he could answer Jess was distracted by a knock at the door.

"Your supper is ready dear, shall I come in and leave it on the table for you?"

A soft voice spoke and she recognized it as one of the elderly kitchen staff who worked there from time to time, a loving woman who reminded her of her grandmother;

"Yes, come in, and thank you I'm absolutely famished." The door opened and a tray was placed on the table nearby, she nodded and smiled at both Jess and Kyle;

"Thank you so much, I can't wait to see what you've prepared for me this time."

She stole a peek and saw that Kyle had told the cooks how to prepare one of her favorite dishes. One she'd prepared for holidays time and time again and for special celebrations.

"I thought you'd love to indulge in a taste of home, since tonight is going to be a glorious exploration for us all."

Jess ran towards him and leaped into his arms, straddling his lap, he laughed endlessly at her precocious nature. She kissed him repeatedly, wrapping her arms around him and suffocating him in her breasts;

"Thank you my darling, for the glorious meal and for giving me my beloved slave back, I'll never quite find words to express to you how grateful I am for your endless devotion, gifts, and offerings of love towards me in every form."

Kyle leaned back and welcomed her kisses, delicately holding her ass and dragging the rose down her back;

"She's yours for tonight, when dawn approaches she's mine again to do with as I wish, is that understood?"

Jess's eyes suddenly went from glowing to somber, she suddenly realized that Sara would never be taken off the hunting list, she'd already been here too long. She'd known and seen far too much to not be the ultimate risk and liability to Kyle and his entire world. The children, his reputation, all that he'd built over a lifetime in this empire that was forged from blood and serrated steel. He couldn't risk losing it all for one woman no matter how attached Jess was to her.

"It's tragically understood all too well, regardless my gratitude never ceases my Lord."

Jess slowly rose from his lap and stole the rose from his hands, smelling it and swooning for its endless scent of passion;

"Are you eating with me tonight?"

Jess raised the silver tray and contently inhaled her own recipe of roasted acorn squash with shallots and rosemary, mashed potatoes, asparagus and a dinner roll.

"I'm afraid I'm not quite hungry for food tonight, though I have yet to have my fill, of other mouthwatering tastes."

His smile sinister in nature leaving Jess blushing all aglow;

"Ah and here I thought you were giving me a night alone to share with my beloved to say our goodbyes, but I'm sure neither of us will mind giving you a show."

She winked knowing full well that he'd soon be deep inside of her while she was deep inside of every wet gaping orifice of Sara's.

"Well then I'll need all of my strength to endure such a carnal night together, do you mind if I call cook to request another plate be brought up, I'm sure it's been ages since Sara has eaten and I know she'll be hungry for far more than good cooking tonight." Kyle crossed his leg at the ankle on his left knee;

"Consider it done my pet."

With a wave of his hand the order was placed downstairs below. The house instantly producing yet another order that nobody questioned nor took from him in the first place, too hypnotized in their formalities to ask questions. Jess wrapped the silk sheets around her and feasted like there was no tomorrow, knowing full well that for Sara it may be her final meal, she felt his strong hands around her shoulders, leaning forward and kissing her neck;

"I love watching you eat, so delicate and sensual, like you're fucking my hard cock with every single bite you take."

Jess smiled and continued eating, the shower water still running and the steam continued to fill the room, a long hot shower was just what Sara needed before she gave herself to her Mistress one last time. Every so often the soft moans of a woman swooning in the throes of hot water caressing her body was heard from them both, as Kyle continued to watch Jess eat, looking at her in the mirror before her standing behind her with his all-encompassing presence. She smiled taking each sensual bite with decadent coquettish charm while her mind whispered to his;

"Mmm, she's hungry tonight, I can feel it in my pussy, so warm, ripe with the sweetest juices that I know my longing slave is thirsting for me."

Jess continued eating passionately while Kyle pressed his hard cock behind her back and shoulders in the chair as she smiled her fangs extended and her eyes glowing menacingly, she couldn't help but lick her lips leaving him in such a ravenous state drove them both mad with passion. Tonight would be a night they'd soon never forget.

Chapter 24:
OTHERWORLDLY REUNION

THE shower water slowly turned off and the sound of dripping water beating down on hot tiles was echoing throughout the bedchambers of the mystical fire goddess that awaited her just outside this bathroom door. Her shaky hands reached for the shower door, a soft towel waited nearby, Sara wrapped herself in the terry cloth and felt a sense of comfort for the first time in far longer than she could recall. She smiled looking around and seeing all of her beloved's mementos. She gently opened the medicine cabinet to see so many pictures of them together, next to her favorite handmade perfume that Sara gave to her years ago when they first met. Sara reached in and pulled out the scent of *Le Bouquet a La Reine* a marvelous scent of every flower that kissed the delicate pale flesh of Marie Antoinette herself.

Opening the ornate bottle Sara adorned her neckline and wrists with the heavenly scent, along with the small of her back and inside of her thighs, knowing her Mistress would crave to devour her after missing her taste. She reached down between her thighs, her sweet sticky honey already kissing each wrist, she wanted to surrender to the woman she loved, mind, body and soul.

She never imagined after all this time kept as a prisoner that she'd ever see her ever again. The tears welled up in her eyes as she smiled and tended to her long raven locks of washed hair, combing the strands down into sheets of black silk, and slathering her skin in layers of moisturizing cream. Slowly turning around to see the scars, lashed and whipped into her body, a permanent reminder that Master Darkeel was nearby, she trembled at the thought of seeing him again, not in fear, but in masochistic rage, how could she crave to serve a man that tried to kill her so many times? It made no sense, there was no rhyme or reason to her logic, she felt compelled to drop to her knees at the sight of him, to kiss his boots and lovingly thank him for such a generous farewell. Where her final resting place would be she'd never know, but tonight all she wanted was to merge and meld flesh and soul once more with the woman who knew her better than Sara even knew herself.

She reached towards her reflection in the mirror, still looking at all of the photos of them together, smiling and knowing that just beyond this door she was waiting, fully rested and well fed, aching in wanton anticipation of this divine reunion that neither woman ever imagined would become a reality after years of mystery and captivity. Denying all shyness or need for foolish shame, Sara dropped her towel and smiled that sexy feline grin, her delicate fingers wrapping around the cracked door and opening it to reveal to Jess in mirrored reflection a goddess floating from the clouds, her figure was shadowed in layers of steam that gently dissipated.

Sara's form stood behind her, regally centered in her sexual energy she sauntered into the room maintaining eye contact and a firm gaze with her Queen. Jess instantly smiled finishing the last bite of food on her plate, she washed it down with a glass of red wine, feeling her muscles relax at the mere sight of her pleasure slave. As Sara approached the side of her bed she noticed that he was there nearby seated and smiling;

"What a pleasure it is to have you join us this evening."

Before Sara could control her urges she found herself on the floor on all fours, crawling to Kyle and kissing his planted boot profusely;

"Thank you for bringing us together, I'll never be able to express how much this night means to me."

Kyle's sinister smile matched the glowing grin that Jess had across her face, tending to her lips pressing the cloth napkin closely as Kyle leaned forward gently caressing Sara's cheek;

"I'm impressed that you've finally found your place, perhaps my love was right, unruly pleasure slaves need twice the discipline than the average slave who easily surrenders to the will of her Master; or in this case her…Mistress."

He leaned into her ear whispering to Sara those three precious words she'd hoped to hear more than anything in this world;

"Go to her."

Sara's eyes welled up in tears, as she turned towards her mistress and smiled, they rolled down her cheek effortlessly, and Jess's eyes began to fill with the same urgency to cry.

"Come to me my darling, Oh how I've missed you for so long."

Sara instantly started to crawl towards her mistress, her head raised to keep eye contact, Jess instantly beckoned;

"Walk to me my beloved, rise from your knees and approach me as your Queen."

Sara rose from the lush red carpet like a phoenix from the ashes, her illustrious hair falling down to her ass and flowing like the dark waters of hades. Jess opened her silk sheet that she'd been wrapped in like a makeshift kimono and the moment Sara was in arm's reach she pulled her close on top of her lap, her hands wrapped around her back and waist, reaching up with her neck and kissing her on full lips with ravenous fervor, both creatures of the night forgetting that the *Brides of Dracula* were under watchful eyes of Dracula Himself nearby.

Sara's breasts swelled and her nipples hardened into two perfect mounds, her hungry mistress couldn't keep her lips or lip ring off of them, tormenting them each with sensual drag of cold metal against hot flesh, she watched as Sara's back arched followed by deep throated sensual moans. Her body in full surrender to her beloved *Mistress Bella*, her blood pumping hot, her veins filled with the coursing flow of lust that only she provoked in her base instincts. Like a writhing animal she was her helpless victim, everything she ever wanted in life, to be captive and tortured by the one she loved; the one she gave herself too completely, in darkness and light.

Jess suddenly remembered in the surreal clouds of carnality that Kyle's delicious eyes were watching mere feet away from their writhing sex show. As Sara's eyes closed in sweet surrender, her back arching violently, Jess stared penetratingly deep into Kyle's eyes.

He watched as she kissed between Sara's breasts, down her stomach and slowly reached around to slip her fingers into her glorious asshole.

"Oooo, Mistress, yes, Goddess I've missed your touch, my ass needs fucking, Oooo, please take me my Queen I beg you, I am ripe with your favorite juices, please take me!"

Sara viscerally reached into her mistresses' hair and tugged it from behind, looking carnally into her eyes and screaming these words out in utter desperation.

Jess smiled and laughed aloud;

"Mmm, hmm hm, I'm so glad you haven't lost a drop of that insane vampire lust, I'm going to fuck you to the brink of death tonight. You'll beg me to stop far sooner than you ever have previously before…this I promise."

Kyle resituated in his chair, soft groans and grunts escaping from under his breath, his hard cock was pressing so tightly on his jeans he couldn't see straight. He wanted nothing more than to please these whores long into the night, hearing their moans and screams of pleasure echoing into one another's like the sweetest melody that any man or woman could ever imagine. His hands gestured to keep going to Jess while his mind entered hers to whisper;

"I'll be right back, with supper for your Sara slut, don't start without me my pet, I wouldn't miss this for the world."

As he rose from his chair and reached down into his now achingly tight jeans he repositioned his cock and slowly emerged from her bedroom, closing the door as he continued to watch Sara writhe on top of her. Jess's thighs were gently parted, her crimson hair already soaking wet, she watched as Sara teased and tormented her full lips watching Jess's nipples harden as Sara drank from her tits suckling the sweet milk from her breasts and moaning serenely intoxicated by the taste of her;

"Mmm mistress you're so sweet, I've missed your perfect tits, you grow sweeter by the year my love. The perfect blend of cruelty and kindness."

As the door slowly shut and Kyle's glowing eyes vanished he smiled into Jess's gaze and watched as Sara's gaping asshole pulsed waiting to be filled by her mistress completely.

Chapter 25:
DYNASTIC JOVIALITY

KYLE wandered down the stairs to find cook before she found herself witnessing quite the overwhelming sexual exploit. He did his best to walk without looking obvious, but he'd never felt his cock in such torment nor pain any time in this life that he could recall. He was ravenous and hungry for pussy, thirsting for the sweet sounds of beautiful women screaming his name, he did his best to focus on something else. Any distraction to allow him to focus on taking dinner up to his sensual whore's bedroom to ensure her slave had plenty of sustenance to survive the night.

Kyle entered the staff kitchen to see his two closest and oldest chefs, one's that cooked for him as a boy in this very place, still slaving over a hot stove.

"You might want to double that recipe now, I'll be eating after all." They both smiled, amused but not the least bit surprised;

"You're just like your father, always a last minute eater, it must be the curse of a writer."

The kindly old woman continued to cook and Kyle sat down nearby on the barstool waiting to take up both trays upstairs;

"She must be hungry tonight, never imagined cooking so much for a single woman." Kyle smiled and looked up, "She didn't eat much yesterday and slept most of the morning, she works much too hard, but her efforts never go unnoticed. Thank you for preparing her favorite dish, it really brightened her mood after she realized she slept all day."

The soft spoken man chimed in, "Sounds like a woman after your own heart."

His eyebrows raised with his smile before chuckling to himself and tending to the additional meal. Kyle looked up;

"I hate to admit it Luther but you might be right about this one."

His smile was one that glowed;

"It's nice to see you happy again Sir, it's been a long time." Kyle continued to smile and sighed contently, "I must be in an agreeable mood today Martha, she truly is the light of my life."

Kyle started to text James;
"Will you for the love of god come in here and break up this conversation, as much as I enjoy others noticing my happiness, this is unbearable."
James was nearby in the office, he was suddenly heard laughing as he walked into the kitchen, "Mmm, whatever that is, it smells incredible! Any extras or is it just for you Kyle?"
James sat down next to Kyle immediately distracting the loyal late night kitchen staff with his interruptions, Martha instantly piped up;
"Not for you hooligan, we take orders around here for supper not surprises, well at least not from anybody but that one next to you." Luther, Kyle and James instantly started to laugh out loud.
"You'd think I was just somebody who works here and not the lord of this manor." Kyle smiled as James chuckled alongside.
"Seriously though, what *is* that smell?"

Luther responded to James inquiries;

"It's a recipe Miss Jess created that Kyle's having us make for her tonight. She's been under the weather so he thought something from home would cheer her up." James responding;

"Ah, I see," before looking at Kyle with a cocky self-assured smile.

"Don't even start." Kyle said instantly before James burst into laughter.

"I wouldn't dare, I prefer to be on your good side." Kyle laughed at the coy response. "Good, that's where I like to keep you." He waited with face still flushed looking down pretending to be on his phone, knowing dinner would be ready any minute now.

Chapter 26:
PARADISE LOST

ABOVE in Jess's bedchambers an entirely different scenario unfolded. One that Kyle never would've suspected from his owned property; a plan that was starting to unravel in full. Sara provoked by this moment of solitude with her beloved found herself instantly stopped mid swooning from pleasure and begged her mistress to go. To run. To leave this place with her, side by side.

"Oh Goddess my love, we haven't much time, he'll be back any minute now. We have to go, we have to get out of here before it's too late. Where are we? I don't remember a single thing since I was drugged that night by him in the snow. I woke up here, in the dungeon below. Are we still in Europe? Oh God who care's! We have to go, we have to leave now, please I beg you."

Jess reached up embracing Sara, kissing her cheeks and waiting for her flesh to stop trembling.

"My darling we are very far away from home now. There is no place to go, this is our home now, and the only chance either of us have of surviving this ordeal is to stay together here, forever…" Her mistress continued:

"I know it's not ideal, after I was hired here and found out that you were the reason why. I tried to find you below and succumbed to him beyond any conceivable understanding. You know I've always had a weakness for Stockholm syndrome, though you my darling are quite the opposite, always fleeing from any form of captivity that keeps you under strict control." Sara cried in her arms, doing her best to keep her composure;

"*Shh, shh* my darling, he'll be back soon to dine with us before you and I enjoy each other. Just as we did together on those cold winter nights near the Carpathian Mountains. I promise, listen to me and do what you're told even with the cruel fear of not knowing if you'll soon be hunted down in the snow like so many others before you. He's fallen for me and I for him, but you will always be my beloved slave. I will do whatever I can within my power to ensure that you stay alive and with me for as long as we live; however long that may be." Sara smiled and hugged her mistress close, as Mistress Bella whispered into her ear;

"I promised you I'd never stop searching for you until I found you. He almost killed me for trying to free you the first time. It's only for his love for me that we are alive right now to enjoy this glorious night together. We have to focus on the glimmers of light in this dark immersive ether."

Jess wiped the tears from Sara's face and lovingly tucked her long hair behind her ears, leaving her smiling:

"Rise my darling, and come with me, I want to hold you, soothe you and remind you where you'll always belong."

Sara stood from her crouched, spread state, Jess stood and gently took her hand walking her towards her bed, "Come with me my love, I'll kiss all of your beautiful new scars and make everything alright."

Jess pulled back the comforter and unwrapped the sheet from

around her and tossed it onto the bed. She leaned forward kissing Sara deeply, slowly making her nerves calm and her body swoon.

"You leave me drunk on your wine soaked kisses, it feels like home. Your love, your touch my Queen, oh how I have missed you… words do not fully express."

Jess leaned back pulling Sara on top of her and rolling her to the side and wrapping her arms around her, pulling her close, kissing her neck and shoulders, "I will die before I let anyone hurt you, ever again. Do you hear me? If you are on his list, so am I and we shall die together in one another's arms. You have my eternal word, I promised you years ago and I mean it to this day."

She felt the weight of the world melt from her beloved Sara's shoulders, "Thank you Mistress, only you have ever known how to truly comfort me."

Sara reached back and held Jess's face;

"Goddess I have missed you more than life itself." Jess smiled kissing her neck and entering her mind with her words;

"I know precisely how you feel my pet, my existence has been cold and without laughter since the night he stole you away from me carrying you across the universe."

The Lord of Burnett manor carried two trays upstairs that silent night in the slaughterhouse hills. The world was sleeping and so were his children, both in deep slumber. The silence would soon be interrupted by the cooing sounds of two women nestled together in one another's arms, waiting for his glorious return.

As he ascended past the chandelier the twinkling in the night instantly reminded him of Jess's smile, her eyes and how they twinkled when she laughed at one of his incessantly dark jokes. No woman ever felt comforted by his true nature, most revolted. Apprehensively realizing they were in the presence of a murderous killer whose violence percolated just beneath the surface in volcanic pools of hot blood and the visceral nearly orgasmic urge to kill.

His soul couldn't help but feel complete. Even the urgency in his nature that Darkeel provoked from the depths of his slumbering heart were calmed by this night. He was far too hungry for another voracious feast in the world of carnality and satiation. Oh yes, tonight he'd give her everything she ever truly wanted, and hoped she'd prove herself worthy of his final test for her.

The dungeons were filled with wild creatures to tame, and the blizzards would soon approach. As the season of light dimmed towards the seasonal wheel turn of the months of darkness, this predatory foreplay was just what she needed to be persuaded to fully immerse herself in his world; tonight she'd be the *Red Queen of Burnett Manor* and her dear Sara her royal courtesan. His powerful steps approached the top floor, Jess felt his presence nearby instantly adding to the voracious sexual energy coursing through Sara's hot lips and filling up her soul with the warmest wine any maenad could ever dream of.

"He's nearly inside my darling, we must wait for his command before proceeding. Plus mistress desires you to be well fed for what I have in store for your gorgeous flesh on earth's warm bed."

Sara rolled from on top of her scarlet queen, as her carnal eyes feasted upon her plump German pout. Jess smiled and appeared in feline form just to betwixt her lover into smiling the way she did in their decadent cabin in the snow. With a wave of her hand the dimmer lights were off and she wiggled her fingers in a filthy way that instantly rose the darkness into candlelight. Her fangs were protruded as she stared at Sara's full breasts as they hung heavily in flickered light. The room looked like a pool of blood and they we're entombed within it. Sara turned around and placed her back near the headboard, just as Kyle walked in, the door opened from the mere thought in his mind that resonated...

"*Mine.*"

Chapter 27:
QUIVERING DESCENT

THE dark shadow appeared from the hallway, the silhouette instantly transforming Sara's radiantly confident self into a timid trembling kitten in Jess's arms;

"*Shh, shh* my darling, I know it will take time to adjust to such drastic changes. You're safe in my arms my pet whore." She gently stroked Sara's back and ran her fingers through her long raven locks until her vibrating flesh softened into a melting state of bliss.

"My deepest apologies my Lord, I'm still adjusting to my new way of life in your home."

Kyle walked in setting a tray on the same table that Jess's meal was previously on, walking across the bedroom at the foot of the bed, the door closing and locking gently behind him without a touch.

"Wow, Mistress his powers mimic yours in such an uncanny way, I can't begin to imagine how incredible you two are to watch, Mmm the mere thought of such a sight leaves my pussy swollen and aching to cum."

She bit her lip and smiled wickedly at Kyle before laughing and blushing burying her face in Jess's breasts;

"I knew she was hungry tonight, but after that comment, I'll assume *starving* is a much better word for you instead."

She leaned in whispering this to Sara and staring Kyle in the eyes with a salacious grin and wink of her left eye.

"You wicked whores, we must gain our strength first before I destroy you both tonight. In the morning walking won't be a part of either of your new lives…Only crawling, begging and pleading for me to cease in pounding every hole in your body as roughly as I see fit."

Kyle sat his tray down on Jess's built in dresser. The long mirror doing wicked things to her mind, making her imagine how it would feel to clone him and to have his mirror twin pumping inside of her tight asshole while his thick, heavy cock was tickling the bottom of her throat and challenging her to breathe as tears of pleasure leaked out generously from such a filling experience. He kicked his boots off and sighed contently he gently unzipped his jeans. Kyle moaned;

"Oh, much better, leaving you two in such a state, my jeans have never been tighter."

Sara and Jess laughed as Jess rose from the bed, completely naked, dashing by and swinging from the four poster bed towards Sara's food. She reached for a rolling wooden tray that allowed Sara to eat from bed, she was already sitting up her long hair draped over her breasts. She smiled radiantly looking forward to indulging in a meal that she and her mistress enjoyed over many holidays together near *Castle Dracula*.

"It amuses me that you still forget I can read your mind…" Kyle said cheekily to Jess as he looked in his reflection as if even he was competition, Jess instantly laughed blushing;

"I haven't the slightest clue as to what you're talking about my Lord." Kyle laughed aloud;

"If that's the best you can do at lying, my love you'll have to try much harder."

His eyes turned to a predatory state that sent chills into both women leaving their nipples hard and their spines tingling. He slowly revealed what was under his tray and waited for Jess to do the same for Sara.

The silver trays rose, both Kyle and Jess let them go to leave them hovering above the banquets, leaving Sara smiling, laughing and clapping at such a sight.

"Oh my God, everything looks and smells so good, thank you. I cannot begin to express how much I've missed this meal, it was the first one mistress ever taught me how to prepare for her on special nights." She sighed in nostalgia she said aloud;

"Memories, I look forward to making many more of if I'm fortunate enough to earn such a right in this life." She dropped her face and nodded at Kyle, her eyes slowly lifting up to meet his, he smiled, his lips curling ever so wickedly;

"You may eat *untamable whore*, tonight you'll find a new name after we're done with you."

The trays slowly floated over towards Jess's desk and makeshift dining table and landed delicately on the wood. As Kyle bit into his first bite of roasted acorn squash, he moaned aloud;

"Oh dear God, and I thought you were the most delicious thing I've ever tasted."

He continued to eat and Sara joined in. Jess watched as they both devoured her special recipe, never knowing that every acorn squash was laced with a special concoction that she personally blended and soaked them in weeks prior as they were ripening in her garden out back fresh on the vine, ensuring that these long passionate nights would overwhelm the senses of everyone present. Leaving even the most seasoned sex addict exhausted in pleas of safe words.

"Oh mistress how I've missed your cooking, I do appreciate the IV's Sir but there's nothing quite like this meal, it turns me into *such* an insatiable sex kitten."

Kyle smiled and entered Jess's mind;

"Another one of your *special meals* I assume? No wonder my cocks harder than iron after a single bite."

Jess' mischievous smile appeared on her face;

"I hope you don't mind, I told you I've missed her, and I want you to enjoy yourself; you work too hard." Jess bemused by her coy response waited for his laugh and instantly aloud his voice was heard.

"Your mistress is a wicked whore Sara, and I look forward to punishing her tonight in front of you." Jess smiled;

"It's true your beloved Bella for years now has, well added a special potion to this dish, I'm sure it makes sense why our holidays have always been so... how shall we say *memorable?*" Sara's mouth opened and she was in awe;

"You drugged me! You bitch!" The room filled with laughter, instantly Sara said;

"Oh well, I really can't complain, I mean there were times I physically was prepared for death from your forced orgasms, and I was more than ready to die that way, Oh could you imagine? Sheer fucking bliss."

Sara continued to eat and Jess noticed she tried her best to hide the deep and massive scars across her back and left arm that were only there after Kyle brought her to this place.

"My poor darling what happened to your back, how did you get such deep scars?" Sara replied;

"I honestly don't remember or know, I just recall waking up down below in shackles and covered in them after they'd fully healed, it's still the strangest thing to me, by the looks of it, I should be dead."

Kyle lifted his sweater to reveal similar scars on his left abdomen that wrapped around his lower back;

"Honestly we both should, I had to kill that fucking animal, whatever it was with my bare hands, and then drag us both under barbed wire fences to safety. I had you on antibiotics administered through IV's for at least six months or so before you even woke up. I thought you would've died from the infection. I know I felt like I did; six weeks in bed, the entire empire nearly crashed trying to ensure your safety here." Jess walked over to Kyle and gently examined his scars;

"Why haven't I ever noticed these before? I've touched you here a thousand times at least." Jess astounded by the deep brooding gashes, she leaned forward and kissed him on his temple, hugging him close;

"Mmm, now this I can get used too. What other awful stories do I have to share that will inspire more adoration from my concubine?" Sara was astounded;

"I really do owe you my life. That phrase always infuriated me when I was held captive, but now it makes so much sense."

Kyle smiled, "I've always been an honest man, even if the cruelty of such words are presently lost by those who hear them. It always makes sense later on I assure you, though most don't stick around long enough to find that out about me." Jess continued to rub his shoulders and watched as his cock jumped from such pleasurable banter;

"Oh God, you know how to soothe the beast inside, Darkeel rarely takes over anymore, ever since you arrived."

With a deep contented sigh, the room fell silent as both Sara and Kyle tended to the final portions of their meals. Sara started to cry softly as she spoke.

"Sir I hope you will forgive me and at the very least accept my apologies for all the complications I have added to your life. All along I thought you were taking me away from my beloved Mistress Bella and instead you were trying to smuggle me into this country to ensure that I'd always be by her side. Words cannot begin to express my gratitude as well as my humiliation for such heinous behavior down below in the dungeons. If there's any way I can make things better I will not hesitate to surrender to your will to pay off my debts." Jess smiled and said;

"That is the nobility that I instilled within you, you make your Mistress proud with such declarations of devotion to this household my darling."

Kyle smiled and responded, "Serve your queen as she serves her king. There is no added complications to such a flawless dynamic, if you please us both with the fullest in satisfaction a world of carnal wonders awaits you. But if you displease me or your beloved, you will regret it unlike any other mistake you've ever made in this life. Apologies will not be enough to save you after you've betrayed my kindness. You put not only my world at risk, but hers as well with even the slightest of transgressions. Remember your place Sara, never ever forget it. You of all creatures of the night know what happens to women who displease me."

Her body shuddered at the thought of other women in cells near hers who'd she tried to help escape, the echoed screams strangled her nerves into submission.

"Yes, Sir." The only words Sara's lips could mutter after such a revelation.

Chapter 28:

CIRCUS BLOODBATH

"MMM you're wicked. You're scaring her." Jess leaned forward whispering playfully into his ear, as he gripped her firmly by the wrists he said;

"Good, I hope you're both scared, left trembling and weakened by the adrenaline coursing through your intoxicated blood tonight. I want you to feel the power that's deep within me. The dark penetrating ether that envelopes me, mind, body and soul."

Jess's heart quickened, along with an audible gasp that left Sara tremoring in her place between her beloved mistresses' sheets.

"By tonight you will fear me just as she does my darling, not to worry, you'll meet Darkeel personally, he's been asking about you for months now. Especially while I watch you bathe and pleasure yourself behind two way glass." Jess gasped aloud once more and shuddered looking over at Sara;

"Where would you like us my Lord?" She waited to feel Kyle's hands slowly release her wrists from around his shoulders.

"I am here for the show, at least for now. I didn't realize you'd have ways to lace my food with bewitching poisons that leave my voracious will faulty with visions of writhing concubines. Show me what's in your mind, go to her and take her as your whore again. Please your master with a show, I'll soon, never forget."

Jess looked at his reflection in the mirror, his piercing gaze left her paralyzed in place. He reached back and up towards her neck, slowly caressing it from collarbone to nape. His dark disposition softened into a carnal grin, leaving her body vulnerable to surrender, her nipples pulsed, her flesh quaked and she craved him more now than she ever previously had in this life.

"Mmm, that's my good girl, she's all yours Jess, introduce me to Mistress Bella. Let me bask in the glow of your salacious creations."

Jess bit her bottom lip sensually her eyes fluttering closed. Her long eyelashes floating in stasis, with one final gasp of contentment. She opened her eyes and stared right into Sara's, leaving her trembling slave as a wanton whore suddenly overwhelmed by desire.

"Oh mistress, those hungry eyes of yours, how I have missed them,"

Instantly Jess's fangs protruded and her tits perked up as she slinked towards Sara on the bed. Gently crawling towards her ass and fresh pussy displayed directly in Kyle's face, a mere foot away from his hard cock and his adventurous hands. She felt him smack her on the ass towards her wanted direction, tearing the sheets from in front of Sara. Her tray sent flying towards her desk, instantly floating to its desired location.

"Spread your thighs, I've missed your taste my sweet harlot. Every drop of you will be mine tonight."

In an effortless motion the sheets flew into the rafters above the bed. Kyle was having more than enough telekinetic fun, watching the women frolic naked underneath waves of red silk that mimicked an ocean of blood. He watched Sara's head as it dug back into the mattress, her tits swelled instantly and he watched as Jess licked her fangs slowly. Her face so close to Sara's sweet dripping pussy that she could almost taste it, she watched Sara's tortured face contort as she began to blow softly at the folds watching the juice flow freely. Jess kissed her thighs, slowly at first and then ravenously with both hands wrapped around her thick thighs, pressing them closely to her cheeks, "Say it, you filthy whore, tell me what your Mistress wants to hear." She peered over at her Master as his carnal eyes were glowing in this ravenous state of live debauchery between Dracula's writhing, carnal and hungry brides.

"Fuck me! Oh Goddess, break me, beat me, and use me as your toy. Oh god, plea…se. Let me cum! I beg you!"

Sara's soft requests transformed into tortured pleas of desperation, as the final word left her full pursed lips, Sara's fangs finally revealed themselves in all their porcelain glory. Two long sharp and fierce canines, protruded from beneath her full upper lip, her nails elongated, each sharp tip slicing into her breasts and torso with the slightest of effort, her hips bucked and contorted wishing her mistresses warm breath would finally inch its way into her soaking wet cunt, she couldn't take it much longer. The poison teasing her blood like hot fire, in that moment when she knew Sara's heart couldn't pump any harder, Mistress Bella plunged her tongue, lips, cold steel lip ring and nearly her entire face into her drenched slit.

"Oh thank Goddess, I felt my life was about to end."

Sara's screams and moans filled the air, Mistress Bella's pussy leaked down her inner thighs, leaving Kyle's cock bulging from pleasure to pain. His blood coursing hard into the thick veins of his dick, his beautiful erection so swollen that audible gasps of pain escaped his lip each time the girls came in front of him.

"Oh god Mistress, Fuck! I can't stop cumming, Oh god, I'm going to gush, Oh God! Oh God! Oh God!"

In that moment Kyle's obedient whore took on a much different persona, her regal nature was bewitching, seeing her ferocity as she bit firmly into her sexy whore's thick thigh leeching the most rampant blood from her while simultaneously fingering her deep. Three fingers plunging in and out of her tight cunt, while the forth dove into her ass effortlessly. Leaving Sara gasping for air, her hands clawing at the headboard, her fingers tearing into the wood and leaving marks as a permanent reminder of what exploits took place this very night. Sara gushed buckets all over Mistress Bella's face, as she gasped for air and suckled on her juicy clit, more juices started to squirt not from Sara but her insatiably horny mistress that couldn't contain her pleasure anymore, this taste was far sweeter than any ambrosia in existence.

She found herself drunk on Sara's ceaseless energy. Her warm blood now pooling through her body she rose above Sara as Sara's arms embraced her mistress in sheer desperation. Jess covered her lips in blood soaked juices and continued to fuck Sara hard. Their bodies writhing on top of one another, their pussies rubbing in such a delicious sight, the full lips of each woman's vulva folding in and on top of one another's before yet another bucket gushed forth between them at the same time. As their moans matched one another's in a haunting echo of high pitched singing that left Kyle hypnotized.

He couldn't take it a moment longer, he needed to feel them both. He craved to be overwhelmed by pleasure and intoxicated by the raw power of sexuality in this moment. He stood his cock hard, walking towards the plump and juice soaked ass of his writhing whore. He watched as she feasted on the lips of her beloved pleasure slave. He used his powers to raise them both inches above the bed, he watched as they both smiled and laughed at such decadence. The blood silk sheets soaking in juices wrapped around them as they continued to fuck one another writhing in every drop. They couldn't help rubbing it all over and into their breasts and suckling at each other's tormented nipples until the milk flowed and squirt all over the bed. Each one shooting streams of sweet white honey into each other's mouths, the blood and milk pooling together in an intoxicating drink that quenched their thirst, but not their hunger for hot flesh.

"Would you like feeling his cock between us? Or would my pet prefer to feel me get fucked as I continue to fuck her until she dies? Mistress Bella craves it all, and you my darling will love the feeling of our energies mixed together in this room of whores."

Kyle stood behind them and watched their sweet pussies sliding across one another's;

"Yes mistress, use me, fuck me, break me in, I want to earn the right to sleep at the foot of your bed, now and always." In one final gasp she screamed, "Take me to your paradise!"

Kyle plunged his cock between these two slippery whores, his moans heard echoing in the room alongside their melodic songs of pleasure, both Sara and Jess were left shaking in pleasure, their cunts gushing gallons of juice forward. An ocean of sweet perfume filled the air, and Kyle gripped Jess's hips, floating them both towards him on the side of the bed. In that moment of weightlessness he teased the tip of his cock between their clits making both women moan, scream and tremble from pleasure, Jess kissing Sara ravenously and Sara's nails digging into Jess's soft porcelain skin and tearing it apart. Her back pooled with drops of warm blood, slowly sliding down towards her ass, Kyle leaned forward, his hands reaching for the fresh kill, and tasting her elixir. In that moment Jess moaned in a way that he had never witnessed by her before. Her mind whispering incantations to his;

"Mmm, I'm now a part of you Master Darkeel, your darkness, your strength, your virility, I'm inside of you now, just as you're about to be inside of me."

Jess smiled and winked looking over her right shoulder, her long red locks cascading down her bloody back. In that moment Kyle plunged his cock deep inside of her, painfully reminding her in that body shuddering moment just who really owned her in this world.

The audible gasps filled the room, and the bucking and hard fucking from behind that Jess was taking like a Queen added to the visceral pumping that Sara felt beneath her.

"Oh Goddess you're right, the combined energy of you two, Ugh! I have never felt such power before, Oh Mistress here I cum, again, Oh Goddess this is it, I'm going to die!"

In that moment Kyle's grunted yells were heard echoing through the bedroom, striking pleasure into the pussies of both vamp whores that shuddered in ecstasy now, limbs and bodies uncontrolled by the state of ecstasy that was pumping and coursing through their veins and every cell. Gushing juices continued to pour down the side of the mattress spilling on the floor, Kyle braced himself on the bed post nearby, still clinging to Jess's ass, still deep inside her, unable to move. Sara was left panting and trying to regain her strength as she felt her arms being forced above her head and watched as Mistress Bella pierced her soft supple tits, watching the blood squirt into her mouth along with the sweet milk that flowed freely behind.

Jess asked coyly, "My King, could you reach into the top drawer of my nightstand and hand me both the lube and my delicious triple dildo?" Sara's eyes filled with drunken pleasure turned to fear and the desire to flee.

"Ah, ah, ah, my pet, you said you wanted to earn it, I am not done with you, just yet."

Kyle grunted still deep inside his warm, wet, sticky whore's pussy, reached over and handed her the desired devices that she craved to show him how she used them on her beloved cum slut.

Kyle leaned forward holding her hips and pulling her head back by her hair;

"Mmmm, I guess you won't be needing this right now…"

As he pulled out, Jess collapsed on top of Sara her hips uncontrollably tremoring. Her cunt spewing juices all over Sara's clit leaving her moaning out loud with audible gasps of pain stricken pleasure that made her gorgeous brown eyes roll back into her head, as her breasts heaved and her lips parted, panting for sweet surrender.

Jess straddled Sara as they floated back down to the surface of the bed, Kyle stumbling back towards the wall and resting his head on it for stability.

"Woo, I have never came so fucking hard in my entire life."

Jess floated a glass of water towards him watching him smiling, laughing;

"You're getting much better at that, such a quick study my intellectual sex kitten."

He gorged on water grasping for his senses and stumbling to the chair for regained composure. As his head leaned back, his smile drunk and glowing in satisfaction. He watched as Jess lubed up the smallest of the three connected dildos, she smiled as Sara continued to catch her breath;

"Do you need a drink my darling? I wouldn't want to leave you without enough fluids in your gorgeous body."

Sara's eyes rolled open slowly and her eyebrows raised;

"Mmm, when have I ever stopped you in the middle of your work my queen? I'll die before I interrupt you."

Kyle smiled and chimed in;

"What a devoted slave, I'm impressed with her affection towards you, yet I understand it all too well. Before I met you I was focused on my pleasure and satisfaction, now all that I concern myself with is your pleasure, which seems to be endless and easily explored at any moment."

He continued to drink his water and watched Jess spread Sara's thighs apart, hearing her hiss, moan and swoon in cooing bliss.

"Do your worst my Queen, after so many years apart, I'm ready for you tonight."

Sara's carnal eyes bantered with Jess' both girls laughing, cooing and kissing with sensual moans of enjoyment. She just couldn't get enough beautiful women, pleasure and the rough and dangerous men of this world that satiated her carnality to completion.

"Spread those thighs apart my beautiful whore, tonight we ride, just as we did in the forest, when your back was ruined by the trees, those trees that I fucked you brutally against, as the wolves howled in the full moonlight."

Mistress Bella moaned, her head falling back and her hips bucking as she inserted the largest cock inside of herself leaving two sticking out in a precarious way that left Kyle instantly smiling;

"Mmm, I can't wait to watch what happens next my pet."

His feet firmly planted on the floor, his hands crossed, each elbow at the knee, his sinister eyes peeking over his wickedly crossed hands glowing brightly for the next view of this carnal show. Jess smiled over her left shoulder to her glorious Master and said;

"This one's for you."

As Jess bit her bottom lip, she looked back into Sara's eyes and said, "I have always loved you, there wasn't a moment in time that I haven't thought of you, missed you, and longed for your touch, your sweet taste and your beautiful scent. You were the first reason in this life I ever had for living, and he is my last. Together we will finally be the family I've always dreamed of."

Mistress Bella's breasts softly kissed Sara's pert tits and their lips fell onto one another's as Sara's thighs raised instinctively around the hips of her buxom Goddess.

"Take me my Queen, break me in and remind me who I eternally belong too."

In that moment both cocks entered Sara's aching holes, she gasped and moaned in unison, her warmth and comfort seeped out into every limb spreading her heat into her beloved mistress's core.
"You will always belong to me, until your dying day."

Kyle leaned back stroking his cock slowly. He was fascinated by her sensuality, her soft regal and refined disposition that provoked his mind to remember this precise scene from centuries before. He knew that Jess and he had conquered beautiful women together in many lifetimes, but he forgot how vividly she reminded him of himself in his earliest days as a young man. So romantic and passionate leaving his lovers swooning and heartbroken after the sun rose over the snowcapped Colorado hills as the sun rose. With each slow all-encompassing pump inside of her, he watched his beloved concubine transform into a strong, powerful queen. Relishing in the fawning affections of rampant whores that ached to be chosen as her favorite new confidant. To later be swept away into her bedchambers late at night, to hear such beautiful phrases whispered into their ear, as she filled them with hand carved cocks that were sent to her from the most depraved experts in Italy. In a flash he was suddenly back to the present moment, the bloody silk wrapped around their flesh, clinging to it a midst the sweet juices and sweat that were thriving between the glistening bodies of his beloved Jess and her eternal pet Sara.

He watched in splendor as these two creatures of the night, writhed, and pumped against one another's gorgeous dew kissed bodies. The glow of candlelight adding to the ambiance of this carnal show. This three ring circus that she created entirely for his pleasure; in turn satiating her own. In one fluid motion Jess raised Sara up by her lower back and shoulders, embracing her close and pulling her breasts against hers. Kissing her as she bucked and rode her wildly, her back arching and her legs stretching out behind Mistress Bella in an extraordinary feat that resembled an *old world circus*, if only the contortionists weren't wearing their costumes.

As Sara reached back and gripped one of the wooden posts on the four post bed, she saw her mistress lean back and in that moment both women came hard. Screaming in unison, their bodies jerking violently as their pussies squeezed the cocks from their gushing cunts, each woman squirting so violently that they shot oceans above one another's heads. The liquid landing in a spray across Mistress Bella's tits and Sara's face. Like a feline in heat Sara ravenously licked up and sucked the juices from her queen into her mouth, and her mistress reaching forward to jerk the cocks out of their holes to toss this wicked device aside, for the sheer sake of survival.

Jess's tits still soaked in Sara's sweet juices both women panting and gasping for breath, their thighs still quivering uncontrollably. Echoes of moans filling the air along with their fragrant scent of feverous passion.

Kyle stood up, erect and soaked in sweat and the sweet juices of two beautiful sex kittens. He wandered to the bathroom and said;

"That was incredible. Would you two care for a shower after making such a ravenous mess everywhere? You've ruined these sheets."

He smiled and watched the girls laugh together, blushing from exasperation.

"I promise I'll replace them my King." Jess said smiling and winking at Sara as she continued to laugh and blush.

"That won't be necessary my darling, I just love teasing you. I'm still speechless from the filthy show I just saw."

He struggled to tear his clothes off over his gorging erection, they heard the water turn on and watched his tall, muscular body enter and closing the door behind him.

"He really is gorgeous mistress, I can see why it'd be hard to kick him out of bed."

Sara smiled and curled up in her arms as they waited for their legs to return.

"You have absolutely no idea, my love. From reading my body, random thoughts and answering me within the chambers of my own mind. To the sheer intellect and brilliance he displays constantly, it takes all of my power not to walk around naked and beg for his cock every.., single... moment of my life."

"Join us my pet, it's time to wash. He mentioned a special surprise that he has to show us, I already thought this was it but perhaps I've been mistaken."

Jess rose and walked towards the shower door, Sara approached her and ran behind to hug and embrace her, kissing her neck and cheek feverously;

"I think I'm going to like it here." Jess reached back to comfort her slaves adoring face, gently caressing her cheek;

"Good, because I honestly couldn't be happier than I am in this moment right now. To have you home again, truly with his presence in my life has made my entire existence complete."

Jess reached for the shower door and opened it to see Kyle's glorious body covered in hot water, his cock slowly stroked by his hands, he opened his eyes and said;

"Mmm, good I was hoping you'd join me."

As Sara and Jess entered the steam filled shower, Kyle reached for Jess's head, pulling her close and kissing her intensely. Sara wandered around the back of Kyle and began to wash, looking into her mistresses eyes for permission to grab his hard cock and to drop to her knees to thank him for such a wonderful night.

"You may do as he commands, it would please my voyeuristic appetites greatly to watch you serve him as I tend to further his pleasure."

"Ugh, possessing such fortune such as this, a dark beast with two writhing whores, open your full lips Sara…my darling Jess, you are far too generous, ever finding new ways to impress me, and I crave your mouth against mine more than ever."

Kyle's hands wrapping around Jess's shoulders and up her neck, began kissing her ravenously, whispering into her ear;

"I can't wait until we're alone in the morning, I'll show you how much you've pleased me tonight. You've made me more proud than I ever dreamed a woman could, I never knew you possessed this side of your sexuality. The best parts of a man's mind sequestered within the body and soul of a temptress. You've stolen my heart and after this night, quite possibly my dark splintered soul will belong entirely to you."

Jess swooned as she watched Sara smiling with her eyes closed as the water trickled over her face, mouth stuffed full with his raging cock, she teased and tormented his shaft, jerking it off while she licked his balls, Kyle hissed in Jess mouth at every debilitating moment of satisfaction.

"Good girl my pet, you're pleasing both your mistress and her master, I'm so proud of you, you bring my soul such joy on this dark winter night."

Kyle continued to kiss Jess, teasing her pussy with his hands and fucking her tight little asshole with his thick fingers, making her moan in every kiss, succumbing to bliss fully, she squirted all over his fingers as he plunged himself deep inside her asshole, feeling it gape as her hips jerked towards his warm wet body.

Sara plunged her mouth deep down to her throat around his cock feeling his warm cum welling up, about to explode. Just moments later leaving her with his regal taste, filling her mouth so fully that it spilled forth, soaking her plump purple lips in a layer of silk. She jerked his cock off ensuring every drop was spilled and Kyle grunted, growled and shuddered under the immense overload felt by the energies swimming around him in the form of Jess and Sara.

"Holy fuck."

Kyle's head fell back and Jess fell to her knees to tend to kissing his balls, licking up the last few drops of cum and kissing Sara deeply to taste them both as they swam inside of her. Kyle watched mouth smiling, feeling both girls' hands swimming up his thighs to his knees, feeling their hands exploring his hips and gripping his ass.

"Oh, I do love a man with a nice ass." Sara said giggling, and Jess remarked;

"A girl after my own wicked heart."

As the shower water continued to wash down onto them, Kyle leaned forward reaching for them both and pulling them up into his arms where they continued to kiss. He reached for the soap and began to wash them and himself before these two succubae had a moment to recuperate their losses, both seeking him out for supper once more. The water continued to flow, the steam billowed out of the bathroom and into the bedroom, and the private tunnel entrance still cracked open, wafting hot steam down into the dungeons to warm the cold victims that shivered long into the night. The Lord of Burnett Manor was exhausted, yet the night was still young.

He knew they'd love the surprise he had in store for them after this long delicious night together. A private retreat for two female vamps to enjoy all alone in hallowed grounds of their beloved earth in his private, haunted cemetery.

Chapter 29:
ACRIMONIOUS AWAKENING

STANDING in the mirror Kyle looked into his eyes, still hearing his darling Jess's giggles and moans of pleasure erupting softly from the cracked shower door. A faint whisper of skin peering through and waves of long wet black and red hair. He saw his concubine's pleasure slave face deep buried between her thighs;

"Just one more, Master please? I promise we'll come out and fulfill our duties."

Jess gasped and moaned between each word, her cadence building in adrenaline and desperation. Kyle smiled his hands gripping the top of the counter firmly, a wicked smile on his lips. His eyes pierced the fog and he watched once more as his beautiful scarlet queen's head fell back, her hand gripping over the shower. He gently touched her fingertips, watching her lips purse as she swooned, her thighs wrapped around Sara's shoulders, her beloved pet gripping her luscious ass and forcing herself between every wet quaking fold. Kyle reached into the shower and grabbed her firmly by the neck, forcing a kiss to her lips that caused her to shudder as her climax rushed oceans of pleasure over and underneath her body simultaneously.

"I felt more than one my voracious whore, out of the shower now. You and the fuck toy, I have a surprise for you."

His eyes changed from piercing blue to a menacing glowing green, Kyle was no longer here, not fully anymore. She felt the darkness consuming him, slowly penetrating into every hallway, corridor and dark chamber of his heart and invading his mind, body and tortured soul. Jess knew she was much too late. She thought the pleasure would be enough to keep him fully present, but the remnants of Kyle were slowly disappearing into the dark bleak nothingness that drove his very existence for breathing... *Darkeel*.

Sara saw the look of alarm in her lover's eyes, she knew in this moment the strictest of old guard protocol would be required to ensure her safety as well as the one she loves. Jess penetrated her thoughts gently and serenely on a vibrational frequency that was far from the dark seeded etheric wave that Darkeel frequently functioned on.

"My darling, Kyle is no longer with us, at least for now, perhaps we can seduce him back out but until then. This is life or death, do whatever he says without even a nuance of hesitation."

Sara instantly fluttered her eyes in a coded way that informed her Mistress that she was in full understanding of the reality of the present situation.

Darkeel's rhythmic hands slinked into the shower, holding two long black and red robes, both hooded. In each robe a golden mask dangled shimmering in jewels. Jess instantly reached towards her love's hands and thanked him for the beautiful gifts.

His tall foreboding figure now peering down in all black. His stare was blank as if Kyle was carved out of his own flesh with a freshly sharpened hunting knife. Jess had never been more terrified in her life, but she did her best to remain composed to feel some sense of comfort and ease to assure him;

"Once you've finished getting ready, wander down your closet, through the secret passage and follow the torches, they'll lead you to your final resting place."

Sara's eyes filled with fear, but she did as she was instructed, reaching for the red robe she started to wrap it around her naked, wet shoulders. Her long hair still drenched was now resting under the crimson hood soaking up her long tresses and instantly warming her to the bone. She hesitated and placed the gold mask on her face, tying it firmly underneath her hood and behind her raven locks. She exited the shower and took her Mistresses robe and waited for her to turn around. Her glorious shapely ass shining in the dim light, Kyle suddenly came too and remembered that tonight he'd have to fight to be present, this time of year was ruled by Darkeel.

This is usually when Kyle said he'd be gone for months on business when in fact he'd dwell deep within the center of his house, buried in old papers of his work, and leaving the house under the mask of night and piercing cold to hunt the hills for every woman he could get his claws into that wouldn't be safe tonight.

"I'm sorry my darling for suddenly vanishing, I usually have more control over him than I do tonight. I should be sleeping but I have a feeling I need to be near you to ensure your safety as well as mine."

He fell to his knees and cried into her beautiful ass, kissing it and spreading the cheeks softly as Sara continued to robe her beautiful scarlet queen. Jess felt his tongue teasing her tight asshole, she gasped suddenly, her tits perking up;

"My love, I'm here to protect you, I know I can save you, even from yourself. It's the only gift I have to offer in this life."

Kyle wrapped his arms around her thighs and gripped firmly as he continued to tongue fuck her tight pink little asshole until she buckled and reached for the shower wall to brace herself from such tremendous pleasure.

"Oh yes, remind me of paradise, and keep the demon away, Oh Jess, you taste so sweet."

Kyle felt himself growing more predominantly into his body again, as if he had just awakened from the deepest of slumbers. He knew this woman was the anecdote to his poison, she always had been for as long as he could remember in this life and previous ones. In dreams far too many to count, he felt her near him, with him, inside his soul, always calming, dare say taming the beast within. Sara tied the mask on her face as soon as she was finished climaxing, and adorned her red locks, now long straight and wet with the black hood cloaking her queen in a mask fit for royalty.

Kyle watched Jess turn around slowly, her nipples were hard and escaping the robe, revealing her porcelain flesh in delicate glory. Still on his knees he reached for her, wrapping his arms around her thighs once more and placing his face onto her body. She felt him tremble and she ran her fingers through his hair.

"I want desperately not to hurt you, but I don't know how much longer I can hold back anymore. I've never been out of my body that long, I should be sleeping or hunting right now. I was a fool to ever think I could control this part of me in any other way, my love…please forgive me."

Jess smiled and reached down embracing his face, Sara was watching from the doorway, slowly walking away to ensure her safety. She never felt safe anymore, she wanted to flee even in this early snow fall she didn't care the risk of such a venture. She wanted to be far away from this place and to never look back. Kyle reached up and looked deeply into her eyes, his face filled with anger and intensity, his blue eyes once more fading out as the green flowed back in, Jess humbly bowed and said;

"How may I serve you tonight Darkeel? Take me to your paradise Demon King."

Kyle's body rose preternaturally, he stood before her appearing slender and skewed, each affectation of his facial expression more elongated and sinister in appearance than ever before. This powerful creature was doing his best to fully take over this brilliant man, whom he found wandering in the snow that day in morbid childlike curiosity. His hands rolled in the direction of the doorway and Jess wandered out through it towards the closet. She reached for Sara's hand and held her arm in hers, insinuating that she wanted her to walk first, to ensure she was the barrier between Darkeel and her beloved slave.

Sara descended down into the hollows of the earth below. The torches already ablaze leading these wandering victims into the dark recesses of the soul of Burnett Manor, to a place that most women would find themselves in a state of sheer horror if they ever stumbled upon it by persuasive force, never by accident. They passed his secret office that Jess has penetrated in her previous investigations, acting as if she'd never seen it before; she walked by head down pretending to see in the dark corridor. She sparked no interest in Darkeel, as he was still at the top of the stairs waiting for them to not follow instructions as he decreed, so he could finally take them both savagely at once. He was a being of calculated barbarianism. The merest utterance of ill perfection in following an order was the initial terror that invoked a forest elemental to finally cross into the material world. Slashing his victims to shreds in the snow and watching the warm blood flow free. It was this weakness for structure that gave these two well trained masochist's full reign to conquer the hollow soul of *The Slaughterhouse Hills Hunter*. The only thing keeping Jess alive was her sacred connection to the dryads; it was the nearly identical familiarity in paranormal bloodlines that prevented Darkeel from tearing her apart limb from bloodied limb.

Sara walked into a dark stone chamber deep beneath the earth's crust. A hidden mausoleum with a center stone, the size of a bed. A place where one usually displays a coffin of a loved one that still means the world to them. She entered and walked towards the door that existed and stood before it.

On the other side a statue with an urn and what was obviously, a woman's ashes. The other two columns found on both sides of the entrance were adorned with candelabra's that gently illuminated this underground sanctuary.

Jess wandered slowly into the room her jeweled mask dancing with the light and casting colors a midst the stone ceiling. Each one was hand painted with filigree and a date that followed with the name of somebody that was truly loved. Darkeel entered and stood at the entrance, his glowing eyes and wicked smile with crossed arms the only appearance his body desired to make in this haunting and somber place. They both stood there like statues for what felt like forever, he waited and smiled, his laugh slowly built and erupted into a hysterical banter of egomaniacal proportions.

"It's funny really, I thought you two cunts would slip up by now, defy me in even the slightest of ways so that I would finally be allowed to consume this body as my own and take you as my tributes, adding your bodies to my collection that you find here in this very vault."

Darkeel continued…

"But you just won't! You're both fucking well trained. Never have I seen anything in my dark and twisted life that both appeases and provokes me in such a way. The worst part is Kyle will be back any minute now, and I have no choice in the matter, you two have behaved far better than I gave you credit for, you're lucky. At least for now."

Kyle's body collapsed in the doorway, his hands gripping the cold stone floor and both women bolting to his aid, ensuring his safety. His body weak, covered in sweat, his breath was rapid and his heart beating fast;

"Jess, it's too late, I can't hold him off any longer, I have to kill or he'll take over for good, it's the only way. I'm so sorry, this is what I've tried to keep you and every woman that's in this tomb away from, please, please, save yourself."

Jess reached down and looked into his eyes;

"Kyle, I won't leave you, just stay here, I'll be right back, Sara hold him for me, as I would you, I'll be right back."

Jess tore her robe and mask off tearing up the stairs and towards her bedroom she could see the glowing vile of atropine in her mind's eye it was resting on her closet vanity. She knew a few drops would subdue him and Darkeel until sunrise. It would be just long enough for him to rest and find the energy to once more fight against the part of himself that sought to destroy everyone in his wake.

Sara tore her mask off and threw it to the corner of the mausoleum, her hood fell back and she started to cry. How she could be here now holding this man's face ensuring that he wouldn't die after he tortured her for months, she couldn't take this anymore. She wanted so desperately to end his life right here and now, knowing it would separate her and her Mistress forever she cried desperately;

"Sara, I'm so sorry, I wish I would've known a better way, I've been alone for far too long. She was the only one that ever turned the lights on for me."

Kyle's eyes closed, he was still conscious, Sara leaned down and kissed his forehead;

"She is the only one that kept my light burning, this I understand all too well...Shh, Shh."

433

Her lips formed into the first smile of acceptance that she'd experienced in all of her life and she watched as her mistress came instantly kneeling and asking Kyle;

"Please, let me give you just a few drops, you'll sleep until morning and I promise we'll both be here when you rise. I'll take you to your office."

Kyle's eyes opened in fear;

"Oh god no, not near the children, you can't take me up there, not now." Jess shushed his fearful feverish voice;

"Not that office my love, the other one. I'll put you on the couch and I'll even turn on your favorite television." She smiled knowing that would spark his mind's eye, he smiled back at her for a moment and said,

"Ah, you know about that one huh?"

His head fell back into Sara's lap and she stroked his hair mouthing the word *children* in question with wide eyes. Jess smiled and mouthed back *the ones in the pictures*. Sara remembered seeing the photo she just thought they were out in public volunteering somewhere. Jess was known for blending in by assisting those in need, it was the most honest outlet to information about missing people, missing women, like Sara.

She realized in that moment that her beloved was happy in this world, and that Sara truly had no place here in the traditional sense anymore. She tried to strike out at the thought inside tormenting her sense of comfort in this moment.

"What shall we do my queen? He's starting to fall asleep."

Jess leaned forward and gave Kyle three drops of atropine to further sleep's arrival, he reached up and suddenly changed into Darkeel gripping her by the neck and screaming as his eyes glowed;

"More!"

Jess dropped two more into his mouth before she saw his energy escape Kyle's soul. Kyle's eyes suddenly changed to blue and heavily fell shut.

"What are we going to do with him Mistress?"

Sara looked shocked, this tall broad built man now completely out cold in her lap.

Jess smiled;

"Let me take care of that, I've been practicing since I've been here, I've had too in these conditions."

Jess instantly started floating his body up into the air, a few feet above the stairs. Sara watched as she slowly curled him into the fetal position to make transporting him easier through these slender halls.

"I'll be right back my love, until then, lay down on the earth's bed and prepare for your Mistress."

Sara smiled and stood, redressing her face with the jeweled mask she left on the stone bed. Feeling her pussy swell and her nipples harden, she craved the touch of her beloved. In their favorite place, she recounted the endless memories of being fucked with the howling of wolves ringing in the air, on the graves of ancient strigoii. Thighs spread, legs in the air, moaning in tandem with death and carnal life. Sara breathing her last breaths filled with ecstasy and filthy phrases in German that left her mistress weak hearing her surrender so completely.

Jess penetrated her Master's mind, while his body floated before the threshold of his hidden inner chambers and private dwellings of his house of torture. Uttering the phrase *Slaughter,* the hidden office door slowly opened, and Jess navigated his floating and heavily sedated body into his most private of rooms. The newspapers were piling up, the latest editions were just a few months old, with new stories about the infamous hunter. He'd already killed three times more since she arrived here this year, and this was after he showed her his captures down below.

She saw his scattered notes about missing time and wondering when this victim was captured because unlike all the others which he has clear recollections for, these ones were still missing somewhere. Kyle had no idea where Darkeel hid these bodies or their missing parts. Jess reached for the wristband with Kyle's key and slowly turned the panel of the desk to reveal the closed circuit television. She turned around and centered his energy over the couch and gently rested him there. Walking over to him and covering him up with his blanket that was disheveled on the back of his chair, she stroked his hair and kissed him tenderly. He was out cold but still his mind was strong enough to tell her;

"You're so strong now, I've never been prouder."

She smiled stroking his cheek. She turned towards the television and waved her fingers, instantly the image of Sara appeared and she smiled saying aloud;

"Ah, no wonder this is your favorite room in the house. I left it on your favorite channel, with audio, another way to settle your mind while you sleep; knowing where all my ultimate loyalty lies."
Jess walked to the doorway and said;

"I'll be in your room by sunrise, and I'll lock Sara up below to ensure you have time to sleep in. Rest well my weary king, this terrifying night is nearly over; if you get lonely just open your eyes and look into mine, I'll smile when I feel you watching."

With a giggle of affirmation towards the raw power of her sexuality, she exited the room and watched as it slowly closed shut behind her.

Chapter 30:
INFLAMED DECEPTION

JESS descended down the secret passageway wandering slowly, dragging her fingers down each intricate stone that lined the corridor of this hidden realm underneath the sleeping earth. Beyond the world that breathed life into the hallowed existence of this parallel world that awaited her within this tomb, filled with a divine creature that longed to serve her every desire. She felt her fingers warm like fire, she knew there were many more openings and secret passage ways that were connected in the inner chambers of this haunted manor. But there would be plenty of time to search for all of these secrets and revelations of her Master's truest disposition another night. For now the clock struck midnight and they'd only have a little while before she regretfully lead her to the place just above their heads. That place where all the other victims still rested waiting to see what dawn would bring them. Another day of twisted agony or sweet release found in death, in the climactic ascension of the imminent slaughter.

Wiping such horrid thoughts from her mind, knowing Sara had a penchant for realizing something was wrong, even in the subtlest of nuances that were displayed on her face. She instantly flashed back to that surreal floating bloodbath that both succubi thrived from in carnal nourishment. Feasting on one another as if they were in another world just hours before in her decadent boudoir chambers, that she imagined would house a lovely hand crafted cage which would sit so beautifully within the opening of this hidden passageway. Each night releasing her wild and lovingly tamed whore into her bed once more to greet the nights with the pleasures and passion of female energy entwined to find herself ravaged in the early morning light, serving her captivating king.

She rounded the corner into the room, seeing the sparkling jewels shimmer a midst the haunting flicker of candlelight she realized that her wildest dreams were about to take place. At long last, a mausoleum all their own, to appease their darkest fantasies, to explore ones that have yet never formed into existence. Kyle was deep in slumber his eyes were unable to see the vision that walked into the room that night, but he felt her swimming inside his mind, soothing the beast within along with a dose of atropine that would've been lethal to anyone else except him. Sara's eyes were sparkling, the dark browns were fiery reds that let her mistress know deep down just how badly she craved her in this moment. Her luscious breasts were full and Mistress Bella smiled wickedly hand on the doorway whispering aloud;

"There's no way out, you're my prisoner, now and forever, spread your thighs and pay tribute to your queen."

In that moment Sara fluidly opened her thighs wrapping them around Mistress Bella's waist and moaning aloud as her head fell back feeling her soft hands wrapped around her backside, Sara was in ecstasy.

"Oh Mistress, do your worst, I've waited so long for this night, *our* night together."

Mistress Bella molested every crevice and crack that displayed itself on Sara's gorgeous flesh, her pert nipples each one in between wandering fingers. Her lips dragging across her chest and up towards her neck to that special spot that always made Sara surrender without control.

"A grave yard all our own, Oh goddess; fuck me until I bleed. I never want to forget this night." Mistress Bella leaned back and looked deep into her eyes;

"It very well could be our last, let's make it one we'll never forget even in death my beloved harlot and insatiable whore."

Sara fell back onto the cold stone, lifting her mistress onto her wanton flesh, instantly Mistress Bella fell forward writhing on top of Sara, hearing her moans and yells of overwhelming pleasure escape in the form of pain;

"Oh yes, fuck me to oblivion. Fuck me until I cannot remember who I am anymore. Oh Goddess! PLEASE! *FUCK ME!*"

In that moment Mistress Bella plunged her fingers deep inside of her, forming all four into an elongated conical shape. She was determined to fill her up completely, she wanted all of her juices to explode, to cover this entire room in tribute to her God... Darkeel.

Sara's back arched violently and she screamed;

"Oh yes Mistress, fist me! Oh god yes, fist my fucking cunt, make it bleed!"

Mistress Bella spread her lips and enveloped her clit and swollen labia into her mouth suckling firmly on her electric spot that threw her over the edge of carnal seduction. Her hands gripped the stone viscerally and her thighs spread. Both feet firmly planted on the stone bed beneath her, in that glorious moment Sara screamed;

"Please Mistress, I beg thee, let me cum!"

Mistress Bella slid back off the cold stone monument of pleasure to reposition herself in front of this wet and wild show that would take place any second now. She could feel her body tense, her pussy swell and her heart beating fast;

"Gush for your Mistress. Oceans of pleasure just for me."

Sara instantly buckled under the pressure and an ocean of sweet juices gushed, squirted and flowed upwards, showering her Mistresses face with sweet juices. In that moment Sara ripped the mask off and threw it aside, her robe now fell back covering the grey stone and leaving the entire mausoleum drenched in juices and an ocean of blood as dark as the abyss.

"That's my beautiful Sara, my beloved concubine and eternal slave, never have I been so satiated, you serve your Mistress well my love."

Sara gripped her tits with the grandest, most beautiful smile that glowed brighter than the stars in the sky in the dead of night. Her red eyes now dimmed back into their usual hypnotic brown, her cheeks flushed red, now blushing, she was a lover of compliments and ones that were aided by the pleasure of her Queen were ones that left her speechless. Without words, she smiled with passion soaked lips.

"Oh Mistress, you still leave me blushing, even after all these years. Now I must appease your appetite my love, I live to serve."

Sara slowly reared up and Mistress Bella pulled down her jeweled mask and let the flowing black robe fall off her shoulders to the ground. She crawled onto the cold stone and placed her plump ass in the air, her precious slave's pussy still inches away from her lips, she smiled wickedly. Sara leaned back on her elbows, her heaving breasts each adorned with hard nipples were filling each hand, she began squeezing and pumping each one, Mistress Bella watched them grow and instantly started to leak sweet juices down her soft ginger curls, the shiny juices coating her swollen folds with honey.

"That's right my darling. Pump those glorious breasts, I want to see milk flowing without your fingers even touching them, lie back and find your comfort. Mistress is so fucking *hungry* tonight."

Sara's lips parted softly she knew her Mistresses tongue would be the death of her. Nothing made her weaker than feeling her tongue, lips and lip ring teasing every fold. Making her juices flow ceaselessly, leaving her Mistress soaked in an ocean of Sara's taste.

Sara's breasts continued to swell, and Mistress Bella leaned forward slowly teasing her pussy with soft kisses and tender licks. Tracing each delicate fold and finding each nerve that sent her body into instant shuddering, forcing her lips to scream vulgar things in German that still to this day Jess never quite knew the entire translation too. Sara's hisses and moans were followed by heavy breaths that echoed off the chambers of the stone mausoleum, leaving Mistress Bella covered in chills, her hair raised and her body trembling. She craved to play this beautiful woman like a violin, slowly, deeply and penetrating her in ways that felt as if time was stretched out far longer than just mere minutes. Each orgasm felt like a slow steady crescendo that built towards climax in such a way that Sara felt like she'd been here on this cold stone slab in tortured pleasure, for what felt like centuries before.

Both women were moaning and writhing, Sara loved watching her Mistresses robust ass shaking slowly from side to side, she knew she was tormented just as deeply as she was by her Queen's hot explorative tongue. Sara reached forward and brushed the hair aside from her lover's face and said as she was about to cum once more;

"Look Mistress, just for you my Queen, my sweet milk flows effortlessly from your kiss."

Sara's torso stiffened and her thighs undulated, her feet dug into the stone for dear life, she gasped and panted rapidly as she felt her sweet death approaching.

"Cum for me Sara, I'll drain you completely before sunrise."

Sara gushed once more, her body pulsing in waves each crescendo creating another ocean of juices flowing and squirting forth to shower her Mistresses, lip's, chin, face and breasts.

Mistress Bella gently kissed Sara's pussy one last time before raising her head mere inches away. Her warm breath was felt with every word that followed;

"After you've recovered I want you to rise and stand behind your glorious Mistresses ass, pump those delicious breasts that I own completely and squirt your sweet milk all over my fucking pussy. If you don't I'll slaughter you myself tonight, is that understood?"

Sara's breathing continued heavy and intermittent, her juices instantly flowed at the concept of her owner killing her tonight and taking that sweet privilege away from the man above who could never tame her.

"Don't stop until I tell you too, and be generous my pet, with your fingers, your tongue, nose I want every piece of your pretty face inside of me."

Mistress Bella leaned forward once more and continued to kiss her pussy, Sara instantly swooned, buckled and came again and again, doing her best to eject herself from the stone, knowing this forced gratification was a test of her mental fortitude. She squirted once more, cumming and yelling aloud;

"Fuck, Oh Fuck!"

Her body shuddered, her milky tits squirt and gushed delicious elixir while she continued to tremble and stumble off the grey stone. Her cheeks left blushing, her Mistresses wicked hands reaching back and slapping her ass hard to remind her of her ultimate direction.

Sara approached her glorious Queens's ripe and luscious ass. Her milk still flowing uncontrollably, spilling down her stomach and thighs, a gorgeous sight to behold by any man or woman who craved a glass with their chocolate chips cookies. Sara heard her Mistress moaning knowing she'd soon be inside of her tight aching holes. She reached forward, her hands pulling back her long flowing onyx strands and throwing them over her shoulders, as they cascaded down her body like a river of ink, her tits swelled. Sara leaned forward and inhaled Mistress Bella's sweet ass, she began to pump her full breasts, each nipple already squirting streams of hot milk onto her Queen's sweet pussy;

"Oh yes, that's the spot my pet, that's the melody. Pour your sweet sugar all over me."

Mistress Bella's cunt undulated uncontrollably rocking back and forth, filling the sweet flow of milk teasing and tormenting her clit until the honey flowed and she squirt all over her slave's pretty face. Instantly Sara plunged her face into her beloved mistress's pussy, spreading her folds with her nose and lips she squeezed her breasts and shot the milk towards her clit, as she buried her nose deep into Mistress Bella's gaping pink, little asshole. She gasped in pleasure of endless measure, spilling forth onto the cold stone, Mistress Bella gripped her fingers firmly onto the stone shrine, and smiled wickedly above to the place where she knew his eyes were watching.

Above in the secret inner chambers of *The Slaughterhouse Hills Hunter's* private office, the beast within was subdued and fast asleep. Yet the man that owned the world above felt his cock stirring at such delicious sounds that echoed from the depths of the tombs below.

Jess's orgasmic song filling the room like a sirens haunting echoes, he smiled and gently eased his body over towards the television screen.

"Oh what a wondrous sight to behold, show me what's in your mind, my beautiful Jess."

In that moment down below Jess smiled and winked, biting her lip as Sara continued to plunge deep inside of her ass and pussy with fingers, nipples and nose pressed firmly inside her luscious cheeks.

"Oh yes Sara, make me squirt, make your mistress cum until I forget what a naughty whore you were that night. Wandering off when your mistress asked you not too, creating this splintered tale for this demon that dwells within the walls of *Burnett Manor* to torture us until the end of time."

Sara guiltily remembered how she was captured that night, she should've remembered but it wasn't easy to remember anything after so long underground. She did her best to focus on pleasure instead of scolding, she hated disappointing her beautiful Bella. Nothing mattered to her in life, not even the possession of her own existence, if her Queen wasn't happy, her duty was to create a world that would inspire happiness to find her.

"I missed you for so long Sara. I searched for you over oceans and countries, wondering if I'd ever see you alive again. This is why you're here now, why we're both here, so I can keep you safe for eternity, never worrying about you vanishing again without a trace."

Sara feared that her dreams for escape would never arrive, she was truly a slave, trapped here against her very will, never realizing that this was the truest adoration for one who was owned completely.

Kyle felt a twinge of panic, he could sense that the only loyalty in this room that persevered through the darkness, shifts in personality and moods of monstrosity was provided in full by Jess, but never would it be given to them by Sara.

"She's too far gone my darling, it's too late, how will I find a way to break it to you at dawn, that there's nothing more I can do, Sara has to die."

Kyle disheartened by the choice that had to be made, continued to watch these two creatures of the night claw and writhe in echoes of pleasure, twisted in contorted positions to reach their ultimate satisfaction.

"Mount me and rub that silken pussy all over mine!"

Mistress Bella commanded in utter desperation, aching to feel the weight and forceful grip of her strong slave writhing uncontrollably on top of her. Jess moved forward, sensually rolling over her cunt, still raised with thighs spread and waiting. Sara crawled up on top of the stone bed and reached her left thigh over her beloveds while wrapping the other beneath hers their pussies instantly kissing.

Pressed together firmly, both women gripped each other's thighs and began to move forward and backward, side to side, slowly building circles that violently pushed both women to the edge of insanity as they lashed out towards one another's breasts and necks. The succubi gripping firmly to hold their position as Sara started bouncing violently on her Mistresses cunt.

Both women screaming, covered in beads of sweat that trickled down their bodies soaking the floor along with the puddles of pleasure that pooled down below. Mistress Bella reached forward with her other hand slapping Sara across the face hard and pulling her lips towards her firmly;

"You will never leave my side again without permission do you understand me? It nearly cost us our lives, and I almost lost you forever!"

Her eyes welled up with tears and so did Sara's, she cried endlessly in her Mistresses arms;

"I'm so sorry my Queen, I should've listened, and I should've known that your feelings are always right. Please forgive me, I cannot stand it when you're angry with me."

Sara and Jess both violently came in that moment, their moans of pleasures turned towards tears of pain and agony filled with sexual release, leaving Sara collapsed on top of her Mistress, crying into her milky breasts and hugging her endlessly wishing she'd never wandered off that night so many years ago.

"Will you stay? If you will I'll forgive you, Sara you must stay. It's our only chance for survival, and to be together the way we've always hoped we'd be without worry, fear or want of anything but the time when the sun goes down and we're together again once more. It can be like this every day don't you see?"

Mistress Bella waited for her response of agreement but heard nothing, she felt Sara's breath heavy and short, rapid and quick. She knew the fear inside her, she felt it pounding against her hitting her heart like a heavy stone. Kyle saw in her eyes in that moment what he'd always feared, she really was untamable, and no amount of love or torture would ever be enough to satisfy the wandering soul of this ancient whore. She'd tear down the house by the foundation with her bloody hands, if it fit into her plans of following her whim. Jess felt the dread building inside her soul, she knew he was watching and she felt his decision ticking by quickly like the sounds of an old pocket watch that was close to breaking. She knew by sunrise she'd know Sara's fate, but until then she did her best to help her see through painted picture just how perfect life could be here, if only she'd just believe.

Chapter 31:
WRATHFUL INITIATION

FOR hours Jess held Sara in her arms, whispering sweet nothings and endless memories into her ear. Brushing the hair from her face, her long nails dragging softly through the beautiful woman's endless river of black, gently touching her head and tormenting energy softly, serenely down her neck and spine.

"You know that I love you Sara don't you? After all these years, no matter what either of us have had to do to survive, you will always be the one that stole my heart and set my soul towards an endless path of rampant obsession. I should've turned you in and locked you up along with those you were working for at that time. But I couldn't help myself though, after reading your files from headquarters, you were everything I dreamt of and wanted to obtain in this life, you've always been worth sacrificing everything for just to be with you."

Sara smiled and reached for her mistress; "I love you more than life itself, whatever happens I am finally at peace, knowing that we've had this time together, and that the twisted man above is tormented by something dark and sinister that in turn left me in pieces without you. I see now what glory there is in such realizations in life, but mistress there's a part of my soul that will always stay wounded and broken so long as I am here. The things he did to me, or whoever that was inside of him when you were gone. I want to kill him with my bare hands while he sleeps, and nothing in this world, not you or the time that passes will change this visceral feeling I have for revenge. I want to carve out what's inside of him and leave it in the snow for the wolves to feast on it. We have to leave this place before it's too late, please my beloved, and come with me?"

Her eyes heavy and weeping filled with tears for the answer she already knew awaited her that escaped her delicate petal lips, so full and sensual. She couldn't take yet another cruel word from them without collapsing into a pile of tears and agony.

"My love, my place in this world is here, for centuries I have dreamt of his face, felt his energy coursing through me in the night, waking me from the deepest of sleep to call out once more hearing his voice inside my head, the moment I stepped foot here I knew I was finally home. All that is missing is my prized feline beside me and without your surrender, I fear what will happen after he realizes that you are unable to comply with my wishes, but more importantly ours." Mistress Bella lovingly embraced her;

"I can never expect you to love him, to forgive him or to even find space in your being not to desire to feast on his flesh for the sheer pleasure of sweet revenge. For it's the same pain I feel deep inside my being, the same desire I've always had the very moment I knew that you were gone that dark, cold frost bitten night."

She continued, "It was devastating to realize that the one who made me in another life into the vampire queen that you worship to this day, was the same predator who captured you and took you away from me leaving me alone in this universe my entire world vanished the night you ran out on me. I never stopped searching and I never will stop searching if you again flee like your tormented gypsy soul demands you too every time peace or solace arrives in our world together.

She pleaded with her; "But Sara know this, if you leave I may not be able to rescue you, he may keep me away from you, he has a power over me that you have witnessed that nobody else on earth has possessed and still to this day I have yet to understand in full comprehension what abilities he uses against me that I am forced to surrender without will. Promise me you won't do anything irrational even in this tortured state you must stay with me, I'll never forgive myself if I watch you die."

Mistress Bella watched her slave crying freely and softly knowing that the look in her eyes signaled that they had truly never been alone. He was always watching, sensing, listening and searching for that moment that she would fail, her basic instincts would provoke a wild and rampant need to flee into the dead of night, without any warning, just reckless abandon that would surely leave this untamable creature to meet her precious death for the last time. Above the stirrings flowed forth from a dead man's heart, Darkeel was pleased to hear such ramblings of protest from the slave he knew that was ripe for the slaughter.

"Mmm, I knew she'd never break, you thought you did your worst but it's up to me now."

His hallowed throaty chuckles echoed in the mind of Kyle waking him from his catatonic state, his fists pounding deeply into the stone wall nearby cracking it and shuddering layers of trophy papers onto the back of the couch.

"Fuck! Why does everything have to be so complicated?!"

Kyle stood and slammed his hands on the desk, watching the closed circuit television screen, he knew Jess could feel his eyes upon her, she instantly teared up and looked back. She stared heartbroken into the camera before closing her eyes, and turning her head in dismay.

"I traveled through vast oceans of time and space to find her, to capture that whore just to bait you my pet, to ensure you'd have everything you needed to keep you in my arms forever, and this is how she repays me?!"

Slamming his hands on the desk in a fitful rage that effervesced slowly like lava bubbling to the surface to instantly change his eyes deep red. Two glowing embers raging with the need to kill, two beings once again working together as one. Atropine be damned nothing would stop this thirst anymore, there was no waiting for sunrise, tonight the untamable whore would find her fate at the bottom of Royal Gorge. As his eyes illuminated throughout the room, penetrating the darkness, the papers began to burn, the television screen went black and as his hands gripping together tightly formed into two vengeful fists, the screen cracked, split and shattered into a billion pieces. Darkeel's voice escaped Kyle's lips for the first time in his life, laughter dark and haunting filled the smoky air, instantly suffocating the fire and leaving ash scorched papers in an ocean of darkness, as he snuffed out the light.

Two boots booming towards downstairs, the dungeons were as silent as the grave, yet the victims inside were stirring. They've grown accustomed to his energy, and felt his coursing fury striking through them like lightning. As he passed by they started yelping and crying simultaneously weeping in tear soaked screams, alerting the women below, Mistress Bella feared what would happen next, but it was far too late the moment her voice rang out, "Sara, I love you."

Jess was already fast asleep, her body floating once more in the air against her will, she felt her consciousness suffocated in darkness. She wondered if this was what it was like to be in a coma by then her body was floating up the stairs at an alarming rate. Stealthily through the hidden panel in Kyle's bedroom, resting her body on the dark hunter green sheets, she felt her limbs revive and her mind wandering back into imprints of reality, feeling herself awaken to the fact that she was now in Kyle's bedroom, all alone, without any certainty as to how she arrived here in the first place.

Darkeel emerged in the doorway of the mausoleum, Sara's trembling state left her curled up wrapped in the red robe in tears, clinging to the corners of the room wishing she'd never made the mistake of letting her emotions get the better of her one last time.

"Oh God! Please, No!"

Her screams echoed in the hollowed underground chamber, but it was too late, before she could flee, plead or grovel for her life his hands were already around her throat. Her body slammed into his hands from across the room, he never took a step, and he forced his victim to come to him, defying her mind, body and will completely.

"No Please, No!"

His smile never changed and neither did his glowing eyes. Burning the infernos of hell with an evil grip that drained the very life force of his victims from the center of their crushing hearts. Sara was choking, her eyes bulging as she looked Darkeel directly into the eyes;

"Kyle, if you're still there, she'll never forgive you, you must know this, and you'll lose her forever this way."

She waited and saw the beautiful face of the one she loved the only hope she had to hold onto, her beauty, and her smile, the laugh that was both delicate, vivacious and contagious. Darkeel instantly stunned into subservience to Kyle's will instantly recoiled from such light, his eyes changing back to green and his face confused yet shocked found himself slowly lowering her to the ground, releasing his grip on her delicate freshly bruised neck.

Sara started to cough violently, she fell to her knees on the stone floor, kissing his boots graciously and reaching for his strong thighs begging him for forgiveness.

"Please, I wish I didn't feel this way towards you, but after being here for so long, it repels me to be near the one that has tortured me, please just let me go, I know she'll never leave your side, I want her to be happy, but I just can't be here anymore."

Sara collapsed into a devastating pile of tears beneath his feet, he could've easily crushed her, one swift blow underneath his boot and she'd never regret anything in life ever again. But instead Kyle weakened by her devastation and wounded by the fact that he'd drive a permanent wedge between him and the one he loved, found himself compelled to wrap her gently in the robe, to pick her up and to lovingly carry her to her resting place; her iron clad cage.

"Please forgive me, I don't even know where I am, there's no possible way that anybody will ever believe me, I'll disappear and go back to the old world, you'll never see me again."

Sara tried to bargain, negotiate as best as she could, knowing full well with abundant vitality she had the ability to persuade even the most powerful of men to compromise to her ideas, her desires and even her will.

"You mean *she* will never see you again…"

Kyle's eyebrow raised challenging her naïve ideal when she knew full well that the moment she disappeared that Jess would do everything in her will to find her.

"If you leave, so will she, and I can't risk losing her again, we've spent so many lifetimes apart. Searching, haunted by the distance and the mediocre connections that pale in comparison, leaving us awake in the middle of the night, furiously writing, trying our best to appease the very part of our soul that will never truly rest."

He continued to carry her up towards the dungeon floor, her head nestled against his chest, eyes closed, tears flowing endlessly as he continued to give her the only closure she was allowed to have in this bizarre world that for now, was her only home.

"You are the missing puzzle piece to her happiness and ultimate fulfillment, and in turn you are the missing piece to this entire world that I've spent a lifetime building and with one decision you plan to tear down everything I've ever worked for. My hands have bled, I have endured centuries of torture and backbreaking work to ensure my empire and my legacy would be in pristine condition for my children to inherit after I am no longer walking this earth. Your whims and wild antics cannot be tolerated any longer, you've left me no choice Sara. You will be hunted for slaughter, as I've discovered in this life, to save the many, sometimes we must sacrifice ourselves in the end."

She felt the door swing open, Sara recognized the lighting and the creaking sounds of this iron cage, the room she'd spent years in, against her will, wondering, hoping and wishing she'd see her mistresses face one last time.

He placed her gently onto the floor and stepped back out to lock her inside, where he left her with a final phrase that would haunt her until the end of time.

"At dawn you shall have your formal sentencing, you have one final chance to prove your worthy, and we'll see each other again soon. You have my word."

Kyle slowly closed the iron barred door, his hood over his shoulders his lips the only apparent image in the darkness of the dungeon in early morning. She watched him disappear into the unknown, his heavy steps vanishing and leaving the torture chamber filled with its tormented victims in complete and utter silence.

"Oh, Goddess give me the strength to surrender to him. I cannot see those desperate eyes of hers anymore, I must break free from this fear to flee."

Sara's voice softly whispered in tears in her room, she felt all alone far away from the world above with all its earthly problems and predilections. She curled up and fell fast asleep on the cold concrete floor beneath her warm body, wrapped within the soft delicate folds of the crimson robe that adorned her flesh like a soothing river of blood.

Jess was still fast asleep in a catatonic dream state above in the sumptuous folds of Kyle's sheets, waiting to be revived from her intoxicating dream. *The Slaughterhouse Hills Hunter* wandered below downstairs, visiting his private office within the heart chamber of his haunted resting place, to survey the damage that he left in his infuriated state.

"Well, it's not as bad as I was expecting, at least he left the data I gathered, there's more bodies missing than he wants me to know about. I can't let them pile up around us, burying us in and exposing what I lack in self-control."

Kyle leaned over towards a cabinet that was resting there covered in dust and books filled with his writing. He opened it and pulled out his hunting bag, his additional arrows, ax, rope, traps and a rifle with enough ammunition to ensure that even if luck was on her side that he'd be ready for her. Darkeel's voice chattered in his mind;

"Now we're talking, it's been too long old friend, you owe it to me."

Kyle snapped back aloud; "I owe you nothing, you're lucky I don't let her carve you out of me, leaving your piss soaked husk on the snow for me to set on fire, to be rid of you once and for all. A dream among dreams my sick friend."

Suddenly without warning Kyle fell to the floor violently seizing uncontrollably.

"Fuck!" He yelled in agony.

He felt his breath quicken and his body doing its best to stabilize beyond the searing pain in his eyes, he stood up slowly, shaking and buckling under the pressure he quickly grabbed the back of his chair and stabilized himself until he could breathe normally again.

"We hunt at dawn, until then fuck off you piece of shit. These last few hours of early morning are *mine!*"

Kyle yelled aloud hearing for once a strong resonating silence that to him signaled that his dark parasite was subdued. Listening for the moment in possession of any sign or semblance of lack of self-control.

He left his bags packed, with his weapons loaded and ready to go. Slowly he took his cloak off and left it strewed across the couch on top of the pile of blankets and clothes that he had on earlier in the evening. Leaning forward he untied his boots kicking them off and setting them aside near his hooded cloak. He slowly wandered up the stairs to his bedroom, tearing off the layers of clothes that he had on. Jeans, sweater, boxer briefs and socks, he wanted nothing more than a scalding hot shower and to find his way into his crisp, clean sheets, to pleasure his beautiful Jess until the sun rose high over the mountain side. With Sara safely locked down below and Darkeel provided with the outlet of his darkest pleasure arriving this very exhausting, and brutal day. He finally felt a sense of peace inside, he felt this story was on its final chapter, knowing it would all be over soon. At dawn he'd finally say goodbye to all of his problems once and for all.

Chapter 32:
RAVENOUS SUCCUBUS

IT was hours since Jess was entwined within the locked arms, thighs, hips and twitching quim of her treasured possession. She awoke softly to the sound of water running in the shower nearby, feeling disoriented from the exhausting energetic take-down, yet oddly rejuvenated in this small span of time sleeping soundly within the dark hunter green sheets of *The Slaughter House Hills Hunter*. She felt her dark lord nearby, his magnetic energy coursing through the room and into her body, preparing her for his passionate embrace that she longed for since the moment she first knew of his existence.

She wanted his lips desperately, ached to feel his weight mounting her and spreading her thighs apart with his strongly sculpted hands. The somber light peered through the bathroom, she could tell he was trying to unwind after peril invaded his body and veered away from duality control in all senses. Deep down she feared what would happen if he could no longer harbor the demon inside, beating swiftly with his heart within the confines of his sturdy rib cage. Was she brave enough to love a man who shared his body with a demon against his will, losing control at any time and relinquishing her to the afterlife with so many others scattered about the cemetery and across the snow drenched hills of Colorado?

Even more than her concern for her own skin, she feared that Sara wouldn't be around anymore. She wondered if that was the last time she'd ever say *I love you* to her ever again. She knew that she spilled her vengeful pride to much, exposing her truest self. A wild succubus that will do anything in her power to set herself free from detainment, it was what she loved most about her, what inspired her and left her in a state of awe and heightened arousal. But she knew years ago in their cold brothel home far away in the *Carpathian Hills* that she'd never be able to tame her, not then, not now, not ever. Sara was and always would be a free woman, no matter how well she played the part it wasn't in her nature to serve for eternity. She always hoped this gift wouldn't catch up to her in life like the wanderlust curse that it always was, but she felt deep down in the very pits of her stomach and every fiber of her being that this would be the final moment she'd ever see her beloved Sara alive ever again.

Slowly her eyes opened and peered towards the bathroom door, hearing the water splashing around she waited to sense if he felt her, sensed her, knew she was awake and waiting patiently for her king to enter into his kingdom once more and to show her every piece of his empire. She yearned to meld with his being completely, searching the vast spans of space and time in his eternal memory bank. Being reminded why she'd always been drawn to these birch trees, the forest, the haunted hillsides of the world no matter where they might be and all the cruelest monsters with eyes peering into the darkness of her very soul relishing in snuffing out the light.

His head rested gently on the cool tile walls, the hairs on the back of his neck instantly stood the moment her eyes were open. He smiled wickedly, knowing her voyeuristic eyes were just as curious as his were. Finding the strength and mental fortitude to focus on doors that were left slightly open. He slowly pulled a vortex of energy towards himself in his mind's eye, hearing her voice softly moan as she watched the steam rise revealing the open shower door and his gorgeous ass glowing softly in candlelight. He smiled and laughed softly not wanting to disturb her private interlude, how easy she was to please, how effortless her ideals for passion.

She took profound reverence in the nuances of life, draining passion and pleasure from seemingly ordinary experiences to others, each time her head filling with the rising sounds of violin, in a cadence that hypnotized her into a living dream world where her wildest fantasies were only a moment, a mere touch away. If only others could see the world at this different angle that she viewed incessantly how easy it would be to thrive forever in the underworld.

Jess rolled delicately towards the shower door, getting the most delicious peek at his strong arms. His right arm reaching back and washing the water from his face and hair down his shoulders. She smiled delighted by the fact that he knew what he was doing. Teasing her, tormenting her, seeing rivers rushing over his tight ass, leaving her warm depths aching severely, she needed to be filled completely. He wanted to torment her, wondered if she'd have the courage to wander into his trap or to watch helplessly waiting for what he'd do to her next. The hunter was already stalking his prey and she watched as his strong hands started to reach down towards his cock, slowly teasing the tip with his fingers. His silky hands stroking every inch from tip to base, cranking his hard meat and gripping it firmly as it bulged, the shower door left too much to the imagination, before Jess realized it she found herself wandering into his private bathhouse, instantly dropping to her knees and peering inside the cracked door watching him pretend to ignore her as his lips parted she heard his moans, it drove her... *absolutely insane.*

Never had she felt her cunt plump instantly to such glimpses, her nipples hard and her breasts swelling before her very eyes, she placed her hands gracefully on her thick thighs and waited and watched, his balls rising and his cock as hard as granite. She heard his moans change to guttural sounds of pleasure, his lips hissing as he pressed his lips together. She longed to taste him, to feel his power between her parted, ravenous lips. She wanted him more than anything in this life, she'd never felt so drawn to another human being so long as she lived. She sat in service position with both hands resting on her thighs quivering at the sight of him. Taking him in and relishing in this sensual memory that she'd long to revisit each and every time she pined for him inside of her, when he was busy working and slaving long into the night.

Kyle reached up and flexed his abdomen, his cock grew and swelled. The blood filling up every chamber in his shaft, she felt her lips water, it'd been so long since she ate meat… years perhaps. This was the only time she ever broke her rule, the only meat she ever indulged in anymore. Which made it even more satisfying to her ravenous soul whenever she was provided with such a warm feast. As the water rolled down his chest and stomach, he reached for the shower handle and slowly turned it off. The drops of water still dripping from his body were ecstasy to her ears, hearing and seeing each drop fall from his flesh as his thick iron dick was more than she could take.

By the time he smiled opening the door completely to greet her with his longed for desire, she was already trembling biting her lip and doing her best to regain her composure. She appeared to be in a ravenous state of sexual frenzy, controlling every impulse within her to tear into his cock and to feast from it the ever flowing fountain of his eternal life force. Her teeth protruded;

"Forgive me my lord, the mere sight of you has left your aching succubus in a state I have not seen myself in since I first changed. I'll do my best to retract them for your sake my king, to please you like the God that you are to me is what I long for more than anything or anyone else in this life."

Jess's body still heavy breathed, her eyes peering up towards this six foot tall menacingly gorgeous man. He stepped forward wrapping a towel around his shoulders and drying his hair briskly before reaching for her jaw and delicately touching her to leave her body covered in goosebumps.

"Leave them out, *for my sake.*"

Kyle's cock was now a breath's distance from her parted lips, without warning, he gripped the back of her head cradling it forward, as she felt every glorious inch enter into her warm wet pout, violating every bit of space within. She heard his voice booming throughout the bathroom, echoing against the marble countertops in one guttural command he said;

"Show me your teeth."

Kyle growled moaning endlessly as he plunged his cock down her throat, feeling her tight warm mouth wrapped around him, barely able to breathe, she suckled on his cock as if it provided the first breath of air to ever possess her lungs in this life. Pursuing every vein with her tongue in a rhythmic cadence that echoed the passion and fire that he felt from her whenever he was inside her. He turned his head towards the mirror and looked down to the beautiful creature's plump ass, now firmly stationed upwards, swishing like a ravenous feline waiting to kill, her tits dragged up his thighs and her head and face were buried into his cock. Waves of red curls flowing like fire on kerosene, her sharp teeth piercing his cock and dragging tiny pin pricks down his hot loins. Jess instantly lost herself to pleasure, eyes closed, ravaged by the taste of his sweet blood. A fountain of memories, flavors and aroused states of being entered into her mind, she slurped, licked, sucked and swallowed unable to contain her want for human flesh. His hands reaching for her head and gently running his fingers through her hair, teasing her neck and resting his fingertips on her upper spine. He played her body like a master musician, transitioning from rhythmic drum beats, to tender dancing flows that felt like her body was nothing more than the keys of a piano. She reached behind and gripped his ass, forcing more of him inside her, feeling her nose pressing into his stomach, she no longer cared to breathe, she wanted every inch of him, and she wanted to feel her body distort to compromise such a violently arousing intrusion.

"Oh my sweet Jess, my beautiful love, never have I felt such peace within this dark soul, you are the key to existential bliss. Yes, just like that, pay close attention to the tip. Oh God, you suck cock as if it's the only thing in life you truly live for. Mmm, yes, that's my girl, that's my beautiful whore."

Kyle brushed the hair from her face, watching her eyes open and twinkling that magnificent green blue. Two jewels sparkling in the candlelight, each center glowing like two minuscule suns, they reminded him of Krypton. His mind wandered towards thoughts of *The Man of Steel*, never realizing until now how much Jess reminded him of Lana Lang. The familiarity was enticing as he felt his blood raging and his cock preparing to explode, he softly pulled her lips from him and smiled gratefully. Before she could say a word she was in his arms, his lips pressed against hers tongue deep inside flicking and relishing in the taste of his own blood swimming on her full lips.

Before she knew it she was tossed sensually onto his bed, she felt his hard cock dragging down between her thighs. He leaned up still kissing her and smiling wickedly, his eyes glowed green and she feared in that moment that perhaps he wasn't the one in control all this time after all, "Kyle? Is…is that you?"

Jess trembled waiting for his response;
"Yes my pet, I'm sorry if my ravenous need to fill you completely startled you, to ensure you feel more at ease, let me share with you that Darkeel has never enjoyed this pleasure in life, it's not what he desires, No this early morning like all the others belongs entirely to us."

With one final kiss she moaned passionately and waited for further instruction. "Lie back, rest your weary head, I want to show you what I've craved for so long, it's been centuries since your sweet taste has quenched my thirst, give yourself to me."

Kyle rubbed his face beneath her crimson pubic mound, kissing her thighs and hearing her moan tremendously beneath the energy she felt coursing from his lips. Before her head even met the pillow beneath, her body contorted and her eyes rolled back, thighs gripping his face as he plunged his tongue deep inside her.

Jess shuddered, her breath changing rapidly her heart beating swift, her voice shaking in waves. Her entire being overwhelmed with his feeling of hunger, she'd never been devoured with such all-encompassing thirst before. His tongue was possessed, teasing and flicking at her delicate folds tormenting her body to shudder, she felt her cunt lunging itself towards his face, his strong hands reached around each luscious thigh enveloping his eyes in a menacing forest of crimson hair.

He maintained eye contact with her until her furrows of passion were too much to endure, her head once again fell back towards the bed, screaming in a mixture of torment and endless pleasure, her body bucked uncontrollably, quaked and quivered releasing an ocean of sweet juices into his wanton mouth.

She heard him moaning in bliss, every drop of her sweet peach now flowed endlessly inside of his being, she could feel his pleasure, his darkness and his soul piercing her deeply like that of his favorite bloody hunting knife, slow at first then menacingly deep.

"Oh God, Kyle, I can't take much more, my heart is pounding so fast, I'll do anything to feel you inside me." Jess eyed him in desperation, hoping he'd conquer her in that moment in ways she remembered and in a rough manner that she never knew before.

"Who is your Master?" He raised his chin from her sweet pussy beckoning her to play his game, this interlude to their mutual desire.

"You are."

Jess said looking into his eyes, already feeling his longing for her wrists bound above her head. He watched as she slowly positioned her wrists above her long locks in ways that forced her tits to protrude in the most delicious way. Kyle smiled wickedly as he kissed her clit and said once more, "Who is your Master? Who is your King?"

Jess bit her lip and blushed her eyes closing, she always felt weak in such exposed states of being. As she smiled and felt his strong arms pulling her closer to him, dragging her body across the bed effortlessly she parted her lips as he buried his face inside her honey soaked cunt once more;

"You are!" She moaned desperately under his penetrating exploration.

Before she could exhale she felt him on top of her, he moved effortlessly into position. Straddling her body and holding her wrists above her head, relishing her soft thighs that wrapped intuitively around his waist in angst to what he would do to her next. With one booming voice that escaped his lips he asked her wickedly;

"Who is your Master? Your King? Your *God?*"

His head raised in a regal and noble way that shined light to his inner workings, her heavy breath was pain stricken, barely was she able to mutter the words from beneath her stifled pleasure, "*You are, Master Darkeel…You Are!*"

In a single breath he plunged his hard achingly stiff cock inside of her. He felt her warmth, her soft delicate body both strong and sensuous in all its glory. He moaned endlessly burrowing himself inside her. Each time he entered her it felt like the very first time, she was excruciatingly tight, trembling in fear for eternity provided sumptuous benefits. He found himself intoxicated by her sweet scent, her perfume that wafted through the cold night air on a breeze of hot sweat soaked flesh that was aching to be used and discarded; after pleas of release were heard echoing off the walls into the night.

"Oh God! So big, I can feel my insides stretching, oh God! How will you fit?" She smiled deviously into his eyes, feeling his teeth instantly plunge to that spot on her neck that made her a writhing whore.

"Mmmm, that's how. So fucking wet you are for me; *just me.*"

Kyle continued to stretch, tear and pound his way deeper inside, her moans and cries of pain and pleasure resonated inside of his darkness, reviving the part of him that never dared enter into his body when he was in the midst of such pleasure.

"Ooo, now I see why you like her so much, reading you like a novel that you wrote yourself, she'd make a delicious companion for me."

Darkeel's murmurs were heard in the minds of both Kyle and Jess in this unified moment of shock and fear. In that moment Jess said aloud;

"I belong to Him."

She reached up and kissed his forehead, instantly his hands freed hers he'd never felt so understood. She kissed Kyle on the lips and pulled his hips, burying his hard cock deeper inside to the brink of her fill.

"I belong to you Kyle, You are my Master, you are my King, YOU ARE MY GOD!!!"

Jess fell back, her arms around his shoulders. Her thighs parted and ankles wrapped firmly around his hips. Her feet digging into his ass by the heels, she felt Kyle fully present while all of his flesh and soul was deep inside of her. In that moment their eyes never parted, and when the precipice of climax arrived in waves of ecstasy, they both stepped onto those waves together hand in hand as they slowly drowned alive. The sounds of heavy breath and heartbeats swiftly exchanged in tandem were echoing through the dark green room that was his paradise and her safe haven.

He reached for her face and pulled her lips towards his, they met in such an explosive union that both beings fell to the bed utterly exhausted. Smiling speechless without the ability to exchange anything more than eye contact, hands tracing one another while being held tenderly. He rolled off of her and towards his side of the bed, she quivered, quaked and moaned aloud in a possessed state of ecstasy. Kyle smiled slowly teasing her body with his fingertips, tormenting her body as it continued to shudder.

"You're…su…ch…a….Sadist!" Jess trembled uncontrollably, smiling and blushing both breasts still heaving, nipples hard doing her best to survive what felt like the nuances of death serenely approaching.

"You have yet to see my *Sadistic* side…" Kyle dragged her body to the end of the bed and tossed her over onto her stomach.

"Oh God, what's my safe word?" Jess begged her kitten claws tearing into the sheets doing her best to stabilize herself, as she tried to flee she crawled onto her knees and instantly felt his hands on her hips.

"Now you're just making this *too easy*…" Kyle smirked as he dragged his bucking filly to the position he desired most.

"If you thought I felt big inside that tight, soaking wet pussy of yours, just imagine how large my tool will feel as its pressing into your delicious ass."

Jess turned her head and gasped with animated eyes;

"Oh God! Whatever you crave my king, it is a pleasure to serve you."

Her voice quaking in what was usually confidence and pleasure was waiting now turned towards a timid disposition wondering just how he'd fit himself inside of her.

"Soaking wet for me, that tight asshole already puckering and gaping at the thought of having my cock inside of it. Mmmm, what a sight to behold."

Kyle's fingers started to tease her ass, he used his other hand to gather and move copious amounts of soaking juices all over his cock, slathering her ass, he couldn't take it a moment longer, and he had to fill her completely. He wanted to feel all of his power, tension, pleasure and pain find release in her glorious ass. Her rounded mounds were soft yet firm, pale and gorgeous, he wanted to mark them up, carve his name into her with a knife, never had he seen flesh so pristine and untainted, he wanted to leave his mark.

He wanted her to think of him now and always when the cool breeze teased her, blowing her skirts and dresses towards the sky. He leaned forward and blew gently a cool breeze onto her delicately soaked pink petals, hearing her moan and exhale in utter ecstasy. He felt his hands spreading her ass and his curious eyes filled with wonder as he drug his cock up and down between her plump cheeks; tormenting that tight abandoned little hole and watching it as it gaped open, puckering and fluttering waiting to be filled as he plunged himself inside of her once more; finally owning every piece of his property the way she needed it most.

"Beg for me, beg for me to violate this tender little hole of yours until you beg me to stop."

Kyle instructed her with firm command, Jess instantly gasped and shuddered doing her best to comply with his wishes beyond the blinding hunger that she had for him.

"Oh Please Master, fill me, take me as your wanton whore." She spread her cheeks contracting her pussy, her ass still fluttering open and shut;

"I need you so desperately Kyle that it hurts, I want to drain your balls, to feel you shudder intoxicated, falling onto my flesh as we both feel the fires burn in waves deep inside and washing over us as we come together. Please fuck my tight ass Kyle! Oh God! I cannot take it!"

She continued to writhe in uncontrollable sexual tremors, her pussy bucking wilding underneath her and her ass gaping open and shut begging for his stiff cock.

"I need your roughness, I want to be reminded time and time again who could take my life in a single moment but instead uses my body, mind and soul to fulfill his dark desires time and time again. Possess me!" Kyle watched her body jerk, quiver and tremble beneath his firm embrace, "That's my whore, my filthy, filthy, filthy little whore...You finally know your place. On your knees, serving your life's ultimate purpose in this world..."

As the tip of his cock unlocked her tight ass, she felt him entering slowly, deeply with all-encompassing glory that resonated up her spine and through her eyes and lips in that moment he uttered that final word in his sentence that transformed her into a writhing puddle of pain seeking pleasure; "*Me.*"

Kyle's lips formed the word of ownership in that single moment as he dived hip deep inside of her. Jess's echoes of pleasure were endless, her moans matched his guttural cadences in unison, leaving these two without the ability to focus on anything else other than the overwhelming fulfillment that arrived in the depths of this beautiful woman's ass. He felt his climax approaching, spurring hers on to join his to writhe, moan, buck and to cum harder than they ever have in present or previous memory.

"Oh God, Yes! Harder, faster, deeper, just take me!"

Jess yelled one last time before she felt them both explode endlessly, his hips jerking. Further plunging himself deeper inside of her, his balls raised firmly against his abdomen, his hands gripping into her hips, his left one slapping her ass hard instantly leaving a prominent handprint.

"Oh, My God!" Her upper body lost its ability to stay raised upon the surface of the bed and she fell face forward into his sheets, body still shuddering beneath him.

Kyle had never felt such existential release before, he felt serene, light, and endlessly filled with hope, the same feeling that he had when the sun rose delicately into his window in the early morning, that feeling that he always tried to capture but fleetingly disappeared as soon as the sunrise transformed into radiant dawn. She encapsulated every feeling that he dreamed of that usually escaped him as darkness returned once more.

"Where have you been all my lives?"

Kyle lovingly looked over at her, as she rolled her eyes to peer from beneath a wave of red hair. She smiled and blushed shrugging her shoulders in such a way that made her indescribably beautiful. He slowly pulled himself out of her while matching her tortured moans with his, he fell to her side and reached for her face, hoping she'd bury it into his chest so that they could both find much needed sleep long into the afternoon.

As he embraced her and kissed her on the head, face, lips and cheek he smiled endlessly, seeing her glow as she was spent, her eyes softly closed. She leaned towards him and wrapped her arms up around his chest and shoulders, teasing the side of his neck with long sensual strokes.

"Here, no matter where my body wanders this earth, my soul has always been, right here. I just didn't know it until now."

Jess smiled one last time as her eyes grew heavy and the light began to peer into the bedroom signaling it was time to rest after such an arduous journey the night before.

"Rest my love, there will be plenty of time to talk about such incredible memories shared between lovers that have found each other time and time again along the timeline of eternity."

Kyle continued, "Sweet dreams Jess, I'll be waiting for you when you wake up."

Chapter 33:
INFINITE ELLIPSISM

LITTLE did they know that something stirred deep below the twisted inner workings of this haunted house, waiting to get out, waiting to escape this realm of torture and uncertainty was fast at work the busy hands of a beautiful, inescapably talented woman who could no longer reside here anymore. The fear, the torture, the mind fucking sense of lost reality, she couldn't rest, tonight was the night. She had to try, she might die trying but at least it was worth it to see the look in his eye before she vanished from this world forever. Tonight was the night Sara, the *untamable whore* had to say goodbye to everything that rested here deep within the walls of this forbidden and forgotten place.

Kyle embraced her long into the afternoon, rising only to shower and wander downstairs to check in on his staff, all busy in the offices below, updating him briefly on progress in his creative endeavors that would take weeks to complete. He was pleased that this house continued to run like a well-oiled machine. The food's fragrant scent traveled through the floors from the kitchen, he heard the laughter of children in their wing as he wandered back upstairs, knowing that a late lunch was in order. He entered the room and all three of his beautiful lights in his life were there, laughing, a movie in the background playing while they caught up on all the fun they had during summer. Surprised by the appearance of his eldest daughter he opened his arms as she walked towards him in glowing smile, "I didn't know you'd be home so soon, I wasn't expecting you until next weekend."

Kyle hugged his daughter, kissed her on the forehead as she replied, "I called and left a message with the kitchen staff, I'm sure they just forgot to give it to you. I could've sworn it was the voice of a woman I've never spoken to before but I was really tired when I called, midterms was murder on the brain this semester."

Kyle felt that tingle up his spine, was she the one who was leaving things out all over the grounds? Moving things in the dungeon down below? No. It couldn't be the untamable whore. He watched her constantly on screen, her menacing stare and her angry gestures of vulgar insults. There's no way Sara would be able to do this without being noticed. Could she?

"Dad what's wrong?" Tiffany inquired, "Oh nothing, I was thinking. Tell me about your summer, over lunch. I'll see if Jess is awake to join us. She's been working during the late night hours on her own creative projects, it's been nice having somebody awake at that hour in the house besides James."

The smile on his face and the spark in his eyes when he spoke about her was obvious to his eldest daughter.

"Ah, so the staff isn't checking in on her anymore then, *you are*."

She winked precociously with a smile and a giggle of self affirmation to what she already knew would happen. She was a writer, a strong, nurturing and beautiful woman, everything her father has a weakness for, the only thing in life really that she ever noticed he was able to compromise his focus and dedication to his work for.

"I'm glad she's kept you happy while I've been traveling, I was worried about you."

Tiffany sauntered towards the television and turned it off. "Come on you two, Dad wants us downstairs for lunch. I think Jess will be joining us, we'll see."

Instantly his son and youngest daughter turned around and started making kissing noises and laughing giddily to poke fun at their father.

Adie spoke up; "Oh, so *that's* why Dad's been so happy lately."

Derek chimed in, "Told you, I knew she was a good fit."

He smiled sending thoughts to his father's mind, "*I know she's here for you Dad, she's passed all of my tests with flying colors, even the more astute ones usually show their true selves, and her mind is always filled with images, of you.*"

Kyle smiled endlessly he finally felt that all of these shattered and broken puzzle pieces from his haunting past, his troubled youth and detrimental childhood were finally forming into a mosaic, a rich tapestry of his life finally coming together fully and completely at long last.

"I believe your sister told you to do something for me." His eyebrows raised and Adie and Derek started to run downstairs, Tiffany walked behind them, first stopping and asking;

"Can I knock?" She smiled cheekily. Kyle shook his head and laughed,

"Yes, but only I will enter. We'll be downstairs in half an hour, keep an eye on your brother, he's been most curious lately." She nodded in agreement after knocking on the door and smiling as she left for downstairs.

Kyle laughed knowing full well her daughter knocked on the wrong door, but he didn't desire such a conversation with her at this time. As he watched the top of her head disappear downstairs below, he wandered to his office and shut the door.

"I don't remember leaving that open, and I know she hasn't left all morning. What the fuck is going on?" He firmly shut the door and used his mind to lock it from the inside.

If somebodies in there I'll have a chance to catch them later. He thought to himself as he entered his bedroom quietly.

There she was in all her naked glory, her full breasts flowing forth out of his hunter green sheets and comforter. Her long red locks spilled around her face in a haunting way, for a moment she looked like the naked corpse he found in the snow all those years ago.

He felt a hunger stirring inside of him, he knew tonight he had to kill, something, anything, anyone for that matter. He had to chase one of his groomed hunting trophies early. Before the first snow fell and he was left buried in this dark place without a means for his appetites release. For a moment the scenery changed and he saw her resting on a mountain of snow, he was aroused and frightened by this image, was it a vision of the future, or his dark parasite returning to find ways to provoke his outlet into full expression?

He shook his head quite literally and hoped the image would fade when he opened his eyes. Once more she rested in the river of green, the fertile goddess of dreams, visions and creativity that flowed through her soul endlessly washing over him, a purifying river of presence in a world where past and future collided in horrific ways.

"My beautiful Jess." His breath slowed and his body sighed effortlessly, he knew she was his salvation. His illuminated sanctuary in a forest of darkness and river of endless blood. He walked slowly, watching her rest so peacefully was one of his favorite voyeuristic indulgences. Her eyes still fluttering in sleep, he watched her biting her lip and smiling,

"Mmm, I knew I felt you…sensed your power. Good Afternoon my King."

As her eyes slowly parted along with her lips, her nipples hardened while her tits swelled and her busy fingers found themselves teasing the soft folds between her thighs without notice. She woke up often violating her body with his image in mind, often times he recalled while watching her on closed circuit television late at night in his hidden office below the sounds of her voice moaning softly. Struggling to form his name on her lips as her hands found ways to touch her the same visceral way he would if he was there, just as he was in this moment.

"Oh my darling I wish we had more time for that. The children are waiting below and lunch is nearly ready, I'd love to watch you shower. Will you do that for me?" She smiled and blushed, "I'll do *anything* for you."

She reached for his hands and kissed them lovingly, slowly opening her lips and suckling on the tip of his forefinger. Her eyes menacing and feline in nature, glowing and revealing that her darkness was present as well tonight. Perhaps she'd enjoy this final phase of her initiation more than he thought. Only time will tell. He wondered what she'd look like helping him dispose of a body, his jeans felt tight and he watched his beloved concubine as she wrapped herself in rivers of green, teasing him as she slowly turned on the shower and smiling over her shoulder as the steam filled the room.

"Is *this* what you want Master?" She smiled cheekily flirting with him as layers of green fabric slowly melted off her body piling up on the floor.

"As if I'd ever have to instruct you how to seduce me." Kyle raised his eyebrow smiling, he wandered to the doorway of the shower as she stepped inside.

"I realize we haven't much time Sir, so I'll tend to washing only the most delicate parts of myself for your enjoyment."

She reached for her hair clip and pinned her curly locks above, a few escaping as the steam touched her skin she felt the hot water washing over her body. She lathered the soap in her hands and teased her breasts, Kyle's cock began to swell as she bit her lip feeling his arousal deep inside her pussy and every nerve in her pulsating ass.

She washed the soapy water over her backside, feeling the water wash down her breasts in a soothing nature that instantly awakened her mind, providing full clarity for what was to be engaged in down below. He watched as her delicate fingers invaded her ass in the cracked open door of the shower.

"Mmm, tormenting me to no end, fuck it. I can't take anymore."

Kyle walked towards the shower and ripped his clothes off, he tore into the shower and grabbed Jess out covered in soap, picking her up and setting her on the counter, he shoved his cock deep inside of her, her thighs wrapped around his ass, her arms embracing his strong, broad shoulders and holding on tight.

"Oh god, tearing me to shreds, Mmm you know just how I like to be ravaged." She gasped, "My God!"

Her lips forced shut instantly by his passionate imploring kiss, she felt the hot fire of their orgasmic ecstasy building. In that moment they looked deep into each other's eyes, her neck exposed and covered in kisses, she felt her fangs retract, "Bite me, you need to feed, I want you well behaved for our family luncheon, you've been such a salacious whore lately."

In that moment she bit down furiously on his jugular. "Ugh! Fuck."

Kyle hissed aloud as his cock swelled engorging every crevice of her tight pussy. She moaned in bliss, the sweet taste of him combined with such a forceful invasion left her in a decadent haze of intoxicating proportions.

"Drinking from you leaves me drunk for *Power*, I want to conquer the world with you."

She leaned back her lips stained red, trickles of blood down his shoulders and chest appeared. She leaned forward kissing and licking every drop from his body.

"Here I come, are you ready to be filled?" He moaned aloud in her ear,

"Fill me, oh God Master, *please fill me.*" She kissed his neck feeling her gushing climax approaching. In that moment they both softly mouthed the words together, *"I'm coming with you."*

Their breath matched the rhythmic cadence of their heartbeats. Kyle shook himself from his deepest temptation. "We have five more minutes."

He watched as her hands gripped the countertop behind her, breasts heaving towards his face, he couldn't help but to kiss her from neck through that delicate path between her parted breasts, to her tense abdomen that was still trying to grasp breath. He knew she couldn't resist such serene bliss coursing through her.

"I could devour you for centuries and never get my fill."

Kyle smiled at her, Jess's head rolling up and looking into his eyes. She kissed him one last time before her legs parted and slowly reached towards the bathroom floor.

"Time to finish getting ready."

Jess winked and smiled leaving her hair up and adding the smallest bits of makeup to accent her natural beauty. She wandered towards her closet and threw on one of her favorite dresses, long and flowing. She never desired to show that side of herself in front of his children or anybody else in this world in all honesty. There was something so captivating about this dualistic world that she shared with this brilliant man.

"I'm assuming our eldest has returned? If so I'll bring down this gift I found for her. I already gave things to Adie and Derek so they wouldn't feel neglected." Kyle smiled,

"Ah, so you were the one who answered and heard she was coming back early." Jess looked at him with a peculiar expression.

"No, I haven't heard from her since she left, I just felt her energy this morning and testing my abilities each day is how I continue to provide such accurate readings." This alarmed Kyle more than anything.

"She's not in her cage, I can sense it, *feel it*. Fuck." Jess was alarmed.

Was it her worst fears taking place? Was Sara really this reckless? She thought it'd take time to acclimate but this was strange, quite out of character for a woman who was used to never being noticed even in the midst of her blindingly sultry beauty.

"If she escapes…" Before Jess could finish Kyle's hand's formed into fists, "There is *no escape*."

His eyes widened and his peril was devastatingly clear to her unlike ever before. She knew if Sara was down below finding ways to explore, that soon she'd try to make her escape. It was no secret to either of them that she was determined to flee this place once and for all. Kyle nor Darkeel would have anything to do with such a reckless risk against his entire empire, his world and his twisted ventures.

"If that ungrateful whore is still untamable then she must be put down. Do you understand me?! I will not allow her to ruin everything that we have, she's been given every opportunity to excel here. We'll discuss this later, after lunch when the children are in the city, Tiffany has a special adventure she wants to take them on. Which leaves us plenty of time to figure out what the fuck is going on around here."

Kyle kissed her on the lips and said, "Let's go, the children are waiting for us."

Jess followed dutifully realizing that, this was not the first time she wandered, she knew far too much the inner structures of this house. Sara had been trying to escape for years now, Kyle just never knew how in tune she was, how powerful her instincts at avoiding death truly were. The Sara she knew was far better at cloaking her mind than even herself. With the ability to absorb any preternatural powers of anyone male or female that ever penetrated her mind, body and soul. This was her final revenge, she wanted to flee, begged her Mistress to lead her and instead was left with an answer and solution that didn't quite suit her. Sara was never known for settling, she was famous for getting exactly what she wanted out of life, no matter the cost, the price was never too high.

Chapter 34:
DWELLING DUALITY

"WE'LL worry about her later, whatever the circumstance that arise, we'll deal with her accordingly." Jess firmly stated to appease his mind and to prevent him from worrying the way she was in this visceral realization.

"Ah yes, here it is." Jess wandered over to her vanity and picked up a journal covered in symbols of travel.

"I thought she'd be inspired to pursue the world if she remembered where she ventured." Kyle lost that rage in a moment of tender reflection,

"That's really sweet Jess, she'll love it I'm sure."

He wrapped his hands around her waist and ushered Jess downstairs below, opening the door and wandering a few paces behind her.

"Enjoying the view?" Jess said trying to keep him focused and present in the tasks that this afternoon catered too.

"Yes." he responded.

He knew he was distracted but he couldn't help but fixate on all the private places in his world that Sara's hands had now explored. Kyle walked downstairs slowly with an eerie vision down below.

"What if she releases all of them, a mutiny would rain down upon us tonight." Jess entered his mind and replied;

"I'm sure we'd have noticed by now, the others aren't as inclined to rebel against you nor are they strong enough in their imprisoned state. Calm your thoughts my love, I'll remote view and see what she's up too, then we'll both punish her tonight. Once and for all."

With that Kyle smiled realizing that he'd persuaded Jess to the dark side. He knew she was open, had a penchant for grey areas of interest in morals and ethics, clearly it was easier for her to see his much broader view of the world than Sara could in this moment.

As Jess tuned into her writhing concubine and rebellious whore down below. She saw her curled up in her cage, her eyes opening and smiling seeing her lips form the words, "Mistress I can feel your eyes upon me, you'll never catch me, neither will he. Tonight after the sun goes down I *will* make a break for it, meet me at the mausoleum if you wish to say goodbye."

She smiled wickedly and closed her eyes cuing her Mistress to knowing she was in need of deep sleep to recharge her with the strength to escape. Sara could tell each year when this lull in weather dipped down into the dungeon leaving it stale and dreary that the first snow of the season was fast approaching. She has but a week's window, possibly less before the snow would plummet to the ground pouring over the trees and preventing her from fleeing until late next spring unless she risked being buried alive.

Jess not wanting to startle Kyle anymore, doing her best to prevent provocation of the dark creature within that was ready to tear Sara's throat open ravenously with his bare hands for her arrogant display of topping from the bottom. She reached once more into his mind as they rounded the final hallway towards the dining room near the kitchen.

"She's in her cage, for now, we'll check on her the moment the children are gone, I'll tend to it myself I assure you. Tonight she'll be broken into, or left broken for

the wolves to tend too. I refuse to make time or hold patience for such trivial acts of rebellion."

Kyle felt empowered and reinforced unlike never before. He knew he could count on her to carry out his will, no matter how dark the challenge would be ultimately, he finally had full faith in her abilities. She was ready for her final test. Her initiation awaited tonight and she was ready for wherever this adventure in the wilderness took her.

"Tiffany! I thought I heard your lovely voice this morning, I swore I was dreaming." Jess walked in, the beautiful young woman walking towards her with open arms.

"I've missed you, and I have something for you. Tell me of your travels I want to live vicariously through all of your adventures."

Tiffany looked at the journal and smiled widely;

"Thank you! I was just telling my friend I needed a wanderlust journal to inspire me to travel the world. I can't wait to fill out what my latest adventure instilled in me. It left me feeling inspired to go to college this fall instead of feeling afraid to leave home." Jess glowed hearing her confidence.

"I'm so pleased to hear that, for us to embrace culture throughout the world we have to first enrich the soul. I find traveling and reading to be the most beneficial methods in life for such pursuits."

Tiffany smiled and Jess instantly inquired, "Did you meet anybody handsome?" Looking over her shoulder she realized instantly and winked, "Oh, never mind we'll talk about that later, just you and I." Jess laughed and walked to her spot at the table where Derek and Adie were already waiting. Kyle sat down and watched the staff bring in food to appease their growling stomachs.

"Oh god, my daughter's dating now." He sternly sat back in his chair and smiled, "So when do I get to meet him?"

Tiffany blushed wisecracking aloud, "Thanks Jess." sarcastically she laughed and Jess made a grimacing face of apologies.

"Sorry, I can't resist ruffling feathers I suppose. Perhaps I was a fan dancer or a peacock in my past life." Adie laughed out loud picturing this and Derek chuckled as well. Kyle shook his head and waited for Tiffany to continue, "We just started talking dad, as soon as I feel like he's even worth introducing I'll let you know, I promise."

He grinned and responded, "I'll expect him over for dinner by the time you start school in the fall." Tiffany laughed as she started to enjoy her salad, "No pressure."

Kyle and Jess started laughing the meal carried on long into the early evening, filled with banter, catching up on all of the stories and adventures each one enjoyed this busy season.

This is what I've always wanted, I just never knew it before.

Jess thought to herself between listening to the children and Kyle share what they had enjoyed as she filled them in on her current projects a midst the adventures she had with Derek and Adie all over Colorado when Kyle was busy with work.

In that moment when her peaceful thoughts effortlessly escaped in her mind's eye, Kyle reached over towards her hand and touched it gently. He responded, his voice soothingly filling her mind.

I'm glad to have you home.

Tiffany shared her adventures until she realized what time it was. "Well, it's time for me to kidnap these two for a few hours, I have a surprise for you guys, get good shoes on and we'll go for a drive. I discovered something on my way home that you two just have to see."

Excited by the element of surprise, Adie and Derek started to run as fast as they could out the door. The moment Kyle was about to remind them to say goodbye first Jess already instructed them.

"What? No goodbye?" Instantly Derek and Adie came in and hugged her, she kissed them lovingly on the forehead.

"Have fun, and take pictures for me, I already know where you're going." Sticking her tongue out and teasing them, they both laughed.

"I can't wait, I want to know where we're going."

Adie hugged her dad quickly so did Derek, as they bolted towards the stairs towards their rooms to find their shoes.

"It was great catching up, I missed you both so much over the summer." Tiffany leaned forward over her dad's shoulders hugging him, Jess stood and wrapped her arms around her.

"You've blossomed into such a confident woman this season, I can't wait to see what paths in life you choose this autumn." Jess hugged her and whispered into her ear,

"The world is lucky to have you."

Tiffany glowed and smiled nodding her head and blushing. She gently waved and wandered out the door before stepping back in for a moment;

"Oh yea, dad, I'll text you when we're on our way back, it probably won't be until after ten o' clock or so, the tour is a few hours and I wanted to take them out for something to eat afterwards, you know how Adie gets when we make her wait."

Kyle laughed and said, "Great idea, have fun." As the children left the haunting expression of fear and vengeance was painted on Kyle's face as clear as day.

"It's time my pet, sun sets in less than an hour, prepare yourself, tonight we hunt, tonight I see once and for all, just where your loyalty truly lies."

Chapter 35:
TRAINED LACHESISM

"OH God! Not now, I thought I've have enough time to see her off, at least give her a head start in the right direction far away from his hunting ground. Oh God No!"

Jess saw a vision of Sara in the near future, fleeing from the chamber door of the mausoleum down below. Burrowing out from the layers of the snow to the surface of the star kissed sky. Her face glowing with the ripe opportunity to escape, never realizing the direction she fled towards was right where he wanted Sara in the first place.

"I have to gather my equipment and get ready, it should take less than an hour. I'll be in my room, when do you desire my presence?"

Jess inquired already focused on a million tiny things that had to be done which required precise timing. Kyle noticed a moment of hesitation in her expression, he wondered then if she'd be foolish enough to disappear alongside her. He banished the thought immediately doing his best not to alarm her with the brief moment of silence that felt like an eternity to the woman he loved who knew in her scarred heart that this was the only chance she'd ever have to say goodbye to her beloved concubine. She had to try, one final time before she let her go to watch as Sara marched rebelliously towards her own demise.

"You have until nightfall that gives you just less than an hour. I'll be waiting for you down below in my private office. When you approach the sigil on the door whisper your desires for me in your mind's eye and the door will open."

Kyle smiled and watched her eyes glow along with her expanding aura. "It pleases me to the very core of my being to see how honored I am with such acts of sacred trust." Jess embraced him closely, lovingly and looked up into his eyes with words that soothed his soul in ways no actions could, at least for now.

"Whatever your eyes see tonight, know that it's what has to take place to ensure that I have a chance to kill her as humanely as she deserves. What may at first appear to be me fleeing by her side, just know that I'm ushering her to the exact spot that I know you've had picked out for her since I came into your world. I will never betray you. You are my reason for breathing."

A single tear streamed down her cheek and she smiled, he knew this was the hardest decision she'd ever have to make, he hoped deep down that she could follow in her own mental footsteps, it was the only way she'd emotionally survive a night like this.

As Jess hurried upstairs, she saw the office door open once more, and felt her energy. She smelled her fragrant scent wafting in the breeze, why was she in there? What could Sara possibly need from his personal office that would be of any use to her? Jess wandered in to see what was missing, misplaced or scattered to the winds, a single piece of parchment was sticking out of his shelf of personal works.

Jess knew Kyle had a collection of local and worldwide maps nestled in here for personal research that aided his writing.

She reached for the parchment and saw the X marked on it in red. She recognized those red lips from anywhere. Sara boldly dressed and ready to flee kissed the location of where she planned to run towards, knowing full well that her beloved mistress would never watch her flee after saying goodbye.

"Oh my beautiful fool, of all the places you decided to run, why did your twisted little mind end up here?"

Jess boldly placed the map underneath her arm and swiftly ran out of his office, shutting the door and realizing there was no way she could lock it from the inside. She didn't know which energetic protocol was required and telepathy was never her strongest ability, especially when pressure, time and adrenaline were coursing through her veins. As she fled towards her room she felt his presence ascending, she knew if he entered her bedroom he'd have questions as it looked as if she hadn't done a thing in the previous ten minutes to facilitate making things move swiftly in the direction of his dark will.

Fortunately for Jess, Kyle was more focused on tending to his office and his bedroom, he left his over layers and hunting gear in the private hollows below but he still needed his boots and under layers. He looked outside his bedroom window and watched as the snow began to fall along the horizon of the mountainside. He felt the frozen chill deep in his bones, he'd lived here all his life and Kyle possessed the innate ability to detect the changing seasons before anyone else could. Leaving him with the power to control when and how he would kill, to hunt down fresh meat with fervor in a silent graveyard without another human being on the planet to intrude.

"Perfect timing." Kyle said with a contented sigh, watching the snow fall in sheets now as he continued to pull on his warm leggings underneath his jeans, adding extra socks under his boots and layers of thick sweaters under what would be his cloaked jacket and armed bow and arrow.

"Cougars detest the snow, yet the wildest most *untamable* ones seem to stick around far beyond their approaching expiration."

As Kyle cinched his belt he sighed contently knowing that he was ready, he lurked in the hallways ensuring no staff or other unexpected employee or co-worker would randomly choose to come up here for some unapparent reason. The halls were dark and silent, he walked like a shadow towards his office door, realizing now that this was unlocked. His blood instantly boiled.

"Fucking cunt, I'll personally finish you off, even if she does have the stomach for it."
Kyle couldn't tell what was misplaced or missing, but he smelled her scent, mixed with another who he knew most intimately.
"Jess was here too recently, I wonder if she found anything."

His mind continued to grind and churn like the cogs and wheels of an old industrial factory machine. As his heart started beating fast he walked towards her door, feeling her visceral presence inside. He let out a sigh of contentment, he couldn't endure her vanishing without a trace on the frost bitten winds of this dark initiatory night. This night was what he'd been waiting for, aching to share with her for centuries. If she only knew how long it took to construct such a dream, the patience facilitated over the year, was maddening.
Kyle reached towards her bedroom door for the handle, first knocking gently to ease her energy instead of alarming her with a sudden entrance resonating with power.

"She's been in your office, I found this in there earlier right before I came in to get ready. She begged me to come down to the mausoleum before sundown but we were with the children, I'd hoped it would've provided me one last chance to instill some sense within her, but then I found this."

Jess was adorned head to toe in her latex catsuit, her hair invisible in the casing of her gear. Her eyes already covered in her night goggles, her bags were sitting on the bed now, still unzipped open to reveal all the tormenting devices she had to use if Sara made this simple execution as impossible as Jess expected.

The map was tossed on the desk table beside him, and he saw the large X painted in red lipstick along with her arrogant lip print. In that moment Darkeel took over, his eyes glowing bright, that wicked, devious smile cracking over and revealing his innate desire to kill.

"A living sacrifice who even desires to serve herself up to me on a silver platter, of all the places she had to choose my favorite hunting grounds."

Kyle instantly snapped back into his body yelling out loud;

"I thought we had a deal, you stay the fuck out of my head until we get to Royal Gorge.

Got it?!"

He heard the billowing growls and hisses building up inside.

"We'll see if I can wait. I'd rather play with the red head, she's much more my type."

Jess held him close even in this risky state of daemonic battle. "Kyle my darling, I know you're here, I know Darkeel wants to kill me, I've felt that fear ever since we first met in that kitchen that afternoon. Whatever happens know that I belong entirely to you." Jess kissed Kyle's lips passionately, instantly filling him up with her warm, brilliant light.

"Mmmm, thank you, I promise I'll never let him hurt you." Kyle's face grimaced, he did his best to tell her his ideals, but his fears were confirmed as she spoke;

"Don't keep promises you can't keep." She brushed his face gently and smiled, "Whatever happens tonight, know that I have never been happier and more fulfilled than I have been in your arms. Even if those strong hands of yours strangle the very breath within me from my lips. Leaving me lifeless in the snow, to blend in and wash away in the cold rivers of spring; know that everything you have given me is everything I've ever hoped for or could ever dream of."

Jess kissed Kyle again holding him close and filling him up with as much light as she could share with another being without snuffing out her own flame.

"That is much as I have to spare. I hope it holds your monster at bay, at least long enough to ensure that we can spend the rest of our lives together, haunting these hills and slaughtering all who dare cross our paths."

Kyle reached for the map and eyed her closet door, Jess instantly grabbed her gear and used her mind to dim the lights. She walked towards the closet and gently pressed the secret panel open and wandered back down inside the secret passageway that now felt far more like home than any other place. Jess waited idly by a few steps below in the bowels of Burnett Manor. She watched as Kyle's mind shut the closet door entrance behind them, once more kissing him and whispering to him,

"I never knew it could be such an honor than to serve the dark will of *The Slaughterhouse Hills Hunter,* until my last breath, I am yours."

Jess turned and walked towards his private internal office. His ransacked trophy room with his gear waiting for the skillful hunter to gather his necessary provisions to hunt long into the dead of night. As he watched her sultry ass enter into his sacred inner temple, his mind whispered within;

That is what I am afraid of my darling, that tonight you risk using that last breath in my honor. Here's hoping I finally am strong enough to conquer you Darkeel, once and for all.

Chapter 36:
ARCHAIC VENERY

JESS collected his bags watching him in her mind's eyes. His bottom lip secured and bitten by his teeth, just watching her pert ass bent over; to retrieve his items invoked a dark arousal over him.

"I can't believe it, for so long this night has been planned in your honor, I envisioned so many variables getting in the way and tearing us apart, seeing your hands calmly collecting what will soon be *our* hunting gear, for the kill tonight; I'm walking into a dream that's finally connected to what I've been working on for centuries. Waiting and hoping that you'd be mine again to train someday."

In that moment her mind flashed back to a time when she spoke no language or knew nothing of outsiders. Those glowing eyes in the dark haunted hills of the black forest waiting for her as she gathered firewood to burn a midst the blizzard in the harshest snowfall that Germany had ever seen in pre-recorded history. He watched her from a distance shrouded in darkness as she slowly pulled her arrow from quiver, drawing her bow back. Her eyes shined and her lips parted into a satisfied smile, when she wandered over towards her prize for that night's meal she instantly felt herself slammed against the trees, her back scraping upwards feeling her throat crushing in. His eyes glowing menacingly from across the way, hers now bulging out of her skull wondering how this supernatural moment would take the breath from her very lungs leaving her a meal for the wolves in the middle of the snowbank.

"It was you."

She smiled in sudden epiphany as her previous lives continued to flash before her very eyes time and time again. There he was hidden in the background, prominent in the foreground of the times. Resting, waiting, and watching his prey waiting for the perfect time to slaughter her when he found them coincidentally alone.

"It's always you, *isn't it?*"

She continued to gather his bags, lifting quivers on shoulder and bows up and over her neck, dragging them both over her luscious breasts and resting them further down onto her waist.

"The real question is, why didn't I let that arrow fly where I first intended it to go... straight, in your heart?"

As her eyebrow raised and she turned towards him, Jess's eyes glowed, her fangs protruded and she smiled wickedly.

"You know I wasn't aiming for that rabbit that was just a fortunate coincidence until I blacked out. What did you end up doing to me afterwards?" Her glowing blue green eyes inspired a smile across Kyle's face.

"You wouldn't want to know..."

He turned his head in regret and tried to center himself in the present, his mind was once more locked away deep inside. Far away from Jess and her powerful ability to penetrate deep into him, finding his truest and darkest nature that he fought relentlessly to hide from those he treasured more than life itself.

"I suppose it truly does take a special or more accurately worded, crazy woman to continue to find you. Lifetime after lifetime, you think I would've wised up by now, recognized your face and learned to flee more stealthily. Perhaps love truly is the darkest form of madness in this world, cloaked in a guise of passionate layers. Any sane woman would've fled by now, perhaps Sara truly isn't as crazy as I've always thought she was. I by all rational and logical account should've tried to escape the moment I knew who you were with Sara in arms. Running across these hillsides in the dead of night. Never worrying about Royal Gorge or the fact that this entire region has been mapped, with traps set entirely by you. She doesn't stand a chance. Neither would we if I would've left with her hours ago the way she planned."

Kyle suddenly sighed aloud in a most disconcerting way, this was the last thing he wanted to discuss right now but he realized this rebellious thought pattern would be his demise tonight if she suddenly switched sides.

"In those times my gift was dark, uncontrollable and far too strong for me to understand fully especially at that young age. It was the only way my base instincts understood how to keep you with me forever. Unfortunately I had the displeasure of watching you die in my arms in more lifetimes than I'd ever like to recollect. There's only been a handful before that we lived both a long and happy life together, including this one… *hopefully*."

"What we sew, so shall we reap. Tonight I prove myself to you once and for all. I only hope I have the strength to measure up to your desires and expectations. I can feel my initiation calling to me. The very idea haunting my dreams now for weeks. I've known its approach was coming, I just never knew it would arrive so swiftly." Jess let a tear stream down her face.

"I've always known I had the ability within me to kill if necessary, but to take the life of the one I love? This will be the biggest challenge to my soul in all of my existence on this earth. Tonight I say goodbye to who I ever truly was, it's the only way for me to find strength in letting go of Sara in such a brutal but well deserved way."

As she wiped the tear from her face she looked into his eyes, Jess was geared up and ready to go, handing him his cloak her words quivered as they left her trembling lips, "I know what must be done. Please I beg of you, let's go before I lose the courage to do what I must."

Jess descended the dark staircase, for once never fearing the darkness in search of the light. The flames flickered above head after she passed by, she already knew Sara was out there, though she ran down once more to investigate her cage to see if anything else was left behind. Her boots invoked fear and whispered gasps from the many caged victims and prey to *The Slaughter House Hills Hunter,* as they saw her approaching Sara's now empty cage they started to cry. Shivering and shaking knowing he'd be here soon to torture them for answers to questions of Sara's immediate location. She walked towards the locked cage door she saw it open without provocation, as she entered the cage she heard the cries of the prisoners build. It was obvious to her that they saw the same foreboding being walking slowly, silently in darkness. His booming silhouette leering down as he approached Sara's now empty cage.

Jess continued to rummage around through the cage looking for tools of escape or even a last note of goodbye, but she saw nothing. As she turned around she heard the door clicking shut.

"What is this? What's going on?! This can't be part of it." Jess looked alarmed as the eyes of Darkeel glowed bright.

"I can't have you getting in the way. Messing this kill up with your precious love. No, too messy for this world. Too busy risking everything we've worked for,

centuries of me strangling the breath out of you with my bare hands and you still haven't learned a thing."

Jess reared back in anger slashing her claws at his bare hands and causing them to bleed. Kyle's hands dripped all over the stone ground and that's when she felt it. His blood soaked hand reaching for her neck and lifting her off the floor.

"Give me the gear and I'll let you live, for now at least. I look forward to playing with you when I get back." Jess choking, her face turning blue and eyes bulging, tears forced down her face.

"Please, let me do this with you Darkeel, let me kill her for you and then take me in return. It's what you've always wanted isn't it? To let him watch me die in his arms again after you've taken over. What do you say old fiend, shall we dance again?"

The words barely audible yet strong enough for him to hear. His wicked laugh echoed through and clashing off the walls of the room causing all the girls still alive within, to cry.

"Shut the fuck up you stupid whores! I'm speaking." Darkeel released Jess and she fell to the ground choking incessantly waiting for the color to return to her face, her fangs retracting viciously.

"I knew you'd come around, with an incessant will to die trying to save him. What a pitiful existence. You can come, but I want a head start."

In that moment he reached for her and dragged her to the cage's entrance once more slamming her skull hard against the cage and pulling her remote viewed screen into his mind, now he could locate Sara much swifter than he would've by hunting down her fresh tracks in the snow. Jess instantly passed out her body slumping to the floor. Warm blood pooling by her a mixture of Kyle's and mostly hers seeping onto the stones beneath her, clotting; as she fell unconscious while the swift feet of Darkeel moved downstairs and out towards the mausoleum. He crawled through her hand carved tunnel and out of the mausoleum door with bow and quiver locked firmly into place. Sara's footprints still vivid in the snowbank above lead off into the north eastern direction exactly where he wanted her to go all along; his favorite hunting ground for those who refused to submit, a ravine so deep that even those who claimed immortality now rested in the snow covered graveyard thousands of feet below; never to be seen from or heard of ever again.

As she swam unconscious, Jess's head fell back onto the cold stone floor, trickles of blood seeping from a small wound on the back of her head. As darkness fell to bleak existences of snow laden hell which expanded across the countryside and haunted hills of Colorado. Jess left her mind forever in tune with the ticking time clock and heartbeat of Sara's. Feeling her fear, watching glimpses of snow covered trees passing by in her panicked breath that streaked across the skies, twinkling in the stars above. Jess felt her heartbeat, the ferocious pace continued to pound in twisted tune with each and every one of his calculated steps. She could see his large shoulders slinking through the snow tunnel that was carved out by her now bleeding blue fingertips. She watched his lips curl into that demonic smile as he pulled his body through the hole and effortlessly dragged himself up with gear intact on menacing form.

Jess watched as he reached down and saw drops of blood right next too fresh tracks in pristine snow banks. This was going to be a much swifter kill than he ever imagined. So many traps set to ensure that she'd never escape, yet she was making this so easy on him. Jess's head moved across the cold stone floor still swimming with dark visions of what was taking place mere feet away from her in this very moment. Still powerless to move, unable to waken herself from this horrible slumber, she watched and heard the haunting sounds of whistling winds howling in the distance, pouring sheet after sheet of icy snow onto the hillside. In that haze of white that imminent wall of snow that masqueraded the things that go bump in the night. She watched as Darkeel walked off slowly towards the distance, his dark silhouette disappearing without a trace over the hillside towards Sara's final resting place.

Chapter 37:
FOOLISH LOVE

SARA turned around and Jess heard her gasp, she knew he was close. She felt him approaching her from behind but she didn't stand a chance. Jess knew Sara had a resourceful way of fashioning weapons out of practically anything on hand, but this was different. There was nothing in that cage to use. Not even as a method to escape this world through the power of her own hands, she would've taken her life countless times if she had the chance. As her eyes peered through the trees behind her she saw a flash from the corner of her eyes. Watching as an arrow landed overhead, she knew he was in range, felt his distance closing in on her even though he appeared to be miles behind her. She instantly fled under a hillside covered in fallen trees. Hoping to cloak herself in the pale snow, she never imagined that it would've fallen this swiftly. Dressed in black and wearing so little to keep warm she panted and breathed heavily as the tears streaked down her face. She knew he was coming for her. Sara felt the wrath of the beast inside that sought to finally tame her once and for all. Like a lame horse unable to move after falling and breaking its limbs, shattering them to pieces. She knew that she was a bright target in a pale landscape just waiting for the moment that that arrow would land and end her without a single consequence or hesitation.

In that moment Jess awoke gasping and choking on her own air, the blood now dried pulled and tugged at her scalp when she rose to the bars. Still shaking and blinded by the migraine that now rested in the front of her skull. She closed her eyes and focused, watching the cage unlock she pushed it open and stepped out. Searching for the first aid kit that Kyle had hidden down here for himself; in those rare and brutal moments that Darkeel took over in ways to torture him for his refusal to surrender to greater powers, not fully understood. She opened the metal box and popped a few pain pills and downed it with the water she found nearby resting on the floor behind this overseers desk.

The monitors were off and the girls were as silent as the grave. They never moved, or even rose from the shroud of darkness that kept them at a safe distance a midst this hellish place. Jess slowly slid her hood back on, hissing with the pain;

"Motherfucker, I knew I shouldn't have gone in there, a set up from the start. Now I'm going to have to play dirty just to keep my promises."

She threw her equipment over her shoulders and ran upstairs, she knew that the neighbors would be gone until next week, they'd never notice their fastest horse missing. Not in a blizzard like this. Jess stampeded up the spiral staircase towards the surface of the twisted manor resting on a thousand corpses still wailing in the graveyard for sweet revenge. Before she realized she was already hopping over the fence and mounting the horse without a second thought. Fortunately the horse was bridled for she had no time to care about the saddle, she didn't need it. She charged the fence and felt the air lifting her up, his body crashing down to the ground and his cadence swift, but challenged with the thickness of fresh snow under hoof. She realized she'd have to push him to the limit if she was going to make it to their location in time. It was only twelve miles away from here and she wouldn't even have to ride the entire way, just enough to give her the advantage, she had to make it to Sara before he did...*at all costs.*

The trees streaking by in a flash of green coated in white she felt the snow piling on top of her, feeling the steed beneath her thighs breathing hard as they attempted to find any place that was hard enough to run across without having to trample through feet of snow slowing her pace to walking. She focused intently and saw her beloved's tears, she could see through her eyes that she was nearing Royal Gorge, the eerie vanishing horizon made Sara frightened as to where she was going, she thought she knew the way. She researched it as best as she could in the last week, not realizing that this entire place looked quite strange and mysterious after heavy snowfall. Her fingers clung to the trees and she rested beside them breathing and trying to find a better way out of this place. It would only be a few more hours until sunrise, and she was already hauntingly close to where he wanted her. Jess yelled and charged towards the side of a trail that was still visible but wouldn't be for even minutes longer. Even if it was frosted in ice, the horse could take it, but he'd soon give out and suffer from exhaustion or worse a heart attack if she pushed him any further.

In that moment, that one brief moment of relief, she saw the steed climb forward, up and over neighing loudly, determined to be on solid ground he trotted across the ice; slipping sideways here and there but steadfastly charging forward. As the echoes of that horse rolled over the hillside, two miles north Darkeel stopped and she felt a haunting penetration into her own mind that she'd never experienced until this day. It was his form shrouded in darkness turning around and staring directly into her soul, she felt his being force himself into her mind, casting aside all other reality that was currently within her psychic field of sight. She felt the charging of the horse going forward but all she could see in these haunting gallops and haze was his face, not Kyle's, but *his* face. A vexing expression filled with rage, she was more than certain as to who this was, she'd felt him whenever Kyle couldn't keep him at bay;

"I thought I told you I wanted a head start? She's mine, you're just here for the cleanup. That is the only purpose I allow you to have, to clean up my messes after I've enjoyed a fresh kill."

His menacing smile expanded and contorted, his green eyes glowing and his long black hair flowing in all directions. Jess instantly saw him where he was transmitting from, a hellish existence, a planet of sulphuric smoke and menacing disfigured faces shaking and screaming in torment, moving so swiftly that no facial expressions were recognizable, if they even had facial expressions at all. The rivers of blood and lava were flowing towards one menacing set of castles on top of a dark abandoned hillside. Instantly through front door Jess felt she was whisked within unable to do anything but stand before him in all of his dark and irreverent glory.

"Darkeel? So that's what you've been calling yourself all these years, when you came to me and tormented my life for so long in my youth? I knew you as *Lupin.*"

The sinister being with legs crossed at ankles, covered in layers of black armor and long rolling fabric of red and black bleeding into one another to remind Jess of the blood soaked abyss. He smiled his porcelain face and long fingers curling towards his chin with pointed nails.

"Ah, my sweet child don't you know that we come to each of you in many forms. We are called by many names. Your powers differ vastly from his, this is why you and I have a much more *special* connection that Kyle and I have never had."

In that moment she felt him inside of her, swimming and stirring, tormenting her body, the most pleasurable parts of her flesh, leaving his poisonous stains inside of her, filling her with rage and ecstasy blindingly mixed in a concoction that left her head swimming now more than ever.

"It really is you that I feel inside of him pushing him to the brink of madness, taking me over and over again and lashing me with your twisted hands upon my silken skin." She heard his menacing laughter and his whispers of cruelty;

"Mmm yes, I never took a liking to pleasure before I brought the two of you together, but now I have a *taste* for so much more on this planet. I must express my gratitude to you, such a seductive feline masquerading in human form."

In that moment she flashed back fully into her body, though she felt his presence deep within her, pushing her powers forth and making her shift. She felt her teeth elongate, her eyes slit and glow, as she felt every hair on her body tingle, stand up straight charged with electricity, she watched as his horrifying energy seeped forth out of her. Slamming back into the back of Kyle's head causing him to fall forward into the snow gripping for mercy. In unison they screamed and Sara heard their voices closing in on her. The sounds of two banshees clashing in rhythmic cadence, leaving the hillside streaked in blood, snow and the songs of harpies. Sara closed her eyes and grabbed her knees, her ass pressed hard against the birch trees behind her, she started to weep.

"Please my love, find me before he does. I know you can hear me, feel me, sense me."

As Sara raised her eyes towards the night sky, the snow finally stopped. The howling was replaced with silence that seemed louder than the whistling on the winds of time. Her eyes bleeding, Jess didn't realize until now just how long it'd been since Sara had fed. Those stains on the snow weren't from her fingers but her tears, her tears of abandonment, hopelessness and isolation. Jess felt an overwhelming amount of guilt rearing up inside as she charged the horse forward.

Neighing furiously it began to stampede over now frozen packs of snow.

Kyle breathing heavily, his arrows tucked away safely in quiver, his bag still over his shoulders filled with his tools, devices and favorite ax. He looked down at his hands and saw them gripping the snow as if it was actually something to hold onto.

"Fuck! You fucking bastard, leave her alone, Jess is mine! I'm already giving you Sara, it's going to tear us apart and I've already accepted that you fucking prick! Give her to me!"

In that moment Kyle saw the memories flashing by in her mind, the years of giving herself over to this dark wandering visitor from another world that beckoned and beguiled her into pleasures against the very volition of her will. Kyle looked up mortified realizing that he'd been fucking her for years now in their preternatural world of dream fueled nightmares.

"But how? How is this fucking possible?" Shaking his head in awe and shocked silence he waited to hear the words of confession that spilled across the lips of his haunting conductor.

"You see, demons have a way of arriving to each of their minions in an intrinsic way, quite specialized and designed for each and every one of your darkest fantasies. She wanted to be taken, needed to be ravaged, captured and mercilessly destroyed. You needed to hunt, you ached for the kill, it was the perfect solution to both of your problems, as well as my own. I've been waiting to finish this game of chess for far too long, and perhaps I'll even show you my final masterpiece."

In that moment Jess felt herself next to Kyle even though he was over two miles to the west. She'd never had the ability to hear in stereo surround sound what it was like for them to speak to one another but as her powers were heightened by Darkeel's torture, she found herself listening into his words of response to Kyle's sheer rage at such a revelation.

"What the fuck do you mean, *your* game? I've been waiting for centuries, spanning time and space and endless lifetimes just to find her again. Do you fucking think I'll let you come near our empire? After all this time forging it into existence? I want to strangle the life out of you with my bare hands!"

As Jess passed by he felt her energy and instantly peered towards her direction miles away and their eyes met on that profound plane of communication that their souls shared like no other two in this world.

"Don't do it Jess! You belong to me, don't listen to him!"

For the first time in his life Kyle heard her voice respond, her voice echoing inside his mind clear as day, *"A girl must do what she must."* She smiled softly and sauntered forward, inching closer and closer towards the direction of where Sara was still hiding.

"My love, I'm coming for you, but you have to trust me, trust me more than you ever have in this life, and we might survive this. I know it seems crazy but no matter what happens, trust me."

Sara's eyes turned towards the darkness as the snow stopped falling her beautiful face was streaked in dried bloody tears, her body pressed firmly against the birch trees. She tried her best to find the courage to move towards the next set of hills covered in trees, she wanted at all costs to be far away from the voice that kept yelling in the night at a man who she could not hear, see or even feel with her abilities. Sara and Jess both knew sunrise was fast approaching, as twilight broke their eyes, Jess knew in her heart of hearts that Sara wasn't going to be able to hide. Sara was a blinding black target that radiated her location along the vast spans of porcelain hillside. She saw as Kyle stood over the horizon his menacing shadow form stretching towards the sky echoing yells of anger that were unable to be deciphered at this distance.

Jess charged forward on her valiant steed feeling her heart crushing as she closed the distance and knew she'd make it to Sara before Kyle ever stood a chance. Her haunting soul sang whispers of adoration towards him hoping he'd embrace the sanctity of her soul.

"If everything works out according to plan, I won't have to break promises to anyone tonight. Trust me..."

Kyle's eyes caught her in the distance, she was such a small figure charging towards her dark destiny. He watched and waited to see where she was going before charging forth to the northern tip of Royal Gorge. He was mesmerized by her courage and conviction, never did he imagine her forging a dark path in life for herself alongside his, and this epiphany was never formulated into his plan. As he watched her steed leap forth towards the direction of the lines of birch trees, for the first time since he'd stopped; He saw her there, sitting in the form of a rock, stirring suddenly he watched her rise, back against the trees still peeking forth to show the parts of limbs still exposed for the kill.

Without hesitation his hand reached back and pulled an arrow from his quiver, before he could blink the arrow was knocked and ready to fly. Before Jess ever made it to Sara she heard that shattering sound of screams filling the woods. She tapped into Kyle's mind and watched the arrow land directly into her left shoulder. Sara's screams filled the trees scattering sleeping crows to the winds, as they flew overhead towards her final resting place. Before Jess could calm her or reach her to throw her onto the back of her horse, she saw Sara bolting towards the gorge at an alarming pace.

"No, please my love, not that way! Any way but that way! Sara

No!" Jess's siren voice echoed in the trees, Kyle bolted ahead and Jess watched him disappear over another hillside covered in snow.

Disappearing beyond the trees, she felt her heart racing as she sensed Kyle's presence along with Darkeel's fast approaching. Now realizing the terror in every woman's heart who'd ran in fear across the haunted forest of *The Slaughterhouse Hills Hunter*. Never before in all of her lives had she felt hunted like this before. The impending doom caused the adrenaline in her blood to spike, forcing her fangs and eyes to glow menacingly, her powers were tainted with Darkeel's toxic potion. She felt the pain rushing forth into her neck, her chest and down into her sides. Her ribs growing tight suddenly throwing her from her horse and onto the snow, her ribs crashing onto the broken tree limbs he'd planted there just weeks before knowing that it would create an impossible landscape for anyone to navigate through.

Jess' painful screams echoed through the forest, Sara was charging forth towards Royal Gorge for her very survival and Jess now winded with three broken ribs stood up slowly with gear still on torso, looking around for her horse that was now running off in the wrong direction alone. She stood gripping her ribs, barely able to breathe she spit fresh blood on the snow and yelled;

"Fuck!" She felt her legs sinking in with every step, but she clung to tree branches and shook the snow overhead, leaving a trail back to where she started so that she could find her way home again when all of this was finally over.

As she followed the blood soaked tracks of her beloved, she felt herself getting closer. She could smell her, taste her, the iron in her blood tormented this hungry vamp to hunt harder, to kill faster and to move swiftly towards the direction of her sinful fate. Before she could make it to the next clearing she saw his form standing in full ominous figure like a giant black bird ready to swoop in and carry her away far from her beloved; leaving her somewhere without the ability to reach her in this perilous moment. She stood and stared directly at Kyle knowing full well that he was no longer here.

He was gone, swallowed in the dark ether, the powerful current of Darkeel was fully present and there would be no mercy this early morning. She smiled lovingly and looked into him, her green eyes glowing, making the perfect target as she ran towards Sara defying the very odds that stood against her, equipped with devices of finality that would soon desire to meet her.

"I dare not ask what I already know the answer too, please forgive me Kyle, but Darkeel and I have unfinished business to attend too. Forgive me my love. Oh God, please forgive me."

Jess with one final absolution of guilt fled towards the horizon and trees where Sara was bleeding and crying on the snow fearing her ultimate demise. Jess bolted fiercely forward using her equipment as a shield to her body. She heard the screams of arrows flying overhead closer and closer they landed, behind each step, over her head, trailing in front of her very eyes and still she charged forward without hesitation. She could feel the deepest parts of Kyle still active inside somewhere, altering his aim, changing the direction ever so slightly to ensure that she would be missed.

"Fucking whore! I'll add you to my collection, have your pretty little head to fuck and stare at whenever I please, spitting on you to remind you of your place, beneath me!"

In that moment Darkeel bolted towards her direction, sending chills of sheer horror up the spine of Kyle's beloved, her eyes widened as his pace was preternatural, moving effortlessly over the snow like a shadow, so swiftly like a man running in a hand held flip book. His demonic staccato rhythms came closer and closer towards her, still

Jess ran. Looking down in the snow below she saw the drops of Sara's blood soaked tears leading her to where she was needed most in this lifetime.

"Mistress, is that you? Oh God please hurry, I'm so cold, the blood is everywhere."

Sara's beautiful voice was shaking violently, hypothermia and frost bite was setting in. Her beautiful pale skin now tinged in blue and black, Jess leapt forward to reach her and in that moment the screams escaped her lips unable to move. She fell to the snow pack just feet away from the love of her life, now bleeding before her eyes, doing her best to hold on long enough just to say goodbye.

"My love it was never supposed to take place this way. I'm here, I'll be here until your final breath, hold on Sara...just hold on."

Jess looked down and her vison started to blur, she felt the sweet escape of atropine filling her blood with insanity. She knew he prepared these to be fatal doses, and for Sara it was certain that she wouldn't make it. It would be a miracle if Jess even woke up after the adrenaline coursed this much poison through her veins. The arrow stood out of her back, directly in the meat of her shoulder blade, fortunately a minor flesh wound if only she had a tolerance that could endure.

Kyle's smile appeared, he was present, Darkeel was present, together they stood side by side simultaneously relishing in this decadent show of horrors that was prepared just for their eyes. He knew it would take time to convince her that Darkeel was a separate being but he never realized how deeply she'd fall head over heels for him, never realizing that the two beings were one in the same. His ominous presence stood over the northeastern hillside, he started to walk towards them. Sara looking over and seeing him, she started to cry. The blood still pooling forth from her chest, the tip of the arrow sticking out six inches forward and through her artery, Sara didn't stand a chance. Jess looked over to see Kyle releasing a shower of arrows in their direction, whistling ahead over trees, crows cawing in the distance fleeing this haunted place. She felt them land around them, once more piercing her flesh and hitting her in the back of her thigh. Jess' screams echoes throughout the woods and she slowly drug herself to Sara's side.

Jess screamed and stood up, tearing her claws at the trees for momentum and forcing herself forward towards her. Hearing her screams of fear echoing against the wooded sanctuary that they now found themselves in. Resting near Sara and watching her eyes focusing on the snow as it started to fall, they could both hear his footsteps approaching but the only thing Sara could say was,

"Isn't it all so beautiful?"

Jess curled up next to her, arrows protruding out of her back and thigh, leaving blood to gush forth in spurts her body feeling weak and subdued.

"Don't give up on me now my pet, we have to make a run for it." Sara laughed manically. The sheer idea of even moving was agonizing let alone running for any short period of time.

"Can you stand? If you can stand I can drag you to our final destination. We can go together just you and me, for old times' sake?"

Sara smiled and reached for her Mistresses lips, kissing them passionately for what might possibly be the last time she whispered to her warmly purring in her ear;

"As you wish my Queen, I'll follow you to the ends of the earth and beyond, you have been my greatest reason for living."

Off in the distance, his menacing approach started to close in on them. Kyle wandered over with his bag over his shoulders, his quiver still half full of atropine laced arrows and his bag of toys still firmly gripped in his tightly clenched fist. He marched forward each lumbering step he took sunk into the earth's bed. Each foot of snow reaching instantly upwards towards his hips, a dark phantom shadow drudging forward towards his longed for kill. It was bittersweet this twisted twilight morning, as the snow continued to fall; he watched as Jess leaned forward, pushing her body upwards and doing her best to refrain from screams and yells of agony. He watched as she pulled herself up one of the birch trees that was now decorated in poisoned arrows. She looked over her left shoulder, a single wisp of red hair trailing down her porcelain face. She'd never looked so pale before, without the latex catsuit she would've blended into the mountain side like a delicate winter hare.

Out of breath and utterly exhausted she smiled in his direction, watching as he once more pulled his legs up and dug them forward towards her direction. He was so close, she could feel him more powerfully now than ever before. The pain in her head from his presence stalking closely and coming for her was radiating through her skull. She couldn't help but smile, she relished in this sweet agony, knowing that she'd never be able to have it all, even if she was given a small taste. A small taste of this dark paradise would never be enough for her, she wanted to rule it, she wanted him to fall to his knees and beg for her lips in confidence; for all the dark and twisted adventures that he enjoyed thoroughly, and completely alone.

"Even after all this time, you still don't trust me?"

Jess watched as Kyle's eyes glowed and his sinister smile curled as he started to laugh under his breath. Still digging towards the snow and thrashing his limbs faster into the layers of fresh powder, watching as she defied all logic and reason. She should've been out like a light, Sara should've easily bled out by now, but beyond all understanding he watched as she stood and walked dragging her left leg alongside her, screaming as she picked Sara up, her agony echoed as she started to drag them both towards the horizon.

"Agh! How the fuck can I trust you, it's obvious you're trying to save her, you're throwing away everything we've ever worked for, sacrificing yourself once again for the wrong fucking one!"

Kyle's voice echoed in the chambers of her mind, rattling and bouncing off of every doorway in her haunted mind. Jess gauged the distance to the side of the cliff, it was only a few hundred feet away, and Kyle was closing in, at the same distance to their left they heard his voice echoing against the rocks nearby. Sara laughed out loud, it was obvious that the blood loss had done its damage, she was slowly losing her mind, and Jess had the unsightly privilege of watching this horror show unfold right before her very eyes.

"Sara, stay with me my darling, remember the time we made love in the cemetery after we first met?" Sara started to smile and focus on nostalgia, "Mmm, it was incredible, it was snowing that night wasn't it Mistress? Just like it's snowing now."

Jess turned around just in time to feel the sailing of an arrow slicing into her forehead before she gasped fiercely and bolted towards the Cliffside, she looked down to see Sara dozing off, slowly falling asleep.

"We're almost there my darling, stay with me, we'll be together for eternity, very soon; trust me."

Sara was barely breathing, she knew better than to turn around anymore, she could hear him now a mere hundred yards away. The sound of his violent yells as his limbs forged his path towards them. In her mind's eye Jess watched as Kyle threw down his bag and moved incessantly quicker. Darkeel was flooding his mind with images of bloodlust and torture, he couldn't play this game anymore, there was no pretending, in the heart and soul of this brilliant man, lied the heart of a killer, there was no mercy on this mountainside. As they all made their way to the highest peak of Royal Gorge, Jess watched through his eyes, she saw her backside, saw that it blocked and protected Sara completely and could feel the impending arrow's arrival closing in on his mark.

"Argh! Move! I don't want to do this, you've given me no choice…"

Kyle knocked another series of arrows, all seeping thick liquid, these were never meant for Jess, they were meant for the kill. Jess leaned forward and woke Sara one last time;

"My darling it seems as if our road has come to an end, what do you say? Want to spend eternity in my arms?" Jess leaned over Sara and smiled, Sara's eyes opened one last time as she smiled the snow fell around Jess's expression leaving her glowing face to appear divine to this nearly dead woman's eyes;

"You are an angel Mistress, take me to our paradise."

Jess leaned down and cradled Sara in her arms. "I love you, no one in this world will ever possess the power to change that… *No one*."

She leaned down and kissed her passionately on the lips, she felt Sara reaching for the back of her neck, moaning and swooning into her warm life force. Jess stood lifting Sara with her, both embracing one another as they continued to drag themselves towards the cliff. It wasn't much farther now before they could say goodbye to all of this, once and for all.

Kyle quickly removed the arrows from knock and through them down into the snow. He reached into his coat and pulled out a long piece of metal affixed with grip hooks, he aimed it high above their heads and launched the hooks high into the trees, as he gripped his hand firmly on the trigger he watched it sail through the air, the steel line instantly retracting with a touch of his fingers, hoisting him into the air and sailing him towards the Cliffside of Royal Gorge. He landed ahead of them and turned around with a violent force that sent them both into shock, instantly leaving these two shaking souls to stiffen and pause silently as they watched as the sound of his boots echoed on the rocks just before them.

"This is how you repay me? After *all* that I've done for you? For us?! This is the thanks I get?"

His voice changed into that demonic tone that she heard ages ago in the dead of night when Lupin came to visit without warrant or formal invitation.

"You're not the only one who enjoys playing the long game. We'll see if you have the strength to watch me as I reveal *my final masterpiece.*"

In that moment Jess's feet shuffled and slipped, the rocks starting to give out beneath them, in that final moment she looked Sara deep in the eyes and with one final whisper of her hearts deepest sentiments escaped, "*I love you.*"

She looked over her shoulder for the final time to see his arrows knocked and waiting to fly, the sun started to rise over the horizon. It was the most beautiful thing she'd ever seen before in her entire life. She smiled into his eyes and turned towards Sara, she shoved her off, watching her eyes widen in shock and fear, seeing her beautiful body flying and falling over the cliffs of Royal Gorge she turned to Kyle one final time and said...

"A girl must do what she must, someday you'll understand."

Her final words echoed in the chambers of this dead man's heart, filling his mind in a swimming ecstasy of truth that he'd never been struck down with until now.

Without warning Jess closed her eyes covered her chest with crossed arms as if she was already a beautiful corpse, heels against the very steep edge of Royal Gorge, she fell back serenely; Calmly over the edge towards the snow covered graveyard of *The Slaughterhouse Hills Hunter* still resting below.

"NOooooooooooo!"

Kyle's voice screamed in sheer terror, his arrows flew and struck Jess in the shoulder, hip and front of her left thigh, reaching for his batter rang Kyle instantly dropped his equipment and flew through the air down after Jess, watching her soar like a skydiver without a shoot to her impending doom. She opened her eyes and smiled wickedly, turning a full one hundred and eighty degrees she started to soar towards Sara like a speeding bullet. She caught her in mid-air as they continued to soar to the bottom of Royal Gorge. Sara reached for her Mistress and clung to her body, the two women wrapped in one another's embrace. Sara's lips parting in sorrow;

"I'm so sorry my love, will you ever forgive me?"

Jess started to cry, tears of blood seeping down her face in time to join Sara's as they warmly kissed. Holding one another a flurry of gray, green and white flashed by as they sped faster and closer to the ground. She felt their bodies turning her now resting beneath Sara, looking up in the sky she saw the dark cloak slowly moving farther and farther away, unable to reach them anymore. Kyle's ominous silhouette stood along the side of the cliff haunted by the image before his eyes.

"It was never supposed to be this way, how will I ever replace you? No one can compare to you. I love you Jess, you're the only one in this world that's ever captured me."

Kyle's voice echoed in her mind, Sara and Jess's bodies continued to spin in a surreal state of suspension as they continued to plummet towards the frozen river below. This frozen terrain was covered in rocks and layers of fallen trees that were pushed there with calculated intent, she knew this had to be it. There was no conceivable way she was ever going to survive this. The odds were completely against her. As the ground came closer and closer, the tree line passed by and she knew that upon impact neither of them stood a chance;

"Take me, take me away from all this pain."

Sara in her final moment positioned herself beneath Jess and smiled knowing she'd made the ultimate sacrifice to the one who sacrificed it all to rescue her, even from herself all those years ago. The ground was solid, and the snow kept falling, suddenly for these two star crossed lovers it all went black. The horrifying sound of two bodies thudding to the ground was the only haunting sound that filled the gorge and the sun kissed horizon on this cold dawn in Colorado during the first day of snow fall. The crows fled and cawed overhead, Kyle watched mortified as the love of his life lie down below in a heap of bodies that he relished throwing away like last night's half eaten meal.

The wind howled and screamed, whistled and shook, the snow started to fall in a silent flurry, it was as if the entire forest cried for the magical being that was now resting for eternity down below. A single tear fell from Kyle's face as he climbed up the cliffside thousands of feet in search of his equipment, and now his horse. In that moment he remembered a night when Jess and he were curled up by the fire and talking about secret places they both have kept to themselves all these years.

"I wonder, would she? No. It's not possible, she's dead, there's no way she could've survived the fall." He paused, *"Is there?"*

Kyle stood at the top of Royal Gorge and remembered telling her in detail about his hidden cabin, a shack really that he'd kept even after all these years, which not a single soul in the world knew of, until that night. When he told Jess in detail about its remote location. Realizing he was still without equipment or resources, and still searching for a missing horse, he knew it would take hours to get down there and then back to the house before the entire manor was worried wondering where he was this time of day.

He reached into his jacket and for the first time ever he broke his own rule, never before during his dark rituals had he ever used a cellphone or even had one on him but this time was different. He needed somebody to count on and the one he usually relied on so heavily was now a pile of blood and broken bones at the bottom of this cliff.

"James, please see to the house, staff and children today, I'll be back as soon as I can."

He instantly hung up before he could even respond Kyle turned the cell phone off immediately. In the distance he saw his bag, arrows and quiver, everything he possessed still in the spot he left it. A few hundred yards to the east the horse was still standing nearby the tree line, picking at bits of grass here and there completely absorbed in his own world. He walked towards it and easily leapt onto his back, marching him towards his equipment he dismounted and secured all of his belongings to his newfound transportation and started heading down the trail towards the bottom of Royal Gorge, he had to see for himself if she was crazier than he'd ever given her credit for.

The sun started to rise above the snowcapped hills, the only sound in the world was the footsteps of both steed and killer slowly descending to the bottom of the most treacherous gorge in all of the Rockies. There was a rich history of death at the foot of this densely forested hell. So many had tried to conquer it, never expecting to freeze to death before nightfall. Every thousand feet Kyle descended he felt in the pit of his stomach for the first time a sickness that permeated through his soul.

He'd always had a taste for this life, one filled with solitude and dark indulgences that most in this world would be incapable of on such a palate. Usually this ritual this planned and calculated cadence towards his deepest primal release was met with a cathartic satisfaction, leaving him hungry for life once more, thirsting for the sweet juices of many beautiful women, but without her he felt lost, empty and hopeless inside, the procession towards her final location felt like a funeral for one lost soul in this expansive terrain, leaving him to feel more alone in life than he'd ever previously remembered.

The cold morning air bit at his neck, even the horse started to slow his pace, shivering every so often and trying to find the courage to continue moving forward. It wouldn't be much longer now before he could hold her in his arms for one last time before she made him say goodbye. The rocky mountainside trailed twistedly into a ravine below, as Kyle circled the trail around a very familiar corner he saw a light glowing nearby in that cabin that not a single soul in this entire world knew of, except her.

"How is this possible?"

He stood there for a few moments silenced by the mystery beyond this impossible circumstance. Darkeel tingled through the back of his skull, slithering up towards his spine he leaned into his mind and spun a tale to mind fuck his chosen vessel one last time.

"How long has it been since you've been down there? It's been more years than even I can remember..."

Kyle stood there frustrated by this cryptic piece to a puzzle that was no closer to being solved, at least not by standing here.

"What the fuck are you going on about now? Nobody, not a

single fucking soul has ever ventured down there, ever. I have alarms everywhere, even the smallest creature would trigger it and let me know immediately that someone was in *my cabin*."

With a rather tormenting cackle Darkeel's voice responded to tease him when he felt the most devastated. This was a torment Kyle was used too, but a type of sadism he wouldn't tolerate in mental anguish.

"Perhaps a girl must do what a girl must." Kyle enraged, clinching his fists, he slammed them against his chest and said:
"Stop. *Now!* I won't hear any more of this."

The voice vanished and a cold silence returned as he continued to travel downwards towards the bodies, now probably frozen beside his cabin that still had the light on.

The horse started to bump into Kyle as the steep incline was far too much for him to take anymore. Realizing that he needed to get him to the bottom to rest, he pulled him by the bridle behind him and doubled his pace. The horse started to trot and slide side to side, the eerie clouds overhead transformed the entire world into a white canvas, and the only color was that of the green trees peeking out under oceans of snow. The slate stone of boulders, rocks and cliffside marbled with deep salmon and red. He was only a few feet from the bottom of Royal Gorge, and already he could see them lying there. In that moment a murder of crows flew overhead cawing, making the only declarations of what had just taken place before their haunting eyes. He never realized just how quickly he fell for her, how deeply his love went, and down to the very core of his soul he felt as if Darkeel had hollowed him out. Carved him out whole, yet for once he had so little to do with this death.

"I can't believe I won't be able to give her the world, how can this be? How is she just *gone?*"

Those words were met with shock, wonder and awe, as he stepped towards her he saw Sara's dead body heaped on the bottom of Royal Gorge. The beautiful woman was smiling, blood trickled down her face, cheek and from her nose, eyes and lips, yet never could he recall not even once in his life ever looking that content. Her body was positioned onto the frozen ice, face nestled onto the snow like it was a pillow and she was still warm in her bed. Curled up in such a serene position, her body wasn't mangled, broken, shattered or disfigured she appeared as if she was finally at peace.

In that moment, Kyle did all that he could to turn his eyes towards her body and look at what was left of her. Jess was just a few feet away from Sara, her hands still reaching up towards her direction as if they were holding hands upon impact. Her eyes were closed and her body lie facing up stuck with arrows and as he started to approach her, he saw the snow falling all around her corpse, the white light illuminating her porcelain skin, leaving her glowing, radiant even. Her lips were gently smiling and her eyes were closed as clotted blood pooled all around her. He stepped around the frozen ice and pile of tree limbs that her body now rested above. Walking around her body he stood at her feet, the tears streamed down his face as he fell to his knees.

"What have I done?!"

An ocean of rage and sadness filled the ravine with echoes and cries of grief and tumultuous sorrow. Kyle covering his face and falling apart, didn't realize that the stolen steed had noticed something about Jess that he hadn't the time in his heartbreak to notice. The horse walked towards her right hand, still gently resting to her side. He slowly nuzzled her fingertips and the palm of her hand as her fingers started to move gently and slowly at first before suddenly in violent spasm, back to life.

With a gurgled gasp, Jess suddenly cracked her eyes open to see the snow falling from above and the tree line surrounding her like a halo from nature's most sacred temple. She couldn't move. The sheer pain alone would've probably killed her. As she struggled to breathe she slowly moved her eyelids open and shut, trying to focus her vision. It was blurred still from the levels of atropine still coursing through her veins, tinging her arteries with purple striations that revealed to Kyle that she was already in overdose. As he lifted his eyes, he was without words, all he could do was crawl towards her on the heaping pile of broken trees, scraping his knees, and tearing towards her as fast as he could. He watched her trying to breathe, he could tell she'd punctured a lung, it was the same horrifying sound that he heard and the despair he felt just to breathe that he'd suffered himself in his youth so many years ago.

She smiled, she was in far too much pain to move. "You really got me good with that last shot. Right in the bone."

Her voice rang clear as a bell in his mind and Kyle started laughing, his eyes tear stained.

"Not my finest hour, but at least I kept my promises to you, and to her."

Jess's words rang true in his head as she glanced up with just her eyes and continued, "I gave her that life and now, you and I can have this one."

She started to smile and coughed hard, tears streaming down her face along with cries of pain. Kyle leaned in and held her head under his hands, trying his best to be near her around all of the arrows sticking out of her now like a captured kill. He leaned in close and whispered to her;

"You won't make it out of this alive, I can already see the signs of overdose in your skin, in your eyes." Jess's lips slowly moved to what would've been her shy laugh if they were at the dinner table.

"You still after all this time don't trust me. I've a taste for atropine, she and I play well together, you'll see."

He watched as her fangs slowly protruded and the striations of toxic poison coursing through her veins slowly resided, her eyes glowed a bright and beautiful purple, haunting Kyle down to the deepest chambers of his soul.

"There is so much we still don't know about one another." Kyle whispered to her mind and waiting for her response.

"I left the light on for you, will you do me one last favor?"

Kyle leaned over and waited for her lips to respond, "Kill me."

Kyle leaned back and realized that her voice was changed, it was his, that wretched voice in his mind coursing through his blood and into his brain.

"Agh! Ahh! Why must it end this way?! Time and time again! Fuck!!!"

His screams echoed off the canyon causing the horse to race towards the top of the mountain from the trail they'd just emerged. Before she could say anything more to him, her eyes formed tears, she could see that he was gone now and that Darkeel was the only one left.

As the clouded tears streamed down her face and over her cheeks, the snow began to fall, the crows surrounded her across the tree line. Each one positioned at the top of each tree, depicting a circle of executioner's waiting for the moment when the guillotine fell on her pretty intact neck. She watched the tall, dark being standing over her, his thighs spread and each boot was firmly planted on her forearms. She started to scream in agony, and trembled trying to remain calm after her nerves stopped burning her flesh alive. He bent down and crouched over her slowly breaking each arrow and sending her body into waves of shock. As he reached for her swanlike neck she knew that it was time to make peace with all that transpired here this dark, isolated day.

She could hear herself choking, feel herself losing consciousness, his hands were so strong, yet so comfortingly warm. In this frigid hell it was the last warmth that she'd ever feel from human touch in this life. Jess formed the words *I Love You,* with her final ounce of strength and watched overhead as the crows started to caw, her eyes capturing *The Slaughterhouse Hills Hunter as he* killed another of his victims and the most prized, of his treasured possessions. She felt the darkness floating in, she could barely see his face, his dark form or silhouette now. It wouldn't be much longer before she and Sara were with each other for eternity. As her eyes rolled back towards where her body was lying, she saw her there standing, glowing wrapped in long layers of velvet, and she looked divine. Her radiant smile serenely depicted on her angelic face. Her beautiful hands that created such pleasure in Jess' body for so long gently reached forward to guide her to their afterlife, a midst the floor of bodies and the haunted hills of *The Slaughterhouse Hills Hunter.* She turned around and started to walk along the frozen riverbed, Jess couldn't help but look up once more to whisper one last thing before she was destined to die.

"Goodbye old fiend, I'll miss you." In that moment his dark cloaked form faded into black and all she felt was eternal warmth, finally at long last.

Chapter 38:
BELOVED TRIBUTE

"WHERE am I?"

Jess could hear her voice muttering aloud, a startling discovery for anyone beyond the grave. Assuming this was part of the transition to the afterlife, she waited and wondered why it smelled of the earth. Like dusty, mildew streaked, earth. The scent of petrichor was thick, wafting into her nose, before she could move she heard the sound of clanking metal chains above her head and she suddenly opened her eyes.

"Where the fuck am I now? This can't be, none of this makes sense. I'm dead? Or at least I should be."

In that moment her eyes adjusted and she started to realize exactly where she was. The stone walls were illuminated by candlelight, she saw her face again, this time behind a statue of stone.

"Oh god, Sara?" Jess shrieked aloud, "What have you done?!"

She tried to flee towards her beloved's form, serenely smiling behind stone, a perfect figure and monument to her beauty, her strength and her powerful soul. She was dressed in her favorite outfit.

"But how did he know?"

She started to cry realizing she was utterly trapped, she'd never felt so lost without her powers, something was wrong, until she realized what this metal was made out of. A powerful elemental that would subdue her abilities leaving her helpless as a mortal…*human*. She searched for answers and looked around the mausoleum, the entire room was filled with flowers, endless bouquets of Sara's favorite lilies and orchids, red roses and lavender, in every corner of this haunted place. It was a beautiful tribute to the incredible creature that captivated her in that bar and stole her heart eons ago on this very Halloween night.

"My darling, questions lead to answers and answers lead to courage, with courage you'll try to flee, and I need you trained, docile and subdued for what I have in mind."

Kyle spoke clearly as his boots echoed off the stone floor trailing up the staircase that she knew all too intimately. He walked into the room and calmly placed a kiss on her forehead. Jess was completely in awe she had no words for what was taking place tonight. She only possessed a thousand questions none of which would be answered tonight, or ever if he had any power or control over such confessions. In that moment she heard his boots silently marching away behind her, the sound of the stone wall door being moved slowly into place.

Instantly Jess panicked as she saw the lights dimming, she knew they'd go out following the backdraft, horrified she saw Sara's face fully in the light, her eyes still open, and her face looking towards the heavens in a haunting expression of fear and torment. Her mind filled once more with that terrifying sound, the endless laughter rang through her head, rang and rang against the halls and corridors of her tortured psyche. In a rage she thrashed and tried to move, her body jerking mere inches above and below she was completely restricted to this slab of concrete, this shrined room to her and her beloved.

"No! No! NOooooOoooooooooOOOOOOOO!"

Jess started to scream and instantly she felt her possessed lips pursed together as if he was standing there personally forcing her lips to form the words she desperately never desired to utter again in this life or any others. As Jess lied there in agony, completely alone, the darkness penetrating into the mausoleum that would be her final resting place. The ether crept in at an alarming rate. All she could do is scream, in agonizing fear, her soul shrieked for the final time;

"DARKEEL! DAR-KEEL! DARK-KILL! DARK-KILL! DARK-KILL! DARRRKK-KKIIIIILLLL!!"

Kyle wandered up slowly towards the dungeon floor, today he had no patience or kindness left in his soul. It was exhausted completely and any prized possession of his would be a fool to cross him. He marched into the dungeons just above Jess as she continued to thrash around in utter darkness. The sound of girls was nowhere to be heard until he walked over towards the wall of buttons. Levers and dials turning and pressed. Suddenly once more the house of horrors was alive with the sounds of torture, shrieks of terror, coughing and choking from those who were once more being submerged beneath cold water and lifted again to their safety right before it was too late.

Still dressed in his ominous hunting gear, he turned on the closed circuit televisions, this time the empty screen that was black before was suddenly illuminated with her presence. He smiled and watched her in sheer darkness, eyes glowing green in night vision filter. He loved the look of terror in her eyes more than he ever loved the sight of pleasure. This was his pleasure, his ultimate satisfaction, to collect and keep those who he most desired, and this one was a gift that he'd never again let get away.

Kyle slowly reached towards her face on closed circuit television screen. He smiled warmly from a part of him that he was still quite unfamiliar with, *adoration*.

"One day you'll be ready for me."

As his fingers grazed her cheek she suddenly calmed down, their link was so intrinsic and intense, Kyle felt he had nothing to hide from her. She was the only one that embraced him completely. As his thumb grazed her chin he replied, "Unfortunately for us both...today is not that day."

Kyle awoke hours later in his bed, sound asleep he hadn't slept as silent as the grave in more years and lifetimes then he had a chance to contemplate. Before he could relish this serene solitude and new chapter in his life he heard the phone ring.

"What happened to you last night?" A voice asked in a stance of both worry and fear.

"James, I told you I don't quite remember, I honestly just remember being near the gorge and all of it from there is blank, I knew I shouldn't have gone off like that but I felt compelled too. As if something incredible was waiting for me out there that not a single soul could understand or grasp." James responded a bit more calmly but still worried about his friend and employer.

"You were gone for almost two days, when I saw you coming over the hill, dressed like that with a horse and a *lot* of baggage, you only said one thing to me before you vanished until now."

Kyle asked. "What was that? What did I say?" James continued; "Return this horse next door where he belongs, before they find out, I have things to tend too down below, take care of the house until I'm ready to surface..."

James chattered on stressfully as Kyle continued to lie back listening, pretending to play daft, to the chaos and mystery of this bizarre series of days.

"Before I could even ask where you'd been, you vanished. I'm really freaking out here man, are you sure you're okay?"

Kyle responded slowly, calmly and serenely, "Yes, I'm fine, it's just been a long week, I've been working way too hard, I need to slow down before I go over the edge, that's all." Kyle looked over at the clock and saw that it was already three o' clock.

"It's this late already? Have food ready for us, I'll be down in half an hour, tell the children to come too." James agreed and hung-up, wondering what transpired in those hours that his best friend went missing.

Chapter 39:
IMMORTAL OPIA

THE formal dining room was lavishly set, the sound of laughter echoed through the halls as the lord of Burnett manor descended to his beautiful and loving family once more to share time and space with those innocent beings in the world who had no idea about the dark nature of their beloved patriarch. Tiffany chimed in and asked;

"Dad? Where's Jess? Isn't she eating with us?" Adie and Derek started to look his way, his youngest letting her sister know.

"Hey I was just going to ask him that question. Weird." The children laughed and waited for their father's response.

He smiled warmly and said, "Unfortunately for Jess, a dear friend of hers from youth passed away recently and she's quite devastated. I put her on a red-eye flight late last night, she'll be gone for some time as she needs to tend to many things regarding all that goes into funerals and assisting families through hard times such as these." The children somberly responded with warm affirmations of love and affection.

"I'm so sorry to hear that dad, I can't imagine how much pain she's going through it's never easy to lose someone we love." Kyle reached for his eldest daughters hand and lovingly held it.

"I'm sure she'll appreciate your affections when she returns. I'll keep you informed I promise."

In that moment the staff entered with pre-ordered meals from the kitchen. The banter of jokes and games between his younger children were shushed and debated by the sounds of his eldest daughter trying to keep them under control.

Kyle sat there menacingly quiet, calm and calculated, yet seemingly unnoticed by anyone in the room, his elbows resting on the table firmly placed. His strong hands pressed together by just the fingertips, his eyes penetrating with their ominous gaze, searching, looking out into the eyes of those who are reading this very twisted tale, right now... His eyes glowing, staring ever so deeply into the depths of every corner of your soul, expelling and pulling out ever secret that you've kept quiet and deep within where you thought nobody in this entire fucking world would ever find it.

As the rooms of his mind echoed and filled with the sounds of begging, pleading and screams of absolution, *The Slaughter House Hills Hunters* eyes continued to glow meeting your gaze in this very moment as your heart still beats swiftly. Can't you hear him?

Kyle's eyes glowed as Darkeel's voice echoes fill the room with sounds of *"Someday,"* his voice whispering.

The Slaughterhouse Hills Hunter was never heard from or seen ever again, after that day.

The End...

Epilogue

IT all originated with two morbid questions that begged by my dark soul to be answered...

Why do they kill?

Do killers love?

It was in the midst of that dark epiphany that I found myself within a self-imposed exile from the rest of society that never cared to ponder let alone explore or question such ideology that I discovered the very depths of depravity that a single tortured human soul can explore and by the rare circumstances that have left me here wondering just how I survived all of this in an entirely new body. It's left me with questions answered by many prolific minds and uncaptured serial killers which has brought me to the end of my insane journey and right back to the beginning again; where it all started, into an entirely new chapter of my life thriving within the underworld. To witness just how vividly this adventure of carnage and carnality has taken me over the past thirteen years, as well as realizing just how fortunate I am to have survived the haunting circumstances in the end.

For as I've lost so many over the years, including a few of the precious monsters, madmen and madwomen who illustrate the macabre pages of this anthology collection that you've read with your very curious eyes. I find solace in the solitude and comfort in the fact that they're all still out there, existing, thriving and enduring and some even surviving themselves while still seamlessly blending in with society without question; from those of you who work and exist right along beside them in your seemingly ordinary lives.

Where this thirteen year exploration of madness and mayhem, carnality and carnage takes us in the future I cannot be certain...

However, with visions as dark and as grand as the ones I have for transforming *Darkeel* into a real life serial killer in the realms of independent horror cinema, I am not only sure but absolutely certain that in time those monsters and madmen will be knocking on my door once more in the dead of night, beckoning me to come assist them with bringing our most debauched visions to life within the co-conspirators work to a silver screen slaughterhouse near you.

To further entice prying yet curious eyes, to wander of their own volition into the dark forests on cold brutal nights, never to be seen from; or heard from...ever again.

About The Author

What some have coined as a *true renaissance woman* of the modern era, when Bella BloodLust isn't busy fleeing from shackles in desolate dungeons and burying corpses in remote locations, she finds herself immersed in historical iconography, spirituality and bringing aesthetic visions in all realms of media production to life. As a multi-generational shaman she spends the majority of her evenings helping the worldwide spiritual community and solving cold cases as a psychic detective and medium.

However this doesn't prevent her from following her old world dreams of bringing new bohemia back to the golden age of humanity through burlesque siren performances in a venue for children of the night near you; to traveling across the country for more scintillating work in the underworld as a professional lifestyle mistress and BDSM educator.

In her spare time at home in her penthouse studio that she calls *Catwoman's Lair;* she enjoys intensive research in various fields of philosophy, metaphysics, reading, cooking gourmet meals and exploring gourmet pastries in the French fashion. In the end the core of her bloody and beating heart will always belong to writing, it's still the one place that truly in this world of monsters and madmen that lurk behind the dark corridors of her illustrious mind; that feels entirely like *home.*

For your private invitation to the 3 ring circus and one woman show visit:

WWW.BELLABLOODLUST.COM